Uncanny Times

Also by Laura Anne Gilman

Uncanny Times

HUNTSMEN: BOOK ONE

Laura Anne Gilman

SAGA PRESS

London   Sydney   New York   Toronto   New Delhi

SAGA PRESS

AN IMPRINT OF SIMON & SCHUSTER, INC.

1230 AVENUE OF THE AMERICAS, NEW YORK, NEW YORK 10020

First Saga Press trade paperback edition October 2022

SAGA PRESS and colophon are trademarks of Simon & Schuster, Inc.

For information about special discounts for bulk purchases, please contact Simon & Schuster Special Sales at 1-866-506-1949 or business@simonandschuster.com.

The Simon & Schuster Speakers Bureau can bring authors to your live event. For more information or to book an event, contact the Simon & Schuster Speakers Bureau at 1-866-248-3049 or visit our website at www.simonspeakers.com.

Interior design by Davina Mock-Maniscalco

Manufactured in the United States of America

1   3   5   7   9   10   8   6   4   2

Library of Congress Cataloging-in-Publication Data is available.

ISBN 978-1-5344-1592-8
ISBN 978-1-5344-1593-5 (ebook)

Janet M. Gilman

1935–2020

Thank you. For everything.

One

*N*OVEMBER HAD SETTLED into New Haven like a petulant child, alternating between raining tantrums and bitterly cold sulks. That afternoon, a storm had wrapped around the house on Crider Street and was busily rattling the windows, an occasional scrape of hail mixing with the rain. After one particularly windy blast, Rosemary Harker looked up from the newspaper she was reading, mentally gauging the probable damage to the roof.

"We can afford to fix it," her brother said, not lifting his nose from the book he was reading. "Assuming the boiler doesn't also break. Would you rather stay dry, or stay warm?"

She made a humming noise deep in her throat. "If we keep the books dry, we can burn those to stay warm."

Aaron lifted his head sharply, first to glance worriedly at the books lining the walls between windows, and then to glare at his sister. "You are not a good person."

Her brother was so easy to rile, it almost wasn't amusing. Almost.

"You know I would never do that." She scanned the nearest bookshelf, burnished leather spines squared neatly behind glass panes. "I'm not sure any of those would be safe to burn, anyway." It was a Huntsman's library: there were things on those aged pages that were not safe to be spoken out loud, much less set free in a puff of smoke. "Your novels, on the other hand . . ."

When her brother simply continued glaring at her, she chuckled and went back to her newspaper. President Wilson had made a speech down in Alabama, claiming that the United States would not seek to claim more territory through conquest, a promise everyone must know he would break. She sighed and turned the page, looking for lighter fare. But the news had been cast under a bad moon that week. Even word of a peace treaty ending the war in Serbia now seemed overcast with doubt.

Aaron thought she worried overmuch about what happened in the larger world. He preferred to focus his studies on things that he could affect directly, the more intimate picture. Their differing approaches made them a good pair, an effective Huntsmen team. But she wished she had someone to discuss events with; the ladies of New Haven hosted the occasional radical speaker, but their efforts were more often bent to the matter of the vote rather than the unrest beyond America's borders.

She lifted her gaze again to see what it was that he was reading tonight. The book was newer than most on their shelves, and slender. He felt her gaze and lifted the book so that she could see the cover.

"*Der Tod in Venedig.* Thomas Mann. You'd dislike it."

She didn't doubt it for a moment. Novels were not to her taste.

She shifted, and a prickling in her limbs told her that she had been sitting still for too long. She flexed her feet, pressing against something heavy and warm. A low moan of complaint came from the brindle hound collapsed on the floor by her chair, heavy head resting on his paws. She pushed at his flank again with her toe, the fabric of her house shoe barely making a dent in the thick muscle under short, plush fur.

"Poor Bother," she said fondly. "Such a hard life you lead." The hound had a kennel out back, warm and dry even in such foul weather, but he was as often inside as out.

His head turned to look up at her now, one triangular ear flopping over while the other remained erect, giving him a rakish look at odds with his impeccable bloodline.

"He's getting soft and lazy," her brother said. "It's been too quiet since summer." He closed the book he had been reading and placed it on the table next to his chair. "I've half a mind to put in a call to Uncle Bryan and see if there's anything happening down his way worth checking out, just for the excuse to do something."

Rosemary rested her foot on Botheration's side and waved her hand in languid dismissal of her brother's suggestion. "Nothing ever happens in Baltimore. It's far too civilized."

"There were grindylows, back in '02."

"Grindylows hardly count."

"They ate seven people."

"Papa said three of them were sailors, so they didn't count," she responded primly.

"And because you always believed what Papa said."

Her mouth twitched. "Well, I did when I was fifteen!"

Aaron scoffed, pushing up out of his chair and walking into the kitchen. She heard him pouring water into the kettle, then setting it on the hob to boil.

"The Keemun, please," she called out. "And the cookies in the tin, there should be some left."

A grunt was the only response she got.

"Your master is a grumpy old man at the ripe age of twenty," she told the hound under her feet. "But he makes a decent cup of tea, so I think we'll keep him, yes?"

The hound let out another heavy, grumbling sigh and got to his feet, dislodging hers, then padded over to the door that led downstairs, where he waited.

She narrowed her eyes at the beast. "It's cold out there, Bother, remember? Cold, and wet, and windy."

As though to make her a liar, the sound of rain on the roof slope slowed to a faint patter, and she glared up at the ceiling like it had betrayed her.

The hound whined once, and she gave in, getting up as well and reaching for the thick wool shawl draped over the back of her chair. "All right, all right. Have I told you recently that you're well-named?"

Botheration's papers said his full name was Eisenblut-Morgendämmerungstreter, Ironblood Dawn Treader in English, but he'd been Botheration since he came to them, a solid chunk of six-month-old puppy already reaching her knee. He was a Foundation Molosser, smart enough to take himself out to do his business and come back, but he still needed her to open the doors for him. "Come on then, let's go."

The house they'd let had an empty flat on the first floor, which the owners occasionally used for purposes unknown, while the Harkers' quarters took up the second and third. It was a solidly built house, and she liked it well enough, the three years they'd been living there, but the stairwell was narrow enough that Botheration's shoulders nearly brushed the walls, and steeper than Rosemary felt comfortable with, wearing skirts. Thankfully, there was also a sturdy railing along one wall, and the electric sconces were turned up bright. Watching the beast in front of her, she could make out the play of muscles under his fur, see where the scar tissue he'd gotten during last month's work was still healing on his left haunch, and made a note to massage it again with salve. He was no longer a puppy, and that scar would only ache more as time went by.

Botheration reached the door before her and settled again into a waiting pose, his left ear flopping over once more.

"You are a ridiculous beast," she told him, opening the door to a blast of damp cold. "Now go on, get busy. I'm not going to stand here and wait on you."

From upstairs, she heard her brother call out that the tea was almost ready.

"You hear that?" she said to the hound. "Go, do."

Botheration shuffled down the porch steps to the street, and she shut the door against the wind, waiting for the sound of his claws against the wood asking to be let in. In weather like this, he would not linger.

Instead, after a few minutes there was a solid thunk on the porch, and then the sound of knuckles against the door-frame, followed immediately by a chiming upstairs as their unexpected visitor found the bell.

Rosemary's right hand dropped to her waist, but she had dressed for a quiet day at home, and her knife was upstairs, safely sheathed and put away. She reached up to find a long, sharp pin nestled in her braided hair. It was a close-in weapon, not ideal, but it was better than opening the door empty-handed.

Not that she expected trouble—this was a decent enough neighborhood, and most of the local toughs knew Bother, or at least *of* him—but for Huntsmen, not being prepared could lead to being dead. Even at home.

"Hello?" A man's voice carried through the door, and then she heard the sound of a familiar, heavy thud, and the man's voice again, louder and higher. "What? Um, good dog? Hello?"

The tension eased from her body: she did not recognize the voice, but whoever was out there was now more at risk than a risk.

Rosemary replaced the hairpin and checked her appearance in the pier glass on the wall, then opened the door to rescue whoever it was from Botheration's attention.

The man standing on her porch wore the brown uniform of the Messenger Service under his gabardine coat, and a politely terrified expression on his face.

Rosemary held out her hand, palm down. "Bother, sit."

The beast settled on his haunches but kept his eyes focused on the stranger, jaw hanging open to let his tongue loll to the side, a sure sign, if you knew the hound, that he was amused.

Clearly, the messenger did not know, as he looked near ready to pass out. To be fair, the mass of muscle and fur, even seated, would give the bravest man pause. There were very few like Botheration anywhere in the States; his bloodline was Albanian, his dam from Russia, and the pups went only to Huntsmen families.

The wind had let up slightly, but the rain still pattered softly on the porch's roof, and unlike the deliveryman, she was not dressed for the outdoors. "Just don't make any sudden moves, or yell, and you'll be fine."

The messenger did not look reassured. "What—what does he do if I yell?"

She rested her hand on the back of the hound's thick neck, giving it an affectionate shake. "Mostly, he licks your face," she lied. "But he'll knock you down to get there."

As she'd hoped, that put the man a little at ease, enough that he recalled why he was standing there, dripping with rain.

"Are you Miss Rosemary Harker?"

She smiled politely, but tension returned to her limbs, and Botheration let out a faint rumble that had the man blanching again. "I am."

"Then I have a letter for you, miss."

Letters, in her experience, meant either bad news or worse news. But she took the letter from him with a polite thank-you, managing to restrain her amusement as he then backed up off the front porch, never taking his gaze off Botheration, who watched him go with placid menace.

"Are you done?" she asked the hound, who sneezed once and shook himself, splatting rain, then pushed past her to head back up the steps.

Aaron was waiting for them, the tea poured and ready on the tray with a dish of shortbread. She lifted the letter so that he could see it, and he plucked it from her fingers as Botheration padded past them both, shaking the last of the rain from his fur before settling on the rug.

Aaron looked at the envelope, then looked back at her, frowning. "Brunson, New York? Who do we know there?"

She sat down in her chair and took a sip of the tea, letting the warmth of it push away the lingering effects of being outside, however briefly.

"The name on the return is Lovelace." She frowned, thinking. "Dr. Lovelace? Remember? Father's cousin, the one who was fond of Mother." She made an imperious gesture with her free hand, and he passed the letter back to her, huffing.

"You mean, the one who didn't turn up their nose at the southern trash Father dragged home?"

"Not all of them were rude."

He made a sour face but let the subject drop. Rosemary placed her cup back on the tray, then slit open the letter and unfolded it. "It's from his wife."

"He was married? Do we have cousins we didn't know about? Cousins would be nice." Aaron sat down, this time on the divan, and leaned forward, forearms on his knees. "So what does it say?"

"Oh." Her expression softened slightly. "He's dead." She read the paragraph again, scanning the words as though they might change between one look and the next. "The funeral was two days ago."

"Huh. So. No cousins? Are we in his will?"

"Aaron."

Her reproving tone failed to quash him. "It seemed an important question."

Their finances were only now recovering from the Panic of '07, so he wasn't wrong. "All she says is that it was sudden, and . . ." Her voice trailed off and she read that passage again.

"What?"

"He left word that we should be contacted in the event of his death."

Aaron made a hopeful gesture. "So we are in the will?"

Rosemary made a face at him, somewhere between exasperation and worry. "He left a note on his desk for her to contact us. The night before he died."

She could see the moment Aaron understood. He ran

fingers through his hair, rumpling the once neatly combed locks into disarray, then rubbed his palms over his cheeks, rough with a day's shadow. "An uncanny death."

She shrugged agreement, folding the letter back up carefully. There was only one reason to inform Huntsmen of a sudden death, and that was if the uncanny were involved. If the death had been uncanny-*caused*.

"So." Aaron had a smile on his face, perhaps unseemly so soon after the news of a relative's death, however distant, but she knew her brother, and understood him. "We're off to . . . where are we off to?"

"Brunson." Rosemary'd always had a better grasp of geography than him. "Upstate New York, on the shores of Lake Ontario."

"In November. Joyous is the life of man." But his grin didn't waver, and after a moment, Rosemary felt a smile of her own joining his. The man's death was a tragedy, of course, but they were Huntsmen, and Huntsmen were not meant to sit home by the fire.

Two

HUNTSMEN WERE ACCUSTOMED to travel at the drop of a note, plans put into motion with smooth efficiency, but in this instance the Harkers were at the mercy of the train timetables.

There was no direct line from New Haven to Brunson; to go upstate required them to travel down to New York City in order to catch the evening Lake Shore Limited train back upstate. Neither humans nor hound enjoyed the hubbub of the city, although the newly opened "Grand Central" terminal was as elegant as advertised, and it was with relief that, several hours after leaving home, they boarded the overnight train that would take them north.

The train itself was a shabby relic of grander days, but their tickets gave them a private car with two narrow bunks, and comfortable chairs by the picture window, and the porter, on request, brought an extra blanket for Botheration to lie on.

Aaron thought that the train's employees would not be so accommodating were they to investigate the contents of their luggage, the heavier, locked case being filled not with garments but several blades, and an unstrung crossbow and bolts, weapons not suitable for carrying in public. His Colt and an iron dagger were on his person, as always when he left the house, and Rosemary was likewise outfitted with her Browning, but they would have no need for any of them on the train, with luck.

Once the porter had departed, Aaron placed his overcoat and hat on the rack, then took his sister's coat as well, while she coaxed Botheration onto the lower bunk. The hound's bulk took up the entire space, square head resting on crossed paws as he settled himself, keeping both humans within view.

Aaron eyed the upper bunk for himself, then considered the armchairs, trying to decide which option might be more comfortable. The journey would take them some time, and he never got enough rest when they were working.

"Would you be terribly offended if I slept until our arrival?"

"I doubt your snoring could be louder than the sound of the wheels." She had already claimed one of the armchairs and opened her writing kit, despite the steady jolt-and-lurch of the car. He slumped into the other chair, stretching his legs out as he watched her select a sheet of paper, add water to her pen, and begin writing.

He tried to doze, as threatened, but the uncertainty of what they would find at their destination interfered, and eventually he gave up, pushing himself upright and watching his sister work.

"You know that most of those will never arrive." The letters going to Huntsmen overseas, he meant. When the unrest in southeastern Europe began a few years ago, the uncanny had become restless as well. Creatures that had avoided human towns for decades began hunting once more, spaces that had been made safe were suddenly dangerous again. Ordinary folk, or worse, the local police, could not be expected to deal with the uncanny, to know which were dangerous, and which merely annoyances, much less how to be safely rid of them all. Volunteers had been sent to aid those towns, most from England and France, but not a few from the States and Canada.

Some of those volunteers had been friends of theirs.

Nothing had been heard from them in months.

It might have been poor mail service, or they might be too busy to reply. But Aaron wasn't as ignorant of the situations overseas as Rosemary thought, and he'd always been more pragmatic than she. America had its full share of the uncanny, but many of them had made truces with the Indian tribes, truces that had been negotiated to cover settlers as well.

Those in the Old World might once have had similar truces, but if so, they'd been long forgotten, and only grudges remained.

Rosemary kept writing, only the slightest ducking of her chin sign that she had heard him. The lamp overhead made her dark curls shine, the skin of her cheek and hands seem more delicate, which was a damned lie if ever he saw one.

Accepting that she had no intention of responding,

Aaron sighed and reached for the book he'd placed in his satchel as they were packing. He'd left the novel behind, choosing instead *The Blackburn Compendium: New England and Environs*, a history of the uncanny known to live along the northeastern borders. Their parents had made sure they knew all the uncanny to be found in their region, from Montreal down to Philadelphia, but it never hurt to refresh one's memory. With luck and a little bit of work, he would be able to identify what they were up against as soon as they arrived, making their job that much simpler.

Unfortunately, he'd forgotten that the *Compendium* had such a dry, academic tone, and between that and the steady clacking and screeching of the train, he soon had a raging headache. Closing the book carefully and setting it aside, he shifted his chair to watch the night-dark scenery go by instead. The monotony of hurtling in a single direction, plus the steady scratching of Rosemary's pen, and the familiar sound of Botheration's breathing finally lulled him to sleep, waking only briefly when the conductor called out a new stop, then dozing off again.

The overnight train took nearly eight hours to reach their destination, Aaron and Rosemary stretching their legs and letting Botheration relieve himself whenever a stop allowed. By the time the conductor called out their station, and the screeching of the brakes against the wheels filled the air, they'd grown heartily tired of their car, the noise, and each other.

Aaron tipped the porters to carry their luggage out, while

Rosemary clipped the leather lead to Botheration's collar, bribing him with bits of dried liver from her pocket as they made their way to the car's exit, stepping down onto the platform along with a handful of other travelers.

Brunson, at first glance, did not impress. The station was nothing more than a simple wooden platform, with a small square hut at the far end. A thick copse of leafless trees stood across the road, looking as though nothing had changed them since Indians claimed these lands. Turning, Aaron could make out a series of rooftops in the distance, the number thickening where the town must be.

The winter sun was just rising over the tree line, and the air was briskly bracing, making his skin tingle with the cold. Aaron drew a deep breath in, and immediately regretted it, wrapping his muffler more closely around his neck and chin, even as Rosemary slid on fur-lined gloves. They'd had snow here, not rain, and the ground was still thinly coated with it, the remnants icy and slick-looking.

Aaron placed his carpetbag valise on the platform by his feet and stretched, raising his arms over his head and drawing another deep breath before dropping his arms abruptly and making a face.

"I thought the country was supposed to smell better," he said, lifting the back of his hand to his nose as though to block the odor. "What is that?"

Warned, Rosemary took a shallow breath through her mouth, grimacing as she caught what he had, a harsh, acrid smell filtering through the cold. "Factory of some sort, I suppose. I wouldn't have expected it out here, but it's hardly the worst thing you've ever smelled. Or smelled like, for that matter."

Aaron tilted his head to the side, considering her claim before acknowledging the truth to it. Hunts were generally messy affairs, particularly with uncanny that fought back.

Botheration seemed unworried by the stink, investigating the nearest tree growing at the edge of the platform and finding it worthy of his attentions.

While they were looking around, the porters made quick work of unloading luggage, piling it on the far end of the platform. This was a quick stop: no sooner had the last trunk been deposited than the train let out a warning whistle and chugged its way onward toward Rochester.

The travelers who had disembarked with them seemed to know exactly where they were going, some walking down the road, luggage in hand, others climbing into a shiny Model T waiting for them. Soon enough the three of them were the only ones left on the platform, save for a hunched-over figure closing up the depot's office, locking the single door with great solemnity. Theirs had been the only train scheduled to stop at Brunson until the evening.

The Harkers exchanged a glance, and Rosemary sighed, leaving her brother to guard their belongings while she walked toward the stationmaster.

"Excuse me? If you would be so kind as to direct us to Mrs. Wesson's Boarding House?"

The old man turned, giving first her, then the others, a

cautious once-over, thorough without being impolite. His gaze lingered for a long moment on Botheration, who had seated himself by Aaron's side, jaw open and tongue lolling to the side.

"Do you better than that," he said finally, raising his voice so they both could hear him. "Can take you there myself, if you don't mind the beast going in back. Otherwise, it's a bit of a walk for the missus."

It wasn't the first time they had been taken as husband and wife, and it was never worth the trouble of correcting the error. "We'd appreciate that, thank you," Rosemary replied.

The depot hack parked behind the hut was a battered machine, more wagon than car and smelling of must and iron, with an engine that did not so much purr as argue with itself. But the seats were well-padded, their bags and Botheration fit securely in the back, and by the time they pulled up at their destination, Aaron was thankful they had taken the man up on his offer. As the crow flew, it was likely only a mile or so to their destination, but the macadam road was pocked with snow and mud, and twisted and turned like a snake before finally making its way into town. Walking would have been deeply unpleasant.

Rosemary made conversation with their driver, but he'd ignored her discreet attempts to draw him into gossip, instead merely pointing out the business district as they passed through it, telling them that the river, and the source of the earlier smell, was on the other side. "Paper mill, new-built. Most days the smell don't carry, some days it does. Not much else on that side of the river save the ironworks and the bury-ing yard."

"Imagine they don't complain much about the smell," Aaron had said with a chuckle, then bit his lip and looked away when the driver gave him an odd look. Rosemary always warned him, his humor put people off.

Thankfully, the town itself offered some distraction. To his surprise, Brunson was not the backwater village he'd half expected. The storefronts they passed looked well-done-by, the streets dotted with healthy if now leafless trees, and de-spite the overall winter gloom, the houses all had the air of being well cared for, although few with the look of money.

The vehicle turned a corner and slowed, the engine pop-ping as it rumbled to a juddering stop.

"There ya are."

Aaron jumped down and reached up to help his sister from the seat before going around back to collect their carpet-bags and the weapons case. The old man didn't offer to help, which suited Aaron fine. Botheration leapt out over the side in one mostly graceful bound, padding around to rejoin his mistress even as the driver took off again, the car chugging and grumbling as it rattled away.

Aaron glanced over at his sister, one gloved hand pressed against her cheek as she studied the house in front of them, likely memorizing every detail well enough that she would be able to sketch it perfectly later, if required.

The house, like its neighbors, was neatly painted with

bright colors, the white lace curtains in its windows giving it a welcoming look. It was an unremarkable building on an unremarkable street; exactly what they needed.

Aaron took a breath of the cold morning air, then exhaled, settling himself into his body, preparing for the role they would need to play.

The moment they went through that door, nearly everything out of their mouths would be a lie.

He offered his sister his arm. "Are you ready?"

Rosemary nodded once, her face letting go of some of its sharpness, transforming into the smooth, pleasant features of a well-bred young woman. His own practiced facade slipped into place as well, and he led them up to the front door, where a small painted sign announced that they had arrived at Mrs. Wesson's Boarding House.

———

The door's bell had a deep, pleasant chime, and it was only a moment before they heard movement on the other side of the door, then the sound of a lock being turned. A young woman with olive-toned skin and sharp black eyes opened the door. Under her assessing gaze, Aaron resisted the urge to straighten his spine or check that there was no stain on his collar. They'd dressed for the part: respectable but not fancy, with enough wealth to pay their bills but not so much that they might draw attention. Like their destination, they were utterly and absolutely unremarkable, the sort of pair that you'd converse with and then forget by the time you turned away. There was no reason for this young woman to look so searchingly at him; he did not like it.

Rosemary shifted, drawing the girl's attention to her. "We had a reservation under the name of Harker." They had the confirming telegram in her carpetbag, in case there was any trouble, but the girl nodded, the shadows under her eyes at odds with the practiced, welcoming smile on her lips.

"Yes, miss. You're a mite early, but your rooms are ready. Leave your bags there. Bernard will come round and bring them up for you. I'm Jan, and if you've any questions or requests, you just come to me. Oh." Her chatter came to an abrupt halt as she noticed Botheration, and her face underwent a sea change from polite welcome to uncertainty. "The dog . . ."

"The hound is well-trained and will be no nuisance," Aaron said. "We were told that there was a kennel for him?"

"Oh, yes." The girl collected herself, nodding. "It's not fancy, but secure. I'm sorry, he's just . . . quite a large dog, isn't he?"

"Yes." Rosemary's tone was dry, much the same as if someone had commented that the sun was warm, or the night dark, and the girl flushed a little.

"We'll take him out back then?" The girl's voice rose, hesitant. Aaron smiled, used to that reaction.

"Put your hand out, palm down, just in front of your body," and he demonstrated for her, until she echoed his movement. Then Aaron tapped the top of the beast's blunt head. "Botheration, sniff."

The hound lowered his squared-off muzzle and took a deep snuffle, then washed the back of her hand with a broad, wet tongue. She giggled faintly and drew back her hand, wiping it on her skirt.

"Botheration, this is a friend." The hound looked up at Aaron, then at the girl, and his entire stance softened. "He'll follow you now."

"Friend" only meant someone not to be attacked without orders, but there was no need to tell the girl that. She took the leather lead Rosemary offered, then cast a look over her shoulder. "Gert!"

The girl who came down the hallway was slighter and younger, lacking the first girl's confident bearing but similar enough in coloring and face to be her sister. Gert's eyes widened at the sight of the hound, then she visibly steeled herself, stepping forward and reaching for the lead. Aaron coughed and shook his head gently at Jan. "Let me do this, Gert," the young woman said. "You get the folk signed in and show them to their rooms, please. Seven and eight."

The girl nodded, looking slightly disappointed, before putting on a cheerful expression. "If you'll only just sign in here, please?"

The desk with the registration book was by a window, and under the bleak winter light Aaron could see that the younger girl's lips were cracked, as though she'd been biting at the flesh there, and the skin under her eyes looked bruised, suggesting that she too had not been sleeping well.

He glanced at his sister, who nodded slightly; she had noted it as well. It was likely nothing, but they were walking into an unknown situation. Everything was potentially something.

"Bernard will bring your things up to your room, Jan told you? Breakfast is served at seven sharp," Gert said, blotting the ink in the ledger and handing them their keys, one each. "Mrs. Wesson sets a nice table but if you're late, you'll miss the muffins. Guests are expected to help clearing the table, and bringing their bedding down to be washed every week, but Jan and I will bring it back up and make the beds fresh."

"We're only booked for the week," Rosemary said. "But thank you."

"My pleasure, miss. This is the best place in all Brunson to stay, you'll see."

"I wouldn't have thought many were needed," Aaron said, as they followed the girl up the narrow stairs.

"Oh, all sorts of folk come to Brunson these days," Gert said. "Ever since the train came through, and they built the new mill."

The stationmaster had mentioned that as well. Aaron had no idea why a factory would bring visitors, but it seemed to be good news for the town.

"Them as come for business, they stay at the Rivers, mostly, to avoid the smell every morning, but you don't notice it much after a day or so." Gert had dimples that appeared as she grinned, her tiredness lifting for a moment. "And for all its fancy airs, between you and me, the beds are more comfortable here."

There were six doors spaced along a wallpapered hallway, three to a side, the electric sconces on the wall giving off a clean, bright light. The rooms they had been assigned were next to each other, and Gert pointed out the washroom at the far end of the hallway.

Rosemary thanked the girl and opened her door, disappearing inside with her satchel. Aaron gave the hallway another glance, making note of the closed doors, presumably housing other guests, then followed suit into his own room.

The space was simple, with a bed, a narrow wooden wardrobe, a straight-backed chair of similar wood, an iron washstand, and a braided rug on the floor between the bed and door. There was a narrow window, too small for even a child to climb in or out of, that looked out over the front street, which was currently empty save for two women walking arm in arm. The walls were a pink-tinged white, scuffed but clean, and the glass in the window had been washed recently. He sat on the edge of the bed, testing the mattress, and gave an approving nod.

"My compliments, Mrs. Wesson," he said out loud. Gert, for all her youthful enthusiasm, had been correct. They had stayed in far worse over the years.

It took only a few minutes to unpack his bag and hang his clothing in the wardrobe, placing his straight razor and comb by the washstand. The mirror was badly silvered, and he scowled at the distorted reflection before smoothing his features again.

"Play nice," he told his reflection, echoing Rosemary's advice, itself echoed from countless hunts before. "We'll get more with honey than steel."

The mysterious Bernard had not appeared with the weapons case yet. Hopefully the boy would not be foolish enough to try opening it; the lock was sturdy, but that could raise a question of *why* it was so heavily locked.

Which reminded him that he was currently under-armed. Fine for travel, less so once they were on the hunt. After changing from his travel outfit into less creased trousers and waistcoat, he checked the pistol holstered under his shoulder, then retrieved from his bag a palm-sized silver-edged blade that matched the iron one at his ankle and tucked it into his inner right jacket pocket. Shifting back and forth to make sure they were properly weighted for ease of movement, he twisted the silver cuff links in his sleeve and adjusted the matching bar in his tie to make sure they were secure. Honey might gather more, but silver, lead, and cold iron were the ways to win arguments.

He looked around the room to ensure that everything was where it should be, then reached into his pocket and drew out a piece of calcite. The wallpaper was difficult to work on, and it took longer than anticipated, but he managed to inscribe a protective sigil on each wall, just above eyesight.

Sigils were old folklore, predating Huntsmen. Rosemary disapproved of him using such things, but their mother had used them, saying they were tools, nothing more. And he did not particularly believe in his immortal soul, to be worrying about what the Church would doubtless say.

Huntsmen, according to the Church, were damned anyway, their blood unclean, unholy.

Aaron scoffed. The same Church labeled the uncanny as children's tales, or biblical beasts no longer an issue in the modern world. He'd sooner have a coal-boy at his side than a priest or preacher, dismissing true threats as superstition or magic.

Too much had been forgotten. Even common sigils relied on half-understood mysticism and a heavy salting of wishful thinking, and were as like to backfire as not. This one, though, he'd learned at his mother's knee, and knew that it worked.

The sigil would not stop anyone from entering the room—or their hostess from throwing them out for writing on her walls—but it should dissuade them from taking anything from the room. More importantly, it would tell Aaron if someone other than himself had entered.

Returning the calcite to his pocket, he checked his watch, then picked up his hat and coat and left the room, closing the door securely behind him. A moment later, Rosemary exited her room as well, as though she'd been waiting on him. She had shed her wide-brimmed traveling hat for a smaller cloche and fixed her hair back into a smooth chignon that made her seem younger than her twenty-six years. Still, add a few wrinkles around her eyes and some silver among the soft black curls, and she could have been the image of their mother in the last year of her life.

"A young brute I assume was Bernard brought the case to my room," she said. "Which is a bit Spartan, but not unpleasant. Yours?"

"Probably identical, down to the starched pillowcases. Bed's comfortable, though." He wondered why they'd thought the case should go to Rosemary, then shrugged it off as unimportant. As easy for him to retrieve his rifle from her room as for her to take the bow and bolts from his, were they needed. "Still want to question the widow first?"

"Since we have no idea how he died or where, yes. Unless you've reason to suggest otherwise?"

Aaron shook his head. She was right; the widow was the logical place to start. He just hated talking to the bereaved.

"Do you want to bring Bother with us, or leave him here?"

"Leave him here," she said, without hesitation. "There will be work for him soon enough, and I can't imagine he'd be a comforting sight to an old woman."

Of course, that raised the fact that they had no idea where to find the Widow Lovelace, having no idea where Molly Lane, the address on the letter they'd received, was.

A quick conversation with Gert, who was sweeping the hallway, revealed that the Lovelace home was only a few minutes' walk from the boarding house.

The girl kept her gaze determinedly on the floor, as though worried a speck of dirt might escape if she looked at them, but when they asked for directions, she glanced up, startled. "You knew Dr. Lovelace, then? Terrible shame, him dying so sudden like that, even though he was so old."

"Yes," Rosemary agreed, without answering the question. "Yes, a terrible shame." She supposed to a girl of barely fourteen, at most, Lovelace would have seemed ancient, although he had been only slightly older than her parents. "I don't suppose you know anything about what happened?"

"Oh." Gert blanched and looked down at the floor again. "No, miss. Have a good day, miss."

Her lips twitching at the firm dismissal from a girl a decade younger than herself, Rosemary wished her the same and followed Aaron out the door. His hat pulled low against the winter sun, Aaron waited while she pulled on her gloves, then said, "You think she knows something."

"The fact that she mentioned it made me hopeful, but I suspect she knows it will be her job, and perhaps her sister's as well, if she's caught gossiping with guests about something so gruesome." Rosemary shook her head. "It's never that easy."

"Maybe the widow will be able to give us enough to identify it."

"And maybe the uncanny will meet us at the front door and confess to all," she retorted. "Left at the end of the street, Gert said."

The boarding house was in the southeastern portion of town, which appeared to be purely residential: rows of square-faced, slant-roofed houses of timber and stone, two or three stories high and set directly on the road, as though they had been there first and the road had trod on their hems.

Mid-day on a Thursday, there were few people braving the cold, and those who were walked quickly, bundled into coats and mufflers, not pausing to stop and chat with neighbors or take note of strangers. A dog barked from behind a low stone fence, and a truck puttered past, battered and splattered with mud. Aaron, walking on the outside, sighed as slush and mud were kicked up by its wheels, splatting the side of his trousers and coat.

"Lovely. That and the noise, it's enough to make you miss horses."

"It's really not," Rosemary retorted. "Automotives don't leave piles in the middle of the road."

Gert's directions had been accurate; they'd barely time to properly start bickering before they found themselves at 13 Molly Lane.

They paused in front of the cottage, its gate propped open and the door still draped with a black wreath.

"Iron gate," Aaron noted. "Hazel and ninebark planted by the way, and dogwood at the window. Lovelace took precautions."

"He was family," Rosemary said. "Distant, but family. His wife . . . Margaret. I think I met her once, when I was very young. Dr. Lovelace came to see Papa, and she and Mama and I had tea." Her eyes were shadowed, the way they often were when she spoke of their mother.

Aaron hated when she talked about things he didn't remember. "And where was I when this all happened?"

"Asleep in your cradle, most likely. It was a long time ago." She took a deep breath, the air frosting the skin of her mouth, and pulled her shoulders back as though bracing to go into battle. "I hate this part of the job."

"It's better than having to deal with the police."

"Barely."

The woman who answered their knock looked older than the sixty-two her husband's obituary had stated, her face deep-lined and her eyes deep-set with sorrow, silver curls loose around tortoiseshell combs. She was dressed in unrelieved black, but a cameo set in a silver chain hung around her neck, and her withered fingers were burdened with heavy silver rings set with stones.

"Mrs. Lovelace? My name is Rosemary Harker, and this is my brother, Aaron. You sent us a letter. . . ."

"Yes." The woman blinked slowly, as though she were thinking through a haze. "Yes, I did. I . . . had somehow not realized you'd be so grown up now." She attempted to smile, the expression strained. "Come in, please."

The woman escorted them into the parlor, a solemn-looking room filled with an assortment of lamps but otherwise bare of most of the decorative clutter Aaron would have anticipated, every table instead hosting vases of lilies that made his nose twitch. There was another odor in the room, but he couldn't quite place it. Dried flowers, maybe, and stale lemon.

Rosemary sat with the widow on the sofa, a stiff-looking

thing covered in floral cloth, while Aaron settled himself gingerly into an armchair of the same fabric. The more comfortable-looking armchair, set at an angle to the sofa, was so clearly the deceased's chair Aaron would have cut off his left leg before sitting in it.

You might not know if the ghost lingered, but it was always safer to presume.

"Oh. Would you like some tea?" Mrs. Lovelace made a gentle gesture at the tea stand, a graceful thing of ebony and brass, supporting a teapot and several cups, plus a covered dish. "I'm afraid I'm out of biscuits at the moment, but there's still some plum cake left."

Aaron would have declined, but his sister shot him a warning glance. "That would be lovely, thank you."

The widow made as though to rise, and Rosemary coughed gently. "If you would allow Aaron . . . ?"

She looked dubious at the thought of a man pouring tea, but nodded, sinking back into her seat. He stood, using the opportunity to look around the room, scanning the windowsills, ceiling, and floor for sigils or other markings. It was unlikely there would be anything, but Rosemary was right: Lovelace had been a cousin, if distant. Not all family members became Huntsmen, but they all knew what they were, and what was out there. And if he'd left a note to send for them, if he'd thought to grow those plants outside, he'd have reason to know if something uncanny lurked in his town.

"We are so sorry for your loss," Rosemary was saying as he returned his attention to them, serving them each a cup of sweet, milky tea, suitable for calming nerves. "It must have been a terrible shock."

Mrs. Lovelace clutched at a handkerchief in one hand, while reaching for the tea with the other. The kerchief was not the delicate black lace thing you'd expect from a recent widow, but a larger cloth square, dark blue and worn. Her husband's, most likely.

"It was. It still is. I keep expecting him to be sitting there, with that terrible pipe of his. I tried to get him to switch over to cigarettes for years, but he just laughed and . . ." Her voice cracked, and she clenched the kerchief more tightly, the teacup trembling until she set it down, untouched, on the table. "I'm sorry, I—"

"No, no." Rosemary was so much better at this than he was, her voice just the right amount of soothing and sympathetic. "Such a loss, it needs to be mourned properly, but our loved ones need to be remembered too, yes? The good things as well as the sad."

The older woman touched the kerchief to her lips. "Yes. Thank you. And thank you for coming all this way, it seems silly now, but—"

"But he asked you to tell us what happened."

"Yes." She sniffled, and lifted her wrinkled chin firmly. "Yes, he did. And you came. . . ." She turned her gaze to Aaron, as though he might have the answers she was looking for. "Why did he leave me that note? I thought about ignoring it, but it was the last thing he wrote, and I couldn't bear to ignore his last wishes."

It looked for a moment as though she were going to dissolve into tears, and Aaron tensed, but she gathered herself back under control.

"Mrs. Lovelace, do you still have the note?"

"Yes. I thought . . . I couldn't bear to throw it away. It's right there," and she nodded to a small side table made of gleaming dark wood, where a sheet of paper rested, folded in thirds, the creases still sharp. Rosemary reached for it, unfolding the paper to reveal thick black ink strokes, a sturdy, no-nonsense hand. With a glance at the older woman, she read out loud, "'My dearest, I would not leave this on your shoulders. In the event of my death, from whatever causes, I ask that you reach out to the young Harkers and let them know the manner of my passing. They will know what to do.'"

It might not have made sense to the widow, but it was almost bluntly obvious to Aaron. But *what* had he feared? Aaron supposed the man couldn't have come right out and said something like, *A Redcap is stalking our streets*, but it would have simplified matters if he had.

"Do you know why he left that note?" The old man hadn't been Huntsmen himself, but he would have been trained in caution. How much had he told his wife?

The widow shook her head. "No. Tucker didn't like to bother me with his worries. I assume it was something to do with the matters your father used to look into. He would never tell me about that, either. Only that it was important, and secret, and I should never speak of it to anyone without his say-so. I used to tease him, say that he must be a government agent, or—well, it was the foolishness married couples say to each other. But I trusted him, and he trusted me."

The woman looked at them, her soft eyes worried. "Did that . . . did what he did with your father have something to do with his death? Was he working on something for your father? Can you tell me why my husband died?"

They could. But they shouldn't.

"Your letter was the first we'd heard of him in years," Aaron said, as gently as he knew how. "Our father . . . is no longer with us. But we will learn what we can." And tell her what they could. "Is there anything you can tell us about the days before his death? Anything that seemed strange, out of character, or simply . . . odd?"

There was fire still left in the widow, the way her eyes narrowed, not so much in anger as frustration. "I wish there was something I could tell you. Back in the days when he and your father corresponded, he would tell me if there was something I needed to keep my eyes open for, strangers hanging about, odd occurrences, that sort of thing, although he never told me *why*. But the past few years, there's been none of that. It's been quiet. Peaceful. He'd retired a few years ago, closed his practice. People go to Dr. Miller now."

She frowned, her wrinkled mouth thinning and turning down at the edges. "But the past few weeks, no, almost a month now, he'd seemed troubled. He started keeping a journal again, and I would come down in the morning and find him at the table with it open in front of him, a cup of tea already cooled. But he would laugh it off when I asked him about it, tell me that it was nothing I need worry about. So I didn't."

Aaron leaned forward, elbows on his knees. "Do you still have the journal?"

Mrs. Lovelace shook her head, a single silver curl coming loose from under a tortoiseshell comb to dangle along her jaw. "The police asked the same thing, and I gave it to them. Although I don't know what use they'll have of it, unless they read Latin. Tucker used to laugh, said he'd started doing so in school, to make sure he kept his skill with the language, and then just kept doing it."

Aaron looked at Rosemary and gave just a hint of a nod. Unlike the local constabulary, he had enough skill with the language to translate the journal, once they had it in their possession.

The trick would be getting it from the police.

"But that last night . . . He never came to bed." She blushed slightly, looking down at her hands, as though betraying something deeply personal. "I never heard him leave the house, but when I woke up, he was gone, and then the officer came and . . .

"He never walked outside at night. His eyesight was beginning to fail, and darkness made it worse. That is why we had so many lamps. He couldn't even read without—" Her voice cut off. "But he must have gone outside, mustn't he have? Because that's where he . . ." She took a deep breath. "That is where he died. Was killed."

Now she did break, although only a few tears escaped,

wetting the soft skin of her cheek. "Something killed him, on the streets of our own town. And nobody heard or saw a thing."

Aaron looked at Rosemary, feeling the first stirrings of panic at the old woman's tears. She rolled her eyes at him, then reached over and took one of the old woman's hands between her own. "Ma'am. Mrs. Lovelace."

"Margaret, please."

Rosemary nodded. "Margaret. You said it happened on a street . . . near here? Do you know which one?"

"I . . . of course. You want to . . ." And she swallowed, then sat up straighter. "You will want to see where it happened. He had a route he walked during the day. He must have been following it. They found him . . . they found him on Culpepper. By the Broughtons' house . . . oh, which would mean nothing to you, my apologies. The white house with the dark green trim."

Her face crumpled. "They, when they took . . . They said that it was likely a cougar, gone hungry in the winter. That he must have gone under a branch, and . . . It was a closed casket. I never had a chance to say goodbye."

Aaron was afraid they'd be treated to hysteria, but while the look she turned on them both then was filled with grief, it was no soft, weeping thing, but rather a fierce, hard determination. "They told me it was a cougar, but they took his journal. They wouldn't have done that if it had been an animal attack, would they?"

"It may be that they are simply being thorough," Rosemary said. Aaron didn't believe that, and neither did she. But neither of them knew what it did mean. Yet.

"You'll find out." Mrs. Lovelace sounded certain. "You'll tell me?" She turned and spoke directly to Aaron now, as though she'd been waiting for a man to lay her problems in front of. "You'll find out what killed him? It won't bring him back, it won't change anything, but . . . I need to know."

Aaron and Rosemary exchanged glances. If Lovelace had left a note for them to be called in, if it was related to whatever left him worried at night, there was no way they could tell her the truth.

And even if they could, it certainly wouldn't bring her peace.

Three

ONCE OUTSIDE THE Lovelaces' home, Rosemary took a deep breath, the cold air somehow kinder to her chest than the stifling, lily-ridden air inside.

"I believe they use those flowers to make us envy the dead," she said. "There's no other explanation for it."

Aaron looked at her blankly. "What?"

She shook her head, drawing her gloves back on against the bitter chill. "Nothing. The street is that way, Mrs. Lovelace said."

They walked for a bit in silence, each working their own way through what the widow had told them. At least, Rosemary was. She loved her brother dearly, but even she could not always say what went on in his thoughts.

"A catamount would break a man's neck, wouldn't it? Jumping down from a branch? That would be quick, certainly, but unless the creature took actual bites from the body, why not let the widow say goodbye properly?"

"And even if it had started to eat, clothing can hide the

worst damage," Aaron said, nodding. "It may be that they underestimated how tough the old lady was."

"Maybe." He didn't sound convinced of his own theory; neither was she.

The house with the dark green trim was easy enough to find. However, there was nothing to set that particular patch of street apart from any other. The macadam itself looked undisturbed, any trace of violence long since washed away by snow and wind, and whatever traffic traveled down this residential road.

"He didn't walk far. Five minutes, even injured; he could have made it back to the house? Or run, called for help. No one was awake, getting ready for the day, unable to sleep, maybe up with a baby?" Rosemary turned in a slow circle, looking at the houses as though one of them might offer an answer.

"Easy enough to pretend you didn't hear anything," Aaron said. "Not at that hour, in the dark. Maybe it was a cat or a fox. Or a neighbor's fight you don't want to know about."

Rosemary made a rude sound but didn't disagree.

"The branches aren't strong enough to hold a full-grown cat." He studied the trees growing on either side of the street, their branches mostly bare of leaves. "A city cop, maybe they wouldn't know that, but up here?"

Their breath puffed white in the air, the temperature dropping as the sun made its way west. "It's possible," Rosemary said, "that a cougar, on spotting an elderly man walking at night, moving uncertainly because of vision problems, would consider him a potential meal. Especially in winter when there are fewer options."

"It's possible," Aaron agreed, but in the tone of voice that said he didn't believe it for a moment and was merely humoring her for the sake of the argument. "But if she doesn't believe it, I'm not going to either."

Rosemary hummed her agreement. The Widow Lovelace was old and grieving, but there was fire in her still, and intelligence to spare. If the locals thought her a frail and delicate woman to be coddled or bamboozled, they were fools.

"And if it was a cougar, why was there anything left to find?" Aaron continued, warming to his argument. "The body was discovered in the morning, at dawn. If nobody came by, it would have dragged the body off, and if someone had come by to disturb it before then, everyone in town would know it by now."

"A body, probably with its neck broken, and claw marks, if not bites taken from it, left abandoned in the street for anyone to find." Rosemary took a few steps in silence, running through every uncanny she could think of that might do such a thing. "It's more likely that the police think that it was a human, maybe with a knife that mimicked animal claws. An old man, uncertain in the dark, would have been easy prey to anyone younger and stronger—or angry enough."

"And they don't want to alarm the widow—or the rest of the town—with fear of an unknown killer, so they make up a story about a cougar? That's thin, Rosemary." Thin, but logical. The outside world was always more comfortable blaming the known than the unknown, even when the known could not possibly be the cause.

He shoved his hands into his coat pockets, obviously regretting not having brought gloves with him when they left the boarding house. "Think it's worth bringing Bother out to sniff around?"

"After how many days?" Rosemary shook her head. "If we knew what we were hunting, I'd say yes. But too many people would have crossed the scene already, to set him on a cold trail."

Two young boys dashed down the street toward them, veering into the road to go around them; an older woman following at a slower pace gave the Harkers an apologetic shrug, calling out to the children in German until they slowed their run and came back to her.

Rosemary looked at her brother with eyebrows raised, as though to say, *See?*

"We can't overlook the possibility that the attacker was human," Aaron said once they were alone again. "And if it is a human attack, there's nothing here for us."

Huntsmen did not interfere in the actions of man against man; that was for the police to handle, as best they could.

"What could an older man like Dr. Lovelace have done that inspired such a rage? And a rage that his wife would know nothing about?"

"Assuming she wasn't lying to us? She admitted that he didn't tell her everything. His journal might be the key. And if it was an uncanny, odds are good he would have left more detail there."

"Dear God." Rosemary put her free hand to her mouth, as though trying to keep anything from slipping out unguarded. "If they are able to read his code, and he said anything about the uncanny, or Huntsmen . . ."

"Then they'll likely think him an old man with an old man's delusions," Aaron said, dismissive of the risk. "They'd rather believe it a catamount than a man, and they certainly have no desire to consider the uncanny world; any evidence they find that upsets them will likely be ignored."

He said it with the confidence of history. Huntsmen dated back, more or less, to the sixteenth century, and in all that time they'd never become more than fodder for fairy tales.

"But they took the journal."

"Because the widow mentioned it. They'll hold it for a while. Then, once enough time has passed, the police will give it back to her, with profuse apologies." But they needed to see it before then, in case Lovelace had left clues for them to follow.

They had been walking for some time now, following Dr. Lovelace's steps. The houses were becoming smaller and less well-kept, the paint on trim faded and chipped, low stone walls overrun with vines. On one doorstep a ratty-eared dog slept, curled against the cold, and a child's cries could be heard from another of the buildings, heartbroken over some slight or pain.

"I wonder if he had a patient here, among the workers," Rosemary said. "If that's why he walked this way, rather than keep to his own part of town. It certainly wasn't for the view."

"You get used to this, the girl said?" Aaron asked, sniffing the air. The bitter taint was back again, a low-level tang on the tongue, sulfur and smoke, like a burnt-out match. "Odds are it will only get worse, the closer you are to the river." He eyed the houses around and ahead of them. "You're probably right; workers live here."

"Do they have a separate store for them to shop at, too?" When Aaron glanced at her, confused by her bitter tone, she waved him off.

"If Dr. Lovelace had been associated with the mill owners, I might see a worker attacking him, but he was a medical doctor. And from what we've heard, one who actively helped those less fortunate, even retired. He should have been perfectly safe here." He took his hands out of his pockets to rub them together briskly, then shoved them back in again.

"We need more information," Rosemary said. "Anything that might have given him cause to worry, anything odd or off. We need that journal."

Aaron gave a half-shouldered shrug. "I *know*, Rosemary. I know." He made a face to match hers, frustration and annoyed exasperation. "If she'd just kept quiet . . ."

Rosemary gave her brother a look but didn't bother to call him on his callousness. Their father had more than once said he was a throwback; Aaron found it easier to use sigils and spells, and harder to understand how people thought and reacted. If it hadn't been for Rosemary—she cut that thought off at the root. They had each other.

"Her husband had just been killed," she reminded him. "I doubt she was thinking about preserving evidence for us."

He took the rebuke without flinching. "I can go to the station, play the grieving young cousin called by the widow to help her settle the old man's estate. It we're lucky, they'll decide that it's easier to give me his journal than argue about it. Particularly if they are determined to call this an animal attack."

Neither of them had a high opinion of the police officers they had met over the years, although they admitted that most of their hunts were well outside those gentlemen's realm of competence. The simplest answer and the least amount of work was always preferred by law enforcement, especially when there was no benefit to hard work: the man would still be dead.

"Central station will be closer to the well-to-do," she said, tugging at his arm to change direction. "If you're to beard them, you might as well do it now."

Aaron tsked. "Criminals' cant from such a genteel young lady. Shocking."

"Oh, hush, that's hardly cant. While you are sweet-talking the local officials into handing over evidence, I will, as usual, hunt down the keepers of local history. If we're very lucky, there will be legends of an infestation of some creature who kills for fun, not feeding." Each hunt was different, but the first step was always the same: gather information. "Did you happen to notice—?"

"Corner of Main, just down from the bakery with the blue-striped awning. Police station's catty-corner across the street from there." His tone suggested that she should have noticed that as well. "And don't look so sulky. You know you're more likely to find something than I am."

He wasn't saying that simply to make her feel better; Aaron didn't think that way. It might have been more interesting to question the police, but there were few sources of information so reliable as librarians, particularly in these small towns. If there was anything askew about the town's history, recent or past, a librarian would know and likely be more than happy to talk about it.

They turned onto a street that seemed familiar. Rosemary thought it might have been the one they'd driven down on their way to the boarding house, but seeing something from an automobile did not place it in her memory the way walking did.

"I never thought I would be nostalgic for a bloody troll massacre," Aaron said, seemingly from nowhere. "At least then we knew what and why immediately, and all we had to do was find where."

"Didn't you break your arm during that hunt?"

"No, that was the kelpie roundup, when Joshua lost track of what he was doing and let them stampede." He sounded almost wistful about it. "Joshua's where, now?"

"Livonia," she said. "For almost five months now, almost six."

Joshua was a cousin on their mother's side, full-blooded Huntsmen on both sides the way they were, and Lovelace had not been, and another who had gone overseas when the call for aid came. She had received one letter from him, early on, and then nothing.

They had reached what looked to be the center of town. More people were out and about here, doing whatever it was folk did with their days on the far edge of America, and the Harkers were getting curious looks, immediately recognizable as strangers. Rosemary smiled, polite but cool, at a woman who was sizing her up, and the woman blushed and looked away.

"Assuming that the authorities are idiots, and Dr. Lovelace had cause to call us in. What do you think it was?"

Her brother did not like to leap to speculation, much less conclusions, but Rosemary knew that he would have ideas, ready to be taken out and sorted against the evidence. "Up here, in such an isolated town? It could be a handful of anythings, from wendigo to werewolf."

He winced as an older gentleman gave them an odd look, and lowered his voice. "Or maybe a snallygaster, although it's rare to find them this far north."

"Not in winter, certainly." Rosemary enjoyed the colder weather, not least because many of the uncanny creatures they hunted did *not*. Uncanny were dangerous, but predictable. There was something in them that did not encourage creativity.

They passed the bakery Aaron had mentioned, and two churches on corners opposite each other, one Methodist, the other Catholic. And there, at the far end of the street, there was a small, two-story building with a sign out front proclaiming it to be the Brunson Free Library.

"And this is where I leave you," he said, letting her slip her hand from his arm and lifting his hat in polite, half-mocking salute before turning to go back the way they'd come.

"Be careful when you speak with the police," she said in return, not without some spite. "We do not need a repeat of the St. Louis incident."

Aaron had the rare grace to flush, although she could not tell if it was from embarrassment or annoyance. "I assure you, I learned that lesson well enough to have no risk of repeating it."

"Good." She smiled then, reaching up to pat his shoulder in a way she knew he hated. He had been shorter than her only a few years ago, but now they could look eye to eye. Rosemary hoped that he was finally done growing; it would be annoying to have to look up at him every time. "Meet you at the tea room we just passed when we're finished?"

He gave a cheeky salute in agreement and turned away, walking toward the police building. She watched him go, exasperation warring with affection as it often did. He was her brother and she loved him, but she worried about him, too. Huntsmen blood ran stronger in some than others, and a heavy dose did not make for an easy life.

But just then she had her own work to do. Taking a deep

breath, she quieted her thoughts and put aside everything save for the most superficial of curiosity. "Folklorist, I think," she said as she pushed open the swinging gate and walked up the path. "They always like that one."

The little brick building behind the library sign was so new it practically squeaked when she walked in the front door, and the smell of sawdust and paper made her nose wrinkle. Built at the same time as the new mill, she supposed, with the money that followed.

Rosemary had nothing against libraries; these little refuges of information were essential to what Huntsmen did. But she found herself resenting them nonetheless, every time she walked into one. Those who worked here did not have to hide their knowledge, did not have to pretend to be something they weren't, but could flaunt it, free and unafraid. Had gone to college and studied among others of like mind.

To be Huntsmen was to be quiet, to be known only to your prey and never those around you, to never speak freely of the things you had done. She could not imagine being anything else, but there were moments she wondered what else she might have been, given a chance.

By the time the door swung shut behind her, Rosemary had put those thoughts behind her as well, every inch alert to her surroundings, making note of every detail.

The first floor was an open space, light coming from the windows set two to a wall, with sheer curtains. The floor was polished wood, and a long wooden table was placed to the left side of the space, two small electric lights set over it, with a series of mismatched wooden chairs alongside. The rest of the room was filled with overstuffed reading chairs and lamps, equally mismatched, and shelving laden with books and periodicals, newspapers laid across long wooden rods at the end of every bookcase. At the far side, there was a narrow staircase and a glass-fronted cabinet displaying oversized leather-bound books. Town ledgers, she thought, or genealogical records.

There were two women seated at a desk, one in a chair behind it, the other perched on a corner, her skirt and jacket dark purple over a high-necked cream blouse, legs crossed at the ankles. It was a cozy enough picture, their heads bent together in conversation, but Rosemary had the feeling that she had stumbled onto a disagreement of some sort.

She coughed gently, as they did not seem to have heard her enter.

The woman seated on the desk looked amused at her interruption, while the woman behind the desk jumped a little, as though caught doing something naughty.

"I'm terribly sorry," Rosemary said, not sorry at all. "I can return another time?"

"No, please, be welcome." The woman on the edge of the desk slid gracefully to her feet, reaching for the hat resting on an empty chair nearby. "I was just about to leave."

"Jes—" The seated woman sounded almost despairing, although her face was now perfectly composed.

"It's all right, dear. You have a guest to help."

Definitely something going on there. Rosemary smiled

politely at the woman who was leaving, noting the expensive cut of her suit and the ostrich plume on her matching felt hat, unexpected so far from New York or Boston. She looked to be in her early to mid-thirties, her face lovely and round, with eyes that were not so darkly lashed without help.

She patted the desk once as though to attract the seated woman's attention. "When you've calmed down a little, we can talk about this again," she said, and with a cool nod to Rosemary, left the library, closing the door behind her with a needlessly firm hand.

The woman behind the desk opened her mouth as though to say something before recalling herself, pasting on a polite, utterly meaningless smile.

"I'm so sorry about . . . that. I'm Miss Baker, town librarian and historian. How may I help you?"

Rosemary was pleased that a woman was the librarian; men were too often suspicious, or tried to tell her what they thought she should learn, rather than what she needed to know. Women could be easily as suspicious, especially if she pushed too hard, but she knew how to turn their levers more easily, and without complications.

She stepped forward, summoning up every scrap of charm she possessed. "I was hoping that you might be able to help me, yes. My name is Rosemary, and I'm looking for some information about the history of the town?" She made her voice rise at the end of every sentence, adding a dollop of sweetness that felt wildly unnatural to her. Thankfully, the woman seemed not to notice anything off.

"Of course. That's exactly what I'm here for." This woman had kind eyes, deep brown and wide-set, with a fringe of dirty-blond hair curled across her forehead and down over her ears where it wasn't swept back into a knot at the back of her neck. She looked to be older than Rosemary by a few years. Thirty at most, her clothing nowhere near as stylish as her guest, though the dark brown dress she wore was perfectly presentable. Rosemary had a thought that when she did smile truly, it would light her entire face, transforming it into something lovely.

"What sort of information in particular are you looking for?"

"Myths, mostly." Rosemary touched her lips with her fingertips, bringing the woman's gaze up to her own face, catching and holding her attention. "It's a little hobby I have, collecting stories about the towns I visit." She gave a light laugh, every inch the harmless eccentric. "So many places have their own local legends, but then they die out and are lost. I'd like to collect them, keep them for future generations."

Aaron should be the one doing this; despite his love for novels, he had the brain for history, for facts and documents. And he was likely making a mess of things with the police, just like he had in St. Louis. But there was nothing for it. She could not step inside the police station. No woman could, not if she expected to be taken seriously, or thought a decent woman. Rosemary would have to trust him, as always.

And he had been right; the police had no reason to help, but a librarian's raison d'être was to provide information. She was far more likely to learn something of importance here if she did her job correctly.

So Rosemary smiled the way she'd practiced in the mirror, tilting her head and inviting the other woman to smile with her.

Miss Baker did, a warmer smile than she'd worn before, clearly pleased with Rosemary's request, and Rosemary had been right: it transformed her face.

"That's a lovely hobby, and an excellent topic of research. The local mythology is quite fascinating! Although there isn't all that much centered around this town, I'm afraid. We simply haven't the wealth of stories you'll find farther south, like Sleepy Hollow or Spuyten Duyvil." She squinted charmingly, and Rosemary felt her own smile warm and become real, helplessly. "Although this close to the Great Lakes, I'm sure you're aware of our Bessie?"

"The lake monster? I've gathered some of the stories, yes." Another Huntsmen pair had spent several weeks up by Lake Erie a few years back, trying to discover if there was any truth to the sightings. They'd come up empty, and the matter had been dismissed. "Truthfully, I thought the stories about her were always a little too detailed. If you were close enough to see something like that, it seems more likely that you'd end up in its belly, not telling the story to a reporter the next day?"

"Exactly!" Miss Baker's eyes sparkled with humor, the delicate skin around them crinkling with easy laugh lines. "Fish tales. Men don't know the first thing about lying properly."

Suddenly, Rosemary didn't mind letting Aaron handle the

police. She glanced at the chair off to the side, where the other woman's hat had rested, tilting her head and raising an eyebrow in question.

"Please," Miss Baker said, gesturing to it. "I may not be able to help much, but I will do what I can."

Rosemary hooked her fingers around the arm of the chair, dragging it carefully toward the desk, wincing a little when the legs squeaked against the polished wood of the floor. They must have just finished this building for the wood to be that unscuffed. Or perhaps the building simply didn't see much use. A pity, if so.

The librarian waited until she had settled herself, then lifted a pen from the blotter and pulled a pad of paper toward her. "If you have already collected our Bessie, what else might you be looking for? There are a number of ghost ships reputed to haunt these waters, though none locally. Or perhaps the Dragon of Lake Superior?" She pursed her lips in thought. "There are fewer stories about him than Bessie, but they date back to the local Indian tribes across the border in Canada. Although they call him the Great Water Cat, not a dragon, and say he's a shape-shifter demon of some sort. Whenever a boat disappears without a trace, the old-timers say the Water Cat ate them."

That sounded . . . like something she and Aaron should likely follow up on, but not just then. One hunt at a time.

"Something a little more local, ideally." She smoothed her skirt over her knees and leaned forward, clasping her hands and resting them in her lap. They were looking for something that hunted on land, and hunted viciously. "Relevant to the town itself, perhaps?"

If Dr. Lovelace had been killed by an uncanny, it was likely the creature had been here for some time. Rovin' Marys aside, few uncanny traveled far from their dens or lairs, and damned few of the large ones could be in any place for long without leaving a mark. If there was something in the woods around town, someone would have encountered it before now, and hopefully lived to tell the tale. Even if they didn't know what it was they were telling.

"Oh dear." Miss Baker turned the pen in her hands. A simple silver bangle glinted on her wrist, a marked difference from the flashy garnet bobs in her ears. "I'm afraid that the town has not been around long enough to gather any truly interesting legends. Our ghosts tend to congregate at Old Fort, and of course, Holy Sepulchre, closer to Rochester." For a moment, Rosemary thought the woman would cross herself, but a hand remained busy with the pen, the other resting in her lap. "Such a terrible thought, that souls remain trapped here, rather than being freed to heaven."

"Yes. Quite." Rosemary had never seen a ghost herself, but from what she had been taught, they were less lost souls than lingering energies of every festering resentment and deep-rooted grudge ever held. There was a reason folk were shriven before death, after all. If the town had ghosts, they would certainly know of it.

She needed to keep the woman on track. "I suppose I was hoping for something of a more . . . physical nature?"

The woman's hands froze on the pen, a little hiccup of movement, then began turning it again. "How so?"

Rosemary wasn't so charmed by the woman that she didn't notice the hesitation, but chalked it up to surprise.

"Less ghosts, more . . . solid? For instance, my mother told me stories of the whip-poor-will men. They are said to be onionskin wraiths, frail but powerful, with the ability to grant a man a wish—or ruin his life, if he disrespected them."

The librarian now looked amused rather than worried. "I admit such a thing would be more interesting than ordinary ghosts haunting the cupboard or schoolhouse. But no, there are no such stories told here. And no elves, either. It would certainly be useful to have someone shelve the books and order my papers for me overnight!" She had dimples, did Miss Baker, and knew how to use them. "Perhaps I should leave a bowl of cream out overnight, and see what happens?"

"Likely you would have a clowder of cats rather than anything useful," Rosemary said. Inwardly, she was wincing; people were often such fools, foolish enough to in fact try such a thing. At best, they might end up with brownies, seeking to trade skills for shelter. At worst . . .

At worst the fey would arrive.

She would not wish that on anyone, much less this librarian with the soft brown eyes and dimples.

"Of course, with recent events, we may have our own ghosts soon enough." Miss Baker shuddered, but if Rosemary was any judge of people, and she prided herself that she was, there was something other than fear or distress behind that shudder. She had the look of a woman who knew she knew more than anyone else and was desperate to prove it. The look of a woman in need of a confidante.

Rosemary schooled her own features, showing a hint more than polite surprise and curiosity as a baited lure. "Oh?"

Some situations, it was better to lead people sideways into indiscretion, implying a shared knowledge so that they need not fear spilling secrets they should not have. That was Rosemary's strength, and why she was usually the one to speak with possible witnesses. But she thought that this woman would rather be the dispenser of gossip than the sharer of same. Power, for a woman who might not otherwise have any past the walls of this library.

Rosemary felt a twinge of regret at using the woman so, but did not let that stop her.

There was a moment where it seemed as though Miss Baker would not speak. Then Rosemary could swear she saw something break behind the other woman's eyes. "An older gentleman was found dead in the road a few mornings back. Terrible tragedy, of course. His poor wife. The police are saying that it was a cougar, and some folk swear they heard it scream in the night. But . . ." Her voice dropped, the woman readying to impart a secret, and Rosemary leaned in, just a touch. "But cats don't leave their food in the middle of a road. Trust me, they don't. And even if once it might have been startled away by a car approaching, or another animal, what about the others?"

Rosemary sat up, all pretense of idle curiosity abandoned. "Others?"

Miss Baker nodded her head, and her voice dropped again, almost to a whisper, so that Rosemary could barely hear. "There were two bodies found, before his. James Underwood, and poor Todd Ottering. And now with the doctor, three in a single month!"

The Widow Lovelace had said nothing of any of this, might not have known. She had not seemed the sort to gossip. But as a doctor, even retired, would he have known about the two before him? Was that what had kept him awake and worried at night?

"That is truly awful," Rosemary said with absolute sincerity. "They died in the same manner? Do the police think a cougar is stalking the town?"

If they did, they were worse than fools. No, she was reasonably sure they thought they were dealing with a human predator. But was this why they were pretending otherwise, to prevent rumors from spreading?

"Not the same way, no. Mr. Underwood worked at the mill," Miss Baker said. "They said it was a terrible accident, and heaven knows it's terribly dangerous work, being around such large machinery. And poor Mr. Ottering was beaten to death. They said it must have been a hobo come on him and become violent. It simply seems hard to believe, here in Brunson. We're not Rochester, after all."

"Indeed."

Miss Baker's face softened. "But I cannot imagine Mr. Ottering being seen as a threat to anyone, even the most benighted of souls. And poor Dr. Lovelace? He'd be more likely to bring the poor man home and feed him. They were both good men." There was something in her voice, as though she was begging Rosemary to say that the deaths were merely rotten chance, that there was no connection, no evil in the world.

"Alas, there are some who will attack for their own meanness or hurt, rather than any cause or insult given. The wrong place at the wrong time, I suppose."

It was a platitude, but something in her words made Miss Baker's eyes widen, as though shocked. Surely she was not so innocent as to think all men kind and good?

"Oh. Oh dear."

Rosemary felt a moment of guilt for worrying the woman, who was clearly taking her words to heart. "I would not worry overmuch about ghosts; I'm sure that their spirits were laid to rest with a proper burial, and their families given peace." And if not, ghosts were simple to dispel. Whatever was lurking here, which might have killed three people now, would be more difficult.

"Oh. Of course, yes." Miss Baker placed her pen down on the paper, fussily precise, her dimples gone now. "I am sorry that I was unable to help you more with your search. If you would like, I could read through some of our older books and see if the local folklore has anything I might have overlooked? Perhaps another town might suit your needs better?"

Rosemary tilted her head, taken by surprise by the other woman's sudden change of tone. Rather than upset, or frightened, she sounded almost . . . angry? Her training told her to dig further. But to continue, after being told quite clearly that this conversation was at an end, would raise suspicions.

"Yes. Perhaps. I do thank you for your time, and your patience. Perhaps I will have a chance to return and browse for myself, before we leave. But for now I must rejoin my brother, before he wonders where I've gotten myself to."

Miss Baker did not stand to see her out, but Rosemary felt the woman's gaze on her as she walked to the door. And yet, when she turned back to wave farewell, the librarian had turned her attention to the papers in front of her, pen working furiously.

Outside the library, Rosemary paused, frowning at a spot of dirt that had attached itself to the palm of her right glove. She could not remember touching anything that had been dirty, but perhaps when she moved the chair. The action allowed her time to wait, counting off the seconds under her breath. Sure enough, after a moment the delicate curtains in a window of the library fluttered slightly, as though someone stood behind, twitching them aside to see the road. Or, perhaps, whoever was standing in the road.

Miss Baker was watching her. To make sure she left? To catch one last glimpse? Rosemary was not unaware of the impression she left, and the librarian, a modern young woman of limited opportunity, had seemed gratified to have an attractive new audience.

"But not at the end," she said to her glove. "At the end, she wanted me gone. Why?"

There was no way to tell. Rosemary could only go with what her intuition told her, and that was that Miss Baker, town librarian, had told her everything she knew, and now feared that her indiscretion might be used against her.

"Never fear," she told the woman as she began to walk away from the building, to every appearance a young lady with nothing more on her mind than a soiled glove and an engagement for tea. "I would not do that to another woman. Not without reason, at least."

She was no radical or suffragette to wave banners and risk arrest for a Cause, but as Aaron would say, she wasn't not, either. And gossip, certainly, was a right both sexes should exercise as they saw fit.

Particularly when it was so useful to her needs.

Rosemary nodded at the pair walking toward her, a young man and an older gentleman, who nodded in return as they passed. They were clearly taking a constitutional for the older man's health, as he was bundled in a heavier jacket than even the winter chill could justify, and the younger man held his arm in such a way as to indicate that he feared his companion might fall.

The elderly died easily, of so many causes. But the other two victims had been younger men, one of them still hale enough to work in a factory.

"Three deaths in a single month." It was hardly unheard of in a town this size, particularly if it was indeed growing quickly. And certainly, an accident and a death by misadventure, although terrible, were not things unexpected in this day and age. Factories could be dangerous places, and murders . . . well, despite what most people wanted to believe, they could and did happen everywhere, even without uncanny influences.

But Dr. Lovelace had been worried about something before his death. He had instructed his widow to contact them. Every instinct Rosemary had told her something was here. Something violent, and uncanny. But were the other deaths in truth connected to Dr. Lovelace's, or were they purely coincidence?

Rosemary exhaled, willing her nerves to settle. With luck, Aaron had been able to learn more from the police. Miss Baker would likely not welcome a second visit.

She checked the hour on her wristlet, surprised to see that very little time had passed. It was unlikely that Aaron was done yet, as it would inevitably take him longer to find someone official who could and would speak with him. But instead of heading to the tea room where they'd agreed to meet, Rosemary turned back toward the boarding house. She had not wanted to bring Botheration with them originally, for good and valid reasons, but if she had time, there was no reason not to give the hound a chance to sniff around. If he found nothing, that would be useful to know. And if he did find something . . .

Well, that would also be useful to know.

Rosemary was late. Aaron checked his watch yet again, then clicked the cover closed and dropped it into his vest pocket, frowning. An hour and a little more past when they had split up. It was not like his sister to dawdle; they had both been raised to be punctual.

"She's likely just having better luck than you," he told the tea steeping on the table in front of him, the cream-colored pot gleaming under the soft lights of the tea room. "If you go in search of her, she'll only be annoyed with you."

It might be that she had found something worth following up on, or merely gotten tangled in a conversation she could not gracefully excuse herself from, and would be here any moment, her face flushed and eyes gleaming, and with a notebook full of information.

He had his own notebook, tucked away in his pocket, and information to share as well. The police station had been surprisingly useful, although not intentionally. Aaron drummed his fingers on the table, the white cloth muffling the sound and turning it into an exercise of frustration. He could do with a cup of coffee, not tea, or better yet a belt of brandy. But that would have to wait. He did not drink while he was on a hunt; he could not afford to have his instincts dulled. One drawback of Huntsmen blood: they did not handle alcohol well.

He poured the tea, then shifted in his chair, aware that he

was being watched. He was one of only two men in the place this early in the afternoon, the other an older gentleman there with his young daughters, neither of them old enough to put up their hair, playing very seriously at pouring the tea for their father. The rest of the guests were women in groups of two and five, and they were all eyeing him with varying levels of interest and suspicion.

Aaron was not particularly vain: the Harker line was a handsome one, making up in good bone structure what they lacked in finances or, according to his maternal grandfather, common sense. Young women, and some not so young, often eyed him as though he were a porterhouse steak, and this was the domain of women, and he the intruder. But even if he were interested, there was no place in his life for marriage, nor any particular interest at this time.

Not that it mattered. Being Huntsmen limited your social reach considerably, and he knew others thought him too much a throwback, too fey in his mind and manners, to be considered an appropriate match. Rosemary would have had better luck, save for the number of young men gone overseas.

It didn't bother him, despite what his sister thought. His parents had understood, had never tried to force him to be other than what he was. Huntsmen blood was tainted blood, that was what *made* them Huntsmen. There was no shame in it.

Freed from the usual worries another young man of eligible age might have, the habitués of such tea rooms amused Aaron. Particularly the older women, solemn, firm-faced ladies who drank their tea and spoke to each other in low, serious voices, their chins tucked in and their hands full of meaning. Rosemary might deny interest in the suffragette cause, but he thought them fascinating, and he enjoyed watching the fluttering of feathers among the hens gathered here, knowing that underneath their lace and flowers they held claws equal to any cockerel in the yard. Let men have their taverns and coffeehouses: a revolution of equal force could be built under tea cozies and corsets, and he wished them well with it.

But politics itself did not interest him, and what-might-be was not his concern. Not today, at least. He was here to discover what uncanny had overstepped its place, and end it. Nothing less, nothing more.

He'd just taken another sip of his tea when he saw his sister through the plate-glass storefront, Botheration's brindle hide visible at her knee. She must have gone back to the boarding house, then. From habit, he did a quick assessment: she did not seem distressed, her attire was perfectly in place, and while the beast was at her side, it was not pressed against her the way it would be if she were upset, nor alert as it would be if she needed protection. But something was wrong.

He waited until she turned and caught his eye, then lifted his left hand slightly, asking if she planned to join him.

Rosemary shook her head once, then tilted her head toward the street, inviting him to join her outside instead.

He nodded once in return, then lifted two fingers politely to signal to a passing waitress, indicating that he was done with his tea.

"Nothing to eat, then?" The woman was twice his age, round-faced and yellow-skinned, with black curls puffed around her face unbecomingly. He resisted the urge to pull at one, the way he might have tugged at Rosemary's ringlets when they were children.

"Afraid not," he said, folding his napkin neatly on the table and leaving money for his tab, then picking up his hat and coat. "Perhaps another time."

———————

There were more people on the street now than when he had entered the tea room, although it was still nothing to New Haven, where there might be more people downtown on an afternoon than lived in this entire town. He nodded politely at two young girls who entered the tea room as he was leaving, hearing their giggles mesh with the gentle chime of the bell overhead. Rosemary had not waited for him but rather strolled on, and he hurried to catch up with her.

He'd been right: he could feel the tension in her body, although her face showed no distress, no expression other than that of a young woman taking a pleasant walk with her dog and her companion. Mother had trained her well. Better than he had been, or perhaps simply better than he could learn.

He fell into step beside her, Botheration easing his body between them as he had been trained, moving a single pace ahead; in perfect position to deter any attacker should one appear, the tension of his leash loose enough to give the humans room to maneuver, if needed. Other folk in the street gave the hound cautious glances, but neither approached nor shied away. Bother seemed to be calm enough, but Aaron kept a patch of his attention on the dog's ears, alert for any change in the beast's mood. If the hound scented an uncanny clothed in human form, it might well decide to attack without command, and that would be difficult to explain.

Rosemary broke the silence first. "Were you successful in getting the journal?"

"I was not." The failure grated on him, but less so in light of what he had learned. "They dodged around the question like they were solicitors rather than cops, until I was worried they might bill me for my time. They are still spouting the nonsense of an animal attack, but they don't actually believe it, not the way they're dancing." He couldn't hold his news in a second longer. "Rosemary, Lovelace wasn't the first victim!"

He'd hoped to surprise her, had *expected* to surprise her, but she merely tightened her jaw and nodded. "I know."

It was equal parts amusing and irritating, and he couldn't contain a brief pout. "Of course you do. Have I ever been able to discover anything before you?"

"Often enough, little brother. Often enough." Her tone was still even, politely controlled, but he could feel some of the tension ease from her, and she lifted her left hand and slid it into the crook of his elbow, gloved fingers tightening in a reassuring squeeze. "Tell me what you learned."

Aaron felt his shoulders straightening, knowing that he was taking what Mother used to call their called-to-duty stance, but unable to help himself after all this time.

"The police are officially listing the cause of the first two deaths as misadventure. And before you ask, our Mr. Ottering has already been buried. The other victim, Mr. Underwood, was taken to Mount Hope to be cremated."

That was a new thing, cremation. Anything that cut down on ghoul feeding grounds he approved of in general, although it made their work more difficult just then.

"Really." Rosemary smiled and nodded at a woman who was walking toward them, and Aaron tipped his hat slightly as they passed, pausing their conversation for a moment. This had been the original heart of the town, he suspected. The buildings were older, wide storefronts and narrow brick-and-clapboard homes set up close to the road, but the sidewalks were wide enough to allow traffic to flow without having to stop and allow the other to pass, as though they'd been designed for wagons to unload and load. The town might not be large, but it was clearly prosperous, despite its isolation.

"However, I made a friend while I was there, and a small donation loosened his hold on the official reports, briefly."

"How convenient, that." Rosemary's tone was dry.

"My new friend said that Underwood was found just outside the new paper mill, as though he'd been leaving long after his shift, although he should have been nowhere near there then." Aaron lowered his voice enough not to be overheard by anyone passing them, but not so low that a whisper would draw attention. They had practiced this, discussing things in public that needed to be private, until it was second nature. "There were marks across his throat and chest, deeply scored. and his head had been cracked open like an egg, and just as messy. Hence the cremation."

"Not much you can do to make that pretty," Rosemary agreed.

"The wounds were consistent with a machinery accident. Or an animal attack, Patrolman Schäffer said."

The look Rosemary gave him told him what she thought of that. Since he shared that opinion, he merely went on.

"Cause of death was put down as suffocation from a collapsed lung. It was suggested that he had been injured by the machinery and staggered to the door, seeking help."

"You said it had been after his shift. Was any of the machinery running?"

"No. Clearly, he was there for nefarious purposes, such purposes unknown but clearly nefarious, because why else would he be there? The implication unsaid was that such a man might deserve such a fate."

"What's the loss of one worker among many?" Rosemary nodded solemnly.

"Nothing so crudely put, of course. I don't know that my new friend believed it, but that is the line he was parroting."

"And there was no one else there at the time?"

"No one who has come forward. Patrolman Schäffer was the one who found him in the evening, and the body was already cold." The patrolman had looked about nervously before leaning in and telling him that, as though the Furies themselves might swoop down on him for speaking.

"Family?"

"None other than his parents. Single, twenty-seven."

"Prime for being fey-touched. Maybe he offended one of them?"

"Near an ironworks?" He gave that suggestion the scorn it deserved, and she shrugged, granting the point. The fey didn't kill their victims anyway, merely left them rattle-witted.

Or with child. That was how Huntsmen had come about, originally.

"The second body, Ottering, was found on the banks of the river, just past the paper mill, though he has no connection with it. The victim was a clerk at MacKenzie's dry goods store; married with four children, a good, God-fearing man."

"My librarian says that they're blaming a hobo," Rosemary said.

"Yes. The death happened just before dawn, near as they could place it."

Rosemary frowned. "Which rules out nightflyers."

"The sun was too close to rising," Aaron agreed. "The marks were across his back, but the depth and fierceness of them was the same as the other victim."

"I suppose it could have been a hobo, or another human with a grudge of some sort against the victim. Was there no sign of an attacker?"

"None at all. And I don't care if it was man, cat, or uncanny, that's impossible. The last serious snowfall in this area was two weeks ago, and it's been cold and damp since then. The banks are all mud and frost. There should have been marks on the ground to show there had been a fight, a struggle, anything. You couldn't clear that away, not without leaving even more traces behind. And even a blind man should have been able to tell if that were so."

"Unless they didn't want to see it. Did your patrolman seem incompetent?"

"Surprisingly, no. Distracted, yes, and uncomfortable. But he had a solid look about him, and his details were concise."

They had reached the end of the storefronts, the road curving slightly, turning back to buildings that looked purely residential, but there was a small park set in the crook of the road, and he indicated it with his chin, a suggestion that they continue their walk there.

Rosemary nodded and, after checking the street to make sure no wagons or automobiles were barreling toward them, twitched Botheration's leash, directing him to cross toward the park.

It was not much to look at, particularly going into the winter, when any flowers were long gone and most of the trees bare-limbed, but the path was gracefully laid out, and they did not look worthy of notice, merely a couple strolling with their dog at their side.

"And then we have Dr. Lovelace," she said, the gravel path crunching under their feet. Botheration moved to the grass, and they waited, eyes averted, while he did his business. "A late-night attack, somewhere after midnight but before dawn. Wounds on his chest and neck once again, deep and vicious, supposedly claws and bites, and no witnesses."

There was too much similarity in the attacks to be ignored, for all the differences in time of attack. Every instinct Aaron had learned to trust told him that this was the work of an uncanny, and he knew his sister believed the same. But in order to track and kill it, they first needed to narrow down what sort of creature might have done it.

"Lovelace was on the road," Aaron pointed out. "There would have been less opportunity for footprints or scuff marks, even if there had been a fight. But he was an old man; the other two victims were younger. If they had no chance to fight back . . ."

"Something strong, and quick."

"And smart. Clever, anyway."

"And nobody saw, or heard, a thing." Rosemary sounded as though she took that as a personal affront, that not a single person in town had witnessed the deaths—or were admitting to it.

"The patrolman who found Ottering had just begun his morning rounds, and found the body as the sun was rising. If there had been anyone out at that time of the morning, I imagine they had cause not to speak with the authorities. But the body was still warm. The attack had not been much before the patrolman came on the scene."

For all that there seemed to be money in Brunson, it was still only a large town, far from any major city. There were few streetlamps, and those only at the corners. By the river, the only real source of light would have been from the moon, and it had been just past new on the night Lovelace had been killed. That was a solid argument against it being werewolves. And they had already ruled out nightflyers and the fey.

Aaron mouthed a quick thanks to whatever looked over fools and Huntsmen that it wasn't fey. They could be cruel and vicious, but there was an uneasy truce between them and humanity, although most of humanity did not know it, which kept folk safe. He did not want to think about the truce being broken.

There were uncanny who could bear both night and sun, but few of them were large enough to take on a grown man, and certainly not one who was young and in good health.

"A pack?" Even a smaller uncanny could be deadly, if there was more than one.

"Packs eat their kills," Aaron pointed out. "Or at least mark them. And they're harder to miss."

"Lovelace was found toward the northern edge of town," Rosemary said thoughtfully.

"And the other two were by the river. The northeastern edge."

"Brass tacks, Aaron. Could it be animal attacks? The scoring, could it merely have been from an overlarge cougar, gotten over its fear of man enough to turn this town into its hunting grounds?"

He half wanted to say yes, but *no*. He shook his head, confident in his opinion. "Nothing about this says cat, or any other natural beast, for that matter."

"Uncanny, then."

"Uncanny," he agreed. He didn't think either of them had truly considered otherwise, but there was a relief in saying it. They hadn't traveled all this way for nothing.

"If the police are attempting to keep this quiet, they've already failed. My librarian knew at least this much, down to the names of the victims and where they were found." Rosemary bent to pick up a short, thick branch and offered it to Botheration, who carried it in his mouth for a few steps before snapping it, leaving the two halves behind without a second look.

"Anything useful beyond that?"

"I'm not sure. She seemed quite knowledgeable, both about local folklore and local doings." Rosemary grinned, a brief flash of sunlight. "She must be an uncomfortable neighbor to have."

That was the kind of woman his sister would find appealing. "But?"

"But . . . she was also . . . nice."

Aaron's lips twitched, but he managed not to laugh at her. "You would have preferred her to be surly, or downright hostile? Is that why you fetched the beast, to protect you from too much niceness?"

She pushed at him, blushing. "I thought it would be useful to walk him a bit, while getting a better feel for the town itself."

He left the matter of the librarian for later. "And?"

She glanced down at the hound, then shook her head, the

ridiculously tiny bow on her hat trembling with the motion. "I walked him through half a dozen streets, and he was alert, uneasy, but nothing seemed to catch his attention particularly. I did have one gentleman ask if he was available to stud, however. He was most disappointed to learn he was not."

"Uneasy." Aaron latched on to that. "Uneasy how? As if he wanted to hunt, or that he needed to relieve himself?" He studied Botheration as though something would suddenly be revealed, if he only stared hard enough.

His sister pursed her lips a little at his crassness. "Uneasy-uneasy. Like he felt something was wrong but couldn't put a finger on it. Paw. Whatever."

He understood what she meant. "You're uneasy, too."

"And you aren't." She wasn't asking a question, but he shook his head anyway.

"But that doesn't signify. We both know that you're more of a sensitive than I am, and Bother's more sensitive than us both."

"A block of wood is more sensitive than you." It wasn't meant to be hurtful, and he didn't take it as such. "But yes, there was something bothering him. Almost as though he knew he was supposed to be hunting, but didn't know what."

"Same book, same page," Aaron said to the hound. "I don't like it either."

They had come to the end of the park. On the street ahead, the houses were larger and more set apart from each other. They'd reached the wealthier portion of town. Botheration had been walking at the end of his lead, but now stopped and turned his square head to look at them curiously.

"Do you remember staying at Aunt Germaine's that summer?" The question seemed to come from nothing, but Aaron knew how his sister's mind worked. They had stayed in a house similar to the ones ahead of them that year, with an ornate, columned porch wrapping around the front, and sunlight dappling through the trees. He had been fourteen, and it had been the last summer their family had been complete, before a hunt gone wrong had taken first their mother, then their father from them.

"Thinking of it does you no favors, Rosie." The childhood nickname slipped out, but she did not seem to notice. "Concentrate on what we can change, or these deaths won't be the end of it."

She scowled at him, the moment of melancholy broken. "I know."

An uncanny that had killed was an uncanny that would continue to kill, until it was stopped. That was why there were Huntsmen.

She tugged gently on the leash, and Botheration came to heel without complaint, turning as they did. They had been walking for some time, the afternoon was beginning to fade into evening, and they would need to hurry to return to the boarding house in time to dress for dinner.

"This is balled-up, Aaron. None of the pieces fit. None of

the victims had any connection with each other beyond living in the same town, nor were they found in the same part of town. The descriptions of the wounds are consistent, but only in the vaguest ways possible. And none of it fits any uncanny I can think of. But it *is*."

"You think this is something new?"

"A new uncanny?" She made a noise of frustrated derision. After centuries of study, the uncanny were all known, even the most reclusive of them; one might as well consider a new species of humans being discovered.

"Something nobody's encountered recently, then. Maybe something come over from Europe." The unrest overseas had stirred up more than one ant's nest, and the uncanny migrated in times of trouble, much as humans did.

She sighed, finally saying the thing they had both been dreading since receiving the post-mortem summons from Dr. Lovelace.

"We need to dig up his body."

Four

B Y THE TIME the Harkers made their way back to the boarding house, darkness was creeping its way through the treetops, electric streetlamps flickering to life on the corners, while warmer yellow lights already glowed in windows, and the few remaining folk on the street hurried to their destinations, heads down and shoulders hunched. A lone automobile went past, headlamps brighter than the lights overhead, but otherwise, the town was beginning to settle in for the evening.

It did not have the feel of a town under siege. Whatever Rosemary and Botheration had sensed, they appeared to be alone in it. She found herself thinking about Miss Baker, wondering if she was walking home confidently through these streets, or looking over her shoulder at shadows.

They made it back to the house moments before dinner was to be served, but Botheration whined a little when they took him back to his kennel, planting his feet square under his body and refusing to go through the gated fence.

"Don't do this," Rosemary said to him. "You have to stay here. They won't let you in the house."

His deeper-pitched whine told them what he thought of that, and Aaron laughed. "You're spoiled, beast. Trust me, your kennel is just as nice as the rooms we're staying in. The only thing you're lacking is a washbasin—oh no, wait, there you have one as well." He indicated the large tin bowl filled with water by the door of the wooden shelter, freshly filled. "If you make eyes at one of the girls, I suspect they'll bring you some of dinner's leftovers, too. It will be just like being at home."

Aaron wasn't exaggerating; the kennel might have been makeshift, but the horse blanket in the corner of the shelter, folded on itself to make a bed, was clean and thick, the straw underfoot was reasonably fresh, and there was enough room for even a dog of Botheration's bulk to move around comfortably, the gate around it allowing room to pace. The only thing that set it apart from the kennel back in New Haven was the latch on the gate keeping him from leaving on his own.

Bother whined again as Rosemary took off his lead and collar and pushed him through the gate.

"No," she told him. "The gate has to stay closed, and you need to stay put. They don't know you here; there will be trouble if you're seen wandering around alone."

Botheration grumbled deep in his chest, then slunk into the kennel with the air of a child being sent to bed without its supper, going to the blanket and settling himself down on it, his backside to them.

"If you smell anything, set up a howl," Aaron told him, and closed the latch gently.

Another long-suffering sigh was the only response, and Rosemary snickered unkindly.

That took more time than expected, and they'd no sooner come through the front door, scraping their shoes on the iron, than Jan whipped around the corner, wiping her hands on her apron as she looked to see who it was. Her expression went from worried to a smooth placidity so quickly Aaron wasn't sure he'd actually seen it.

"You're only just in time for dinner," she said, the aromas coming from the kitchen supporting her words. "Mrs. Wesson hates when guests are late to the table, but I'll delay a bit, so you'll have time to clean up first." She nodded once, as though she'd sorted out the world's problems, and then disappeared back toward the kitchen.

Her words had been clearly directed at Rosemary, but Aaron appreciated the opportunity to wash his hands and face and comb his hair, adding a hint of pomade to keep the strands in place. He was fair-skinned to Rosemary's duskier looks, but they'd inherited the same recalcitrant black curls, and he'd more than once envied her ability to tame them with combs and pins. He checked his shirt for stains or marks, gave his shoes a quick buffing, and knocked on Rosemary's door.

A muffled "A moment!" sounded, and then the door opened, his sister still tucking pins back into her hair. She had changed her blouse but kept the simple dark blue skirt and added a black cameo to the neckline and jet bobs to her ears, a reminder that they were in mourning for a relative, however little they had known him.

He had almost forgotten.

Downstairs, the double doors to the dining room had been opened, revealing a long table set for six. There were two gentlemen already sitting at the table, deep in discussion, when the Harkers entered the dining room, and they stood to greet the newcomers.

"John Baxter," the first man said, offering his hand for Aaron to shake, and inclining his head in greeting to Rosemary.

"Aaron Harker, and my sister, Rosemary." Baxter had a strong handshake, dry and confident, and his body matched it, burly and broad in a well-made sack suit and rounded collar, the picture of a man who had never heard the word "no" twice.

"William Dolph, of the Cape May Dolphs," the other man said, offering his hand in turn. There was a moment when it seemed as though the man meant to attempt a harder squeeze, but instead pumped Aaron's hand once and let go. He was younger than Baxter, although older than the Harkers by at least a decade, and Aaron thought he had a mean look to his eyes, a washed-out gray that matched his complexion.

"Oh, excellent, you've already made introductions." Their hostess came into the room with a swish of skirts, her silver hair up in an old-fashioned pompadour. "I do so hate for people to stand on ceremony at the table, so please, sit where you will. We are family under this roof, for however long we are here."

Mrs. Wesson took her seat at the head of the table, while the Harkers sorted themselves out, Rosemary and Aaron taking two chairs next to each other while the gentlemen reclaimed their seats together on the other side of the table, leaving a single seat unaccounted for.

"Mister Dolph and Baxter are businessmen," Mrs. Wesson explained. "And the Harkers are brother and sister, traveling for pleasure. There is another gentleman staying with us, a return guest, but he has only just arrived and pled exhaustion from the road. You shall meet him tomorrow evening."

Introductions done, dinner began.

They soon discovered that Mrs. Wesson had a seemingly effortless charm, and although she was certainly much older than any of her guests, she brought a bit of the flirt to the table, asking each of them how their day had been as the younger girl, Gert, brought out the soup course.

The older man, Baxter, merely grunted in response, and when his companion began to enthuse about some progress he had made on something, a sideways look shut him down quickly. Seemingly accustomed to their rudeness, Mrs. Wesson turned to the Harkers.

"Did you have a nice walk around town? It's always good to stretch your legs after a long journey, I've found. And your dog, too? Such a magnificent creature, the girls tell me."

"A dog, here?" Baxter looked up as though expecting to see the animal sitting at the table with them.

"Oh, not here, no," Mrs. Wesson assured him. "He has been given his very own room out back. Bernard was able to make a lovely kennel for him out of lumber and chicken wire. Hopefully he does not find the cold too overwhelming."

Dolph put his fork down, squinting at Rosemary as though he couldn't quite understand. "It's woeful cold outside. Surely he could sleep at the foot of your bed?"

Rosemary blinked, trying to imagine that, and let out a peal of laughter. Dolph flushed, and Baxter frowned, looking at Rosemary as though she'd just done something scandalous.

"Botheration is a tad large for such things," Aaron explained. "He's a hundred and twenty if he's an ounce, and all of it muscle and bone."

He could practically see both men digesting that fact, their view of Bother likely shifting from a small bit of lady's fluff to something closer to the truth. Then Baxter's eyebrows rose, and he gave Rosemary a more assessing look. "He's a guard dog?"

"He has been trained to be, yes." She finished her soup, laying down her spoon and nodding when Jan stepped forward to remove the bowl. "His line is best noted for their hunting skills, however."

Baxter still looked as though he'd bitten a raw lemon, but Dolph looked fascinated. "I would be most interested in meeting him, if time allows."

"Perhaps it will," she said with the air of someone ending a conversation, as Jan finished clearing the table, and Gert began carrying in the main course, a roast chicken with stewed vegetables and pillow-top rolls.

"You will discover that no one starves at Mrs. Wesson's," Dolph said, accepting the vegetable dish and placing it on the table, family-style, while the chicken was placed in front of Mrs. Wesson. Apparently having a guard dog had improved the Harkers' standing in his eyes, if not his companion's.

For a few minutes there was quiet, as the plates were filled. Then:

"So, we have determined that you are brother and sister, and that you travel with a mighty dog, but what has brought you two and your four-legged companion to Brunson?" Baxter's earlier disinterest in conversation seemed to have disappeared with the arrival of food.

"Family," Aaron said, as Rosemary had just taken a bite of chicken and could not respond. "A cousin died recently, and his widow asked us to help her sort out his estate."

"Indeed. Are you a money man?"

"I have some experience with legal papers," Aaron hedged. "And Cousin Tucker trusted me, I suppose."

"Tucker Lovelace?" Mrs. Wesson sounded surprised. "I didn't think he had any family."

"Distantly. He and our father were cousins."

"And you came to be comfort to the widow," Dolph said to Rosemary.

"As I may," she said. "But also to indulge a little hobby of mine. I collect folk tales from all across the country." It was a useful story, one boring enough that most people accepted it at face value while allowing her, as with Miss Baker, to ask otherwise odd questions without raising eyebrows. "When Aaron travels, I go with him, and learn what I may."

"Indeed," Dolph said. "You have a most considerate brother, Miss Harker. And once you have collected those stories, what do you do with them? Are you perhaps a lady authoress?"

Rosemary shook her head with a small smile that didn't quite hide her disdain. "It is enough for me to know them. It is a foolish hobby, but one I enjoy. And perhaps someday, someone will take what I have gathered and make use of it."

That amused Aaron, although not for the reasons others might suspect. Rosemary's notes—and his as well—were in fact sent on to Boston, where a clerk would add them to the Huntsmen's files. Aaron rather suspected that those files were locked into a cabinet somewhere and never saw the light of day again, but they had been trained to record and save, and so they did.

Having set their cover, Rosemary redirected the conversation. "And you, Mr. Baxter? What brings you and Mr. Dolph to Brunson?"

"Business," Baxter said, his face a little ruddy from the glass of wine he had already consumed. "We're looking to acquire some land just outside of town."

"You are a farmer?"

This time it was Baxter who burst out laughing, a

rough cough from deep within his chest. "No, indeed. An investor."

Rosemary made a polite noise, and he put down his fork and knife to explain.

"It may not seem it from this table, but this little town is a hot spot of activity. It's perfectly located. Rochester is a growing city and soon will rival Boston and New York for industry. And access to the Canadian markets will only increase its value. And where large cities grow, opportunity appears!"

Opportunity being Brunson, apparently, although Aaron couldn't see how.

"The talc mines are expanding, and there is an increased call for factories that can produce the needs of a modern age," Dolph said, seemingly eager not to be left out of the conversation. "This area has the timber and limestone, and water power they can't match downstate."

"We are a bit of a journey from Rochester," Mrs. Wesson said doubtfully.

"Ah, but with the rail lines up and running," Baxter said, "there is huge opportunity for someone ready to take advantage. Mines, yes, and mills, but they will also need processing plants, and shipping yards. Land will increase in value all along the tracks."

"And so you plan to get in early," Aaron said.

"That is how one makes money, yes."

Aaron had his doubts about the viability of their schemes, but he admitted that his interests were not attuned to such things.

"You are correct, Mrs. Wesson, that Brunson is a bit far off from Rochester," Baxter went on, warming to his topic, "but that only means that it is less expensive to build here. Having a station here already, and easy access to the ships of Lake Ontario, gives the town a leg up."

"Indeed." Rosemary leaned forward, her eyes bright with what an ignorant man might have thought fascination. "It seems logical, but are you counting too much on further expansion by Union Pacific? The recent Supreme Court ruling with regard to them would seem to indicate they might be curtailing their reach, rather than enlarging it. And US Steel has considerable debt, I understand, but they do not seem to look kindly on competition."

Aaron lifted his glass to his lips to hide the smile as Dolph spluttered a weak refutation.

Baxter chuckled, clearly amused both by his partner's fluster and Rosemary's audacity. "The young lady makes excellent points, and I commend her studies. However, I would suggest that enough money could and will fix many of these issues. Industry goes where there is opportunity, and people to grow it."

Rosemary looked ready to debate the point, and Aaron would have kicked her if he thought he could find her under the table without accidentally kicking someone else instead.

"No doubt, no doubt," Mrs. Wesson said, breaking into the conversation with a soft laugh. "I trust your eye for such things, gentlemen, but business talk is not suitable for the dinner table." She lifted a platter and offered it to Aaron in distraction. "More chicken, Mr. Harker?"

"Thank you, yes." He managed to catch Rosemary's eye as he took the platter, willing her to remember that they were here to work, not argue finances. He was satisfied when she dropped her own gaze to her plate, putting forward the image of a chastised young lady through the rest of the meal.

The moment the meal ended, Rosemary excused herself, pleading exhaustion after a long day. Having no desire to linger with the other guests, Aaron soon followed her up the stairs to his own room.

Removing his shoes and placing them just inside the door, he then draped his jacket over the back of the chair and undid his cuffs and collar, sliding his necktie off and coiling it neatly on the seat of the chair. A long stretch, hard enough to hear several things crack and pop in his back and neck, and a few deep knee bends, and his body unwound itself from the long day of travel and the tensions of dealing with the police. It had been a necessary step, lacking information, but the best hunt was one that did not involve official notice.

He went to the sole window in the room and looked out. The roof of the kennel was just visible, but when he pushed the window open, he could hear nothing but a desultory owl's call, and the distant sound of a train rattling past. Botheration was likely sound asleep, but if not, nothing was causing him alarm.

Good. A quiet night would be ideal for what they were planning.

But they had to wait. It would likely take the two girls a bit to finish cleaning up and go home for the night, and some time after that before the rest of the household were sure to be asleep in their own rooms. Eyeing the bed, he thought that a short nap might be just the thing. He glanced at his watch to set the time in his mind, removed the Colt from its holster and put it on the side table, and lay down on the bed, closing his eyes and letting himself sink into the mattress.

It seemed as though he'd barely evened out his breathing when his body was telling him that it was time to wake up again.

Sure enough, it was after eleven o'clock. He listened for a moment, in case a knock on the door had woken him, but there was only silence from the other side. Rising from the bed with reluctance, he shed his clothing and dressed again in rougher cloth pants with a heavy workman's belt, and a knit sweater over his shirt. Thick-soled boots were laced up over woolen socks, and with the addition of a knitted cap, his silhouette was completely different from the city slicker who'd arrived that morning.

Perfect.

He laid his jacket on the bed and opened a smaller case in his valise, taking out a handful of items and placing them in various pockets. He eyed the Colt, then picked it up, loading the chamber with casual efficiency. He did not expect to need it tonight, but at the same time, there was no need to be careless in a town where three people had already died. He slipped it into his left pocket, moved the silver-bladed jackknife to the right, then slipped on the jacket and pulled the cap down over his forehead.

Pausing in front of the door, he cocked his head, listening, but heard no sounds coming from the house around him. Going into the hallway, he saw Rosemary just outside her own door, waiting for him.

They had been working together for nearly five years now. He should not have been surprised.

Rosemary had also changed her attire, the pants moderately scandalous but far more suitable for the night's work than skirts could be. Her hair was caught up in a loose braid and pinned up under a cap similar to his own. At a glance, in the dark, she could pass for a gangly youth.

She nodded to him, then stepped carefully toward the stairs, Aaron following a few paces behind. Neither of them spoke until they'd made it safely down the stairs and out the front door, closing it carefully behind them. A quick sketch of three figures in a circle around the lock, and Aaron ensured that they would not be trapped outside, even if someone were to wake and bolt the door before they returned.

"Lockpicks are a thing," Rosemary said, dropping back into that low voice that did not carry.

"Sigils work faster in a hurry."

"If they work."

"These always work. You just don't know why, and that bothers you."

"I don't know why it doesn't bother you," she muttered, but followed him as they moved away from the house. Like all their arguments, it had no conclusion. Rosemary knew full well why it didn't bother him; she just didn't like the answer.

He was too fey even for his sister, sometimes.

The street was dark, the moon hiding behind thin clouds. Aaron gestured for her to precede him, and they made their way to the yard, where a small wooden shed pushed up against the side of the house. He made quick work of the latch and poked his head inside. The tools leaned against the walls or were hung from hooks, ordered neatly by use and size. He nodded approvingly. There were four shovels by the door. He picked up one of the smaller, flat-edged ones, testing the grip and weight, then passed it to his sister before selecting a larger one with a pointed edge for himself.

Rosemary swung the shovel experimentally, then twisted it up over her shoulder. She could have handled a heavier one, but they were going to have to walk a distance. There was no point in carrying more weight than they had to.

A shuffling noise came from the kennel behind them, Botheration no doubt catching their scent in the air.

"Hush," Rosemary told the hound, her voice just barely loud enough to be heard. "Stay."

There was a whine, but Botheration did not bark, or otherwise draw attention to himself.

"Good boy."

Aaron might have argued to take the beast with them— Bother had been bred to hunt the uncanny, after all—but they were not looking for a kill tonight, only information. And the dog's presence would also make them instantly and undeniably identifiable should they be seen. She was right: better to leave him here.

Once they left the more populated streets and their lamp-posts behind, the world seemed much emptier, the few houses they passed gone dark, or lit only by a solitary window. Creatures rustled in the brush and in the branches overhead, the crunch and thud of their boots on the ground a solid counterpoint.

"One thing this town did right: not putting their boneyard right by the churches," Aaron said. "Sanctified ground never once saved a soul. Would have been a shorter walk, though."

"A pity cremation isn't likely to become popular. Starve all sorts of uncanny out."

"You don't think it will?"

Rosemary shrugged. "People like traditions. You can't do much with a handful of ashes."

The street they had been walking along came to a blunt end, and it took them a few moments to discern the wide grassy path leading between two houses. Past that, they could see the slope of the river, and a hint of smooth, glossy water reflecting the moonlight.

"Just past the bridge," Aaron said.

Rosemary hated bridges. No matter how well-built, no matter how many times she had crossed one, she was perpetually convinced that this was the moment the structure would fail, dropping them to wet, painful deaths.

At the base of the narrow wood-and-stone footbridge,

they both peered cautiously under the arch to ensure that no uncanny lurked, waiting only for the echo of footsteps to reach up and claim its toll. But there was only water, painted silver by the rising moon, broken by the occasional splash of a fish or plunk of a frog hunting its dinner. Rosemary took a deep breath and stepped onto the first plank.

"Running water is supposed to break curses," Aaron reminded her.

"And stop nightflyers. I know. And if any of these kills had been vampiric feeds, that would be useful information."

He just chuckled as they walked briskly to the end of the bridge, giving her a hand down the cold-slick stones to the winter-dead grass on the other bank. Logic was Rosemary's guiding light, but this was a thing logic could not touch. She had to simply get over it.

Away from the town, the single road turned left toward the graveyard, and right to run along the river's edge. The clouds had thickened as they walked, and the air was filled with the gentle sounds of the river flowing, and larger things hunting in the underbrush.

The tension they'd been carrying since they'd arrived didn't ease, but shifted to a different sort of alertness. The attacks might have happened within the town itself, but there were dangers here, as well.

They walked silently through the night until Aaron broke the silence again.

"What was that about, at dinner?"

Rosemary didn't pretend to misunderstand. With the

hand not holding the shovel, she made an airy gesture, conveying a ladylike disdain. "They're idiots."

"They're speculators, which isn't always the same thing. I agree with you; they're likely to lose their money, and the funds of anyone foolish enough to join with them. But you were being deliberately provocative." He was puzzled, not accusing. But Rosemary was used to having to explain things to him.

"There was something about them that annoyed me."

"You mean other than Mr. Baxter's obvious refusal to believe that a little lady could know anything about the market?"

It was too dark to see her expression, but he could practically feel her eye roll. "Men," she said, an exhalation of frustration.

Aaron chuckled, the sound carrying through the night. "I do like seeing you take them down a notch," he admitted. "But—"

"I know," she interrupted him. "I know. Don't make a fuss, don't be memorable. I shouldn't have risen to the bait. But it's 1913. They need to let go of their delicate sensibilities."

"Well, I'm certain you set them on the right path tonight."

She swung the shovel at him in mock offense, and he dodged it with ease, stepping back and then to the side, bringing his own shovel up easily but stopping just shy of touching her. In a fair fight, she had no chance against his longer reach and superior strength, but neither of them had fought fair in their entire lives. She had already turned as he was raising his shovel, swinging her off leg out and tapping him on the shin, a faint echo of the force she would have brought had this been a true scuffle.

"Peace," he said, lowering his improvised weapon. "I'd as soon not collect bruises before I have to."

"Toss salt," Rosemary said, starting forward on the road again. "You have the worst habit of jinxing us."

"It's a simple grave desecration," he said. "What could possibly go wrong?"

"I hate you so much right now."

Despite her worries, they arrived at their destination without issue. The cemetery was larger than they'd expected, with the dark-looming woods pushing in at three sides. The quarter moon slipping in and out of clouds painted shadows past the wrought-iron fence, the old maples and oaks far more sinister than any rooted thing should be.

"It looks peaceful," Rosemary said, but neither of them relaxed their guard. Boneyards were dangerous places. There were reasons why iron was used to enclose them.

"Ladies first," Aaron said, gallantly sweeping the simple gate open and bowing her through, then closing the gate behind him. "Now all we have to do is find the old man."

Five

ACCORDING TO HIS widow, Tucker Lovelace had been buried in the family plot in the southeast corner of the cemetery. There were no lights this far from town, and the moonlight hid more than it revealed, but the graveled pathway was wide enough to be obvious.

"I like this place," Rosemary said, still keeping her voice low, despite there being no living soul beyond themselves to overhear. "No mausoleums or towering monuments to mortal folly, just nice quiet stones. You could have a picnic here and see everyone."

"And nothing for ghouls to hide behind."

"That too. Oh, there he is."

Lovelace's grave had soil fresh-turned over the spot, the snow around it cleared into half-melted piles. There was no stone in place as yet, but unless another corpse had been slotted in between Justice Lovelace and Abraham Lovelace Walker, they were in the right spot.

Aaron let his shovel slide off his shoulder, the metal spade hitting the frozen ground with a hollow-sounding thud. "Huzzah for the freshly planted. Easier to unbury, especially in winter." He made a face. "Worse smell, though."

His sister ignored him, stepping forward so that her toes almost touched the edge of the mounded dirt.

"I'm sorry we weren't able to see you one more time." She always liked to say a few words first, although Aaron had never understood why. "We will take care of this, we promise."

"Don't make promises to the dead, Rosie. They don't care, but if you can't hold to it, you'll feel guilty."

It could have been new-moon dark, and he would still have felt the glare she shot him. He grinned in response, holding up his shovel. "May I do the honors?"

She stepped back, her own tool held at her side. "Please do."

He took off his cap and jacket and handed them to her, rolling up his sleeves to the elbow despite the cold, and flexing his back and shoulders to loosen them up. Then, aware that the night was ticking away, he set the tip of his spade to the soft dirt and began shoveling it aside, careful to toss the dirt to where his sister was not standing.

It might not be seemly for a gentleman to enjoy physical labor, but it certainly got the blood flowing. And the sweat.

"Just once," he said between swings, "it would be nice to arrive before the victim is buried, so we can see the wounds firsthand."

"Yes, the family should absolutely think, first thing on finding the body of a loved one, 'Let's call Huntsmen in.

That's the most important thing. Shock and grieving and calling the police can all wait.'"

"That would be nice, wouldn't it?" he said, immune to her sarcasm. "Just once. And anyway, most times the police already know before the family does, for all the good it does anyone."

"Fine, yes, you're absolutely right. But first we'd need the flat wired for a telephone, rather than relying on messengers and mail," Rosemary said, knowing that would put an end to the conversation. Having a receiver installed had not been a priority in their household budget, not when messenger services were so plentiful. That might have to change soon, however. The world was moving, and changing.

Aaron grunted, having cleared the first layer of soil and reached firmer-packed dirt. "At least it's not snowing. Or raining. Rain would be worse, all the mud *and* cold, and none of the pretty."

"Oh hey, if we wait a day or two, maybe there will be another body we can look at." He considered the idea for another two tosses of dirt, then realized that his sister had gone silent behind him. Aaron took that to mean that he'd said something off again. He did that occasionally, or so Rosemary informed him, often at great length and with increasingly exasperated language.

"Humor, Rosemary. That was humor. I would never put someone at risk," he said, digging the spade perhaps a bit harder into the ground than was strictly needful. "Not unless they had agreed to it."

"Like Corpus Christi?"

He might not have been quite so careful as to where the next shovel of dirt landed. "He agreed."

Rosemary sidestepped the dirt before it could hit her shoes. "You made him think he was going to be the hero, not the bait."

"Standing in front of a raging orc is as heroic as I can imagine." Even among the more distasteful of uncanny creatures, orcs were nasty, all scabby white skin and poison in their claws and filthy teeth, and their single weak spot was the back of their neck, so you always needed someone in front of them, to distract them. They'd no interest in fighting women, and Rosemary had been recovering from a bad cough that made it unlikely that she would be able to sneak up on even a distracted orc, so they'd had no choice but to bring someone else in.

And only the orc had died, so really, why did she keep bringing that up?

She let him dig in peace after that, and he fell into a smooth, experienced rhythm of dig-and-toss until he felt something in his back twinge. He paused, stretching to ease the stiffness, then checked the depth of the hole he'd been digging around himself. To his surprise, the dirt sides were almost shoulder-high.

Almost to the coffin, then.

"You're up," he said, and tossed his shovel up onto the bank before climbing out.

Rosemary took off her own coat and handed them both to him, reaching up to pull the knitted watch cap down onto his head. "Your ears will freeze off," she told him, before sliding down into the hole, her shovel in hand, and setting to work.

Anyone who wanted to claim that women were too delicate to handle manual labor had never seen his sister wield a shovel. The flat blade was less useful for digging, but once they reached the coffin itself, it would be more effective in scraping the dirt away so that they could open the box.

As though he'd been prescient, the sound of metal scraping against wood soon rose up from the hole; she had reached the burial box.

"Got it," she said, her voice echoing oddly as she knelt down to push the last dirt away with her hands, the sound of grave dirt falling away in a dry, rattling slide.

He dug into his coat pocket, fumbling slightly with gloved fingers until he found what he was looking for. The moonlight had been enough to dig by, once their vision had adjusted, but more delicate matters like finding the latch and lock would require closer sight and better light.

Rosemary would like it about as much as she did the sigils, but fairy lights were better here than the newfangled tungsten flash Rosemary carried. A flash was an obvious sign of human interlopers. Palm-sized, and weighing about as much as a handful of feathers, fairy lights clung where you put them, and could be easily mistaken for a will-o'-the-wisp, discouraging all but the most foolhardy, or other Huntsmen, from investigating.

Such lights weren't officially sanctioned tools, of course;

nothing of uncanny origin was. But most Huntsmen carried one or two with them, just in case. Rosemary didn't like it, didn't like him using anything of fey origin, but as with the sigils, he'd persisted.

He held the light in his hand, closing his fingers over it gently, and pressed down into the soft center with the thumb of his other hand until he felt something click. "Laft, pfiit, pheeen." They were nonsense words, fey words, but the right order and the right inflection were what made it work.

When he opened his fingers, a pale pinkish-white light spread, making the rest of the night seem even darker in comparison. "Still got it," he said with satisfaction.

"When you've finished congratulating yourself, could you bring that over here, please?"

She didn't like it, but she'd make use of it. He moved to the edge of the grave, holding the fairy light so that its glow filled the space around his sister, illuminating her face, the shovel, and the top of the casket.

"What a waste of money," she said, as she uncovered more of the coffin's surface, brushing the last of the dirt to the side. "They think the worms and crows are impressed by brass fixtures and velvet linings?"

"A good lock keeps the dead down and safe," he said, shrugging. "But people like to put on a show for the living. Also, even in fair . . . where are we again?"

"Brunson."

"Even in fair Brunson, New York, farthest outpost of civilization, an undertaker must make a living."

With a snort, she struck the latch with a sharp blow with the shovel's blade, and the lock broke open. She took a step back, then lifted her shovel up, placing it on the ground at Aaron's feet, and hauled herself out of the hole with a ladylike grunt, brushing the dirt from her trousers and wiping her hands with a handful of nearby snow.

They waited a moment, just in case they'd misjudged Dr. Lovelace's status, but the lid remained unmoved. Aaron exhaled, then pulled their sketchbook from his coat pocket, a stub of pencil tied to it with a frayed black ribbon, and handed it to her.

"I sketched last time," she said, surprised.

He shrugged. "You knew him." This part was never easy on her, for all that she hid it. Focusing on the wounds rather than the body itself might be better. He might not understand her reactions, but that didn't mean he had to be an ass about it.

She was the better artist, anyway.

Her hand was a gentle pressure against his shoulder, all the thanks he would get.

Aaron waited until she had settled herself cross-legged on the ground, the fairy light resting on her knee. Then he knelt carefully, easing himself prone on the ground, his shoulders just over the edge of the grave. The cold immediately sank through the front of his shirt and trousers, chilling his skin. He should have put his jacket back on, the way Rosemary had, but it would restrict his movement too much. Using the flat-bladed shovel, he angled it into the grave and pried open the lid, pushing it over until it clattered against the earthen wall they'd dug, dirt falling back into the grave and coffin.

As he'd expected, the body hadn't been in the ground long enough for the smell to have faded, but long, deep breaths through his mouth kept cold air in his lungs without carrying the stench to his nose. Aaron had no particular memory of Lovelace the way Rosemary did, but he suspected the man had looked better.

"Do you want me to—"

A faint noise, and instinct, had him rolling over onto his back, bringing the shovel up across his face in a defensive move as the first ghoul fell on him. Long claws dragged across his cheek, hot, maggoty breath making his skin crawl even as he pushed the uncanny away, then swung the shovel in a counterclockwise arc, slashing at the creature's throat. The sounds of scuffling and feminine grunts told him Rosemary was busy next to him, but he had no chance to look, intent on the next wave launching themselves at him.

"We just barely opened the lid!" he snarled, irritated beyond belief. "How do they know? How do they always know?"

He swung the shovel at another one, knocking it back into yet a third behind it, then drove the edge of the spade into the neck of a fourth, buying himself enough time to pull the jackknife from his coat pocket and flick it open, stabbing the second one through the left eye.

Ghouls were scrawny, what muscle they had atrophied under cold skin, but they were tenacious, and the only way to put one down for good was to destroy what little brain it had left.

He pulled the finger-length blade free even as cold, knobby fingers grabbed the back of his neck, and he went down on his knees, the jolt sending a shock through his entire body. But it was enough to loosen the ghoul's grip, giving him time to grab the shovel again and room to swing it sideways, cutting the uncanny off at the knees.

Rising to finish the job, he saw Rosemary stab one of her ghouls through the eye, then kick it several feet away before swinging to deal with the last one standing. He took the moment to stab the downed ghouls through both eyes to be certain, then kicked them into a pile with the others.

Five, plus the two Rosemary had dispatched already. Fewer than usual, but he supposed pickings were scarcer, this far from any city or hospital. None had run away; ghouls didn't have the brains to run, only attack.

Under the night sky, their skin seemed to shimmer with a sick gray light, limbs bent in ways no human joint could mimic. Ghouls were among the most disturbing of the un-canny, human-shaped, but not human at all. And that was before one considered their eating habits.

He used the edge of his blade to pry open the mouth of one, clacking the metal against the teeth until one fell to the ground. He took a kerchief from his pocket and used it to pick the tooth up, wrapping it carefully and putting it away safely. There was a small but lucrative market for such things, if you knew the right buyers.

A final body was kicked to the pile, and Rosemary came up alongside him.

"Maybe"—and he wiped his hand against his pants leg with an expression of disgust—"maybe I jinxed us. A little. I don't suppose you brought matches?"

"You doubt me?" Her voice was slightly breathless, but she reached into the outer pocket of her coat and handed him a roll of matches. "But wait until we are done. I'd not like to have to explain to the local police, if we can avoid it."

Since they had not taken anything from the grave, they could only be charged with vandalism, not corpse theft or grave robbery. But it would make it difficult for them to continue investigations, or indeed, to ever come back to this town. Not that Aaron thought either of them would have any desire to do so, once this was finished, but any official attention to their work was frowned on.

He paused to re-tuck his shirt and fix his collar where it had gotten twisted during the fight. "Were you bitten?"

"Just a scratch, nothing a washcloth and some whiskey won't handle. You?"

He did a quick once-over to confirm that nothing had broken skin. "I'm fine."

A ghoul bite would rot the tissue around it unless treated immediately, but their claws, although filthy, were less dangerous. If they had access to water, or even whiskey, Aaron would have insisted that Rosemary wash out the scratch at once, but she was correct: it would wait.

"I don't suppose we can blame the attacks on ghouls?"

Rosemary laughed a tired, unamused noise. "First, something would have to lure them out of the boneyard, then across running water, and into a living town."

Aaron sighed. "It couldn't be that easy, just once?"

"Never. Back to the body," she reminded him, and he nodded. They needed to get a better look, which meant they'd have to disrobe the corpse, possibly his second-least-favorite activity.

Moving carefully in respect to his inevitable bruises, Aaron lowered himself into the grave, bracing his feet on the edges of the coffin and bending into a crouch. Touching the dead had long ago lost its repulsiveness, although it would never be a thing he enjoyed. Working quickly, he opened the jacket and unbuttoned the shirt, then climbed out and allowed Rosemary to lean in. The fairy light, reclaimed from the ground where it had fallen during the fight, cast its pink-white illumination on the body, and her pencil flew over the pages as she sketched the visible wounds: long, deep tears, three on the chest and one at the edge of his neck.

They had been stitched up prior to burial, but the shape and depth of each was still clear, the edges oddly clean. None of them alone should have been fatal, but he supposed there might be more damage not visible. One thing was certain: the man was very definitely dead.

Rosemary turned the page of the sketchbook and kept drawing. Aaron stayed out of her way, his elbows resting on his knees, and took note of everything he could see. Memory was a fickle servant, but the trained mind was as much a tool as a shovel, knife, or fairy light. He let his gaze drift from the open lid to the body, starting at the feet, the once-upon-a-time shine on second-best shoes now clotted and muted with dust and dirt, and working his way up to the face. The widow had opted against a winding cloth, the body resting on a cushion that might have been white before the dirt soiled it.

He supposed the old man looked good for being dead nearly a week. There was a fashion now for the body to be restored to near perfection before burial through use of wax and cosmetics, so there might have been more wounds on his neck, face, or hands that had been covered up. If there were cuts on the hands, it would indicate that Lovelace had time to mount a defense, however useless.

They would need to check.

"Hold up," he said, and Rosemary paused in her sketching, looking at him in inquiry. The fairy light draped over her arm cast odd shadows on her face, turning her skin the same ashen shade as the dead man.

Once sure she wasn't going to yell at him for getting in her way, he swung his body around so that he was sitting at the crumbling edge of the grave, his legs swinging over the side, feet dangling. A quick assessment of the remains, and he slid back down, dirt and roots crumbling from the side walls and landing in his hair. He planted his feet at the bottom edge of the coffin. A careful walk up, feet braced against the wooden sides of the coffin, and he made it high up enough to reach over, one hand braced against the dirt wall, and scrape lightly at the skin over one cheekbone.

Nothing came away in his fingers save dirt.

Moving lower, his fingers scraped across the chin, then the neck. "Rosemary." He held up a finger, the smudge of something putty-colored on its tip.

She lowered her pencil and squinted. "From his face?"

"The neck. And a lot of it."

"Clear it away."

He grimaced. "Give me your kerchief?"

She reached into a pocket and dropped it into his hands, a fluttering piece of cloth, a corner embroidered with her initials.

He wrapped it around two fingers and set to work, carefully brushing at the putty until he was confident it had all fallen away. The wounds underneath were dry and shriveled to the touch. He grimaced, wiping his fingers against his thigh, then did the same for the corpse's fingers and palms, revealing only dirt and flaking skin. No defensive wounds, nothing to indicate the man had so much as put up his hands.

When he was done, he shoved the filthy kerchief into his pocket and moved back, crouched on his heels over the body. He stared at the exposed wounds, then up at his sister.

"Check me on this?"

Rosemary had to squint under the fairy light, but a few minutes of studying the corpse, and she nodded slowly. "Those aren't claw marks; they're too deep. Or bite marks, not from any mouth I ever saw." And they'd seen a great many over the years, often too close for comfort.

"That's not a bite . . . but what is it?" Rosemary nudged the fairy light closer, trying to see the marks on the skin more clearly now that the putty was gone. It had been sewn up reasonably well, and the putty had disguised the worst of it, but they could see now that the marks on his neck were unevenly jagged and oddly textured, as though the flesh had been burnt or cauterized. But Lovelace had been dead when his body was found; there would have been no need for such measures.

She traced the air above the body with her finger, noting where the wound circled up, as though whoever—or whatever— had struck the blow had jerked away just after the weapon hit home. "The attack was brutal, done to disfigure as much as kill." She looked up at the sky, then back to Aaron. "Not a small weapon, whatever it was. Maybe the size of a bowie knife, or a little larger."

"No knife would cut like that," Aaron objected. "It could have been done by claws, maybe a single huge claw, like a zovatis? But"—and he tilted his head, trying to visualize the angle of attack better—"I can't imagine anything that would leave the skin like that. It's not like any attack wound I've seen before." He paused, then, "Rosemary."

"Mmmmm?"

"Didn't Mrs. Lovelace say that it was a closed casket?"

"Yes. She did." She turned the fairy light on him, to better see his face.

"So why did they go to the effort of covering up the wounds?"

She stared at him, her lips moving in a soundless curse. Then she said, "Maybe it's a standard courtesy? Can't face Saint Peter in less-than-perfect condition?"

"Or they're covering up something more than we know. Damn it." Aaron muttered a few of his worst curses under his breath, pinching the bridge of his nose between two fingers and staring down at the corpse. "You were supposed to give us answers, not more questions!"

"If he answers you now, family or no, I'm shoving you in and running," Rosemary said dryly. She shifted, sketchbook open, and put her pencil back to work catching every detail she could. They had already taken too long, between digging up the coffin and dealing with the ghouls. The wolf's hour was on them; morning would be soon enough, and with the sun rising, there was a higher risk of someone seeing them where they had no cause to be.

"Done," she said, standing up. "Will you do the honors?"

Aaron flipped the lid closed again and took up the shovel to move the dirt back into the grave, the soft thuds of soil meeting wood quickly becoming the softer sounds of dirt on dirt. "Get rid of the trash," he said over his shoulder, and she nodded once, leaving him to finish the reburying.

Hopefully with the grave so new, no one would notice that the turned-over dirt on the mound was fresher than it had been a day before. But even if they did, it would take a terribly paranoid man to insist the grave be dug up again to check the contents of the coffin. And from what they had seen of this town already, the residents seemed more determined to ignore strangeness than investigate it.

No self-respecting grave robber would come all this way north, anyway. It would take too long for them to deliver their bounty, time and distance eating their profits. Especially when there were always bodies to be found in the streets of the cities, in the more disreputable areas where itinerant workers and sailors congregated.

By the time Aaron had finished piling dirt back into a rounded mound and scuffing away any evidence of distinct footprints, Rosemary had gathered the ghouls into a pile and set it aflame. It took several matches before the pyre lit, but once it did, black smoke rose in a thick, gritty cloud before being caught up by the pre-dawn breezes and scattered into the sky.

The stink was not as bad as some corpses they'd disposed of, but it was bad enough.

"You should have waited until I was done to start the burn," Aaron said, wrinkling his nose as he pulled his jacket back on. Even with the sweat of physical exertion, the night air was cold, and he had no desire to catch ill.

"You were taking too long."

"I do beg your pardon," he said. "Next time, you can do the reburying. How would you like that?"

He walked a circuit around the pyre, making sure that the evidence was fully aflame. Rosemary knew her craft; every bit was engulfed, bones popping and skin crackling as the fire ate away. There was little fat or flesh on ghoul bones, so the smoke would disperse soon enough, and even if someone were to notice and come investigate, there would be nothing left that a layperson would be able to identify.

"Coffee and a large slab of bacon sounds ideal right now," Aaron said as he came around back to where Rosemary stood, mainly to see his sister's face scrunch up in disgust. She crouched to pick up her shovel, shaking the last clump of dirt free. "How you can stomach eating after this, I will never understand."

He shrugged. "Meat is meat. It's not as though ghouls have souls to worry about. They're nothing but mindless beasts, and we do them a favor, ending their miserable lives."

"Everything wants to live," Rosemary said. "Although that is not what I would name living, personally."

Another time and place he might have argued with her, but this was neither the time nor the place, nor, he suspected, was she in the right mood for such a discussion. Besides, he *was* hungry. Sooner they got back to town, sooner he could eat.

Six

THE WALK BACK was at a quicker pace, though they were both bone-tired, for fear of sunrise—or early risers—catching them out. Thankfully, they made their way back to the shed without being noticed, replacing their shovels and dislodging the worst of the dirt and dust from their clothing. A low, mournful noise came from the backyard when Botheration heard them, but a "Hush" from Rosemary made him stop.

"You'll need to apologize to him later," Aaron said. The dog was prone to sulk if she was out of his sight for too many hours. "We should have brought him a ghoul bone to chew on."

Her disgusted expression told him what she thought of that idea, and despite everything, he couldn't hold back a chuckle. For a woman who could take a machete to a skinwalker without flinching, she could be surprisingly delicate about some things.

There were noises coming from the kitchen in the back of the house, and they made their way up the stairs with caution, placing their feet carefully on the carpeting to ensure that no treads creaked and betrayed them.

The washroom down the hallway was unoccupied at that hour, and Aaron waved his sister toward it. "Go. I will bring you a change of clothing." A man being seen in rough clothing, unshaven and unkempt, was the mark of a possible eccentric. A woman in the same condition, wearing *pants*, would be a scandal, even within the semi-private confines of a boarding house.

He went into his own room first, dropping his filthy clothing with a grimace of distaste and pulling on his unworn pajamas before going next door.

Her room was the mirror of his own, although her valise was fully unpacked and placed at the bottom of the wardrobe, her clothing neatly hung on the racks and pegs provided. He gathered her unmentionables and a clean blouse, then took the skirt she'd been wearing earlier and tucked it over his arm, hiding the other garments. She could worry about her stockings and shoes once she was back in her room.

He knocked on the door twice, a sharp double-time rap, then opened the door and let himself in. The room was barely large enough for the toilet and tub, a curtain run around the tub to create privacy.

"That had best be you," his sister's voice came over the curtain, "because I'm too tired to scream."

"Hurry up and finish," he said, placing the clothing in a pile on the commode's lid. "My skin is beginning to itch and I smell like grave dirt."

The water cut off in response, and he fled. They might be accustomed to living in each other's pocket, but there were some things a gentleman simply did not see. He gathered up a clean change of clothing for himself, and waited outside the lavatory door, looking as nonchalantly just-woken-up as he could manage. When one of the other doors in the hallway opened and a tousled male head stuck itself out, he gave a curt nod, and the head withdrew back into the room, the door closing softly behind him.

The door at his side opened and his sister emerged, fully dressed and pink-cheeked, smelling of soap. Her hair had been let down from its braid and hung in tangled curls across her shoulders. "All yours," she said, even as he was shutting the door in her face.

The tub was still warm from use, and the spray of water against his head and back felt like heaven. He tilted his head back and let it rain down on him, then reached for the bar of surprisingly fine-milled soap and began to wash the dirt and sweat from his body. His mind went blank as he did so, aware of nothing more than the texture of soap and water and skin, as all evidence of the night's adventures swirled down the drain.

The lack of sleep wouldn't be so easily erased. For all that he'd put up a cool facade, and Rosemary likewise, the night's work had been taxing even before the ghouls had arrived. Digging up a grave was hard work. But there was no help for it.

Food and coffee would put things to rights. He just had to force himself out of the tub.

There was an impatient knock on the door, a heavier fist than Rosemary's.

"Out in a minute," he called, and hurriedly finished drying himself, then pulled on trousers and undershirt and opened the door for John Baxter, who gave him an odd look before nodding a greeting and taking possession of the washroom.

Breakfast was served on the dot of seven a.m., and they slid into their seats just as Gert brought in a platter of toast, crisp-edged and dripping with butter. Aaron checked his first instinct to grab for it, filling his plate with other items while waiting for the platter to make its way down the table toward him. Conversation was less lively than it had been the night before, with the addition of another guest at the far end of the table, the owner of the tousled head he had seen earlier, an older man with old-fashioned sideburns and a decidedly solemn expression. Even Rosemary seemed subdued, although she was normally willing enough to chatter over her morning tea.

He supposed exhuming the body would have taken the starch out of her. She had known the man, after all. Admittedly only as a child, and Rosemary was rarely the sentimental sort, but it could be a contributing factor to her introspection.

Shrugging it off, he took two pieces of toast, layering several strips of bacon on one, then dipped it into his egg. He hadn't been teasing her earlier: their work built up an appetite. He noted with approval that Rosemary had filled her plate as well, despite the sideways glances the new guest gave her. Doubtless he was one of those who thought a woman should never be seen putting food in her mouth, or lift anything heavier than a sewing needle.

Whatever the cause of the mood at the table, their hostess decided that she would have no more of it. "I trust you slept well, Mr. Wilder?"

The older man looked up, and Aaron half expected him to merely grunt and return to his meal, but he seemed to recollect himself, managing, "Well enough, thank you. It is a pleasant change from the noise of the city." He had a surprisingly soft tenor, not the bass Aaron would have predicted.

Mrs. Wesson waited, but when nothing more was forthcoming, she turned her attention to her next victims. "And what are your plans for the day, Miss Harker, Mr. Harker?"

"I will be paying a visit to my cousin, Mrs. Lovelace, to see if there is anything she may need of me," Rosemary answered, politely putting her teacup down to respond. "And then I had thought to take a walk, once the day has warmed up. Botheration needs his exercise, or he becomes sulky. Might there be a path you would particularly recommend? We spent most of the day walking through town, but I'd a particular interest to see this new mill we were discussing last night."

"Oh dear." Mrs. Wesson seemed taken aback by the request. "I'm not sure if . . . well. A young lady such as yourself?

Jan and Gert walk from their home, and I suppose they might be able to suggest a walk that would appeal, but the millworks are no place for a young woman to be walking alone."

Aaron had the sudden desire to tell her exactly how her delicate young lady guest had spent the past few hours, and from the look his sister gave him from under lowered lids, she knew that. He contented himself with taking another piece of toast and scraping up the last of his eggs with it, to Mr. Wilder's very obvious wince.

"Nonsense," William Dolph responded to Mrs. Wesson, blustering up from his toast and jam. "You frighten the girl for no reason. It is perfectly safe for even a child to walk without concern."

Mrs. Wesson smiled, but it was a thin, clearly forced response that ran counter to Aaron's appraisal of her. "Of course, of course. You should be perfectly safe. But I would be a poor hostess if I did not suggest that you stay away from the mills. We have a lovely park. The river paths are not entirely safe, not alone."

Aaron wondered at her reluctance, and insistence. She surely knew of the recent deaths, just as her maids did, but this seemed more vehement than public knowledge should cause. Mr. Dolph, on the surface, had the right of it; they had seen no sign of anything fiercer than a squirrel or owl while walking back that morning.

Excluding the ghouls, of course, but ghouls rarely went after healthy victims. It had been the scent of the dead body that had drawn them, and he and Rosemary had merely been in their way. And the way a ghoul stripped flesh from its victims was nothing like the wounds they had seen on the body. Because no hunt was ever that simple.

No, the surface of things was what Dolph saw. Huntsmen looked beneath. Mrs. Wesson was right to worry: something was stalking this town.

"I thank you for your advice," Rosemary was saying in response to conversation Aaron had missed, caught in his own thoughts. "It would indeed be a most unpleasant and unwanted encounter. For me, at least."

Baxter let out a low chuckle, but nobody else laughed, and Mrs. Wesson's tight smile returned. She knew about the deaths, Aaron decided, if not the uncertain cause behind them, but she had no intention of possibly scaring away paying guests by telling anyone.

Movement caught his eye, and he lifted his napkin to his mouth to hide the turn of his head. In the doorway, the older girl, Jan, was watching Mrs. Wesson, an indecipherable look on her face. She saw Aaron looking and ducked her head, disappearing back into the kitchen.

Curious. He had no experience with housemaids; perhaps they all looked at their employers like that. He would ask Rosemary.

Baxter turned to Aaron, bringing his attention back to the table. "And you, Mr. Harker? Are you also a fan of calm walks along the riverbanks?"

The man's tone was edging on the snide, although his expression was purely that of polite interest. Aaron did not think he had done anything to evoke such behavior from the man, but responding in kind would get them nowhere.

Aaron might not always understand what people felt, but he knew how to manipulate them. Baxter was a businessman; he would respond best to his own language.

"My sister may have time for such casual strolls," Aaron said, dabbing at his mouth where some jam had strayed, then replacing the napkin on his knee. "I, however, must spend some time with my work."

"And what is it that you do?" There was a definite edge to the man's voice now, and while Aaron did not understand where it came from, he could not continue to ignore it, not without giving the impression of rolling over and showing his belly to the other man. And that, his instincts told him, would be a very bad idea. And it wasn't as though he could admit that his plan for today was to speak with the families of the other victims, to determine if there was some connection between them.

"I manage our family's investments." A true enough statement, although Rosemary had her hand in the decision-making as well. She had a decent eye for new trends, and they'd done well to follow a few of them. "As I'm sure you are aware, such things require constant vigilance."

That seemed to be the right thing to say, as Baxter was now nodding, the gleam in his eye shifting from snide dismissal to a predatory look. Aaron saw the trap immediately: Baxter now saw him as a potential mark to be roped into his investment schemes.

Not ideal, but there was nothing for it, and far better than suspicion.

Sure enough, the other man leaned forward, shifting his weight onto his elbows. "Have you considered adding real estate to your portfolio?"

"Mr. Baxter." Mrs. Wesson's voice cut across anything Aaron might have said in response. "You will not bring business dealings to the breakfast table."

"Yes, ma'am," he said, not in the slightest bit abashed. "My apologies. Mr. Harker, if you would care to speak more of this later . . . ?"

He really would not. "Perhaps another time."

With luck, he would learn something, speaking with the families of the dead, or Rosemary and Bother would discover something, and they could kill the uncanny and be gone before this would-be speculator could try to rope him into their game.

But Rosemary was right; he did tend to jinx them.

When Mr. Baxter turned his attention to her brother, Rosemary saw the perfect opportunity to escape. Rising quietly from the table, she nodded her thanks to Mrs. Wesson and received a nod in return, acknowledging her departure. And if her hostess had a knowing twinkle in her eye, Rosemary refused to admit that she was fleeing. Rather, it was—hopefully—a dignified retreat.

Going upstairs, Rosemary closed her bedroom door

firmly behind her with a not-quite-suppressed sigh of relief. She then quickly unpinned her hair from its bun and braided it into a coil, topping it with a simple hat that would be less likely to catch on branches or come loose if she had to run. If she could cut her hair short like a man's, she would, but only the most daring of suffragettes were so bold.

Rosemary had never acquiesced to the ridiculous fashion for hobbling skirts at the ankles; all her skirts were simply tailored but allowed reasonable movement, and the pockets sewn discreetly into the folds were suitable for both her jack-knife and a handful of dried liver bits for Botheration, as well as the leather lead for his collar. Warm woolen stockings went on underneath her skirt before lacing on sturdy walking shoes, the heel suitable for sidewalk strolls and hillside hikes alike. And if her stockings bore a delicate lace pattern and her shoes were a fashionable oxblood, a little style never harmed anyone.

A tapestry drawstring bag held her coin purse, gloves, and pistol, a Browning 1910, plus a small silver knife in the shape of a half-moon, cradled in a sheath of hardened leather.

She chose her cloak rather than last night's coat to go over her outfit, and a once-over determined that she looked the part of a well-to-do countrywoman of respectable independence. Satisfied with her effort, she went downstairs again.

The men were still at the breakfast table, although Mrs. Wesson had disappeared to Lord knew where. Gert was changing the flowers in the vase in the entryway, and the girl startled, almost dropping the vase, when Rosemary passed by. With a whispered apology for disturbing the oddly-skittish girl, Rosemary slipped out the door and headed back around to the kennel.

The air outside was every bit as bracing as she had expected, and she drew one glove on as she walked, leaving the other hand bare.

She opened the gate to the kennel, tapping the side of her right leg once. Botheration was curled on the bed in the corner of the shelter, and did not acknowledge her approach or the command.

"Oh, come on."

That got her a turn of the head, brown eyes considering her reproachfully.

"Yes, all right, I'm sorry we left you out of last night's fun, but you wouldn't have enjoyed picking ghoul out of your teeth again."

He huffed once and lay his head down on his paws.

"Aw, Bother, don't be like that." She reached into her pocket and pulled out one of the liver treats with her bare hand. "Come on, I brought you something."

The dog huffed again, then got to his feet, coming toward the door where Rosemary waited, but stopping just out of reach. She crouched so that their heads were at equal height and offered the treat to him on a flat palm.

"Forgiven?"

You could order a Molosser to do something and it would, but they were partners, not servants, and it was always better to treat them as such.

A warm, wet tongue lapped at her bare wrist once before Bother took the treat and swallowed it whole. Then an equally wet nose rested on her palm, breathing her scent in deeply.

"Good morning to you, too. Ready to do some work?"

That got his ear perked up again, and his blunt muzzle shoved at her arm once before he backed up a step and sat down, clearly waiting for her.

"All right then, all right." She drew on her other glove, then adjusted the heavy collar and lead, making sure it did not pinch, and stood up, waiting until Botheration joined her outside the kennel.

"No scent for you yet, boy, I'm sorry. We still don't know what it is that we're hunting. Hopefully you can help us with that?"

The look he gave her then, if he had been capable of speech, would have translated to *Just get out of my way, woman.*

Not every pup from his line took to the hunt; some made excellent guard dogs, while a few every generation preferred to live a quiet life as household pets. But the ones who did were similar to their human companions; it was better to be working than waiting.

"Let's go, then."

Mrs. Wesson's warning to stay away from the mills had been heartfelt and well-meaning, and Rosemary felt a slight twinge of guilt that she had no intention of listening.

"There have been three bodies, Bother. Three, not just

the one. And all three found in different locations, but with similar wounds. At least we think they were similar. We've only seen the one. They think it's a human doing this, but we know it's not, don't we? So we need to find out what it is, and stop it."

Updating Botheration on what they had learned was often, Rosemary had found, the best way to identify holes in their assumptions. But they didn't even have enough yet to make an assumption.

"So where do we start, Bother?"

She paused at the corner, nodding a vague greeting to a woman walking past her, and looked down at the beast. "Two of the bodies were found closer to the river, and one in town. What do you think?"

Bother lifted his head into the air and drew a heavy breath in, his entire body still as he did whatever it was his nose did. If she'd been asked, Rosemary would have thought Botheration would choose the river. Instead, he exhaled, coughed, and turned to the left without hesitation, heading northwest, away from both the river and the site where Dr. Lovelace had been found.

"All right, then, you and Mrs. Wesson agree," Rosemary said, having to increase her pace to keep up.

The sidewalks turned to snow-covered verge, the houses farther and farther apart, until the road ended in a copse of massive chestnut trees that had likely been there before the Pilgrims landed on this coast. On the other side of the copse she could see where the train tracks ran, connecting city with city and town to town, a lifeline of civilization. Eventually, as the city grew, *if* the city grew, this copse would become farmland, or be given over to factories.

This was likely the land Messrs. Dolph and Baxter sought to acquire, Rosemary realized, and she pulled Botheration to a gentle stop, studying the copse with a wary, experienced eye. Most folk, if they thought of it at all, would assume that this close to town, the woods had been tamed; that nothing more dangerous than squirrels and foxes roamed there, even allowing for the occasional cougar come down from the mountains. But pockets like this too often held uncanny creatures as well, tucked into the trunks and roots or burrowed high in the branches, waiting only for a hapless human to wander into their grasp.

Or, occasionally, venturing out to hunt humans, and thereby earning the attentions of Huntsmen. Was that the reason the hound had led her there?

There was only one way to know.

"Bother." She unclipped the leash and watched his soft ear prick up and his body tense, waiting for the command. "Hunt."

Without a more specific command, the hound would look for any trace of uncanny, no matter how mild, no matter how long-abandoned the den, and lead her to it.

The hound moved forward in a steady, almost stately manner, ears alert and eyes up. His breed used eyes and ears and nose together, his line bred to this one purpose. If there was anything uncanny within the copse, no matter how well hidden, he would find it.

Nearly two hours later, they had gone over every inch of the copse and the surrounding meadows, and Rosemary's feet were swollen in her shoes, her stockings were sagging, and if it hadn't been winter, she would have been certain an entire bevy of biting insects had taken up residence inside her sleeves, the way her skin itched. She would have considered it fair payment, had they discovered anything. But they'd found nothing. There had been no sign of anything uncanny in the woods, all the way to the railway tracks and back again.

"Bother. To me."

The hound hesitated, as though unwilling to give up, then let his head drop slightly and returned to her side.

"This makes no sense," she told him, clipping the lead back to his collar. "Why did you bring us all the way out here, if there is nothing?"

The hound simply stared at her, brown eyes patient, as though waiting for her to solve the puzzle.

Maybe the fact that there *should* have been something here? The trees were old enough, exactly the sort to appeal to half a dozen native uncanny, and undisturbed for years; something should have chosen to den here. Rosemary frowned. Unless the workers who had laid the rail tracks had driven them away?

Possible, but unlikely. Most woodland uncanny were territorial. They did not pick up and move; they had to be removed.

Rosemary felt the skin between her shoulder blades twitch, as though one of those nonexistent insects had bitten her there. The unease that had dogged her the day before had returned at some point, layering under her physical discomfort.

"I wonder if there were any other attacks on the workers," she said, staring thoughtfully at one massive trunk. "Unexplained accidents, equipment that suddenly stopped working, men quitting without giving any reason why . . ."

But if anything had been here once, it was gone now. And there was no one she could ask, not without a reason that would hold water. Even Huntsmen could not work miracles: they needed a place to *start*.

"Everything leaves traces, Bother. Everything."

The hound sat his rump on the ground and scratched busily at his neck, no help whatsoever.

Rosemary stared up at the tree limbs overhead, thinking about the wounds they'd seen on Lovelace's body. The placement of the wounds, the shape and depth, and the odd texture of the skin around them. Something that could take down three adult men, do that sort of damage, wouldn't walk lightly, and very few of the uncanny were intelligent enough to clean up after themselves, so that they left no sign behind. And yet there had been no sign of a violent attack where the men had died.

And something that killed the way Lovelace had been killed, with such precise savagery? That was not a creature that could easily hide along the riverbanks, and certainly not in town. Not without being noticed—and Botheration picking up the scent.

And even if it was new-come to this area, several weeks' residence would leave *some* sign.

But there had been no trace.

"We're missing something, Bother. I just don't know what."

Botheration, finished scratching, rumbled deep in his chest, clearly unhappy. He took it personally when he couldn't pick up a scent when asked. If they'd been in the country, she would have let him chase down a rabbit or two to make him feel better. But they were too close to town, and some people reacted badly to having a hundred-and-twenty-pound beast barreling after rabbits in their yards.

"So much for that brilliant idea." She looked down at her skirt, thankful that snow left behind fewer stains than dirt. A quick sniff of her clothing reassured her that, although she had hardly been sitting idly by while Bother did all the work, she would not need to go back to the boarding house to change clothing before meeting up with her brother.

Having struck out with the countryside, perhaps they would have better luck in town.

"It's near lunchtime, but I wouldn't say no to a quick something to eat," she said. "How about you?"

The look the hound gave her could not have been clearer if he'd been able to speak: he would like that very much, please.

There were two bakeries in town, and although after the long walk back it was well past when their goods would be freshest, Rosemary thought she might be able to cajole a roll or tart for half price, before they closed for the day.

The first storefront, the one they'd seen the day before, did not inspire confidence; the breads looked dull, and the pastries over-sugared, and the way the clerk looked sideways at them both made Rosemary decide to take her chances elsewhere.

The other bakery was several blocks away, and she found herself pausing by the milliner's window, admiring the assortment of winter hats, fur-trimmed and banded, on display there. The woman she'd seen at the library with Miss Baker had likely bought her hat here, to judge from the quality. Rosemary's own felted hat was serviceable enough, but lacked a certain flash these had to spare.

"You've no need of flash," she told herself firmly, and clucked at Bother to get him moving again.

The second bakery, even from the outside, was redolent with the sweet-stale smell of yeast, suggesting that the ovens were still warm. She paused a moment to breathe it in, her stomach rumbling loud enough for anyone to hear, before pushing the door open and going inside, Botheration at her heels.

"Good morning," the clerk behind the counter said, his gaze flicking from Botheration to Rosemary's face with only the slightest wince. "How may I help you?"

Botheration came to attention, blunt head up and tail

lifted and still, and Rosemary's prepared greeting died in her mouth. The beast had scented something, something that had been hiding under the aromas of flour, sugar, and molasses, until they had come to the source.

"Ah." Her thoughts spun wildly, then training took over, and she gave the display a quick glance, then offered the clerk a shy smile, expressly designed to defray suspicion. "I was wondering about your breads?"

As the clerk pulled out a tray of shaped loaves to show her, Rosemary discreetly loosened her hold on the hound's leash, allowing him to explore more of the store without drawing attention. His narrow tail stayed high, but he did not show any sign of alarm, only alertness.

She moved closer to the counter, engaging the young clerk in a discussion of grains and lamenting the high cost of everything these days. The floor and shelves behind the counter were scrupulously clean, as she'd expect, but beneath the crisp brown paper lining the shelves she could just see the gossamer traces of brownie tracks. If you didn't know what you were looking for, it might seem like the reflection of sunlight through the glass, but for a Huntsmen it was unmistakable. Unfortunately, it was impossible to tell without closer investigation how old the tracks were, and if it was just the one, or if there was a larger nest hidden back in the kitchen.

Another day or time she might have done something about it, but unlike ghouls, brownies were no real threat to life and limb; even if you reneged on your deal with them, they merely ruined the individual foolish enough to do so, and then left town. Huntsmen would still clean out nests, of course, but it was never a priority.

Still, this was the first sign of uncanny interacting with humans they had found in town; it couldn't be ignored.

Rosemary had an uneasy thought that what they were hunting for might be hiding in a house, but dismissed it almost immediately. Something that tore and cauterized flesh like that would not be able to hide its nature, and it would take a particularly unpleasant human not to notice, or be willing to ignore it at close quarters.

Not that such humans did not exist; she had intimate knowledge that they did. But those types tended to be known to their neighbors; known, and talked about. Especially once people started to die.

Certainly her librarian would not have passed up such a rag-eared whisper, and Mrs. Wesson . . . Their hostess certainly heard gossip; any guesthouse-keeper worth her salt cultivated it for business reasons, but Rosemary doubted that the woman spilled much, and never unintentionally.

She wished Aaron could ask his new friend, discover if the police had anyone they were keeping an eye on. But that would require another bribe, no doubt, and risk bringing themselves further into the official eye, and every Huntsman's instinct told her that was a terrible idea.

Some officials could become allies. But they were few and far between, and you couldn't know who they were until often too late.

The clerk was still waiting on her, so she gave a gentle tug on Bother's lead, bringing him back to her knee, and pointed with her free hand at the smaller of the three loaves. "That one, please, and also one of your crullers?"

Leaving without purchasing something would make her memorable. The bread she could offer to Mrs. Wesson, or more usefully to her hired girls; the cruller she would eat herself.

"You don't have a basket," the clerk observed, after he had wrapped the loaf carefully in brown paper and taken her money, then snapped his fingers. "A moment."

He turned around, rummaging under the counter, and came back with a cloth bag, soft white and just the size to hold a loaf, with a cord to close it tight. "My father saw these when he was abroad," the clerk said. "They're supposed to keep the bread longer, but you can use them to carry it too."

"How much . . . ?"

But the clerk waved her offer away. "You're new to town, yes?" he asked, and nodded in satisfaction when she said yes. "So you must come in again, to return it."

"Of course," she agreed, and watched as he slid the loaf inside, and handed it and the cruller, wrapped in its own brown paper, to her.

Good product, good service. The baker might be benefitting from uncanny interference, but they were clearly not relying on brownie magic to make their business profitable. She hoped they wouldn't have to come back to deal with the brownies later.

Outside, she paused to take a bite of her cruller, then tucked the remainder into her pocket before anyone could see her being so gauche as to eat on the street like a child. Botheration pushed at her hand, licking the glaze and crumbs off her fingers. "Sorry, boy." She broke off the heel of the loaf and offered it to him. It disappeared in one gulp, leaving the palm of her glove sticky from his tongue.

"Ugh," and she discreetly wiped it against her skirt, looking around to see if anyone had noticed, then checked her timepiece, surprised that it was only just after the noon hour. The walk back into town had seemed longer. She wished there was some way to determine what Aaron was up to, and where. Had he had better luck than her, or had he also hit a dead end, trying to speak with the families of the victims?

"What do you think, Bother? Should we look for him? Or should we go back to Mrs. Wesson's and wait for him to find us?"

Bother whined a little and leaned against the leash, tugging her down the street, away from the center of town and the boarding house both. She let him lead, hoping that he was not leading them on another wild-goose chase.

"It was terrible."

Aaron made a humming noise under his breath, trying to project an air of sympathy and caring into the sound. The woman seated across from him was neither weeping nor angry, thankfully. Her eyes were dry, and she stared at him with the wearied expression of a woman who has come to accept that the world is not kind.

"The body was mangled. We . . . I couldn't bear to put him into the ground like that. His father objected, wanted to hold a proper funeral. A showing of hysterics sent him scurrying." Her mouth twisted, although if it was at the memory or the weakness of men, Aaron couldn't tell. "It was better that way. Jimmy's parents shouldn't have to remember him that way."

He had been surprised at first to learn that she had been the one to identify the body, since the two hadn't been married yet, but no longer. Louisa Batali might have made a good Huntsman, if she had been born into another family.

Underwood's parents, who had reluctantly given him Miss Batali's direction, were not made of such strong stuff.

"You said that it looked as though he had fallen into the machinery of the mill?"

"Yes. There were lacerations all over his body, the front of his body. Deep ones. Like gears had chewed him up and spat him out again." She raised her chin, as though expecting him to mock her, or tell her she couldn't have seen what she was saying.

He'd seen heavy machinery at work a few times, and could imagine the damage even a relatively benign grinder or drill might do to a human body unlucky enough to be caught in it. But. "Is there a machine in the mill that could do that?"

He thought her surprise at being asked was genuine. "I

don't know," she admitted. "They wouldn't let me near the place, after." Her bitterness also seemed genuine. "And the mill owner and the police of course insist that it was a wild animal, terribly sad but nothing to do with them. I've been around animals my entire life, Mr. Harker. My family's bred hunting dogs, and I know what a bite looks like, dog or big cat. What was done to my Jimmy wasn't that." Her face tightened, making her look far older than her early twenties. "I don't care what Chief Schneider has to say on the matter; he's wrong."

She sighed then, strength leaving her shoulders. "They all think I'm overwrought with grief. You likely do, too."

"I think you're a remarkably sensible woman," he said honestly. "But it might be best for now if you allowed them to say what they will. It won't bring Jimmy back, not the arguing nor the knowing. Let it go." He'd seen it before: she might thank him for the truth, but it would weigh on her for the rest of her life. Better to remain in angry ignorance.

She looked at him, dark brown eyes staring into his as though she could determine if he was being truthful, or merely giving her platitudes. Aaron held her gaze, remembering to soften his face around the eyes and mouth, until she gave a slight nod.

"You're right. It won't change anything. But someone got my Jimmy killed, and I know who it was."

Aaron held back his surprise, but it took effort. "You do?"

She nodded once, strongly, and her fists clenched where

they had been resting in her lap. "It was those men staying at Mrs. Wesson's."

As Aaron left the Batali home, closing the door gently behind him, he looked up and was unsurprised to find Rosemary and Botheration waiting for him. The dog was splayed on the ground, head on his paws, while Rosemary was half perched on a low stone column that had likely once been a hitching post. Her hands were folded in her lap, her gaze on something far in the distance. He paused to adjust the muffler tucked around his neck and pull on his own gloves against the chill before coughing gently: he no longer even tried to sneak up on them individually, much less together. Their reflexes were better than his.

Rosemary must have seen something in his face that made her straighten up, which in turn made Bother get to his feet, legs stiffening into "guard" mode.

"It's all right," he told them both. "Walk with me."

Rosemary looked as though she doubted his ability to judge what was all right, but slid off the column and followed him. "How did it go?"

"The first family shut the door in my face." He didn't tell his sister about the wailing baby he'd heard, or the look on the widow's face, pinched and strained, when she told him to go away. It would bother Rosemary more than it had him, and they might yet have to revisit that home, push the widow to speak with them. Better if she didn't carry that weight with her when they did.

"And there?" Rosemary tilted her head to indicate the house they were walking away from.

"His parents would not speak to me, but he was engaged to be married. She . . . had things to say."

He wished for a quiet room where they could sit down with a beer, somewhere warm and private, but this town was too small for such a thing, and they had no allies here. He said as much to Rosemary, who scoffed, slapping his shoulder gently with the back of her hand.

"There's the reason you don't hunt alone." When he looked blankly at her, she prompted him. "Mrs. Lovelace."

"What about her?"

Rosemary's sigh told him that he was the slowest brother on God's green earth. "We can talk there. She knows . . . well, enough. And she's invested in us finding this thing."

Invading a woman's home to discuss her husband's death seemed the sort of thing Rosemary would scold him for suggesting, but strolling back and forth on the streets would likely garner them unwanted attention before too long. He nodded, and they set off again, this time with purpose.

The widow answered the door so quickly after Rosemary's knock, Aaron half suspected she had been sitting by the window, watching for them.

"Come in, come in. I just set a new pot of tea down, and there is fresh-made kuchen; it's almost as though I knew you were coming—oh." And she stopped, having noticed Botheration standing a little behind them, his solid bulk not at all hidden by their bodies, his tail wagging diffidently.

"He can stay outside," Rosemary offered, but the woman waved her off. "No, no, I'm sure any dog of yours is well-trained, and a little fur on the carpets is hardly the worst they've ever seen." Despite her words, she eyed the hound cautiously, and he, aware he was being judged, lowered his head and wagged his tail harder until she laughed. "Yes, all right, boy, you may come in. Please, do come in, all three of you."

And that easily, the Harkers were relieved of their coats and hats and settled back in chairs, thin-rimmed cups of tea in their hands and slices of apple-shortbread cake on plates in front of them. Botheration took a careful turn around the parlor, then stretched out in front of the fireplace as though he'd always lived there.

Aaron took a sip of the tea, welcome after the cold outside, and glanced around the room. Half the vases of lilies had disappeared, and the ones that remained had been moved to tables in the corners of the room. The photo of Dr. Lovelace was still front and center, however, and Mrs. Lovelace was still gripping that man's kerchief. Aaron wondered if she'd let it out of her hand since last they saw her.

"Terrible weather out, isn't it? It's always cold, come November, but the winds have been fierce, and terribly unpredictable, even for the lake. You should see this town in warmer months. People come from miles around. It's so beautiful, with everything in bloom. . . ."

She fell silent, as though realizing anew that her husband would not be with her when spring came around again.

"It's been too soon; I won't ask if you have news. And as much as I'd like to think you are here simply to visit an old woman, I suspect otherwise." She didn't quite smile, the sorrow still too heavy to allow for that, but there was a gentleness in her eyes as she sipped her own tea. "Mrs. Wesson is a dear woman, but she's also a terrible gossip, and she gleans her table for tidbits better than any farmer I ever met. And I suspect you sussed that out about her within minutes."

"We may have noted that she has a remarkable interest in her guests," Rosemary allowed, while Aaron took a large bite of his cake so that he would have an excuse not to speak. Then he took another bite; it was quite good.

"It makes her an excellent businesswoman," Mrs. Lovelace said. "Far better than her husband ever was, in truth. Men never like to hear that, but I have a suspicion you know quite well what women are capable of." That was directed at Aaron, who quirked his mouth up in a smile but declined to comment.

"But your business is the sort that needs privacy, no doubt. A safe retreat, away from such a gossip, however well-intentioned, where you can speak without fear." She waved away anything they might have responded. "I called you here. The least I can do is offer you tea and sanctuary." She did smile then, a soft curve of her mouth. "That's what Tucker used to call this parlor, 'the sanctuary of peaceful thought.' Said it made coming to hard decisions easier.

"I have laundry that needs airing and folding, if you wish to be alone," she went on. "But I admit to a certain level of interest in what you have learned."

Rosemary gave Aaron a sidelong glance, and he nodded once. They could send the woman out of the room, certainly, but there was no need. Huntsmen worked along the edges of society out of necessity, not desire or dogma. And Tucker Lovelace might not have been a Huntsman, but he hadn't been an outsider. He had been family, and so therefore was his widow.

"Are you certain?" Rosemary asked gently. "Your husband was careful to keep you out of what we do, but once you know, it is difficult, if not impossible, to forget. Your life will change, and likely not for the better."

"I may have misled you slightly as to how much Tucker shared with me," she admitted quietly. "Forgive an old woman her caution?"

"Of course," Aaron said without hesitation. "What did he tell you?"

"That your people are . . . soldiers. That you fight in wars people couldn't know about. And he, Tucker I mean, was able to help sometimes, but nobody could know about that, either. I teased him that your father and he were government agents, but . . . it wasn't that, was it?"

"We're Huntsmen," Rosemary told her. "Not government, no. We're . . . There are things in this world. Uncanny creatures. And many of them mean us ill. When an uncanny becomes a known danger, we step in."

Mrs. Lovelace looked upset. "But why you?"

Aaron watched his sister struggle with the words, fascinated. He'd never had to explain themselves before, neither of them had. They just *were*.

"Huntsmen families have . . . a connection to the uncanny." A blood connection, though Rosemary did not say that part. "It allows us to deal with them more safely than others might."

Huntsmen *were* uncanny. Or had been, far and long ago, when the uncanny called fey took mortal lovers, then abandoned them with their half-breed children, leaving them to find their way, generation after generation.

"If they're so dangerous," Mrs. Lovelace asked, "why not deal with them before they kill anyone?"

"It's been tried," Aaron said, when Rosemary hesitated. "But they are many, and they hide. And because not all become dangers, no more than cougars or bears." And "many" was an understatement; there were far more uncanny than there were humans, a fact that lingered in every Huntsman's mind, and was never spoken out loud.

"And you think that is what killed Tucker, one of these creatures?" The kerchief fluttered slightly in her hand. "Was that what he was so worried about? That one of those things was in Brunson?"

"We think so, yes," Rosemary said. "I'm sorry, I know that this is a lot that we're asking you to accept. . . ."

"My dear." Mrs. Lovelace reached over to pat Rosemary's

hand. "I know it is difficult for young people like you to accept, but older folk are not fragile flowers, to wilt in the heat." Her round face was cast with memories for an instant, deepening the shadows under her eyes. "I was a child when the War Between the States began. Even here, the things we heard, saw . . . That there are things of great evil in this world does not surprise me. That they are not all human is almost a relief."

Aaron put his tea down, wondering if they needed to tell the woman that they had disturbed her husband's grave. It seemed the sort of thing that maybe one shouldn't talk about, but if they were going to be honest with her . . .

Maybe not that honest, he decided. And the ghouls weren't a risk to anyone living, so long as you didn't get between them and a carcass.

"But we've looked, and there are no uncanny obvious within the town," Rosemary said, then seemed to recollect herself. "None dangerous, at least." She grimaced a little. "Several of your fellow citizens may be taking advantage of a nest of brownies. If you encounter one, Mrs. Lovelace, I strongly suggest you gently refuse any offer it may make you. It is never truly worth it."

The older woman simply nodded, as though this were only common sense. "Do they come to your door, like a brush salesman, or . . . ?"

Aaron bit his lip at that image, and shook his head. "More likely, you would simply find traces of them in your kitchen one morning. Make sure that you do not leave any cream or butter out on the counter, and don't speak to any you may see, and they will move on."

"Not all uncanny are directly dangerous," Rosemary added. "But none are harmless."

"No dairy on the counter, no to any offers made," Mrs. Lovelace repeated. "And a cross at the door and windows?"

Aaron managed not to snort, but only just. "The uncanny have no fear of human gods."

"Oh." Mrs. Lovelace looked taken aback, but recovered after a few seconds.

"Brownies aside," Rosemary said, "we haven't been able to find a hint of uncanny within the town, and that . . ." She shook her head. "But we are certain that whatever killed your husband, and two other men in town, was neither human nor animal, despite what the police believe."

"Oh." Mrs. Lovelace let out a wounded sound at that. "There were more?"

Rosemary looked guilty. "We're afraid so, yes. There are too many similarities in their deaths to be ignored. Although we've yet to determine what connection there might be between them."

"About that," Aaron said, putting his teacup down on the table next to his now-empty plate.

He grimaced as they both turned to study him, Rosemary with curiosity, the older woman with that and a hint of something else he couldn't quite read. By the fireplace, Botheration moaned and stretched.

"Mrs. Lovelace, before I begin, I must ask you a question, and forgive me if it seems . . . impertinent."

The older woman raised thin white eyebrows, and he could have sworn there was a flush of color on her shock-pale, powdery cheeks. "Impertinence at my age is a rare beast indeed. Go ahead and ask, young man."

"Was your husband a Knight?"

Rosemary cast him a startled glance, but he was focusing on the older woman. Her eyes widened, and her mouth thinned.

"I have a reason for asking," he said, as gently as he could manage. "And it's not to judge."

"He was not." Her voice, rather than the snap he'd expected, was amused, almost tender. "But . . . he was a doctor here for many years. He saw things, heard things. Treated men with injuries that could have been prevented, with illnesses that should not have happened."

Rosemary leaned in. "And these men all worked at the ironworks?"

"Some. Some elsewhere, but all down by the river. There used to be a lumber mill, years ago, before it closed down." She sighed, her eyes gone hazy with memory. "It smelled so much better. They cut the wood upriver, floated the logs down to be shaped at the mill. Better smell. But the men who owned it . . ."

She tilted her head, remembering something. "There

were some who said the wood was cursed, or maybe the river. But Tucker went down there more than a few times, and he always took his bag. And when he came back, he was in a sour mood, a truly sour mood that took hours to lift. And the ironworks . . ."

The thinness of her lips wasn't for Aaron now. "Tucker wasn't a Knight, no. But if you were to ask him, if he were to answer you, I always suspected that he would say that they were doing necessary work."

The Knights of Unity had been socialist agitators, with a mission to stand like old-fashioned knights against the robber barons of a previous age. They had lost most of their membership years ago, after a strike out in the Midwest had gone wrong and bloody. But they'd been powerful in their day—and the rumor among Huntsmen was that they'd used unnatural means to get that way.

Aaron had always discounted that rumor. A man with a powerful natural persuasion could be called a warlock easily enough, and have it mean nothing. But Lovelace, with his knowledge of the uncanny world, and a sympathy toward unions . . . Huntsmen had seen it before, men seeking to do good, using foul means. Even among their own kind.

It was how their own mother had died, trying to end such a folly.

Mrs. Lovelace interrupted his darkened thoughts. "You said you had a reason for asking. What was it?"

He saw no reason not to tell her this truth. "I was speaking with Louisa Batali this afternoon. Her fiancé, James Underwood, was one of those killed by similar means as your husband."

"Jimmy . . . he was killed in an accident at the new mill." She glanced at Rosemary, then back at Aaron. "It wasn't an accident. Oh. Oh, poor Louisa. And his parents, oh." She shook her head. "And the other victim?"

"A man named Ottering, Todd Ottering." Her expression showed no recognition of the name. "The police are claiming that it was a random attack by a hobo, who fled town afterward. But the description of the wounds was nearly identical."

The kerchief in Mrs. Lovelace's hand was crumpled into a ball, blue veins showing through the skin of her wrinkled, too-thin hands. "And the police knew this. Did they insist on a closed casket for those other men, too?"

"Miss Batali convinced his parents to have him cremated, as the body was . . . badly disfigured. I don't know about the other."

Rather than breaking into tears, as he'd feared, her eyes glinted with anger. "I should march down there and give Chief Schneider a piece of my mind. How dare he—"

"It is entirely likely they thought they were keeping a panic from breaking out," Rosemary said. "I'm not saying I agree with them, but they had their reasons."

"Poppycock." Her voice was tart as gooseberries. "They have an obligation to this town to tell us the truth, not ride roughshod over it."

"They don't know the truth," Aaron said. "And even if we tried to tell them—"

"They'd have you locked up at Willard before you could turn around," Mrs. Lovelace said, sighing. "You're quite right, unfortunately. If Tucker hadn't trusted your parents, worked with them, I might have been tempted myself, if you came to me with this tale."

Her husband had done more than trust them. He'd been fey-born, too. But there was no need to explain that to his widow, not now. They'd had no children to worry about.

Rosemary tapped the table in front of her with two fingers, bringing their attention back to her. "What does this have to do with unions, Aaron?"

"Miss Batali said that she knew who had killed her fiancé. She is grief-struck, and angry, so anything she says must be taken with skepticism, but she seems convinced of it." He pressed his hands together and raised them to his lips, considering how best to phrase the woman's accusation.

"Her fiancé was a union man, or wanted to be. She said that he had told her that there were men in town who didn't like him arguing for better conditions for workers, here and elsewhere. Men who were looking to turn the town into a factory town, and to hell with anyone who objected." He did not want to name names, not in front of Mrs. Lovelace, and could only hope that Rosemary picked up the words he was not saying.

"Strikebreakers, before a strike had even been called?" Rosemary sounded not doubting, but dubious. "Does she think that the police were involved?" It would not have been unheard of; the police, or more accurately, off-duty policemen in the hire of factory owners, had gotten their hands bloody before. "In any other situation I might be willing to consider the theory, but Aaron, those wounds."

The gashes had been too clean to be the work of wild animals, too deep and raw to be from a human blade, particularly since there had been no defensive wounds or bruising. And nothing explained the cauterizing.

"She is convinced," he said. "Although not enough to risk contradicting the police."

Rosemary shook her head, and he agreed: Miss Batali, no matter her certainty, was wrong. And yet.

"That might be the connection we were looking for," he said out loud. "If James Underwood was a unionist, and Dr. Lovelace a sympathizer."

"If these were common murders, yes. But why would an uncanny care about such things?" Rosemary wasn't seeing what he was. He might be wrong. He might be reaching too far, connecting the wrong things. And yet.

Men had been foolish enough to bind the uncanny to them before, and for far gentler things than the promise of wealth and power.

"We need to speak with the police again," Rosemary said with a frown. "We need that journal; it's the only solid clue we have to what might be stalking this town."

"It won't do any good. Trust me on this, Rosemary. They didn't want to talk to me to begin with, and that was when I was asking questions about Dr. Lovelace as a family member." He glanced over at Mrs. Lovelace, fixing an apologetic grimace on his face. "Forgive me, we have been telling those who asked that you called us in to help you with the estate, that we were cousins to your husband, and I may have let the police presume a closer relationship than existed."

"Well, you are family, as near as any I have left, aren't you, and I did call you here. It's not as though you can help what they make of that, is it?" She clearly was still indignant about the police's behavior, and half-ready to storm down and bawl them out herself. Under any other circumstances, Aaron would be tempted to follow in her wake and cheer her on.

"I've known half those boys since they were in knickers, and they're none of them what I'd consider great minds. Fair enough, and I don't think they've a cowardly bone in their bodies, but this isn't New York, or even Rochester. Most they have to deal with most days is someone running their automobile into the ditch, or someone going out with seven cows and coming in with eight. You shouldn't count on them for anything."

"Still, they must know something," Rosemary insisted. "They saw all three bodies. They must have some clues that would tell us what killed these men. They can't find it, they don't know how to hunt it. But we can."

"And if this is union related, you think they'd talk to us at all?" Aaron said in disgust. "They'd be just as happy to have every gomper laid out by the side of the road as not."

Rosemary's expression made him back up and look at what he had said. "Oh. Oh, I am so—"

Mrs. Lovelace didn't reassure him that it was all right,

but one delicate hand reached out to pat his knee, as though he were a boy of seven again. "None of this is easy to hear, Mr. Harker. Not the failures of the police who are supposed to protect us, not the idea that my Tucker may have been murdered—certainly not the idea that such creatures exist among us.

"But it's harder still to live with, to wake every morning and remember all over again that he's gone. To live in this house, surrounded by decades of him, and know that he'll never push his chair back, never light that terrible pipe of his. That some thing killed him, and not know *why*. Words can't hurt me, not anymore. So you say what you need to say, if it leads to finding out what happened. I can suffer that."

She paused, then gathered her shawl around her shoulders with her other hand. "But not today, I think. It's gone late, and I find I'm very tired."

It was a kinder dismissal than they deserved.

Seven

WINTER STORMS SIMMERED over the Great Lakes, a northwestern front building and driving east, while along the eastern line, another disturbance shifted and grew. Experienced sailors looked at the sky and shuddered, lashing down everything that could be, changing plans where possible, while along the shore and under the surface, things more instinct than sense nervously sought safer dens. Winter along the US-Canadian border was a chancy thing, often beautiful, often deadly, always changeable. But there was more to the weather's mood the past few weeks than science could explain, some element of rage in the eastern winds that made every slap of the waves, every down-cross of rain, seem personal.

The mood spread, stretching tendrils across Lake Ontario and along the shores, pricking and pinching some, ignoring others.

Inside the Brunson Free Library, Madeleine Baker scratched at an itch just behind her ear, unable to shake the feeling that something was terribly wrong. She glanced out the window, powerless to suppress a shudder when the wind dragged a branch across the glass. Not even the warm lights within could disperse the gloom lurking outside.

She'd burned dinner the night before, filling her cottage with thick black smoke, and when she'd opened the windows to clear it out, the salty-sweet smell of the wind had made her want to curl up in her quilt and cry herself to sleep.

Normally she would go to Jessika when her mood twisted like this, let her dear friend's clear common sense guide her out. But she hadn't seen Jessika since their conversation— their argument—had been interrupted, and the thought of going to her now felt too much like begging for attention. Like apologizing, again.

Worse, Jes might ask about the woman who'd interrupted them. Might ask what they had spoken about. What Maddy had told her.

"Nothing can be trusted. Nothing, no one, no thing," a voice whispered to her, and she shook her head as though to discourage a honeybee from buzzing. There was no reason for her to feel that way, as though she'd done something wrong, speaking with her visitor. The woman had asked harmless questions, innocent questions. There was no way that woman could know. No way anyone could know, and it wasn't as though she'd done anything wrong. . . .

She hadn't done anything wrong.

"You can trust me," she said out loud to the buzzing. "I won't tell anyone."

She didn't know why she said that.

The buzzing faded, but the itch remained, keeping her from focusing on her research. She'd told Miss Harker that she would look things up, and she was a woman of her word, even if the other woman never did come back for them. But looking at the legends of monsters and magic gathered around this area was only making her headache—and her heartache—worse.

Madeleine gathered her papers together and slid them into her satchel, then set about closing up the library for the night. It wasn't as though anyone was likely to come by in this weather, and if they did, they could just come back again tomorrow.

The house felt too quiet after Margaret's visitors had left, despite the wind rattling roof and walls outside. She closed the shutters against the coming night and turned the lamp up higher, filling the sitting room with a deep yellow light. Her hand touched the back of Tucker's chair as she walked past, letting her fingertips glide along the edge the way she used to when he sat there, the fabric rough under her skin. When she saw him now, he was often the young man she'd married, and then just as often as he'd been the night before he died, bald pate shining and a hand lifted to his chest when he coughed.

She knew Tucker wasn't there, not truly, but she took comfort in the feeling nonetheless. And if she did not speak to the memory-specter, it was only because she did not trust herself to remember not to do so when others were around. Being old was difficult enough without folk thinking she'd lost her mind from grief, as well.

The young Huntsmen, the Harkers, would tell her to exorcise the ghost, no doubt. And they would likely be wise and right. But she couldn't. Not yet. Not when it only sat there and watched her, a half smile on its face as though it were bemused to see her, too, bemused and happy and not willing to do anything that might sour their luck.

"There's been little enough luck in this town lately. I'll take whatever I'm given."

She thought the ghost nodded at that.

There was a noise outside, and her hand stiffened against the chair, neatly trimmed fingernails digging into the fabric, her heart suddenly racing. She didn't use to be this easily frightened; she'd once faced off a drunken man with nothing but her wits and a strong chin. But now, it seemed as though every crackle of leaves or scrape of branches made her skin leap. The young Harkers had warned her, but she had thought knowledge better than comforting ignorance.

Maybe she had been wrong.

The noise faded, and she could hear the cries of children somewhere, doubtless running home for supper. Someone passing along the road, she supposed, or someone's cat looking for its own dinner. "Nothing will harm you within these walls," she murmured, repeating what Tucker had said so many times. She'd not understood what he meant for many years, not until he told her about the markings within the walls, the salt and iron buried under every doorsill. Not until he'd told her that he'd done terrible, dangerous things when he was a younger man and Levi Harker had called upon his services. *There's so much I can't tell you, Maggie-love,* he'd said. *But know that I would never leave you unprotected.*

Tucker had never lied to her before, and so she had believed him. But that trust had been shaken when Chief Schneider had come to her door and told her they'd found his body.

There was something wrong in her town, this place where she had lived since she was a young woman newly married. She had tried to tell herself that it was her imagination, that her grief had made her feel things that were not there, that her feelings of loss and anger were creating phantoms in the shadows.

But Tucker had felt something was wrong too. Wrong enough that he'd not been able to sleep. Wrong enough that he'd made arrangements for Huntsmen to investigate his death.

She knew now what Huntsmen were.

The sound came again, but this time it was from her front stoop, as though someone had jumped up the steps and landed hard. She half turned, looking over the room to see if the children had left anything behind that they needed to return for. But there was nothing on the sofa or in the chair, nor on the floor by where they'd sat.

There was a knock on the door, a firm, barely polite rap. She frowned, then glanced to where Tucker would have been sitting, as though he might offer to open the door for her. There was only air there now.

"Foolish old woman," she said, and went to open the door, thinking that perhaps a friend had come to offer lingering condolences, painful and unwanted.

But by the time she had the handle turned and the door pulled open, there was no one there. She clung to the edge of the door, peering out into the darkness, her heart pounding hard enough to feel. This was her home, this was where she had lived for decades. There should be nothing out there unfamiliar, nothing she could not recognize. But for the first time in her life, the familiar bite of winter air and smell of pine did not comfort her, but rather left her deeply ill at ease.

And when she closed the door, she locked it, and then poured a fine line of salt across the sill as well.

Eight

THE HARKERS HADN'T gone more than a few strides from Mrs. Lovelace's house before Aaron opened his mouth. "There is a way we could lay hands on that journal."

"Aaron. No."

"You said it yourself; it's the missing piece, the one piece we need. We *need* it, Rosemary."

He didn't need to elaborate on what his idea might be. It wasn't the first time they'd had this argument. Aaron was always eager to use every tool at his disposal, no matter its origin. And Rosemary was just as determined not to.

"It's dangerous, and it's wrong. Do you not remember—"

"Of course I do." His tone was sharp, and Botheration hitched a step, turning his head to look back at them. "It's all right, Bother. Just Rosie and I having a disagreement."

She wasn't appeased. "I've overlooked your use of sigils. I might even have winked at it a time or three, and that's on my conscience. But those were protective, defensive. What you're suggesting . . . it's wrong."

Aaron shoved his hands into his pockets, the years falling away until all she could see was the sulky child he'd been, forever wanting to know *why* and *when*. "They're just brownies. You've cleared a nest or two yourself before."

"Cleared a nest, yes. If something is a danger to the people around it, I won't hesitate. But you're talking about forcing it to do something, Aaron. Using sigils to bind it."

"It's an uncanny."

She didn't disagree with him entirely, but . . . "It's a living creature. Would you force Botheration to do something against his will?"

He glanced down at the hound. "That's different."

"Not as much as you want to think." She could feel herself practically shaking with something that felt like anger, and she drew a deep breath in, letting the crackle of cold in her lungs distract her for a moment. "You're frustrated. So am I. But not like that, Aaron. Please."

She objected to the use of sigils on any living creature, but more than that, every time she thought of it, she saw her mother in the simple pine coffin, her lovely, loving face gone still and cold. All because their father had thought to bind an uncanny and use it—and then lost control.

Even a brownie could become deadly, if it chose.

Aaron never gave in, he merely moved on. "The only other option is to break into the police department and steal it ourselves."

"Or," Rosemary said, her voice dry, "we could go back and ask Mrs. Lovelace to request that the police return her husband's belongings immediately, since they are claiming an animal attack was to blame and have no need for evidence of any sort."

"Mmmm. And when they refuse? Or they misplace it, to protect the good doctor's reputation, keep him from being considered a madman and a maniac?"

She didn't have a response to that, because he wasn't wrong. That was exactly the sort of thing the police would likely do. Things people didn't understand, they tried to bury. "Then we can steal it ourselves."

It wouldn't be the first time they had committed a crime in the execution of a hunt, although she had a suspicion Aaron enjoyed it a bit too much for decency. But if it distracted him from using those sigils, she would gladly break a few laws.

"Mr. Harker. A word, if you will?"

The hail came just as they turned the corner, nearly to the boarding house. Aaron tensed, and Rosemary instinctively let her fingertips touch the short knife tied within her coat sleeve, the cold steel reassuring, even as her brother turned.

The street was empty save for the figure that had hailed them, and another man standing a half step behind. The men were both wearing the dark blue uniform and peaked cap of the police force, their five-pointed badges placed high on their lapels. Despite the Harkers' conversation of only a moment before, she could think of no reason for the authorities to wish them harm. Still, Rosemary was cautious, aware of their movements and surroundings, anticipating an attack.

"And you as well, ma'am," the foremost officer said, including her in his glance. "If you would."

Their expressions were stern, their bodies telling her that they would be polite only so long, and no longer. She reluctantly moved her fingers away from the sleeve holding her throwing knife, shaping her expression into a surprised but polite look of inquiry, as though she had no idea why the police would wish any word with her.

Huntsmen answered to no authority save themselves, and in truth, what could the police arrest them for? Killing monsters that did not, legally, exist? But their father had been blunt about the risks when faced with local authorities. *The world is sleeping,* he would tell them. *And we do not want to rouse them. They would not thank us for it.*

Also, being arrested would be an annoying, and avoidable, delay. Best to humor them.

"Officer." She slipped her hand into Aaron's arm, leaning into him as a reminder not to do anything rash. "Good evening."

"Ma'am." They drew abreast of the Harkers, and she was able to distinguish them better. The one a few steps behind wore sideburns and a mustache more suited to a gentleman of the previous generation, his coat obviously worn at the seams, and his right hand deep under his coat, where Rosemary assumed he was gripping a pistol. The other man, the one who had spoken, looked sharper, his face clean-shaven and his billed cap tipped back so that she could see his face. His hands were entirely visible, but she did not trust the open look he was giving them.

She doubted that they had come out to have a friendly chat about the weather.

"Easy, beast," she said to Botheration, who had turned with Aaron, pulling slightly at his lead as the two men approached them. His erect ear had swiveled forward, and his tail gone down over his hindquarters in alert-but-not-attacking readiness, so he was reading the tension on the two men as well. She was not certain if that made her feel better or worse.

Sideburns spoke then. "Mighty large dog you have there, sir."

"My sister often travels on her own," Aaron said smoothly. "Botheration is a good companion for her."

Oh, how she hated that excuse, but it served its purpose. A dog owned by a woman was to be less feared than one owned by a man, as though a woman was not perfectly capable of giving the command and allowing Botheration to rip their throats out where they stood.

Rosemary reined that thought in, keeping her face composed, her body polite, and her gaze trained on the clean-shaven officer. The older man deferred to him, but that might be a ruse, to allow a senior officer to watch and assess. Aaron and she had used that tactic enough, certainly.

Aaron was playing his role perfectly. "Might I hope that you have new information regarding our uncle's death? We were just visiting with our aunt—"

Cousin, she thought. *Cousin*. He never could keep their stories straight.

"We know where you were," the bewhiskered officer said. "And what you've been doing."

Rosemary felt her muscles tighten from more than Aaron's slip.

"Indeed." Aaron merely gathered Bother's lead up from her hand, tugging the dog gently to their side as though to start walking again, forcing the officers to fall into step with them. "Then you know that we were on our way to dinner."

"This won't take but a moment of your time," the clean-shaven officer said, stopping them again. "But you'd best listen."

And didn't that half sound like a threat. She willed Both-eration not to react to her unease, her fingers digging into Aaron's arm deep enough to leave bruises through the heavy layers of coat and cloth.

"If it's so important you had to come out here to find us," Aaron said, "then certainly we will listen." He was too young yet to quite manage the tone of "displeased but polite citizen addressing an inferior," but she thought he was giving it a good try. The officer seemed somewhat nonplussed, glancing at his companion before barreling on.

"This isn't New York or Rochester, where they don't mind a bit of trouble. People know their neighbors here, and know what's expected of them. We like it that way. Peaceful."

Rosemary could practically hear Aaron opening his mouth to ask how three violent deaths in recent days was peaceful, and leaned her elbow into his side, hard.

"It seems to be a lovely town," she agreed, stepping into the brief silence. "You've a right to be proud of it. But forgive me for not understanding why you felt the need to accost my brother and me on this chilly evening to tell us this?"

Sideburns spoke then, his voice brusque. "What he's sayin' is that your kind aren't welcome here. Go have your dinner, miss, and then you'd all be well advised to pack your things and go back to where you came from."

"Our . . . kind?" Aaron sounded completely befuddled, and Rosemary struggled to match her expression to his tone. Had Dr. Lovelace's journal mentioned them by name? Had he, dear God, actually mentioned the Huntsmen, written down anything of their work, of what they were? If so, she would dig the man up and put him back down in the ground again herself, for such careless stupidity.

Or were there, by some wild happenstance, Huntsmen within the police force? One who was protective of his turf, or afraid that they would show him to be incompetent? She tried not to study the two before her too obviously, but there was nothing about them, no sign or subtle wink, that suggested a connection. No, she decided. There were few police officers among Huntsmen; even in the larger cities, when things occasionally needed official smoothing over, the very few in the know did what was required. The need for secrecy hobbled them as well: one wrong person confided in, and a Huntsmen could lose their job, their pension, and worse. But all it took was one person to whisper what they knew. . . .

If these men did know of Huntsmen, it would certainly make sense to meet outside the station, to keep this discussion from being overheard. But if they knew about Huntsmen, then they should also know Huntsmen *ended* trouble, they didn't start it.

Her thoughts were chasing each other into the bramble, solving nothing, and she forced them into stillness.

"Look." The younger officer was clearly trying to sound reasonable. "You've been quieter than some, I'll grant you that, but you're still not exactly subtle. We hear what you stir up elsewhere, and we don't want it here. Anyone who doesn't like their job is free to go elsewhere, right?"

For a moment his words made no sense. Then Rosemary followed the thread of them and realized what he was saying at the same time her brother started to laugh.

"You think we're union agitators?" Aaron sounded more amused than surprised, choking down his laughter when he saw the looks on their faces.

"You city folk come into town, don't seem to know a soul but immediately start meeting with the widows of known union men? Dr. Lovelace didn't have any siblings, and neither did his missus, so you're no nephew of his." The man started off with firm words, but Aaron's continued laughter, now muffled behind one hand, seemed to discomfort him.

Rosemary shot her brother a reproving look, then said, "Officer . . ." She waited until he offered a grudging, "Calune, Officer Anthony Calune."

"Officer Calune. I think that there is some misapprehension. I assure you, we have no interest in the doings of anyone in this town save how they affect the death of Dr. Lovelace."

He opened his mouth to say something, but she plowed on. "And you are correct, we are not the children of a sibling, but cousins through our father's side. We call them aunt and uncle out of courtesy to the older generation. It had been his wish that we, as his only remaining family, help his wife settle his affairs. In truth, that is why we are here, and the only reason we are here." She waited a heartbeat, then added, "And if you have further questions, I would request that you follow us to Mrs. Wesson's, because it is too ridiculously cold to be standing here."

Officer Calune almost smiled at that, before recollecting himself. "You're delicate, downstate. This isn't cold at all." But he made a wide-swing gesture with his hand and stepped back. "A bit of friendly advice, Miss Harker? Whatever your claim to being here, my partner's right; you should leave town soon's you've settled matters for the Lovelaces. And not visit with other folk while you're here. Good evening."

The two officers turned on their heels with near-military precision and walked away, the sound of their boots on the macadam echoing in the darkening air.

"They think we're union organizers?" Aaron had gotten himself back under control, but his eyes were still merry. "I didn't see that coming."

"It makes a certain amount of logical sense, from their point of view." She started walking again, and he followed, Botheration trotting at their heels, his ear still alert. "We've met with the widow of a sympathizer with the workers' plight, and the grieving fiancée of a rabble-rouser? Weaker cases have been made from less."

"We don't know that the third victim had any connection."

"The family refused to speak with you?"

"Yes. Even after I invoked Dr. Lovelace's name. I thought at the time they were too deep in mourning, but now I wonder if the police might have visited them before I did."

"And warned them against speaking with you?" She stopped, turning to him and waiting until he stopped and looked at her. "Aaron. I know we dismissed human actions earlier, but do you think that this is another Coalfield, God forbid, or Paterson?"

Two men had been killed during the Paterson silk workers' strike, and the National Guard had fired on Coalfield strikers only a month earlier. It had been in all the newspapers.

"The police tend to shoot at strikers, not organizers." Aaron made a face. "It may be that someone has decided to be proactive. Maybe Dr. Lovelace, even retired, saw something, or knew something. . . . Except the deaths were definitely uncanny. Why else would Lovelace leave our names?" A thought made him chuckle. "As far as I know, the uncanny have no interest in unionizing."

Rosemary wasn't amused. "Bother and I both feel something in town, even if you don't. And I don't think it was the brownie. There's something bad going on here. Something uncanny. And involving workers."

"Not disagreeing with you." His tone had gone from amused to terse. "And I know what you're thinking, because I'm thinking it too, but if someone were harnessing an uncanny to their own agenda, they'd need to use sigils, strong ones. And they'd need to know what they were doing. Where would they have learned them?"

He had a point. Even if someone here had found an old book that had the right sigils, they would need training to use them properly. The odds of that happening were slim, to put it mildly. And for Huntsmen to do such a thing, or teach such a thing, was almost unthinkable; there had been an edict in place since their mother's death, and the punishment for disobedience was shunning. No support from the larger group, no recognition, and no aid if something came after them. It was, in effect, a death sentence.

"We can't rule it out," she said. "It's the only thing I can think of that makes even the slightest bit of sense. The deaths, the feeling of wrongness. The odd wounds. Not being able to *find* this damned uncanny, as though it came out of nowhere and then disappeared again. That speaks to it being summoned."

He raised both eyebrows, amused by her lapse into vulgarity, but didn't disagree with her.

She frowned, pulling her coat tighter, feeling as though a ghoul had walked over her grave. "What do you think the likelihood is that the police know their killer isn't human?"

"Low to nil. If any of them even suspect, they're keeping their mouths shut like smart men." Aaron kicked a rock in the

street and watched it bounce several times before coming to rest. "This should have been a straightforward hunt: find the evidence, find the uncanny, kill the uncanny. I don't like it when the police stick their beaks into our business."

"They're already suspicious. Maybe we should back off. Bring someone else in."

She knew what it cost her brother to say those words. No Huntsman wanted to admit that there was an uncanny they couldn't handle. It was a matter of pride, of professional dignity. But their first obligation was to protect the unwitting, and they would not be able to do that if the police were watching their every move.

She tried to look at it dispassionately, slicing her own feelings out of the equation. "The Petersons are the closest, but—"

"Good Lord, no." His words were equally horrified and disgusted. "Maybe Jacob?"

Rosemary shot him a sideways glare. "We are not bringing that old man back into anything." Aaron was not a sentimental man, but even he must draw the line somewhere. Jacob ben Elizar had been the one to find their mother, moments before she died. Found her and their father, covered in blood and entrails and mad beyond recall.

Jacob would come the moment they called, but there were some things you didn't do, especially not to another Huntsmen. Even one who was retired from the field. *Especially* then.

"I can't think of anyone else," Rosemary admitted, coming

to the rock Aaron had kicked and sending it tumbling again off the toe of her boot. The hound looked after the rock that had attracted their attention, then sniffed, dismissing it as neither threat nor food. "Not in this region, anyway," she went on, "and it would take too long to read anyone else in."

"So we stay."

Rosemary nodded agreement. It might not have been the best decision, but it felt right. From the look on Aaron's face, he had come to the same conclusion. And it wasn't as though it was the first time they'd had to dance carefully around the police. Uncanny were the stuff of children's stories and madmen's tales, and Huntsmen could not afford to be seen as either.

It was nice that Mrs. Lovelace knew some of the truth, though.

They had walked past the street where they should have turned, caught up in their conversation. The street they were on now had fewer houses, more bare-limbed trees, and the moon overhead seemed more distant, somehow, despite the clearing skies and sharp, cold air.

"Rosie." It was barely a whisper, but she nodded. What she felt wasn't uneasy-making, like before. This felt *wrong*, in a way that both Harkers recognized. Nothing to do with Huntsmen, merely the essential human awareness that they had become the prey, that something Else lurked nearby.

An uncanny was watching them.

Rosemary felt her pulse speed up, sweat prickling on her skin, even as Botheration shifted closer, four legs square

under him, head raised and chest bold. Had either policeman seen him in that moment, they would have drawn their weapons on the beast, not stopped to speak.

"Where . . . ?"

"Huntsmen."

The whisper came on a breeze, cold and low, faint enough to be mistaken for the whispering of leaves or the rushing of water.

Rosemary didn't think it had been either of those things. "Did you—"

"Huntsmen." The whisper came again, unmistakable now that they were listening for it.

"Ignore it," Rosemary said. This was the wrong sort of place for a will-o'-the-wisp, but they still had no idea what they were hunting, and listening to any uncanny whisper was a poor choice to make. Especially one that knew what they were.

"It came from over there," Aaron said, turning to follow the sound.

Her brother was an idiot. Rosemary let the knife slip from its pocket in her sleeve and into her left hand, a cool, reassuring weight resting from fingertips to wrist, before she followed. Her nerves might be a little shaken from the encounter with the police, however amusing Aaron had found it, but nothing calling them like that had good intentions.

The street bent left, leading back to the boarding house, but to the right was a low hill, bare of anything save a stone bench that in warmer weather couples might use to watch

the river flowing below. As they crested the hill, they saw the figure standing by the river, waiting for them.

Botheration growled deep in his chest, a rumble of warning.

The uncanny ignored the beast. "Huntsmen."

The presence of two Huntsmen and a Molosser should have sent the creature fleeing, not calling them closer. A trap? Aaron reached under his coat to retrieve his pistol, palming it just out of sight, and, with a glance at Rosemary, started down the hill. She took a breath's pause, then followed just behind him. To an observer it might look as though she lagged, but if the figure made any aggressive moves, she would be in a better position to attack. A bullet might reach farther, but a knife was silent, and her aim was just as deadly.

Closer, she could see that the figure was only human-shaped, the arms too long and the face lacking discernible features save for a round lamprey's mouth set where a nose should be. A hood covered the rest of its head, but strands of green hair could be seen falling to its sloping shoulders. It was barefoot in the slushy remainder of the snow but showed no discomfort, no awareness of the cold. Green hair, fish-mouthed. Water-based. Air breathing. Her mind slotted it into categories, trying to identify the species.

Botheration kept his gaze sharp on it, intently focused. Three against one; if it was a trap, it was a poorly made one. Unless there were more, hiding nearby.

"Uncanny." The word, in Aaron's mouth, was a curse, and the hand holding the pistol began to rise.

"Huntsmen." The thing's voice carried mockery now, and Rosemary felt her hackles rise. Trap or no, she did not like this. "I am unarmed, in a place of truce." One of its arms swept forward to indicate lines drawn with ash on a bare patch of ground, a rounded sigil of some sort that Rosemary did not recognize.

Aaron did, from the way his arm lowered again. "What do you want?"

"Speech. Only speech."

Rosemary presumed the sigil was some proof of its intentions, although she did not trust it. She trusted nothing about uncanny, save that they were a danger to decent things.

Still. Some were more of a danger than others. This looked to be a merfolk of some sort, that much she could identify, if not the specific type. If so, it wouldn't be able to stay out of the water for long.

The thing looked at her, as though hearing her thoughts, then turned back to Aaron. "You are here to hunt the killer."

Aaron nodded once. "Yes."

"You swear to that."

Her brother glanced at her, and she gave back an equal look, having no idea what the uncanny wanted.

"Yes. We swear that we are here to hunt the killer. And we will find it." Aaron's voice deepened into a threat, if the uncanny thought they might be swayed—or forced—from their duty.

The uncanny shivered, although not, it seemed, in response to his words. "This is a place of secrets. Some must be kept. Some must not." It swayed slightly, long arms wrapping around itself. "Stop it now, or more will die."

Stop what? Rosemary felt the itch to throw her knife and repressed it. At least until the uncanny told them something useful.

She controlled her frustration, moderated her voice. "It would help if we knew what we were here to stop."

"We dare not interfere. To be seen is to die. I was sent to tell you this: It grows in power, every time it strikes. Stop it now, or you may not be able to stop it at all."

The uncanny shut its mouth with that, gills suddenly appearing under its eyes, fluttering like lace. Before Rosemary could ask what the hell it meant by that, what secrets it was keeping, it turned, the robe sliding off its back as it dove into the shadows of the river and, without a splash, disappeared.

"Wai—ah, damn it." Aaron cursed, then holstered his pistol again, stepping forward to toe at the discarded robe as though half expecting something to leap from it and attack his knees.

Rosemary exhaled, feeling the cold again as Botheration whined and pressed against her leg. "That was . . ." She struggled for a word. "Unexpected."

"What. No. What the hell?" Aaron stared at the robe, then whirled to stare at Rosemary. "What. The. Hell? Since when do uncanny bring *warnings*?"

"That wasn't a warning," she told him. "It was an order."

The uncanny wanted them to kill one of its own kind.

Nine

ONFRONTING AN UNCANNY, even without violence, took its toll. Given her choice, Rosemary would have found a quiet location somewhere far from prying eyes and practiced her knife work for several hours until her body stopped humming like a telegraph wire. Unfortunately, if they were late to dinner at Mrs. Wesson's, their only option would be to find a café that was serving dinner, and given the paucity of dining establishments in town, that wasn't a pleasant option either.

Her stomach, aware that all it had been given since breakfast was a cruller and slices of shortbread cake, overruled her nerves.

"I don't suppose we could talk one of the girls into bringing us dinner out to Bother's kennel?" Aaron asked, and she couldn't tell from his voice if he was joshing or not.

"Likely not," she responded. "And we need to put a good face on."

He glanced at her, the question clear.

"Think about it, Aaron. Never mind the uncanny for a moment. How—*why*—did the police even think to look in our direction? Yes, you went and asked questions, but even if you'd pushed too hard"—and he made a noise that might have been demurral but did not actually object to her assumption—"the effort of following us around? Watching who we spoke with? That took action, and approval from someone higher than a mere patrolman."

"Miss Batali named Dolph and Baxter as being responsible for her fiancé's death. Not that they did it themselves, but that they were responsible." His voice dropped as they approached the house. "If they are somehow tied up in all this . . ."

"You think they know we're Huntsmen?" She could not fathom those two having any knowledge of the world past what they could buy or sell. "But why—"

"Or, more likely, they decided that we are somehow a threat to their plans, and need to be run out of town immediately."

Rosemary had to admit that that sounded more plausible. More, that it was likely her fault. She never liked to admit when her brother was proven right, but perhaps she should have held her tongue and not baited the speculator at dinner. Momentary amusement always had a cost.

That thought reminded her of what she'd meant to ask earlier. "What did you say to them, when they tried to inveigle you into financing their scheme? I presume that was what they were trying to do after breakfast."

He scoffed. "More, they wanted me to acknowledge their

brilliance and cunning, although there were a few lures dangled my way. I declined to bite."

Or they had been testing him. "Did they ask your opinion of unions?"

"They did not." He hesitated, his foot almost missing a step as he thought, and then sighed. "There may, however, have been mention of avoiding textile industries that employ women, as it is their opinion that women are far more likely to demand better conditions than men."

Aaron was usually quite good at dissembling, but the way he'd said that . . . "And your response?"

His sigh this time was heavier. "That women often prove themselves the wiser of the genders."

Her lips twitched despite herself. "I'm sure they blame my terrible influence on you for that."

"Oh, they're assured that you are a confirmed suffragette and also possibly a Bolshevist. A terrible influence, indeed."

Rosemary shook her head, tugging the lead to keep Botheration from growling after a squirrel dashing across the road. "Bother, stop that. That's beneath you."

Aaron rubbed the back of his neck, scowling up at the sky. "So from all that, have they decided that we are here to rouse the people of Brunson to rise up against their rightful masters and demand better wages and . . . what do they usually demand during these strikes?"

"Safer conditions, more money."

"Huh. We should try that."

"We don't get paid," she reminded him dryly.

"Then we should absolutely try that."

In truth, every active Huntsman received a stipend each month that covered their living expenses, but it was never quite enough.

This time, when they finally arrived at the boarding house, Botheration gave no protest at being taken back to his kennel. He trotted inside, grabbed the blanket in his thick jaws, and pulled it to the door, where he promptly lay down on it, his head set so that he could see the house clearly.

Knowing that there were uncanny nearby, that the uncanny knew that *they* were nearby, would keep him on watch until they took the threat down.

"Good boy," Aaron said, reaching down to knuckle the top of the hound's head before closing the gate. "Dinner will be out soon. Let us know if anything happens."

Any question of whether Messrs. Dolph and Baxter had been talking with the police was laid to rest when they entered the dining room to find the gentlemen in question already seated, and clearly surprised to see the Harkers.

Rosemary wondered if they'd expected the police to have taken them into custody, or escorted them from town already.

"Good evening, gentlemen," she said, smiling at Mr. Wilder as he rose to pull out a chair for her. Aaron took the chair to her other side, and nodded to Wilder before apologizing to Mrs. Wesson. "We regret our tardy arrival, ma'am. I'm afraid tea with our cousin ran long, as we were reminiscing, as one does."

"And how is poor Margaret holding up? We used to see each other in town, but then she switched churches, and, well." Mrs. Wesson gave a helpless little shrug. "And then Mr. Wesson passed along, and my days became busier."

"I'm sure she would welcome a visit," Aaron assured her. "Particularly after we return home."

"And that will be soon?" Dolph said, his attention determinedly focused on the piece of meat he was cutting.

"We are not certain yet," Rosemary told him, placid as a bean. "We are quite enjoying our stay here, and I still have research to do." On thinking about it, Miss Baker the librarian would definitely be worth another visit. If nothing else, she might know if the uncanny they had encountered was native to these waters, and if they had a reputation for violence. The merfolk Rosemary had read about tended to be isolationist, shy, and mostly preferring to be left alone. They were certainly not the sort she would have chosen to run an errand for—

For what? What had the ability to order another uncanny around, and enough concern for others that they would do so? That was the thought digging at her, as much as the warning itself. The fact that the police were watching them more closely than was comfortable for Huntsmen was no more than a mayfly irritant, in light of what else they had learned today. In light of an uncanny approaching *them*.

The incident made Rosemary deeply uncomfortable. Uncanny were beasts, for the most part; only a few rose above with a rudimentary intelligence capable of logic or forethought. This was what she had been taught, this was what she had seen, in all her years.

If this one had only been repeating words it had been taught, like a parrot, the question remained: Who—what— had taught and sent it?

Overthinking. Stop.

Aaron's hand-sign reprimand above the table made her frown faintly at him, her own fingers itching to tell him to *start* thinking.

But he was right. A Huntsman wasn't only training and learning. A Huntsman was *instinct*, driven by the fey remnants in their blood. And her instincts right now were whispering to her that she needed to stay still and quiet, to watch, and wait.

So instead of responding to Aaron, she gripped her fork and knife more securely and directed her attention to her meat, head bowed and mouth closed, every visible inch the demure, chastised woman.

It might be too late to fix the damage they had done to their reputations here, but she could at least not set it on fire as well.

Rosemary was so carefully minding her own plate she almost missed when the conversation took a turn.

"It seems odd that a man of such quiet life would have matters that require so much handling," Baxter was saying, his voice just a hair shy of being condescending. "Surely the estate of one medical doctor could not be difficult."

"There are a number of bequests that need attention,"

Aaron said, equally smoothly, ignoring the implicit insult to both Dr. Lovelace's finances and his own handling of same. "And Cousin Margaret appreciates our company. She has, in fact, asked us to stay longer than we had previously planned, if you are able to have us," he said to Mrs. Wesson.

"Oh, of course. Family is family, no matter how thin the blood between. You should stay as long as the poor dear needs you. And as well for you gentlemen," she said, turning to the business pair, although her expression was not quite so warm when she looked at Baxter. "It would be delightful to have a full house next week, when our new guests arrive."

"Regretfully, we have obligations back in the city before then," Dolph said, a thick-laid implication that he, at least, worked for a living. "But rest assured, you will have your fill of guests soon enough, once the rails set more trains into motion, and Brunson becomes a known name."

That comment was a lure, dropped in front of Rosemary's nose, and on any other day it might have been a near-physical pain to resist it. But today she merely smiled at the man, and turned to offer Mr. Wilder the bowl of creamed green beans.

With so many tensions in the room, no one lingered after the dessert plates had been cleared. Aaron announced his intention to go check on Botheration, and Rosemary used his exit to excuse herself as well, retreating to her bedroom.

One of the girls had been in; the coverlet was straightened and the pillow plumped, her robe draped over the back of the chair. A quick look into the cabinet reassured her that nothing there had been touched, and the chest with their weapons remained locked, the scattering of face powder she had placed on the hasp unsmudged.

Aaron might swear by his sigils, but she had her own tricks, far easier to explain away should someone come snooping.

She shed her shoes and skirt, hanging the latter up carefully so that the wrinkles would fall out, and sat on the edge of the bed in her undergarments, unpinning her hair and letting it drape over her shoulders. She'd had to trim it after a phoenix hunt in Weehawken, and the curls had seemingly doubled their efforts, escaping every turn of a knot and slithering out of every twist or chignon she attempted.

"I should have been born a boy," she told a curl, pulling it away from her neck to inspect the length. "Life would have been much simpler, then." Aaron certainly had the easier time of it because of his gender.

"Maybe I will take up with the suffragists when we go home." She'd told herself that before, more than once. But once home, the weight of her occupation was enough to keep her from following through. You could not shout and raise a fuss, and risk arrest, when other peoples' lives depended on you being unseen and easily forgotten.

She wiggled her toes, still encased in stockings, and wished for the thick robe and comfortable chair back in New Haven. Aaron could live out of a traveling case, and so could she, at need, but still, there were small luxuries that made life easier.

And while this house boasted a very modern coal furnace, the bedroom carried a distinct chill if you weren't already under the covers.

A gentle knock on the door got her up. Gathering the thinner robe from where it was draped over the chair, she wrapped it around her before opening the door just enough for Aaron to come in.

"Well, that wasn't awkward at all," he said, making for the single chair in the room and turning it around to sit backward, leaning his arms over the straightback. "At least neither of them stood up midway through dinner and cried, 'Begone, foul beast!' Do you think they think we mean to murder them in their beds, and rob them of all their belongings?"

"I think they worry more about the theft than the murder," she said. "Or more likely that we will steal their workers out from under them before they can build their empire."

"It's tempting to try," Aaron said.

"I didn't know you were such an advocate of the workingman?"

"I'm not," he admitted. "But those two annoyed me. And it's easier to think of ways to annoy them in return than"—and he put his head down on his arms, dark curls falling forward in disarray, his next words almost too muffled for her to hear— "than what the uncanny said."

She didn't want to talk about it either, but they had not been raised to avoid things that needed doing. Or speaking.

"It knows something we don't."

"No, really?" That made him raise his head, and the look in his eyes was tired scorn. "What makes you think that?"

"Aaron." He had rebuked her earlier; now it was her turn. "It makes no sense, Rosie. Why would an uncanny warn us?"

"Because it was told to. I'm more wondering about what or who could compel it to do so, and why, for the love of God, they couldn't just *tell* us what we were hunting."

Her brother tilted his head back, his expression thoughtful now. "Maybe it couldn't. Maybe it was under a geas, or something that tangled its tongue. It's not as though we know all that much about . . . anything about them, really. Except how to kill them."

"We haven't needed to know anything else," she said sharply, and he nodded.

"I know. But it's a problem now, isn't it? Some of the aelf always speak in riddles, don't they? Maybe this is like that."

"Or it's simply taking orders. The most obvious answer usually is the right one." Aaron was too clever for his own good. He tended to tie things up in knots for the pleasure of undoing them. Rosemary preferred her life simpler.

"I like my answer better," her brother grumbled. "One uncanny compelling another . . . or simply having the ability to send it to do something? A command structure? I don't like that."

They'd been trained to go after individuals who were a threat, or, on occasions, an entire nest, but the idea of more than one species working together was new, and potentially horrifying.

"That's something for other heads to think about," she told him. "We need to focus on the hunt at hand."

"I can't stop thinking about it," he grumbled. "And it matters if there are a bunch of uncanny in the area working together, especially since we haven't seen indications of *any*. Not the sort that would kill a man, anyway." Aaron was in his element now, up off the chair and pacing back and forth in front of the bed. "That was a mer-creature." He paused, and she nodded. "The river here isn't large enough to support more than a single creature, not really, is it? But Lake Ontario . . . the river runs down to the lake, doesn't it? Deep water, plenty of areas for uncanny to hide." He made a face. "Anything could be out there."

Rosemary thought of the deep-lake monster Miss Baker had mentioned. "It's a theory. Interesting, but not particularly relevant. What we know as fact, or possible fact, is that this mer, and whatever sent it, seem to be on our side." It hurt her, physically, to say that. "But," she went on, "it gave us absolutely no useful information to go with the warning, which makes it useless."

Rosemary sat on the edge of her bed, crossing her legs under her with an utter lack of modesty, as though they were children again, telling each other stories. "And possibly a trap."

"A trap with no bait? Telling us there will be another murder without anything else—"

"But it did," Rosemary said suddenly.

"What?"

"It said it was a secret. A secret that must not be kept."

"A riddle?"

"Or a statement of fact. Maybe . . . maybe they don't know what it is, but they're frightened by it. Frightened enough to warn us."

Aaron followed her thoughts, the way she'd known he would. "Because that something is hunting them, too? Or maybe it will, once it's done with humans? 'To be seen is to die,' it said." Aaron scowled at the lamp, as though it were the cause of their problems. "What would go after both humans and other uncanny?"

Rosemary sighed. "All right, get out of here and let me get dressed."

"What?"

"You were right. We need to steal Lovelace's journal."

Enough of their work had to be done under nothing more than starlight that Aaron often wondered if Huntsmen would eventually develop the ability to see in pure darkness. So far, that had not occurred.

With Rosemary at his back, keeping an eye on the street, he angled his body more sharply, so that the fairy light wrapped around his wrist illuminated the lock in front of him, but his body would keep the glow hidden from anyone who might walk by.

Not that he thought anyone would be walking the streets of Brunson at one a.m., unless they had equally impure actions to be about, but it never paid to get sloppy. And there was at least one patrolman walking rounds; they had seen him strolling through the streets a half hour before, swinging his club as though he were looking for someone to use it on. Aaron had thought about suggesting to Rosemary that they start a fire somewhere, to draw attention away, but he knew that was another one of those things she would frown on.

Huntsmen weren't supposed to put others at risk in the pursuit of their prey, but their mother had once embroidered *Needs must* onto a pincushion, and their father had joked that it should be the family motto.

The memory had faded from bitter to bittersweet over time.

"Hurry," his sister breathed, barely audible.

"Mmm. Just a little, sweetheart, there you go," he coaxed the lock, equally quiet, jiggling the pick just so. Lock-breaking might not be a noble art, but it was an art nonetheless, and he felt a glow of accomplishment when the bolt-and-latch gave way, the door sliding open on well-oiled hinges.

"And here we go," Rosemary murmured behind him as they slipped inside the police station, closing the door carefully behind them.

Aaron's fingers flicked in the hand-sign for *silence* and she made a face at him but quieted. Brunson might not be a large city, with the attendant crime, but there would be at least one officer still in the building, and the structure wasn't so large that voices where there should be none wouldn't be heard, unless the man was asleep on the job.

It would certainly simplify their work, if he were.

There was a dim light coming from a lamp left turned on near the door, washing the room with a pale yellow haze. Aaron glanced at the windows, gauging the strength of the glow, and whether it would cast shadows outside. Deciding not, he moved forward, Rosemary at his side, their shoes making a softly echoing noise that couldn't be helped.

The police station was nothing impressive in and of itself: a narrow two-story wooden structure with a staircase leading up the middle. Rosemary went halfway up the steps, cat-quiet, and then paused, returning back down with a quick shake of her head. From the bars in the windows outside and her reaction, he deduced that the jail was upstairs, and with it any likely overnight guard. Thankfully, their interest lay else-where.

The main room was cast in light-haze and shadows, the two rows of desks and chairs darker shapes, the floor under-neath worn slippery by years of rubber-soled shoes. The space smelled of hair tonic and tobacco and a tang Aaron too easily recognized as cold sweat gone stale. This was a place of desperation, not anger.

A tap on his shoulder, and Rosemary pointed toward a door set with thick frosted glass. The fairy light picked up the glint of lettering, and as they came closer the glint resolved into the word "records."

The door was unlocked.

Inside, the smell of tobacco and dust doubled, and he felt Rosemary stifle a cough. There was a line of tall wooden filing cabinets against the wall in front of them, flanked by two desks. With a sigh, Aaron directed his sister to start at the left, taking the right for himself.

The warm white glow of a modern tungsten flash briefly lit Rosemary's face before she directed it downward into the first drawer. Aaron gave a quick glance over his shoulder to reassure himself that it couldn't have been seen from the street, then turned back to his own task. Placing his wrist so that the fairy light shone downward, Aaron bent his knees to better read the labels on each of the drawers in front of him.

Nothing. No journal, no files, no answers.

He'd barely reached the third drawer when a sharp tap on wood jerked his attention toward Rosemary, who was holding a folder in her hand.

"The reports. They put them all together," she said in a low voice. "Convenient, that."

"And also proof that they knew damn well they were connected." He moved closer, adding his light to hers, the better to see the contents.

She flipped open the folder and placed it gently on the nearest desk.

"All the bodies were found during the morning hours," Aaron noted, "but the estimated times of death ranged from late afternoon to just before dawn."

"So no preferred hunting time," Rosemary concluded, and Aaron nodded. They knew that already. He skimmed over smaller details, speaking the pertinent facts out loud to better impress them into memory. "Slashes at the throat and torso consistent with claw marks rather than a knife—" He broke off, exasperated. "Had none of them ever seen a claw score before?"

"Likely not," his sister murmured, still reading. "I'll wager the only scars they have came from shaving too swiftly."

The inappropriate snort that escaped him was entirely involuntary. She might scold him for a lack of delicacy, but the only difference between them was that she was slightly more discreet in her comments. "And nothing about the strange texture of the skin, or the lack of defensive wounds we saw on Lovelace." He lifted his head, letting his eyes rest on the shadowed wall. "Even incompetence couldn't miss those things; they left them out of their report deliberately. Why?"

"They were protecting . . . themselves, probably. Erase any evidence that doesn't fit your conclusion."

"Thank you, Sherlock Holmes," he said.

"Or maybe they're just that sloppy." Rosemary licked a finger and turned a page, then stopped.

"Oh," she said, in a different tone of voice, and he dropped his gaze back to where her finger had frozen on a line.

"Oh," he echoed.

Their uncanny snitch had arrived too late: there had already been another body. The night before, a man had been found dead of similar wounds.

The notes, inked in an unsteady hand rather than typed up the way the others had been, said that the cause of death was blood loss due to untreated wounds, the same reason given for the others. Different stories, but the same ending. But one thing had been different.

He had been a patrolman.

According to the file, the dead man's name had been Archibald Hemry, and he had been twenty-seven, on the job for all of a year. His weapon hadn't been fired; had, in fact, still been in its holster when he was found, just outside the police station.

"Put the folder back," Aaron said when he finished reading, sliding the file out from under her finger and closing it in the folder before offering it back. "Now."

"But—"

"Now, Rosemary." He made his tone as deep and firm as he could, pushing every inch of urgency he felt into those two words.

She knew not to argue with that voice, turning to place the folder into one of the still-open drawers and sliding the drawer shut carefully, while he put his mess to rights as well. Everything needed to look untouched. They had just finished when the sound of a solid thump overhead made them both freeze, heads alert like startled deer.

The sound wasn't repeated, and there was no movement on the stairs. Aaron's heart was racing like a Derby winner, and his skin prickled with the need to move, either to hide or fight, he didn't much care. But he controlled it, breathing in and out through his mouth in counted measures.

Aaron? Her fingers moved in his name-sign.

Not here, he said in the same manner, and could feel his

right eye twitching. You didn't discuss ways to kill a blood-spinner while standing under its web, and you didn't talk about how cops might be complicit while standing in their den. Putting a firm hand between her shoulder blades, he gave a little push and followed her to the front door.

Rosemary didn't speak again until they were several streets away, the station's door relocked and the guard upstairs none the wiser for their visit. The moon was doing its best to light the sky, despite the clouds drifting across it, creating a distracting pattern of shadows. While he had been calm and confident on the walk to the police station, even with all that they knew and suspected, now Aaron could feel the unease Rosemary had spoken of earlier. It churned in his bowels, making him feel the need to urinate, even though he knew he had nothing to pass.

"One of their own. They're covering up the death of one of their own." Rosemary had always been oddly idealistic about the police; Aaron found he was angry at these men for taking away some of that.

"If they admit to anything, it all comes apart." She was puzzling the pieces together, and he waited for her to catch up. "They were willing to close their eyes, and now—"

"And now they're probably afraid to open their eyes," Aaron said. "It took one of their own, left him to die in a pool of his own blood."

"No." Rosemary shook her head. "Not in a pool. Like the

other bodies. There was blood on the ground around him, but nowhere near enough blood from a body that had bled out there. There's a great deal of blood in the human body. Even if they were moved after being killed, there should have been some."

He'd missed that. Aaron snapped his fingers twice, thinking. "A nightflyer would lap up the blood, but they don't leave those kinds of wounds."

"And if it were a sanguisuge," Rosemary said, "why attack Dr. Lovelace? Not their usual type at all." The older the victim, the less nutrition a sanguisuge could take from it. Younger was always preferred, and they were more likely to attack children than adults past their fourth decade.

They had reached the turn for the boarding house, but Aaron paused, taking some comfort in the buzzing glow of the streetlamp overhead. "Did you notice the one other thing that was different in the last report?"

She nodded. "His face was ripped off."

Shredded, actually, but close enough. "The first death, he bled out from wounds that were bad, but not vicious. The second . . ."

"Much worse," Rosemary supplied.

"And then Dr. Lovelace. An old man, it wouldn't have taken more than a single blow to lay him out, and yet it seemed almost like whatever attacked him wanted not just to kill, but to hurt him. And now this, almost destroying the body. Rosemary, it's getting more vicious."

"Angrier," she corrected him. "Not hunger; it's not feeding off them, just killing them. Hurting them before it lets them die."

"Werevolk might kill like that, but the moon phase is wrong for it to go feral. A piasa? Hard to imagine nobody hearing it, though." Piasa screamed when they attacked, the sound paralyzing their prey. "And they're hardly local."

"Any chance that they might have moved? They do that, and they never think to inform us when they do. Not until after the fact." Sarcasm was not her usual forte, but he understood the urge. By now, they should have been able to identify the uncanny and have an idea of where it was denned up. The delay was making them doubt themselves.

"And the mer, or whoever sent it, was trying to head off a rival for territory?" It was a thin theory, and he didn't like it, but it fit the few facts they had.

They started walking again, by unspoken decision heading away from the boarding house, back toward the river.

"Stick to what we do know," his sister reminded him. "Something that attacks humans, slices them open, possibly for fun? No, that violence suggests anger. And leaves the body . . . what happens to the blood? Does it drink it? Wash it away?"

"Two of the attacks happened near the river. If it's a water-based uncanny similar to our informant, maybe, yes. Something less flesh, more liquid?" Aaron tried to visualize the pages of the books he'd read. "There's a mud-based uncanny, the whatsitsname, from Poland. I can never remember those names. And a handful who aren't much more than air. Sailors must have some stories."

"Sailors have endless stories, most of them based in rum, not water."

There was a crackle, the sound of a stick breaking, and they both tensed, but did not stop moving. An owl hooted three times, and then nothing. Rosemary sighed, and Aaron eased his hold on his pistol. There was no way they could have brought Botheration with them tonight; he hoped they wouldn't regret that.

"Anger. What causes anger? Fear." Rosemary shaped the words like they were keys, looking for a door. "What is it angry at? What is it afraid of?"

"And why are the police covering it up? That's what I don't understand," Aaron said. "We know that they won't catch the killer, but they can't know that. So why pretend they have a man-killer cat, when they know it isn't?"

"Fear," she said again. "Fear makes people do foolish things. They panic. They hide. Or they run away. Uncanny, too, apparently. Tell me, Aaron: Who has the most to lose right now from people running away?"

Aaron picked up on her thought. "Our friends Baxter and Dolph were already here when the first death happened. And even if they're not involved directly, they'd want something like this kept quiet, or risk potential investors pulling out. You think they put a word in someone's ear?"

"I think we already know that they have friends on the police force, and a strong desire for this town to shine like gold. And they also have enough ambition to think that controlling an uncanny—especially if they don't truly know what it is—might achieve their goals."

"By killing union activists . . ." Somehow, it seemed worse to him if they were using an uncanny than if they'd done the work themselves.

Rosemary pushed forward. "If they've stumbled onto a controlling sigil, they have no idea what they're dealing with. The uncanny was right: the more they try to hide it, keep it secret, the less control they will have over it. They'll lose control, and it will scour the entire region, in revenge, or sheer pettiness. If Lovelace suspected any of this—"

"He would have called in Huntsmen. Which is what he did."

"The only Huntsmen he knew. I wish—"

"Don't." His voice cracked a little on the word, and he flushed. "Don't say it, Rosemary."

"He'd know what to do."

"He doesn't even know his own name anymore."

Levi Harker had been a fearless Huntsmen, once. A loving father, a brilliant tactician, a patient teacher.

To the rest of the world, Levi Harker had died with his wife in a terrible, violent tragedy, when an uncanny hunt went badly. That was the truth of it, as far as truth went. But the body bearing their father's name still breathed and moved, locked in a sanitarium in Louisiana, where he would never see free sky again.

It was for the best, for him and for humanity, and best for his children to never speak of.

"We've already been through this. There's no one else to bring in, not in time." Aaron didn't want to have this discussion again; there was no point to it, it only made his stomach hurt. "The police are watching us? Fine, let them watch. They'll be looking for the wrong things.

"It's time to hunt."

Ten

Y THE TIME they made it back to the boarding house, the clock in the hallway was marking three a.m. Rosemary could feel exhaustion like lead on her bones, but the suggestion that they wait another day never crossed her lips. She might have preferred a full night's sleep before they did anything more, but what she wanted rarely had anything to do with a hunt.

The first death had been barely a month ago, and there were already four bodies. If they waited even another day, there might be more. And now that they were here, now that they had at least some idea of what was going on, any more blood spilled would leave its stain on their hands.

There was enough there already; she wanted no more.

The house around them had the stillness that came from every living thing being sound asleep, save them. The air was thin; every noise she made seemed magnified, but at the same time muffled, so it felt as though she were moving through a tide of molasses, slow and sticky.

"Wake up," she told herself fiercely, pinching her cheeks to force the blood to start moving, to wash some of the tiredness from her eyes.

She needed to change her attire. They'd dressed normally to break into the police station, hoping that appearances would save them from suspicion, but that would not do on a hunt.

Shedding her skirt and blouse and unfastening her corset, Rosemary took a moment to stretch before pulling the dirt-dusty trousers and shirt she'd worn to dig up the grave from their hiding place under her valise. She made a face at the aroma that still clung to the cloth. They needed several hours dunked in soap and hot water, but that would not be possible until they were home again, and they could not go home until they were done.

Finished dressing, she turned her attention to the case at the foot of her bed. A key hanging on a chain around her neck unlocked it, and she lifted the lid, considering the weapons crated within.

Aaron would likely not want the shotgun, but he'd need more ammunition. She lifted the slender box of cartridges out and placed it on the floor beside her. She considered the unstrung crossbow, running her fingers over the smooth wooden arc, but finally put it back into its wrappings. Instead, she chose another throwing knife and its sheath, this one longer than the one she'd carried the night before, and an already-sheathed iron dagger the size of her palm. The iron blade wasn't sharp, but it didn't need to be; inside the hollow hilt was a vial of poison that dripped down the edge of the blade when it struck something. Wood, fire, iron, silver, they were all effective weapons, but anything with a heart could be killed by this.

Herself included. It was like her Browning: she didn't like carrying it, but she'd like even less needing it and not having it.

Putting the poison dagger in the outside pocket of her coat, she turned back to close the case when the sight of a battered tin box half-hidden under the wrappings and weapons stopped her.

She shouldn't. Rosemary knew she shouldn't. It was a crutch, and when you depended on a crutch, someone could yank it out from under you. But she was so tired, and they needed to have all their wits about them.

Not letting herself waste time second-guessing, she gently pulled the box out and placed it on the floor next to the revolver. It was the size and shape of a cigar box, but what was inside was nowhere near as innocuous. "Blast," they called it: the combination of a drug discovered by a Polish scientist a few years back, and a similar chemical derived from the blood of centaurs. She didn't know what madman of a Huntsman had first thought to combine the two, but she'd acquired some out of curiosity, years back.

Aaron didn't know.

With the ease of practice, she slipped the needle from its case and lowered the waist of her pants, sliding the point into the flesh at her hip. A wince and a sigh, and it was done. She felt the rush immediately, inhaling and feeling her spine lengthen, her heart pumping more strongly, every inch of her body tingling as it spread. Just enough, just enough to wake her up, make her more alert.

She put the kit back together and slid it into its hiding place, then closed and locked the weapons case before arming herself.

Her pistol went back into the inside coat pocket, then she wrapped the new sheath around the outside of her left sleeve, sliding the throwing knife into it. A quick tug, and it fell neatly into her right hand, ready for throwing. A quick flip over her knuckles, showy but effective, and it became a stabbing tool.

"Please, please give me something to stab." She did not think of herself as a particularly violent person, but there was no denying that the act of stabbing something could lift even the most melancholic of moods. Sadly, even the most annoying of humans, named Messrs. Dolph and Baxter, were not to be stabbed. Not because she had anything particularly against stabbing them, if required, but that certainly would get the police involved, for actual cause.

Readied, she pick up Botheration's leather lead where it was coiled on the nightstand, then turned off the lamp and let the room fall into darkness. When her eyes adjusted enough to see, she made her way to the closed door and took a deep breath, holding it for a count of three. The drug had steadied in her system, leaving her tight but loose at the same time. She gathered all other concerns from her thoughts, bundled them up, and then exhaled, pushing them from her. Petty worries, discomforts, even the familiar-yet-forever-strange feel of loose shirt and trousers against her skin, all fled, leaving her focused and honed-sharp.

Opening the door slowly, Rosemary cast a quick glance into the darkened hallway. Seeing no sign of Aaron, she made her way down the stairs, breathing in time with every creak and squeak of the carpet underfoot.

He was not downstairs, either, and she wondered for a moment if he was still in his room, then looked out the window by the front door and saw the red ember of a cigarette butt. Frowning, she followed it outside.

The night had gotten colder, and there was a taste of moisture in the air that made her think it would snow soon. She hoped not.

Aaron was leaning against the far corner of the house, the cigarette in one gloved hand, the other hand shoved into his pocket. He had switched his expensive felted fedora for the flat cap, and even in the darkness she could see that his ears were pink with the cold underneath the brim.

"Give me that," she said and, when he didn't move fast enough, reached out and took it from his hand, then took a shallow drag. She was not fond of the taste, but by now the sharing had become a ritual of sorts. She took a closer look, noting the light tremor in his hand, now that it was no longer holding the cigarette. "Are you all right?"

He took the cigarette back from her, pulling another drag

before dropping it to the ground, grinding it out with his heel. "I was feeling restless."

He got that like sometimes, had ever since he was a child. But where another would stomp and storm, burning their restlessness out through movement, Aaron would become quiet, watchful. Unnerving, others said, when their parents couldn't hear. Almost uncanny.

It never boded well.

"We can do this," she said, although she didn't think she would be able to go back upstairs, undress, and fall asleep no matter what.

"I'm fine. You worry too much," he said, shoving off from the wall and heading toward the back of the house and the kennel.

"I worry just the right amount," she retorted, stretching her pace to catch up with him. He might have made a rude gesture with his free hand, but she pretended not to notice.

A low woof came from the kennel as they approached, Botheration's shadow appearing in the gloom, pressed up against the gate. His eyes glowed like Aaron's cigarette, and faint plumes of white smoke drifted upward when he exhaled, visible even in the pre-dawn dark.

"He always knows," Aaron said, a touch of awe in his low voice. "It's as though a switch is thrown, the moment we decide."

Bother's line was bred for this, for the hunt, but that eagerness was more than breeding; it was bone-deep, back to the essence of the founding stud. On the hunt, he shed the veneer of domestication as easily as Rosemary left behind her skirts and corset.

Rosemary raised her left hand, placed two fingers to her lips, then tapped them against her left thigh. There was the scrape of claws against stone and the cool swoosh of air, and Botheration appeared at her side, ear pricked up and jaw hanging open in anticipation.

"Someday he's going to do that in front of someone and we'll all be sunk," Aaron murmured, but Rosemary ignored him. Bother never acted without command. It was part of his training, from the moment he was weaned.

And really, if you saw a hound move from one place to another without actually moving, who would you tell? Especially one whose eyes glowed red, and whose breath stank of brine and smoke.

"Come on, Bother," she said, slipping the lead onto his collar. "A little walk first." If they knew what sort of uncanny they were hunting, this would be simpler; she would be able to give him that command and he would ignore everything else until he caught the scent. But for now, they would have to take him to the site of the last murder and see what, if anything, he picked up.

They had arrived too late for Lovelace's blood to be useful, even if any had remained on the ground, but Aaron was right; this most recent death had been recent enough that they might still be lucky, and Bother might be able to pick up the scent.

Botheration shook his entire body, irritable at the lead when he'd expected to be set loose.

"I know, I know. Just for a bit," she told him, while Aaron snorted, sounding remarkably like Botheration himself.

"I don't know why you worry about a leash this hour of the night," he said. "Anyone wandering this late likely deserves to see a hellhound pacing through the streets."

"Don't call him that," Rosemary said, walking a little faster to keep up with the tug of the lead. "It's unkind."

"I don't think he cares much what he's called," Aaron said, which was a valid point, but the word still made Rosemary uneasy. What you called something mattered. Botheration was flesh and blood and bone, same as they were. And if there were things deep in both their family trees that weren't exactly as advertised? Best not to speak that where others might hear. Ever.

They fell into an easy pace, taking advantage of the hour to walk two abreast in the street, rather than the sidewalks. When they had been children, it would have been a risk to do such a thing, as the asphalt would be littered with debris from horse-drawn carriages thronging the streets. Autos might be noisier and have less charm, but they also left less mess behind for the unwary.

The pavement here was old-fashioned macadam. The men had spoken at dinner of the need to bring Brunson into the new decade, with all the attendant "improvement," but Rosemary rather liked the soft sweep of their soles on the surface, the echoes a quiet accompaniment as they walked.

There was more activity in the houses they passed than she would have expected, lights flickering through windows here and there. Either Brunson was home to chronic insomniacs, or there was something in the air keeping decent folk from sleep tonight.

She looked at the beast pacing ahead of her, pitch-black nose to the ground, and thought perhaps both causes might be to blame. The presence of uncanny in a town, even ones as mostly harmless as brownies, could affect humans without their being aware of it. Uncertainty and unease keeping them from sleeping might be the least of it. She only hoped that they would stay inside, where it was warm, dry, and safe.

The walk back to the police station seemed to take longer this time, although she knew that the steps between remained the same. It made little sense, but Rosemary had long ago accepted that there was little that made sense about perception during a hunt. What they were, the uncanny blood in their bones, rose to the surface, overtaking normal senses. And despite the unease dragging at her still, the solidity of Botheration in front of her and Aaron's warmth at her side were reassuring; she had no fear of walking in the night, even knowing that there were uncanny about. It was clear to any with eyes that they were hunters, not prey.

Overconfidence is a sure way to die early. The thought was her own, but it carried the echo of her mother's voice, a lesson the woman had repeated over and over, as though she knew the shape of her own death to come.

If she had, if she'd had even an inkling, it hadn't mattered. Knowing what was to come had never once changed anything.

The building next to the police station now had lights behind its windows as well, dim-lit shapes occasionally moving past drawn curtains. There was little reason anyone might look out, and even less that seeing two figures walking a dog would alarm them to the point of investigation, but Rosemary still sent up a little prayer that they would not be noticed.

The alley the report mentioned ran at an angle behind the police station, a ragged stone wall about hip-high, backed by a taller wooden-slat fence of much newer construction. While Rosemary pulled her flash from a pocket and played the beam along the ground, careful to keep it low to not interfere with their night vision, Aaron reached up to grab the top of the posts, lifting himself up to see over the top. He hung there for a few seconds, then dropped back down to the ground with some semblance of grace. "Umph. That used to be easier. There's a bit of meadow behind. Someone's dumped the carcass of an old wagon out there."

"No way through the fence?" Their voices were low; not a whisper, which would carry suspiciously, but cast down to almost a mumble.

"Not unless they can levitate."

There were uncanny who could fly, or glide, but none that she knew of in this area. Still, populations moved, and individuals traveled. Assumptions got Huntsmen—and innocents—killed.

The other side of the alley was the back wall of the police station, and the garage next to it. There was a narrow lane between the two buildings, but barely wide enough for Rosemary to slip between. The walls of both buildings were solid, without a single window looking outward.

"It's completely blind back here," Aaron said. "Convenient, that."

"I suspect they didn't think their backyard needed watching."

"Or they needed a place out of sight to drag prisoners."

"Don't be ridiculous," Rosemary said. "That's what they have cells for. Out here, someone might hear yelling. But that raises an interesting question. Was our patrolman killed here, or killed elsewhere and then deposited here after the kill?"

"The others weren't, so why would this one be?" As usual, he quickly saw what she was thinking. "Left here as a warning? It's not as though the police were investigating the earlier deaths—and not even Lovelace's, not really. And even if they were, how would an uncanny know—and why would it care?" Officers occasionally stumbled over an uncanny, but always by accident, and usually not without high cost.

"I don't know. It just feels . . ." Her voice trailed off as she tried to marshal her thoughts. Aaron waited. He'd always respected her emotion-driven hunches, even when he didn't understand how she came to them.

"The killings. There wasn't enough blood."

He nodded; on that they agreed.

"And there's no real sign of a struggle here, the way you'd expect with a man in his prime, one trained to deal with criminals. Not so near to help, if he could only raise enough of a fuss."

"Men like that, they'd rather die than scream," Aaron said. "Most of 'em wouldn't even know how. Their throat would seize up before a noise escaped."

"Men are ridiculous." She pulled gently on the lead, and Botheration came back to sit at her feet, obedient but clearly still on the job, from the way the skin over his shoulders rippled and his black nose twitched.

"Hound." Bother's flopped-over ear made a valiant effort at lifting, and he whined a little, deep in his chest, to show that he was paying attention. Aaron could give commands as well, but during a hunt they typically defaulted to giving her the lead. It was simpler for the beast to know who to look to when time was of the essence.

She knelt to take off his lead, wrapping it into a tight bundle and handing it to Aaron before giving the hound her full attention, his deep red eyes fixed on her as though she held all the answers in the universe.

"A human died here," she told him. Died or was already dead, it didn't matter. A hound could pick up the scent of cooling human flesh in the middle of a butcher's garden. *If* there was enough for him to start from. "We need you to find his scent, and follow it back to the place where his blood was first spilled."

Explicit instructions were needful, otherwise he might lead her to a charnel house, or a long-empty lair, or—as in one case early in their partnership—the bed of someone newly dead of purely natural causes. That had been . . . awkward.

If the man had been killed here, Bother would not be able to find a trail. But she didn't think that was going to happen.

Traditionally, hounds would announce their intent with a discordant howl, rising to the skies to announce that the pack was hunting. That urge had been bred from Botheration's line over generations, but he still paused to lift his square muzzle to the sky, mouth open as though sending the notes directly to the bone-white quarter moon glinting behind the scrim of clouds. Then he swung his head to look up at her, his entire body tight as a bowstring, waiting to be released.

"Hunt," she told him.

They'd been trained as Huntsmen long before they had Botheration, had learned the hard way, as all Huntsmen did, how to read the sign that meant an uncanny was near, find the clues left behind to lead them to a den or hiding space. But for something like this, when time had passed and any clues visible to human eyes would have been wiped away, even the best Huntsmen needed help.

The hound snuffled at the ground, paying no attention to them, completely focused on his task. Aaron watched him, his head cocked to the side the way it always was when he was intent, his hands shoved into his pockets. He was still enough to pass for a statue in the dim light, his earlier agitation gone.

Rosemary used the moment to inspect her own pistol, reassuring herself that there were iron-tipped bullets in the chamber, then checked it again.

"You keep doing that, you'll lose your youthful vitality and become a sallow old hag."

"Better that than hair on your palms like a werewolf," she retorted.

"Ouch," he said mildly. "I'll have you know—"

"Please don't." She knew many things about her brother, but there were still things she did not wish to know at all.

Botheration stopped mid-pace, his backside quivering once, and she slid the pistol back into place even as Aaron raised his own Colt, stepping forward to see what the beast had found.

"*Woof.*" Bother's bark was low and quiet, a confident statement that he had taken the scent.

"Good boy," Rosemary said, all focus again. "Let's go."

Freed of the leather lead, Botheration could move far more quickly than his companions, and only experience kept them from being left behind as he shot off, intent on the scent. Thankfully, he kept to the road at first, barely pausing before turning left, heading away from the station, not away from town as Rosemary had half expected, but toward the center.

"He was killed in the center of town?" Aaron sounded as

confused as she felt. "All the others were attacked outside town, or on the edges, like Dr. Lovelace."

"And they were all found in places no one would be likely to be walking by. Hemry wasn't. The uncanny is getting bolder." She checked the placement of her knives as they trotted after Bother, a habitual gesture, making sure they were secure. "The patrolman didn't have any connection to unions, or union organizers?"

Aaron could only shrug; she knew as much as he did, which wasn't much at all. It seemed unlikely that Hemry would be pro-union, but they had seen and heard far stranger things.

They were speaking in more normal voices now, away from the police station, but their focus remained on Bother as he moved forward, nose going from ground to air and then back again. He paused a few times, giving them a chance to catch up, then made a low grumbling noise and set off again, as though he had temporarily lost the scent, or been confused.

That wasn't right. He was bred for this sort of work; nothing shy of a massive thunderstorm could dilute the scent enough that he couldn't keep it, once taken up. And yet, the beast led them down the street and then back again, around a corner and back, only the cock of his ears telling them he was in fact following a scent, not merely wandering.

"There's no way something dragged the body around the block," Rosemary said, but she didn't rein the beast in. His skills had to be trusted, or there was no point whatsoever in using him. "Not without being noticed. And Bother didn't find even a trace of any uncanny *in* town, earlier. Well, only the brownies."

She missed a step at the thought, and turned to see Aaron looking equally thunderstruck. Then . . .

"No," her brother said firmly. "Ridiculous."

Brownies might be willing and certainly were able to kill, but the number of them that would be required to drag a human body, much less carry it the distance they'd covered between the disposal point and here . . . No. He was right, it was ridiculous.

"They might know something, though," Aaron said. "We should pay the bakery a visit. Officially."

He looked far too pleased at that thought.

"Woof." Botheration had settled in one spot, a dark patch of road where the snow had either melted or been cleared away at some point, leaving only dirt and gravel behind. He sank onto his haunches and looked at them expectantly, as though to say, *This is where you take over.*

"Good boy," Aaron praised him, pulling a chunk of dried beef heart from his pocket and offering it to the hound on an open palm. A dip of Bother's head and a swipe of his tongue, and the treat disappeared, but the hound didn't shift from his position, watching as Rosemary made a circle around him, trying to see what it was that had made him stop in that particular spot, no different to her eyes than any other. She lifted her hand, and Aaron placed the fairy light into her palm. Tungsten flashes were useful, and to be preferred, but even she would admit that fairy lights were better for some things, like finding blood or body debris on a darkened street.

"No blood. Not even a stain." The annoyance and exhaustion in her voice felt like a physical thing, heavy on her tongue. "Twenty-four hours and there's nothing left at all?"

"Someone could have washed it all away."

"Oh an' for sure," and she adopted a broad mockery of Aunt Germaine's husband, Henry, who had taught them their tracking skills. "We'll just be seeing some blood and sweep it away, never telling anyone."

"If there was unexplained blood in front of my home, and no body to account for it?" Aaron huffed his amusement. "I'd for sure be sweeping it away, and washing it down with soap, too."

"Yes, but we were raised to be suspicious," she replied in her normal voice. "All right, Bother. Thank you."

Released, the hound stood up and took three steps backward before settling again, this time in a resting crouch. His eyes had gone back to brown, but the scent of brine still shimmered around him. She suspected he was unhappy not to have found something he could sink his teeth into, but he had completed his task, and that satisfied the beast, for now.

The air around them was brighter than it had been only a few minutes before, despite the cloud cover lying thick to the north and west. Rosemary felt exhaustion beginning to creep over her bones again, the effects of the drug wearing off, but it was a familiar exhaustion, and she could ignore it for now.

With dawn came people stirring, and more chance of them being seen. They needed to work faster.

"So what does this tell us?"

"It killed here, but not at once," Aaron replied without hesitation. "The blood didn't pool in one place. It probably scattered, drops fine enough that you wouldn't notice unless you were looking in daylight. The back-and-forth wasn't from dragging after death. It came at them from one side, and let them run, then swung around. . . . It played with its food."

"And it moves fast," Rosemary said.

"Faster than a human. Maybe winged?"

"Or more than one."

Her brother made a face. "I really was hoping you wouldn't say that."

"That would be consistent with the strike marks," Rosemary said, reaching into her coat pocket and pulling out the sketchbook, flipping it open to the ribbon-marked page holding her sketches of Dr. Lovelace's corpse. "Not a single killing blow, but many together, weakening the victim until he died."

"Heart failure?"

"Or blood loss, or shock . . . Differing results, but the same cause."

"But none of that explains the cauterizing. They cut, then burn?"

She closed the book, and looked at the ground, then back up at her brother. "Prolonging the game. All four victims. They were tortured to death."

The walk back to the boarding house was quiet, Bother padding silently at Rosemary's side, the lead now coiled in her hand.

"We need to do it," Aaron said, finally. "The brownie, I mean. I know you don't like it, and if there was any other way, I'd take it. You know that. But if anyone knows anything, it's another uncanny. And since we've got no chance of nabbing the uncanny who warned us, unless you'd like to go netting the river . . . ? And don't even suggest what you're thinking. You know it's not going to volunteer anything out of the goodness of its heart. Brownies don't have hearts, just cash registers."

"All right."

"All right?" He glanced sideways at her, checking that he'd heard correctly. He had expected it to take more convincing.

"I don't like it, but all right, yes."

Winning that argument should have made him feel better. But he didn't like winning because Rosemary just gave up. He kept glancing at his sister, concerned about the way she seemed to be dragging. Her head was bowed forward, so he couldn't judge the shadows under her eyes, but she seemed to have gone from full of vigor to emptied-out, far faster than she should have.

That happened to her occasionally, during a hunt, and it never failed to worry him.

Food and a warm beverage would help. Sleep would help

more, but he didn't see much hope for that. He glanced up at the sky, frowning as he noted the ominous swirls in the clouds. A storm was rolling in from the northwest. Because of course, that was all that was missing.

"Bother." The hound looked up at him, and he flicked three fingers toward the house. "Kennel. Go." It was a risk, letting him do that, but he wanted to get Rosemary inside before she fell down.

The hound looked at Rosemary, as though asking if she were certain she wanted to send him away, and she nodded once, tiredly. "Good job, Bother. Go rest."

The hound disappeared, a faint glow lingering for a second after he was gone, and they made their way through the now-familiar door of the boarding house.

"I'd kill for a bath," she said, as they climbed the stairs to their rooms. "At home. With all my bath salts and a glass of whiskey."

"A double," he agreed. "Rosie." And she stopped just outside her door, not looking at him.

"It's the only way. We don't have time to be delicate anymore."

"I know," she said, and closed the door firmly behind her.

Aaron sighed, and went into his own room, shedding his clothing and bundling it away, then choosing a fresh shirt, listening for the sound of Rosemary leaving her room, and then coming back.

Aaron ran a hand over his chin and decided to take the time to shave. It took him too many days for a beard to come in, so letting it grow wasn't an option; they had enough trouble already without him looking like a well-dressed hobo.

The water was still warm from Rosemary's use, and he'd managed to lather his face and strop the blade before a knock sounded on the bathroom door.

"In a moment," he said, lifting the blade to his chin, but stopping just shy of touching skin, in case whoever it was made another noise.

"I'm bringing breakfast out to Bother," his sister said, her voice muffled through the door. "Hurry."

"Not if you don't want me to slit my throat, I won't," he muttered, and went back to work. It wasn't the best shave he'd ever done, but when he patted his chin dry a few minutes later, the face that looked back at him was eminently respectable, despite the dark blue shadows forming under his eyes. Rosemary had cosmetics with her that would hide those, if need be. But for now, for what they were planning for the day, it would not be necessary.

By the time he was ready to go downstairs, there were sounds of movement coming from the other bedrooms. Not wanting to encounter any of their fellow guests, or worse yet, their too-chatty hostess, Aaron quickened his pace down the stairs and out the door. Jan was coming up the front walk dressed in a heavy hooded cloak, clearly arriving to help with breakfast. She raised her face to look at him, her eyes wide again, and he fought the urge to make sure he wasn't splattered with blood, or otherwise offensive. Instead, he merely tipped his hat to her and kept on moving.

"She's an odd duck," Rosemary said, when he joined her outside the gate. "Have you noticed that? Polite as a parson when others are around, but it's like she's looking away even when she's looking straight at us."

He'd noticed but not thought much of it. People often looked that way at him. "I suspect that either she or her sister took our measure that first morning and decided not to be involved," he told her, offering her his elbow. She accepted, gloved fingers curling around his arm, and they walked down the sidewalk, every inch respectable citizens.

Her breath caught as she took his meaning. "You think one of them has the Sight?" Rosemary looked over her shoulder, as though tempted to go back and accost the girl.

He shrugged. The Sight was an iffy thing in humans, even among Huntsmen. "I think she's an odd duck."

By the time they reached the center of town again, the smell of yeast and sugar rising from the bakeries was too much to resist, particularly on stomachs that had not been filled yet that morning. Aaron abandoned Rosemary on the street to go into the first bakery they came to, before she could say anything. He came out a few minutes later with a small loaf of pumpernickel, so dark it was nearly black. He tore it in half, giving one side to his sister, who bit into it with a distinctly unladylike fervor. An older man, rough-skinned and dressed for labor, gave them a scandalized glance as he walked past, but nothing more.

"Better than I expected from them," she said. "Although cheese would be perfect with this. Cheese, and mustard."

He shuddered. "You have the stomach of a peasant. But no sign of brownies there. Where did you see it, again?"

She finished the last bite and shook the crumbs from her glove. "The other bakery."

He shot her a reproving look. "You couldn't have told me that before I bought there?"

"You didn't exactly give me the chance, dashing in like that. Anyway, it's better to eat first," she said calmly, taking his elbow again as they resumed their walk. "I was careful not to react when I was there last, so returning should not alert it." With her free hand, she reached for the now-empty cloth bag she'd shoved into her coat pocket, shaking out the last of the crumbs. "And we even have an excuse to return this, if it's the same clerk. So, you're the proper scholar of the two of us. Any particular defenses we should be wary of?"

"Like you haven't cleaned out a nest before."

"There's a difference between clearing a nest and trying to get one to speak."

That was a valid point. "The books don't say much. They're . . ." And he didn't want to say "insignificant," because nothing that spread that rapidly over such a wide territory could be insignificant, but they were not placed among the first four classifications of uncanny, which were the ones most Huntsmen worried about. "They're not written about much."

"If anything comes of this, then, you can publish a mono-graph," she told him, as she pushed open the door to the second bakery and stepped in.

The man behind the counter was clearly surprised to see strangers in so early, his hands still powdered with flour, and a streak of it across his round, sweat-flushed face. He looked to be the baker himself, rather than a clerk.

"Good morning," he said, hastily wiping his hands on the apron tied around his waist. His accent was heavy, and clearly German.

"Guten Tag," Aaron said in return, his normally-fluent German suddenly halting, forcing Rosemary to hide a grin behind her hand. A shared language made witnesses feel comfortable, speaking it poorly made them feel superior, which often meant they underestimated the speaker. Not Huntsmen training, that, but mere observation of human nature.

"We were hoping to buy a loaf of rye?" Aaron held up the bag, taken from Rosemary's hand, and the baker's eyes lit up. "My sister was in before and said they smelled wonderful."

"Natürlich, ja," the man said, his face flushing slightly under the compliment, and took the bag from Aaron. "There are some in the oven. Let me pick one for you, fresh."

"Sehr aufmerksam," Aaron replied. "That is very kind of you."

Rosemary waited until the baker had gone into the back before pinching his arm. "What did you say to him?"

Aaron just chuckled. "You should have attended better to

your language studies," he told her, and she muttered something in Latin that should never have come out of a gentlewoman's mouth.

They were playing up the rivalry, working for an invisible audience they hoped was there, and their efforts were repaid by a faint noise that might have, if you were expecting it, sounded like a snicker. Lacking Botheration's ears, Aaron could only guesstimate where it came from, but when Rosemary patted his arm and drifted off to look at the long sticks of bread displayed in baskets along the far wall, he turned a little in order to better watch the other wall.

The door the baker had disappeared through was slightly ajar, and he could hear the sound of low voices and a clatter of wood and metal that he assumed was normal for a bakery. The smells of yeast and sugar were nearly overwhelming, but scented now with cinnamon, warm fruit, and . . . He sniffed once but couldn't place the aroma. "Smells good."

Although they were leery of showing themselves, compliments were impossible for brownies to resist. Aaron saw a wisp of movement in the corner of his eye, not at floor level, where he'd been expecting it, but higher up, on one of the shelves. He stepped forward, training taking over before thought could interfere, and closed his fingers around a solid, warm shape, scooping it off the shelf from behind a canister of flour and bringing it into the light.

Barely a handspan high, dressed in flour-dusted homespun, the brownie glared malice out of beady yellow eyes, its bald pate and wrinkled face the color of wheat and yeast.

"What have we here?" Aaron said, bringing his other hand around to reinforce the first, as the brownie squirmed in his grasp, teeth on display and claws out. "A mouse? But like no mouse I have ever seen before."

"That is indeed no mouse," Rosemary agreed, coming up beside him. "Or if it is, a particularly large and ugly one."

The brownie bared its teeth at her, then sank them into the flesh between Aaron's thumb and forefinger.

"That tickled," he told it, hiding his wince. "Be good for a moment, will you?" He handed it over to Rosemary, the leather of her gloves better protection against brownie teeth, and stepped back just as the baker came back, with not one loaf but two, the second one smaller, in his hands.

"Your rye, and also a fruit loaf, very fresh. No, no—no charge for the second, a thank-you for returning to buy from us. We hope you come again soon."

The baker made short work of wrapping the loaves up and sliding them into the cloth bag, then accepted Aaron's payment, oblivious to Rosemary standing behind him, holding a likely increasingly irate brownie in her hands.

The moment the door closed behind them, the wrapped bread tucked under Aaron's arm, they headed for a tiny pocket park Rosemary had noticed when walking through town the day before. They needed privacy for this, but it was too much of a risk to bring the uncanny back to the Lovelace house. The park was tucked in between two houses and half-hidden by a thicket of bushes, and in warmer weather, it was doubtless popular with courting couples, with a carved stone bench set under a graceful aspen. But in winter it was deserted, the perfect location to interrogate someone in relative privacy.

"Watch him," Rosemary said when they reached the bench, depositing the brownie on the cold surface. Aaron's hand came down on the brownie's neck when it would have darted away, tsking sadly down at its sullen face. "Stay put," he advised it. "Or we'll make you stay put."

He'd been right, the brownie's teeth couldn't cut through the kid of her gloves, but they'd doubtless leave a bruise. Rosemary took off her hat and removed several hairpins, then jammed the hat back on with a careless gesture. "Use these."

"Don't know nuthin'." The brownie glared at them, arms crossed over its stubby chest. The effect would be more impressive if it weren't bound with metal loops around its ankles; four of Rosemary's iron hairpins, twisted into shape to keep it still. If it exerted itself, it could probably break free, but where would it go, with two humans watching it?

And if it did run, there were sigils marked in the ground around them, prepared before they went into the bakery. The brownie might be able to break past, but it would not be pleasant.

Rosemary had frowned when Aaron had drawn them, but she had not stopped him.

"So you keep insisting." Aaron tilted his head and smiled,

the same expression he'd used to use to coax his mother into just one more cookie, because he'd been a good boy. "And yet, somehow I don't believe that. Why don't I believe that, Rosemary?"

"Because it's a brownie," she said, arms crossed over her own chest, words laden with practiced boredom. "And brownies are incapable of resisting gossip. Any gossip."

"Hey." The brownie was indignant, its yellow eyes going wide, practically sparking with outrage that nothing they'd said previously had been able to provoke. "You say gossip, I say marketable information."

Aaron smothered a grin behind two fingers. Anyone could threaten and get nowhere. But prick someone's pride, and they'd fall over themselves to prove you wrong. Human or uncanny, it didn't seem to matter.

"Point taken," Rosemary allowed, luring the brownie on. "And yet you claim to have absolutely no . . . marketable information about people being killed in your town?" She made a scornful, scoffing noise. "Come on, little uncanny. Don't play games."

The brownie sneered at her, then turned its head and sneered at Aaron, just in case he was feeling left out.

"I've been in both bakeries," he said to it. "Yours is clearly the more popular. You're doing good work with them."

The brownie puffed up a little. "Best bakery in the entire county. Bread stays fresh days longer than anyones' else. Not that you'd know it, the way people gobble it up. Pies, too. Crust perfect every time."

"Which means you're getting people in all the time," Rosemary said. "Local people. They feel comfortable in there, surrounded by all those delicious smells, warm against the cold outside. And the clerk, he's a friendly sort. Likes to talk. And you, I'm betting, like to listen." Rosemary leaned forward, placing her index finger under the brownie's chin and tilting its head up. "So don't tell me you don't know. Tell me what you *do* know."

Its eyes narrowed again. "And if I don't?"

"Bakeries are such busy places. So much flour dust, such hot ovens. And your humans live over the bakery, don't they?" Her tone was light, conversational, but blood drained from the brownie's face, leaving it an unpleasantly ashen gray.

"Huntsmen. Barbarians. Yeah, okay, I mighta heard a little something. Folk getting torn up in the street, yeah, people whisper. They don't know what's going on, they buy more pies. Ever notice that? You humans like a little sweet with your panics."

"Who doesn't like pie?" Aaron asked, and the brownie tsked at him. "Makes you fat and sloppy," it retorted.

"Still fast enough to take you off the board."

"Enough." Rosemary's voice was like a whip, cracking through the air. "Brownie, we have no case against you or your people. Yet. But you know what is killing humans in this town. And you are going to tell us, before I start to wonder if you're a danger to this town, too."

The brownie looked mutinous, then threw its hands up around its ears. "I don't know. I swear, I don't know. It showed ups outta nowhere. Bad storm blew it in, four, six weeks ago, maybe? It's nothing I've ever seen before, or heard of neither." The brownie's voice fell, the first sign of fear it had shown. "It's a shadow, a dank, nasty shadow, and you just pray it don't fall on you, is all. I've been keeping an eye on my shop, but nothing's come sniffing."

"And you weren't curious about what it was?"

"No. Why should I be?" The brownie looked genuinely puzzled by that. "The Aksha can worry about everyone else, that's Big Deal business, not mine."

"The what?" Rosemary looked puzzled, but Aaron stepped in before the brownie could say anything. "Tall, green, mouthy, likes to come and go by water?"

The mer-creature.

The brownie widened its eyes at them, this time in mock innocence. "You've seen it."

"It warned us," Rosemary said. "Told us to find this thing, but neglected to tell us what it *was*."

"Then they don't know either." The brownie's face scrunched, making it look like a pale, withered apple. "That's not good. Aksha knows everything, or at least, everything the water knows. The mills fall within their territory; when the human died on the banks, it got their attention, I guess. But normally they don't care a whit about what happens on soil." It paused. "Wait. They spoke to you?"

"That's odd?"

"That's terrifying," the brownie said, and Aaron couldn't really argue.

Rosemary sighed, a short, exhausted sound. "What's your name?"

The brownie looked at her as though she'd suddenly sprouted horns. "You're joshing me, right?"

"We can't keep calling you 'brownie.' That's rude."

"You stole me, chained me up, and threatened my home. And you're worried about being rude?"

Put like that, Aaron acknowledged, it did seem awkward.

"And you're Huntsmen. Your kind kill my kind. I'll be keeping my name to myself. You want to know what to put on my stone, you'll have to make something up."

"We're not going to kill you, brownie."

"Not right now, anyway," Aaron said, ignoring the different faces the brownie and Rosemary both made at that. He thought that was hypocritical of her; she'd been the one to threaten the bakery, after all.

"Look. The Aksha talked to you, that's its business. They do the Big Deal stuff. Me? I take care of my bakery. The rest of it's your problem. That's what you do, isn't it?"

"And if this thing comes for one of your humans?"

The brownie shrugged, bony shoulders rising up sharply, then falling in a quick slump. "So long as there's someone left to run the bakery."

"Soulless creature," Rosemary muttered in distaste. "Aaron, come on."

"Hey, wait!" the brownie yelled as they turned to leave. "You can't leave me here like this! There are foxes out here! And owls!"

They were back on the street before Rosemary said, "You think owls will eat him?"

"I doubt it," Aaron said, not without regret. "I broke the sigils as we left. If he can't get out of those pins before dusk, that's his problem. We have a name now, Rosemary. Aksha. Aksha." He rolled the word around in his mouth but stopped before repeating it a third time.

What they could name, they could find. And, if need be, kill.

Eleven

"THERE'S BEEN A small problem."

John Baxter did not sigh as he placed his pen down on the desk and looked up. "I don't like hearing that."

Thankfully, Dolph had gone to meet a potential investor at the train station. The younger man was a personable ass, but his stick was inserted a bit too high to deal with problems properly. Society snobbery, Baxter called it. But Dolph brought in important clients, clients with names as well as money, and names brought in more money.

The clerk shuffled the papers in his hands but didn't retreat under his employer's stare. He was young, and confident the way only the very young can be. John Baxter felt a moment's pity for the boy, with so many disappointments and discouragements waiting for him, but simply waved him forward, holding a hand out for the papers.

The office they had taken in town was over a warehouse, and he could hear the thump and crack of boxes being moved about below. If he closed his eyes, he could let himself imagine that the warehouse was his, that every box came and went with his name stamped on its side. Or maybe his initials, with a curlicue banner around them.

Soon. If everything went to plan.

If he could keep the town's council satisfied, the greedy bastards, and convince that witch to sell him the final acres they needed, and if no further surprises turned up that needed cleaning up. The girl hadn't been wrong; the feds were looking too closely at everything having to do with the rails, and one bad report could set the whole applecart over.

So no, he didn't want to hear about any problems of any size.

"What's the short version?" The papers might tell him more detail, but it was good to hear someone else's take on it first. Even a wet-eared clerk.

"The union organizers haven't left town."

Damn. Still, not entirely unexpected. If they could all be run off with a warning, his life would be much easier. "Have they been talking to anyone else?"

"Not yet. Or, maybe?" The boy looked as though he wanted to check his notes again, but they were in Baxter's hands now. "They went into both bakeries this morning."

"Pffft." He tossed the papers down on the desk. "Nobody cares if bakers organize, Ronson." Well, he supposed someone would, but that someone was not him.

"Yes, sir," Ronson said. "They were also seen," and he stopped, looking unsure.

Baxter took off his reading spectacles and folded them

carefully before placing them on the desk next to his ledger and pen. "Yes?"

"Walking the street just before dawn. Both of them. With their dog." He shuddered on the last word, then looked mortified that he'd done so.

Baxter had not seen the dog, having no interest in animals as a rule, but the maids at the boarding house had been chattering about its size. From the boy's reaction, they had not been exaggerating. But even a monstrously large dog could be taken down with a bullet, if need be.

Still. Bad enough the money he'd already had to spend to keep the recent deaths quiet. He preferred that problems not be solved with violence, if it could be avoided. Violence brought newsmen, and newsmen brought headlines, and headlines of that sort brought further problems. It was an ugly cycle that made him no money.

He scowled at the leather journal on his desk, noting that he was due to meet with the witch again tomorrow, one last meeting before they went back to the city. If she didn't agree to the latest offer, they would have to change their plans, and *that* would cost them money, too.

One problem at a time.

"Did they meet with anyone?" An early morning meeting of itself was not enough for the police to finally roust them, but a whisper of it into the right ear might put a stick in their spokes.

"No, sir. Just walking around." He sounded befuddled by that. "But they came in only long enough to change clothing and right off again." A pause, then the boy burst out, "The woman was wearing trousers like a suffragette!"

Ronson sounded outraged, and Baxter resisted the urge to tell him that he would see far worse and more scandalous things in his life than a woman wearing men's clothing. "Likely she found it more practical than skirts." He didn't care a whit what the woman or her brother wore, so long as they stayed out of his way. "Keep an eye on them. Continue to make note of who they speak with, and for how long. But don't interfere." Agitators could not go long without causing trouble; sooner or later they would slip up, expose their purpose in being here, and the police were now primed to sweep down and sweep them out of town.

Baxter & Dolph Ltd.'s hands needed to be clean when that happened.

Twelve

"AKSHA. AKSHA." JACOB rolled the word around on his tongue, his West Virginia drawl making it sound like the word had melted in the sun. "No, doesn't sound familiar to me."

There was the sound of pages being flipped, then a thump and rustling as Jacob closed that book and reached for another. Aaron shifted, rubbing the back of his neck. He felt exposed, here in the hallway where anyone heading for afternoon tea might come by, but there was nothing for it. He was lucky that Mrs. Wesson had installed a phone at all; he had no right to complain that it was not somewhere more private.

"Please, Mrs. W." He'd not bothered for charm; she likely saw enough of that on a daily basis. Instead, he'd pushed all his worry and frustration to the surface, thinking of the look on Margaret Lovelace's face when she'd asked—no, told him to find her husband's killer. "It's a matter of family urgency, and some sensitivity. I'd rather not transmit it over the telegraph, for anyone to read."

Not that using a phone operator was all the much safer, but this couldn't wait on a letter.

He'd chalked protective sigils onto the desk next to the phone set, and another on the phone itself, marring the polished brass, but he had less confidence in them than he did the ones in his room. Sigils, like most fey tools, were most effective when they worked on an unaware mind; anyone coming down the stairs would see him here at the desk, and their curiosity might engage before the sigils could affect them. And there was no guarantee that the operator would not be listening in.

But there'd been no other choice.

"Give me *something*, Jacob."

"I can't give you what I don't have. You want me to lie to you?"

There was silence, then Jacob snorted. "Didn't think so. Now, there're stories of a serpent with a similar name, supposed to live in the mud of the Great Lakes. But the stories say it stays there, doesn't go wandering around streams, and certainly doesn't come out on land. But it's just some old Indian myth."

"They're all myths until they kill someone," Aaron said.

"Don't you sass me. And why in tarnation would it tell you to keep looking if it was the killer? Uncanny don't work like that." Jacob sounded like he was half a hair away from doubting Aaron's story.

He couldn't blame the old man. Uncanny were beasts. Uncanny were monsters. Uncanny acted on vile instinct, and never to the benefit of humanity. They did nothing that was not in their interest, first, second, and last. Aaron had heard those truths his entire life, had never seen anything to contradict them. Certainly nothing to suggest that one might be playing a deeper game.

And yet. The Aksha had been sent to warn them. To warn *them*, specifically. An uncanny had sought out Huntsmen.

"You sure someone hadn't bound the thing?"

"Sigils like that would glow on its skin, forcing it to do its master's bidding." Aaron hated that he knew that, hated that it was a thing anyone had to know. Rosemary was right: nothing should be bound like that, not even an uncanny.

"Nothing about this town feels right," Aaron said, rubbing the back of his neck even harder, to no relief. "We've been off since we arrived. Nothing feels right."

"You haven't been drinking the water, have you?"

Aaron bit back a sigh but rolled his eyes, secure that the other man couldn't see him. "It's not the city, Jacob. The water is fine, as are my bowels."

There was a crackle of static, and the echo of someone else's voice on the party line drowning out the old man's response.

"What?"

"I said, I'll keep looking, see if I can't find something else. You just keep your pretty head attached to your shoulders, and tell your sister to do the same."

"Yes, sir. If you find anything, call this number," and he

read the exchange off carefully, waiting until Jacob had repeated it back to him before signing off.

That had been not entirely useless, but much less help than he'd hoped for.

Aaron took a moment to wipe the sigils clean. The chalk left a faint waxy trace behind, but he'd no doubt that the next time the girls came by with their rags and polish, it would be erased completely. With luck, they wouldn't even notice it, much less wonder at the cause.

Turning to go back upstairs to replace his marking chalks before reporting his lack of progress to Rosemary, he collided abruptly with another body.

"Oh, Mr. Harker, I'm sorry." Jan, with the sharp eyes and odd-duck behavior. Those eyes were wide now, staring . . . no, not at him, but past him, the way Rosemary had complained about. He checked, subtly, but she wasn't looking at the phone, either, but rather at some point in the air just past him. He wasn't sure if that was better or worse than the way she'd looked at them when they first arrived, like she was grabbing into the soul of him, every secret thought and shadowed act.

Aaron stepped back, lifting his hands to show no harm had been done, but also to get a little distance between them. "My fault," he said, indicating his dark green suit. "I blend too well into the shadows."

"Indeed, sir." She was too well-trained to allow a guest to take blame, but also too well-trained to argue with a guest; he was putting her in an awkward position. He should apologize. If the girl did have the Sight, she might be useful somehow.

Her eyes focused on him again, and he knew for certain he liked that less than when she looked past and through him.

As though reading his discomfort, she cast her gaze down again, then said, "I was wondering, sir. We'll be roasting meats this afternoon, and there are sure to be some bits left. Would your dog like some of them?"

The unexpected change of subject threw him, and his initial reaction was to say yes; Botheration was expensive to feed, and every extra bit would certainly help. But her odd behavior remained, and the thought of her looking closely at the hound . . . it didn't seem wise.

"Thank you, but no. He has a sensitive digestion, and so we prefer to handle his feeding ourselves." None of that was untrue; for a beast that looked as though he could eat through an entire hambone without so much as a burp, the hound was surprisingly finicky. But not finicky enough to refuse a chunk of meat that might have Lord-knows-what tucked inside.

The girl's offer might be completely innocent. The uneasy feeling he had might be paranoia. It likely was paranoia, or an echo of the unease Rosemary had said she'd felt earlier. But Huntsmen who did not trust their instincts most often died younger than they should.

Jan and her sister were odd ducks, there was no doubt about it. And having the Sight did not make someone trustworthy.

The girl nodded, solemn-faced, as though she'd been able to hear his thoughts, and went past him into the kitchen without so much as a glance at the phone. He slipped the chalks into his pocket and went, not upstairs, but directly for the parlor, where Rosemary was sitting with Mrs. Wesson. The former had a daily folded open on her lap but was not reading; the latter had a ball of yarn in her lap, fingers working swiftly with thin needles.

"Well, I don't understand why everyone is so upset," the woman was saying. "Of course men need to earn a decent wage, and it's not as though they don't earn it fairly. Mr. Matthews always said he wouldn't have been able to build the paper mill if there weren't men willing to work it." She stopped, sighed. "Oh, he was a delightful man, Mr. Matthews was. Always candies in his pocket for the children, always there in church on Sunday morning. He had a fine voice with the hymns, he did. Such a shame."

Rosemary tilted her head, frowning. "And he died recently?"

"Oh heavens, no. Near on five years back. His son-in-law, Edmond, took over the mill, made all sorts of improvements. Forward-minded, he was. But then he died last year. Now, that was a tragedy. Left his wife with a young child and no one to look after the business. Jessika is a clever girl, though." Mrs. Wesson leaned closer to Rosemary, as though imparting a secret. "She went to college, before she got married."

"Did she now?" Rosemary's face showed nothing but gentle curiosity, but he knew his sister; there was something in this conversation she was determined to prize out, like the pearl from an oyster.

"Down in Boston. Got a degree and everything. Came back and married Edmond when she graduated, but clever girl, yes. Said she was determined for there to be a mill for Michael, that's her son, to inherit; used her money to bring in men to run it for her until the boy's old enough to take the reins. Took back her maiden name, too, under the Cady Law, and didn't that startle the biddies of the town." Mrs. Wesson laughed a little to herself. "Misters Dolph and Baxter, they've been working on her men to buy into their plans for the town, acting as though Jessika has no say. But they're in for a surprise if they don't mind their ways. She may want their money, but she won't tolerate being ignored."

"And well she should not," Rosemary agreed firmly, and the two women smiled at each other in a way that made Aaron feel vaguely awkward and not a little apprehensive. Before he could be discovered eavesdropping, he moved into the doorway and rapped his knuckles gently on the wooden frame. "May a gentleman intrude on your tea, or am I to be banished to the shed with the chickens?"

"If you will make yourself useful and freshen our cups," Rosemary said, "I think we might allow you to linger."

He came into the parlor and joined his sister on the sofa, shifting to the far side so that his knees didn't knock into the tea table when he leaned forward to pour more tea into their cups. There was a third cup waiting, unused, which made him think that he had been expected.

The tea was jasmine-scented, and warm enough that a curl of steam rose from the cups.

"Your sister said that the call was to your uncle?"

"Yes." Aaron had a brief moment of worry, unsure exactly what Rosemary had said, and decided to keep it as close to the truth as possible. "A great-uncle, actually. He worries about us. Sometimes I think that he forgets we are grown now, and half expects to be called in to mediate an argument."

"Oh, we still call on him for that, on occasion," Rosemary said with a sly smile, and Aaron rolled his eyes.

"You called him in. I was perfectly capable of winning that particular discussion."

"Discussion. Hah. You had already lost and simply would not admit it."

The argument had been real, and heated; the banter about it was a facade, to distract from any further questions about the telephone call. Aaron watched as Mrs. Wesson took a sip of her tea, eyes crinkling with the smile she was making no effort to hide.

"You make me wish I'd had a sibling," she said with a sigh. "And also thankful that I did not."

They both laughed at that. "I tried to exchange him for a puppy when he was born," Rosemary confided with a sly sideways glance at him. "Sadly, my parents declined my generous offer."

"You did get a puppy, eventually," he reminded her.

"Ah, yes, your dog." Mrs. Wesson lowered her cup and shook her head. "I admit, when you asked after a kennel, I was expecting something . . . smaller."

"He was small, once," Rosemary protested. "When he came to us, Aaron could hold him in his hands."

"Both hands," Aaron clarified. "And bits of him sprawled over. But he's a gentle creature. I'd trust him with a baby. His line was bred to be guardians."

Guardians of Huntsmen, which was a slightly different thing, but Aaron felt certain that still fell within the parameters of acceptable honesty.

"I think that may be why Mr. Baxter has taken you in dislike," Mrs. Wesson said, in the tone of someone continuing an earlier conversation. "I heard him say to young Gert that he does not like dogs. A pity, as he seems a decent man in all other ways."

"That is a surprise; I would have thought him a man who admired dogs," Rosemary said. "They are, after all, quite obedient."

The women exchanged another look, eyes lowered and smiles half-curled, that made Aaron certain that the conversation before he came into the room would have been highly entertaining, and would likely have made his ears flush.

"More tea, anyone?" he asked.

Some time and far too much tea later, Aaron followed Rosemary out when she took Botheration his supper. He leaned against a post and watched as she scraped the bits of meat and meal into his dish, scrubbing at the hound's flopped-over ear while Bother ate. The air was cold, but it let his thoughts form, unclouded.

"The mill owner, Matthews, the one who died. You think it's connected to this? A haunting?" Aaron was dubious; uncanny were solid things, flesh and bone and bile. For all the reports of ghosts Huntsmen had collected over the years, not a one of them had ever been proven to have physical influence on the living, shy of scaring them to death. And even that had never been conclusively proven.

"No." Rosemary shook her head. "I don't know. I still think Baxter and Dolph are our likely culprits. If Mrs. Wesson is to be trusted, the first death occurred just after our union-hating friends came to town and started trying to woo the widow's business. If so, honestly, I'm half tempted to leave them to their consequences."

If they, or anyone else, had tried to harness an uncanny, odds were high that it would end in their death, with or without the Harkers' intervention. One slip, one error, and the uncanny would turn on them.

"What did Jacob have to say?"

Aaron allowed the redirection. "He's not certain. The only reference he could find was to a legend about a serpent with that name, associated with the Great Lakes. But that could be coincidence, or some overlap between tribal languages, two names with similar sounds, or . . ."

He left the last word hanging, spreading his hands to indicate his lack of knowledge. "He's going to keep looking. But we shouldn't wait on that. Did you learn anything useful?"

"Just that nearly every soul here is willing to sell themselves for a decent profit, our hostess included. Mrs. Wesson says that when the old lumber mill failed, the town fell onto hard times. The river brings in some work, but they're just far enough away from the lake not to attract the fishing industry, and before the train came through, farmers would take their crops to larger cities, bypassing them entirely. Now, Brunson is watching money flow into Rochester, and they want some of that, no matter what it takes. Grow or die seems to be the feeling."

She shrugged, giving Botheration's ear one last affectionate pull and rising to her feet, shaking her skirt out as she did so. "Bother, you slobbered," she complained, all present utterly unsurprised by the discovery.

"For that reason, the new paper mill is quite popular, despite the smell," she went on. "And there is rumor of another mill to be built, farther upstream. Brunson is making a name for itself, and they circle their financial wagons around it. Like Baxter and Dolph, the residents smell success, and want more."

"Are the workers as happy as those profiting off them?" Aaron wondered.

Rosemary shrugged. "According to Mrs. Wesson, they have been well-treated by the Matthews family in the past. But what she knows and what they know may not entirely match up."

"And it doesn't match with what Mrs. Lovelace said about her husband," he reminded her. "Who do we trust, the known gossip, or the widow of a man who treated those with no-where else to go?"

"Both? Neither? I'm not sure it's even relevant. And if we try to speak to any worker, the police will doubtless take that as their cue to escort us out of town." She shook her head at him. "Stick to what we know, and can do. Hunt the uncanny, and stop it."

Rosemary might be curious about what drove the un-canny to kill, but when it came down to it, she didn't actually *care*. He supposed he should cultivate that perspective as well.

"The only thing we know about the Aksha is that it's water-based, and it used the river to travel. But merfolk—"

"Don't generally live in rivers, particularly not ones that don't lead directly to the ocean," Rosemary finished for him.

"Jacob said that the only thing he could find by that name was a serpent, but it was supposed to live in the lake, not a river."

"Lake Ontario is only a few miles off. How far would it be willing to travel?" She rubbed her nose, then shook out her hands as though to get blood flowing in them again. "There's something slapping around in my head, like a drunk ele-phant. A greased drunk elephant, and I just can't grab at it."

Aaron sighed. He didn't doubt Rosemary's feelings; too often they had been shown to be based in facts she could not identify just yet. But, "Can we try to catch in the morning? I need more than three hours of sleep at some point, and so do you." He anticipated her objection, placing a hand on her shoulder and squeezing gently through the fabric of her coat. "Exhaustion leads to mistakes. Shy of forcing everyone to stay indoors and patrolling every street all night, we can't keep the town safe. Not yet. Not even by letting Bother out to roam on his own."

"If someone dies tonight . . ."

"Then we will have a fresh track in the morning." It was the wrong thing to say, he knew that, but it was also the true thing to say. "Dinner, and then sleep, Rosie. You always are the most clever in the morning, anyway."

She made a face but let him lead her back to the house.

Thirteen

ARON HAD MADE good on his threat to sleep as long as he could, waking only when the sounds of other people using the bathroom down the hall woke his bladder as well. A glance at his watch-piece showed that he'd missed breakfast by half an hour. Grumbling about Rosemary not waking him up, he took possession of the bathroom and made his ablutions, noting as he dressed that he was down to his last clean undershirt. They either needed to wrap this up, or arrange to have laundry done.

The younger girl, Gert, might be amenable for hire. He considered how the girl's sister looked at them, and reconsidered.

He finished styling his hair and studied his face in the mirror, pressing cold water to his skin to reduce the sallow half circles lingering under his eyes. He might not be particularly vain, but one had standards to maintain, after all.

By the time he finally made it downstairs, Rosemary was sitting in the front parlor with the sketch pad on her lap, the other guests and Mrs. Wesson nowhere to be seen.

He mentally calculated the days, and winced: it was Sunday, she had doubtless gone to services. Hopefully, either Rosemary had made their excuses, or their hostess had determined that they were not regular churchgoers.

He paused a moment, studying his sister. Were Rosemary's features more drawn than they had been a week ago, the hollows of her cheeks more pronounced? It wasn't just exhaustion, or worry. She thought that he didn't know about her reliance on that drug, but there was no way you could live with someone and not know, not the way they were in each other's pockets half the time. And Aaron might admit to many flaws, but blindness was not one of them. Not even about his sister.

But he wouldn't say anything to her. Yet.

When he knocked gently on the doorframe and came in, she closed the book and put it aside, then leaned forward to pour him a cup of tea.

"I saved you a biscuit and some bacon from breakfast," she said, pointing her chin at the napkin-draped plate next to the teapot.

"I wouldn't have thought Mrs. Wesson would be so indulgent," he said, taking the plate in grateful hands.

"She wasn't. Gert, however, was. She said something about us needing to keep up our strength."

He stopped, half the biscuit nearly to his mouth, and put it back down on the plate again carefully. His sister shrugged.

"She didn't offer anything more, and I didn't ask. But one of those girls definitely has a bit of the Sight."

He wondered if she would See that their laundry needed doing, as well. "Do you think Mrs. Wesson knows about it?"

Rosemary considered it, then shook her head. "If I were to venture a guess, I would say no. It's not exactly the sort of thing one blurts to an employer."

The Sight was a tricky thing. In some folk it was nothing more than a hunch or a dream; for others it came as clear knowledge, as though they'd read it in a newspaper, or seen it in person. But no one had been able to predict or test what would be known when, and while there were theories aplenty on the how, that was all they were: theories. So while he might find it unnervingly fascinating, as a tool it was useless. And, as Rosemary said, risky to admit to, even in this more enlightened age.

He resumed eating. "Do they know anything about what's happening?"

"I don't think so. All she said was that we would need our strength. And then she played the role of rabbit and hippety-hopped out of the room." Rosemary's expression went from curious to rueful. "Although if one or both of them is only Seeing flashes, that would certainly explain their nerves around us."

Depending on what they had Seen, Aaron could only agree. There were moments of his own life he wouldn't want to experience without context.

Aaron tapped the tip of his nose, then pointed at her. "This town is more interesting than I expected."

"Mmm. I could do with less interesting, thank you."

He shrugged, finishing the bacon and washing it down with a sip of tea, then picked up the biscuit again, drizzling a spoonful of honey over the top before taking a bite.

"Speaking of things being more interesting than desired, Mr. Dolph and Mr. Baxter were both icily polite to me this morning, but their stares indicated that they have not softened toward our being here."

Aaron, his mouth full of honey-topped biscuit, merely waved his fingers in a rude comment to indicate how little he cared about the feelings of Messrs. Dolph or Baxter.

He swallowed and cleared his mouth with the last of the tea in his cup, then asked what he should have the moment he came downstairs. "Was there any news this morning?" Of more deaths, he meant, but was wary of saying so out loud. Even if the help did know what they were about, there was a third guest in the house who might not know about any of this, and Mrs. Wesson should not be alarmed, if they could avoid it.

"There's been no newspaper boy howling outside on the corner," she said, a little tart. "Other than that, I've no idea. But when I took Botheration for his morning walk, while you slept in, there was little activity by the police station, and no signs of significant alarm around town."

All the bodies so far had been found between dusk and dawn. If there had been another death, it would have shown up by now.

Rosemary drummed her fingers on the cover of the book in her lap, a *rat-tat-tat* noise. "I've been sitting here trying to work out our next step. But shy of bringing Botheration into every home in town . . ."

"That would not go over well, no." He took a closer look at her. Her skin was still too sallow, and there were shadows under her eyes that likely matched his own, but the knot of tension between her brows had smoothed out. "You have that look. Did you catch your elephant?"

She grimaced. "Not yet. But I have an idea. Do you know a sigil that could summon an uncanny?"

He stared at her, then blinked, and blinked again.

"I said—"

"I heard you," he muttered. "I'm just not sure I heard correctly. Yes, I know it." He didn't want to ask, but he needed her to say it out loud. "You're asking me to use a sigil? A binding sigil?"

"No." Her rejection was immediate and emphatic. "A calling one."

The difference between calling an uncanny and binding it was the split of a moral hair, and any other time and place he would have been delighted to call her out on it. But this wasn't a theoretical or philosophical discussion: she was asking him if he could do it. Against Huntsmen decree, and her own oft-stated distaste.

She lifted her chin and stared at him. "Can you do it?"

He leaned back, finishing the biscuit and wiping his mouth and hands with the napkin. "I might. I might. Let me check my notebook." He grinned at her, delighted that she had given way but wise enough not to crow. "I told you you were cleverer in the morning!"

———

The notebook he had in his bag had been their mother's, a battered composition book written out in her careful hand, every line filled with a deep blue ink that was beginning to fade at the edges. He would need to copy it over for himself, sooner rather than later, but the notebook itself was a connection to her he was loath to give up. He had made a few marks of his own in pencil, to make it easier to find things, and once he'd retrieved it, he flipped to the pages that he thought might be relevant.

There wasn't anything specific to calling an uncanny; most sigils were protective or defensive, or the simple restraining one he'd used on the brownie. But a few pages after that was something that he thought they could use. He changed his shoes and replaced his vest with a sweater, then went back downstairs.

———

"It's not perfect," he said to Rosemary a few minutes later, showing her the page in question, "but it will work."

"You *think* it will work," she corrected him.

He frowned. "I think that it will work, yes. This was your idea; do you have something else in mind we should try instead?"

She didn't. She'd already admitted she didn't. "Go change," he told her. "I'll gather what we'll need."

Aaron knew he should get permission from Mrs. Wesson before taking anything from the toolshed he did not plan to return, but at this point, seeking forgiveness—or better yet, not admitting to anything at all—seemed to be a better choice.

It took some rummaging, and narrowly missing a concussion from the tools hanging from the ceiling, but he acquired a small jar of white paint and a mostly clean brush, plus some cloth rags. His nose wrinkled as he shook out the mouse droppings and took the cleanest bits he could find. Mrs. Wesson needed a cat or two, clearly. Or the yet-unseen Bernard needed to clean more often.

By the time he made it back to the parlor, his finds stored in a canvas satchel he'd also found in the shed, Rosemary was waiting not only with his coat and muffler, but also a thermos from the kitchen into which she was pouring the remainder of the tea, and a small pile of winter apples.

"It's going to be a cold walk," she said when he raised an eyebrow. "Or did you think to summon up an automobile as well?"

"I'd thought borrow a horse," he said, just to see her expression. Rosemary could ride, they both could; their parents had seen to that, but neither of them enjoyed it overmuch.

Thermos under his arm, and apples carefully packed in their coat pockets, they pulled on gloves and hats and stepped outside to fetch the hound.

Rosemary hadn't been wrong about the weather; when he'd ducked out to the shed, he'd barely felt the cold, but once they'd collected Bother and left the relative shelter of the houses lining the street, the air turned damp and chill, biting into exposed skin. The sky overhead was thick with clouds, and although he wasn't particularly sensitive to weather changes, his earlier feeling that there was a storm on the way only intensified. Hopefully, they would be home before it reached them.

The only one of them not affected by the weather was Botheration. His fur might be short, but it was thick enough to keep him warmer than all the wool coats or cashmere mufflers a body could wear.

Rosemary had a piece of paper in her gloved hands, neatly written directions filling the page to lead them out of town, across the wood-and-iron rail tracks, and due north into open farmland.

"Mrs. Wesson?"

"Mr. Wilder, actually. He is an ardent bird-watcher, it seems, and claims to have walked every mile of this region. He seemed quite pleased that I felt capable of walking the distance."

Aaron snorted as he took a bite out of one of the apples, the white flesh soft but still tart on his tongue. "Yes, you're a delicate little thing, aren't you."

He ducked when she threw one of her own apples at him, catching it easily and tucking it into his own pocket for later.

Once out of town proper, the road widened, but also lost the macadam surfacing, and the Harkers had to be careful to avoid snow-muddy ruts as well as the ice-covered ditches along the side. Several automobiles passed them along the way, but none stopped to offer them a ride. Watching Bother stride forward like a young bear, tugging at his lead, Aaron found he couldn't blame them.

The road wound its way through fenced-in fields, now bare for the winter, and the occasional small herd of cows standing huddled together, then sent them through wooded areas, clumps of towering pines and thick-trunked maples, the occasional chestnut, while squirrels ran along the branches and by the road, chittering their agitation at the intruders. Sweat pooled under Aaron's arms and ran down his back but did nothing to offset the cold. Rosemary's nose was flushed pink, and he suspected his own looked little better. They did not speak, keeping their breath warm inside their mouths, and if Rosemary was running the plan through her thoughts over and over again, trying to find a way to make it better, Aaron could not say, but he certainly was.

But in the end, he came back to their original plan, with nothing better for it.

They drank the tea, and ate a few more of the apples, pitching the cores into the tree roots as they passed, competing to see whose aim was the best.

Past the woods, there was a single farmhouse by the road.

A woman was taking down laundry in her yard. He could only imagine they looked like vagabonds, with dust on their shoes and sweat on their limbs, and the look she gave them was nothing short of suspicious. Rosemary lifted a hand to wave, but the woman did not respond.

Another hill, as the sun arched overhead, and then it was downhill to flatter ground, and the wide stretch of rocks leading to the grayish-blue waters of Lake Ontario. The beach itself was narrow, red-hued stones at their back and marching down to the water's edge like sentinels, interspersed by those that had fallen flat, smaller rocks and pebbles scattered between. It was lovely, in an eerie sort of way.

Wavelets were breaking against the shore with loud slaps, and out in the distance, Aaron could see the storm pelting down on the water, the wind swirling off the lake filled with moisture. It wasn't ideal for what he'd need to do, but shy a downpour, it would do. He just needed to move faster than the storm.

Rosemary passed him the thermos, and he drank the last of the tea, grimacing at the now-chilled bitterness.

"The walk back is going to be horrible," she said, as though it had just occurred to her. He eyed the dark clouds across the lake and kept his mouth shut. Maybe they'd get lucky. But he doubted it.

Botheration was splayed out on the rocky beach, hind legs stretched out behind him in possibly the least-dignified position he'd ever seen the hound take, collar and leash coiled by Rosemary's side, where she was perched on a wide, flat rock embedded into the sand.

Aaron pulled the paint and brush from the satchel and pried the lid of the jar open with the edge of his knife, then dipped the brush in and swirled it about to mix the paint. It was yellowing and watery with age, but it would do the trick.

"We'll be too tired to care how cold it is," Aaron said as he made the first mark on a flat rock the size of his hand. "Or possibly dead."

She grimaced. "Thank you for that incredibly cheering thought."

"If you've come up with a better idea, I'm willing to listen." Aaron kept moving as he spoke, the wet paint glimmering lightly against the red-hued rocks.

There was silence, and when he glanced up, Rosemary had pulled her knees up to her chest, arms wrapped around them, and was staring out into the rippling waters of Lake Ontario, her face half-hidden by the brim of her hat. On a summer's day, it might have been a pleasant sight, but the storm had stolen all vibrancy from the air, leaving it a dull pewter.

"Rosie?" He called her name just to see her move, as though she might have turned to stone when he'd looked away.

"I'm here," she said, her voice a tad sharp.

"Just checking," he said anyway.

And so they were back where they'd been that morning, tight and tense and ready to snap at each other.

Rosemary ate another apple, pitching the core underhand into the water and watching as it sank without a trace.

"Some fish will be rather confused by that," Aaron said mildly, finishing another rock and staring at it critically. He was not seeking to paint a masterpiece, only to mark a few of the rocks with the right sigils, but they had to be exactly right. There was no near thing with sigils; either they did what they were meant to do, or they did nothing at all.

In his quietest, most private thoughts, Aaron acknowledged that what they were was magic, and suspected that belief was what made them work. But it was too difficult a thought to speak out loud, even to Rosemary. Perhaps especially to Rosemary.

She looked over at his work, and a small shudder passed through her that had nothing to do with the wind. "I know I was the one who suggested it, but I don't like this."

"It's just another trap," he pointed out, finishing another rock and moving on to the next.

"It's not the same thing," she retorted, swinging around on her perch to look at him rather than the waters. "Honest traps are one thing, but this, and what we did to the brownie . . . I don't like it. It's coercion. And I don't like that you know so much about how to make them."

"I know you don't like it," he said, shoving the *magic* thought down even further. "But I won't reject a tool that works. Not without good reason."

She scrunched up her mouth. "The Church says that it's magic, and it's wrong."

Hearing her say that word was like an electric shock, and he winced. "Jesus worked miracles."

"Aaron." Her tone tried for scandalized, but he could hear the laughter in it, and he relaxed, just a bit.

"If you're going to bring up the Church, when you haven't been to services since you started wearing long skirts, I'm going to commit as much blasphemy as I can think of."

Neither of them had much use for organized religion, although they held membership with the local Episcopal church in New Haven to smooth the social waters and maintain certain useful connections.

"Still." Rosemary sighed. "We don't know how these sigils work, or even *why*."

"The same way cold iron works to bind an uncanny, and silver to disinfect a wound; because there is some logic in the world that connects them in useful ways."

"In other words, you have no idea."

"None whatsoever," he admitted. "But not knowing the science behind it does not mean that there is no science." Thinking about it that way helped.

"And sorcery?"

"Is what people who didn't know better called science they didn't understand yet. Or it was the work of charlatans pulling wool for money."

Magic, something deep within Aaron murmured again, and he slammed the door on it, hard. That way lay madness, and more arguments he couldn't bear to have.

"Four deaths," he reminded his sister, instead. "Four, and the Aksha said it was just getting started."

"I know." She had turned her back to him again, and the wind muffled her voice. "Just do it."

He painted the last sigil and placed the paintbrush next

to the paint container, stepping back to observe his work. Eighteen marks, three each six times. "One for calling, one for protection, and one for thanking," he recited, double-checking his work to ensure they were all painted correctly, with no drips or smears that might ruin the work. Rosemary got up off the larger rock she had been sitting on and joined him in placing rocks in a wide half circle facing the shoreline, leaving twenty paces from one end to the other.

"We stand just outside it," he told her, "and then call the Aksha. It will be restricted to the half circle."

"Theoretically."

"Theoretically it will work at all," he said. "Worst-case scenario, we stand here for an hour and look like damp idiots."

"No," she said, taking her place beside him at one end of the half arc. "Worst-case scenario, the creature shows up, is not bound by the sigils at all, and eats us."

He had no comeback for that.

That was the plan, as much as they had one. Summon the uncanny who had warned them, pull it from its home, and hold it until it agreed to tell them what they needed to know. He hadn't been wrong that they were splitting moral hairs about the difference between a summoning and a binding, and Aaron was honestly surprised that Rosemary had agreed, once he'd shown the sigils to her, save that she thought he would go ahead and do it without her if she refused.

He might have. He was just glad not to know for certain.

They could have tried this on the banks of the river, since the uncanny had appeared there, but merfolk liked deeper water, and Rosemary had said that the librarian had only known stories about local lake creatures. It was probable that the river was merely a road, while the lake was home, and they'd more chance of finding it at home.

Probable, but not proven. It was all a risk. Here, at least, there was far less chance of being seen. Explaining this would have been awkward.

He held out his left arm, palm up. Rosemary sighed, but flicked open her jackknife and made a diagonal incision across his wrist, enough to bleed freely, but not so much that they would have to bind it immediately. She had offered to be the sacrifice, but he trusted her fighting skills more than his own; if things went badly, he wanted her to have his back.

Three drops of blood swelled up and he turned his wrist over, then walked a few paces along the arc and waited for another three drops, continuing in a ragged half circle until there were eighteen splats of red on the sand to match the eighteen sigils. Rosemary had cleaned her knife and put it away, and was waiting for him, a piece of the ragged cloth in her hand, wetted with lake water. He allowed her to clean the wound, wincing a little at the touch of the damp cloth. Then she used it to put pressure on the wound until he elbowed her aside. "You didn't cut that deeply. It'll be fine."

She made a face, but backed off a little, seating herself on another rock and gesturing for him to begin.

Facing the half circle, he lifted his gaze to the growing chop of the water and recited:

"Aksha. Te povikuvam, ne za šteta tuku za znaenje. Te po-vikuvam ne za bolka, tuku za učenje. Te povikuvam, ne za zlo, tuku za pomošta na čoveštvoto. I summon thee, not for harm but knowledge. I summon thee, not for pain but for learning. I summon thee, not for ill but for the help of mankind."

He had found the calling summons in one of his books years before and added it to his notebook out of idle curios-ity rather than any thought that it would someday be useful. Their mother had always said that there was no useless knowledge, only things you hadn't had need of yet, and he might have taken that saying a bit too much to heart as a child.

The language was Macedonian, near as he could tell, and he had to trust the translation that came with it to be accu-rate. The sounds had rumbled in his ear as he was speaking them, but there was no reaction from the sigils, and when he finished, the shores were as bare and barren as they'd been before they started.

"So." He eased his posture a little, letting his heels settle into the sand and pressing his shoulders down away from his ears, feeling the tension in his back protest. "How long do you think we need to wait before admitting it's a flop?"

"Not long, probably," Rosemary said, her voice tight. "Look at the waves."

He followed her pointing finger, sighting over the top of her wrist, and saw what she had already spotted: out past the breaking wavelets there was a hump of water moving forward at a steady pace, angling not within the waves but diagonally across them.

"It's moving quickly," he noted, astonished that his voice was steady. He didn't want to take his eyes off the lump, half-afraid it would disappear, half wishing that it would, but the glint of metal made his gaze flicker toward her. Rather than the smaller blade she'd used to nick his arm, she had taken the larger hunting knife out of its sheath, holding it ready in her right hand.

"You might want to get your gun," she suggested.

"I summoned it with words of parley. Holding a weapon would put lie to that."

"Fine. Then give it to me."

His Colt was heavier than her Browning, and a smidge more accurate: at the distance they would likely be looking at, her demand made perfect sense, and he handed it to her without demur. The click and snap of her checking the chamber wasn't as reassuring as it normally would have been, however, because he'd just noted something.

"There's another hump."

She dropped the knife in the lap of her skirt and shifted the pistol to her left hand. "Two of them?"

"Maybe." He'd used the name they'd been given but hadn't thought to consider that it might be the name of a species, rather than a specific creature. If so, the sigil would have called any within reach.

Or more than one.

"Oh hell," Rosemary breathed, even as the first lump reached the breaking water and lifted above the waves.

―――――――――

Already the plan was going to hell. Aaron was staring at the rising wave coming toward them, his feet planted square on the rocky shore, his coat flapping slightly at his legs. "That's not the Aksha."

"You think?" Rosemary slid the knife back into its sheath and firmed her grip on the larger pistol, despite being reasonably certain that, shy of a lucky shot, it wasn't going to do more than make the creature unhappy. At her side, Bother growled, deep and low in his chest.

The head that rose from the waters looked nothing like the uncanny they had met by the riverbank, save for the fluttering green tendrils flowing from it. Where that one had been vaguely human-shaped, this was the head of a monstrous beast, with a long muzzle that tapered up from snout to a broader base, lacking visible ears, although they could be hidden by the weed-like streamers. The mouth was open, and while Rosemary could not see into the gap at this distance, she had no doubt that it was filled with teeth worthy of a shark, many and sharp.

And at that distance, she was bowel-chillingly aware of how massive the creature was, that she could make out even those details.

"Holy mother of Jesus."

She tilted the hand holding the pistol toward Aaron, offering it back, but he shook his head, still determined to keep to his side of the summoning.

He was right, though she hated to admit it. Whatever this thing was, if it had come in response to the sigil-calling, then it would be bound by the terms, so long as he held to them as well.

If it hadn't . . . well, they were likely dead no matter what.

She settled her stance more firmly in the rocky sand and lifted her elbows, both hands wrapped comfortingly around the grip. There wasn't anything so uncanny that blood loss wouldn't kill it.

The beast came closer and closer, slipping through the water like a knife, the head lifted above the waves, with the now-visible ripple of a long body behind it. Botheration took a step forward, just waiting for the command to dive into the waves and start ripping the thing to shreds.

"Step back," Aaron said.

"What?" Her voice cracked on the word, and she cursed herself for it.

"Step back, both of you," he repeated. "Let it focus on me, as the one who summoned it. If it does anything—"

"I'm shooting it."

"Agreed, yes, but not until then." He canted his head, staring at the lake's surface. "I want to know what the hell it is."

"If you're dead, you won't be able to tell anyone," she reminded him, but stepped back two steps. "Bother, hold still."

The hound grumbled, but obeyed.

The uncanny stopped just shy of the shoreline, still

mostly covered by water and centered within the half circle of sigil-stones. Rosemary didn't dare hope that the half circle would contain it, but her muscles eased just a hair, no longer presuming an attack would happen immediately. The head, she judged uneasily, was nearly the length of her torso, and yes, the mouth was filled with teeth, small and sharp and on full display as it stared at Aaron.

"Thank you for responding to my call, although I think you are not who I summoned," Aaron said, and if she hadn't known him well enough to hear the quaver in his voice, she'd think he was greeting an old acquaintance. "You are not Aksha?"

A bird cried out somewhere, harsh and angry, and the uncanny's head slid forward a notch, then back again. If it was meant to be in response to Aaron's question, Rosemary couldn't tell if it was a yes, no, or maybe. Or if it had merely been annoyed by the noise.

"Do you have a name?"

The creature moved its neck forward again, farther toward the shore this time, as though it were peering at him. Rosemary's gaze was drawn away from its head, distracted by movement below. She bit back a gasp, seeing the elongated neck lifting from the water, revealing a thicker torso, with what looked to be haunches supporting it, crouching on the lake's floor. Not a snake or serpent, her Huntsmen's mind coolly categorizing it. Some sort of giant lizard? But the skin seemed smooth, more like a seal's, and those teeth . . .

Her gaze went back up to the head, now far too close to Aaron. God's mercy, those teeth.

"Aaron . . ." She hadn't meant to call out to him, the word slipping out, just above a whisper. She didn't want to take her eyes off the uncanny, terrified that the moment she did so it would strike, but she forced herself to move her head, just enough that her brother was in view again.

He stood like one of the rocks farther up on the beach, still as stone, his coat open, bareheaded, hair tousled from its usual sleeked-back look. He looked at the uncanny, and the uncanny looked at him, and Rosemary had to force herself to relax her arms, not to raise the pistol and fire.

"Can you communicate with us?"

They'd assumed the uncanny they were summoning would be able to speak, as it had before. But that had been human-form, with a mouth that could shape words, whatever the intellect behind them. This . . .

This was a beast. A monster.

The uncanny slid forward until its nose was nearly even with the line of sand, and more of its body was revealed. Rosemary forced her fear down, her mind cataloging the details, cool professionalism keeping the horror at bay. Definitely lizard-like, with forelimbs that lifted it up on the sand, but the way it moved was more of a snake's slither, back and forth. She regretted now having never seriously studied the sea-bound uncanny. There were Huntsmen who knew more, but even in port towns, it was rare that any appeared. She'd never entirely bought the tales of massive sea monsters that could take on a military frigate and win, or kraken who posed real threats to the safety of passengers on an ocean liner.

Rosemary thought that she might rather have to apologize for her doubts.

Aaron did not back away from the creature, even when its neck brought it within lunging distance. One dart forward, and it could catch Aaron up in that awful mouth, could bite down, and— Her elbow firmed, the pistol rising without conscious thought. One shot, she'd only have one shot. Not the neck, with its thickly corded muscles, or the head . . . The eye. She needed to catch it in the eye.

Aaron raised the arm nearest to her as though he knew what she was doing, and pointed his fingers down. She shook her head, although he wasn't looking at her, but lowered the pistol again, halfway.

"Can you speak?" Aaron asked again.

A low hiss came from the uncanny's mouth, and her hand pressed around the trigger guard, itching to slip and fire. Sensing action, Botheration took a pace forward, and the uncanny's head swiveled to look at them. The eyes were huge, set to the forefront of the narrow skull and protected by a thin ridge over each, like bony eyebrows. At this distance, they looked to be entirely black, no white at all visible. She did not raise the pistol higher, but calculated what it would take to hit that target.

"Speeeek." The monstrous jaw opened to let the word escape, the massive head dipping once, the long green tendrils hanging from its neck swaying as it moved. Then it reared its neck back up, rising from the water until the head was above them, and one massive paw reached out of the water, thick black claws like a dog's curving out of webbing the same color as the tendrils on its neck, and placed the paw on the break between water and land; not quite leaving the lake, but showing that it could.

"Speek. Ysssssss."

Her entire life, Rosemary had been taught that only the human-derived uncanny had the power of rational thought, that the others were nothing more than dangerous beasts, capable of only the most rudimentary logic, of aping behaviors rather than understanding them. She was finding it difficult to let go of that, even with her heart beating double-time, and the evidence directly in front of her.

Aaron moved on to the next item on the List of Interrogating Uncanny. "What is your name?"

The massive black eyes were covered briefly by a thin film, then heavier eyelids dropped down, closing entirely before opening again, the head tilting to one side as though it did not understand the question.

Rosemary desperately wanted to take the uncanny's lack of comprehension as proof that it was nothing more than a creature, that the summons had merely called the nearest uncanny, or that it had not been drawn by it at all, but random chance.

But the tilt of its head, the way it scratched at the rocky surf, the way it looked at Aaron, then tilted its head again and looked at her . . . that was not the behavior of a dumb creature, but one that simply did not understand the question.

What had those stories said about the sea-uncanny? She

had listened, even if she hadn't believed, so there must be something useful in her memory. . . .

"Bother. Wait." The hound, who had been grumbling under his breath, body tense and waiting for the command to attack, sat on his haunches but did not take his gaze off the beast. He had been bred to track and take down uncanny and did not understand why the command to do so had not been given, but was too well-trained to question it.

"Watch."

His thick whip of a tail thumped once, erect ear pointed forward and eyes unblinking. No matter what the uncanny did, he would stay in position until she or Aaron gave him his next command.

She left him there and moved closer to Aaron, careful not to step past any of the sigil-rocks, or disturb them in any way. "Sea serpents are supposed to be territorial," she said softly. "And Nessie's the only one of its kind ever spotted. Allegedly."

"So?"

"So it may not have a name, because there's nothing out there to distinguish it from." And somehow that was the saddest thing Rosemary had ever thought. "It doesn't understand what 'name' means, not the way you're asking it."

"It came when we summoned the Aksha." Aaron's eyes narrowed, and he turned back to the uncanny. "You aren't the Aksha. But you know it. You sent it to us?"

"Ysssssssss." The head lowered, the neck undulating in a way that made Rosemary think of a snake or an eel, something that flexed and stretched in ways nothing with limbs could match. "Sent Aksha."

"To us?" Rosemary was startled enough to speak directly to it.

"To Huntsmen. You." It seemed to have gained more control over its voice, as though it was remembering how to shape words. The jaw still did not move the way a human's would, but as the head dropped closer, Rosemary thought she could see the flickering of a tongue inside that mouth, and her own tongue moved as though trying to imagine how it was pushing the words out into the air.

"You knew we were there?" Well, that wasn't alarming at all.

"Huntsmen would come. Sent Aksha to find."

"Because of the murders." Aaron took a step forward, his toes butting up against the line of the half circle, enough that she drew an involuntary breath of alarm, but he didn't look down. "You knew about the murders, knew about Huntsmen, knew we would come to investigate. How?"

The uncanny's snort blew warm salty spray onto them, pungent with the smell of fish and brine. All right, Rosemary supposed the reaction was fair; Huntsmen took care to hide their actions from other humans, not the uncanny. If it knew of the murders, it would have to assume a Huntsman would come.

But how had it known, unless—

"You didn't kill them." Aaron made it a statement, not a question, and he was right; there was no way this creature could have traveled upriver without being noticed, come out onto land—assuming it could even move on land—and returned without any excitement. And there would have been traces for Bother to find. "Did you send the Aksha to kill them?"

More plausible, but if so, then why would the Aksha have also warned them? There were too many details that did not make sense, starting with why those men had been killed in the first place.

The uncanny pulled back, the tendrils on its neck rippling as though agitated. She thought she saw gills moving underneath. "Things stir on land. Disturbing air. Disturbing water. Things that should not, that must not." The tendrils fluttered, the gills working more obviously in what looked like agitation or upset.

"Huntsmen find it. Stop it. Or we all die."

"It will kill more people?"

"Kill all. Everything. You stop it."

"We can't if we don't know what it is." Aaron rarely lost his temper, but he could feel it coming to a boiling point, the frustration of the past few days heated by the uncanny's demand. And there was no way around it, it was a demand.

"You stop it."

"Stop what?" He was dizzy with the frustration, his skin tight and aching with it.

"It doesn't know," Rosemary said, barely a whisper, feeling more of the pieces slot together. "It doesn't know what the killer is either. But it scares them. It terrifies them."

The uncanny drew back again, the neck uncoiling until it could look down over their heads, the suggestion of shoulders rising well above the water to display more of the body, thick and sleek, and easily larger than an automobile, if smaller than a train car. It did not glitter under the winter sun like she would expect from a fish or lizard, but seemed instead to absorb all light into itself, the gray of the sky and the gray of the water matched by the gray of the skin. "You cause it. You stop it."

And with that, it dropped smoothly back into the waters, causing ripples to push back against the waves, and slid, faster than their eyes could follow, back into the surf, disappearing into the greenish-gray waters without further sign.

"That was fun," Aaron said, before he wobbled slightly and dropped like a deadweight to the sand.

Fourteen

AARON WOKE TO a very large, very wet tongue trying to wipe his face off.

"Ugh, oh God, off."

"Bother, it's all right, he's awake now."

The hound backed off, but only far enough that he could sit by Aaron's hip, his blunt head even with Aaron's face, clearly ready to swoop to the rescue again should Aaron close his eyes or otherwise do anything disturbing.

His sister was crouched a little distance away, watching him intently. "How do you feel?"

"Like I was dropped into a quarry and crushed with rocks," he said honestly, forcing himself to sit up on his elbows, which caused Botheration to scoot back a little. Rosemary knelt on the sand on his other side, her expression worried but not panicked. She stretched out an ungloved hand and pressed two bare fingers to his neck, feeling the beat of his blood.

"Will I live?" he asked, only half joking.

"Yes," she said. "But you may not be happy about it. At the

risk of you filling with manly bluster, if we see a vehicle on the road, I strongly recommend that we hail it, even if it means Bother has to make his way home alone."

He tried to sit up on his own and groaned. "I won't argue with you on that."

They made it back to the road just as a wagon was going by. Rosemary stepped out into the road and hailed the driver.

He pulled the horse to a stop and looked them over. "You lost?"

"My brother fell. I'm not sure he can make it back to town on his own."

"Hrm." There was a drawn-out pause while the man eyed the three of them and then sighed. "You willing to ride with the hay, get in."

Rosemary had to boost Aaron into the back, then wait for Botheration to leap up before joining them. They'd only just gotten settled when the rain that had been threatening began to fall, a steady, light drizzle that made Aaron's hair curl beyond all control, and the wind picked up enough to almost take Rosemary's hat off her head before she finally took it off and held it in her lap.

Aaron could feel every bump and rut in the road, but he wasn't so stubborn he'd deny that it was better than trying to limp home. And the hay bales, while prickly even through the cloth of his coat and pants, did a good job of cutting the chill of the air.

"That was a complete toss," Rosemary said, plucking at

the band of her hat, a faded blue ribbon that was slightly the worse for the day's outing.

"Oh, I don't know," he said, trying to get more comfortable. "We know more than we did before, and no one got eaten. I'd say that was a success."

Rosemary's glare wasn't diminished in the slightest by the strands of damp hair now plastered across her forehead.

"More, but not enough." She sighed. "If we only had that journal . . . no, we're not breaking into the police house again."

He hadn't, actually, been about to suggest that, but he nodded anyway. "Without knowing where they've stashed it, or if they've kept it at all, it would be folly to try again, I agree. I think visiting your librarian once more would serve us better."

"She's hardly my librarian," Rosemary protested, reaching out to hold the side of the wagon as it went over a particularly large bump.

" 'The lady doth protest too much, methinks.' " He started to tease her further, but something in her eyes stopped him. "If you don't want to go see her again . . ."

"No." Her chin firmed and her lips pursed, before she shook her head. "No, it's fine."

It wasn't fine, even he could tell that, although he had no idea why.

"You're right, she's the most likely to have information. I should follow the lake monster angle, you think?"

"Start there," he agreed. "Shake the tree a bit, see what falls out."

The farmer let them off just outside of town proper, where the road split to head south, and they walked the rest of the way back to the boarding house, thankful that the rain had tapered off to a thick mist. They were still bedraggled as catfish by the time they arrived at their doorstep.

"Back to your kennel," Aaron told Botheration. "Quietly, now." It was a risk, letting him show his true nature in daylight, but the chance of anyone watching the kennel at that moment was low, in this weather, and neither of them wanted to wait even a minute longer to get out of their wet clothing.

The hound whined a little, casting his gaze up at both of them as though aware that he was going to be left out of the next part of their hunt, but both Harkers stood resolute.

"Go," Rosemary said again, and the hound went.

They didn't enter the house as unnoticed as they'd hoped; Jan was coming through the front hall, her hands filled with dried cattails to put in the front parlor. She stopped to take in their condition, and a series of emotions passed over her face, settling finally on resigned amusement. "There's a meanness in that storm. I've brought extra towels up to your rooms," she said. "And I've hung a mackintosh up in the closet for you, miss, not knowing if you'd brought one. You'll want it when you go out again."

When, not if. And with that she disappeared into the parlor, pulling the door shut behind her and leaving the Harkers to stare at each other in bemusement.

"Odd duck," Aaron said again, washing his hands of the matter, and gestured for his sister to precede him up the stairs.

As Jan had promised, there was a towel neatly folded at the foot of his bed, dry and warm. Aaron made short work of stripping off his clothing and draping it over the straight-backed chair to dry, toeing off damp wool socks with a grimace. When he'd thought that their clothing needed a wash, that had not been what he'd meant.

A brisk toweling-down left him dry but chilled, and he quickly pulled on a new pair of pants and shirt, choosing one of his fancier waistcoats and a sack jacket before adding pomade to his hair and styling it in a fashion better suited to town than country. Checking himself in the mirror, he nodded. The perfect facade of a well-bred idiot, if he did say so himself.

Checking his watch, he frowned. It was later than he'd thought. He picked up his coat and left his room, knocking gently on Rosemary's door, prepared to warn her to hurry. But when the door opened, she was already dressed, hair and attire as fresh as if she'd spent all day doing nothing more strenuous than needlepoint, the promised overcoat draped over her arm and an umbrella in her hand.

"I will never know how you manage that," he said, gesturing at her. "Ten minutes, and you look as though you've spent all day in the parlor."

"It's not as though you didn't do the same thing," she

said, as they went downstairs, thankfully unobserved by anyone.

"My toilet is far simpler. One of the great reliefs of being born male is that, so long as I hold my liquor reasonably well and don't insult young girls or matrons, I may do as I please and be acceptable." He smirked at her look of disgust. "Besides, you're the one she's going to be focused on. I'm just the slightly lackwit brother"—and he affected his best vaguely dim-witted expression—"who supports you in your endeavors."

A fellow in England had advocated that affect, saying that it was the surest way to encourage others to speak freely in your presence. Normally Aaron preferred to play alert rather than buffoon, but from what Rosemary had said of her librarian, he suspected confirming a low opinion of men would work better.

"You're far too good at that," Rosemary said, slipping her hand into the crook of his elbow as they stepped onto the sidewalk. "If all else fails, perhaps we should take to the stage. We'd be quite the sensation, don't you think?"

They'd known an actress once, a friend of their father's. She'd told them they would in fact be a sensation on the stage, and cautioned them against ever considering it seriously.

But the tricks she'd taught them had stood them in good stead since then.

The walk to the library was a cold and dreary one, their umbrella fighting a valiant battle against the rain, as though Nature herself had fallen into an irritable mood and sought to take it out on anyone who dared venture into the streets. A mean storm, Jan had called it. It was a relief to turn the corner and see that the electric lights of the library were still on, although the glooming air and rainy mist seemed conspiring to overwhelm them from outside. Rosemary took a deep breath, settled her shoulders, and walked up to the door like a smaller version of the storm overhead, pushing it open as though she were entering her own home, Aaron trailing a step behind.

Before the other woman could do more than look up from her desk, Rosemary had started speaking. "Miss Baker, I am so glad to find you here, and not yet gone home for dinner."

Rosemary handed the umbrella to Aaron to close before unfastening the mack and shaking the rain from its hem, every inch confident in her welcome.

"Well. Hello again." Miss Baker had smiled when she saw Rosemary come in, but that smile seemed to flicker slightly when she noticed Aaron following at her heels, before a polite public mask fell over her features.

Smart, was Aaron's first impression, then: handsome, not pretty. Terrified.

Aaron kept his fatuous expression firmly in place, taking his hat off and holding it in both hands like a supplicant. "Miss Baker, is it? My sister has told me how helpful you were as she indulged in her hobby. She had hopes you would be able to aid her further?"

I'm just here as escort, he tried to convey. *Don't pay any attention to me at all, I'm harmless and possibly a little helpless.*

Her polite smile didn't falter, but she didn't respond to his greeting. If he'd been a betting man, he would have just won himself a five-spot. Suffragette or simple man-hater, she wouldn't react well to his charm. Rosemary's, on the other hand . . .

He'd wondered occasionally if his sister might not prefer the company of women, but it was hardly the sort of question one could ask, not even of one's own sister.

Rosemary seemed not to notice Miss Baker's coolness toward her brother, seating herself on the single chair before Miss Baker's desk and settling her skirts around her while Aaron shuffled off his own coat and took up a nonchalant slouch against the wall.

"I was waiting until the rain passed before leaving," Miss Baker said with a sigh, gesturing with one hand toward the windows. "I'd not been expecting a storm when I left this morning, and unlike yourselves, came without a bumbershoot. I really should know better, this time of year." She shook her head, smiling a little ruefully, then continued. "And not that I'm not pleased to see you again, because of course I am, but I have to sadly admit that I have not made much progress on the items you asked me to research. I thought you might have gone home already?"

There was more than one question in those words, Aaron thought, although he was not entirely sure what they might be.

"Ah, well, we've been rather taken with this town, so decided to extend our stay a little longer." He knew his sister well enough that even with her back to him he could imagine the soft smile and flick of her lashes, inviting her companion to laugh at her flightiness. It was an effective trap even he fell prey to, occasionally. "This morning, while it was still clear, we took a walk along the shore of Lake Ontario. It's quite striking, isn't it? All those pillars of rock, so brightly colored."

"Oh, that must have been a lovely walk, yes, although quite long! Red sandstone, and limestone, and some quartz, I believe?"

The woman seemed oddly relieved to have a different topic of conversation, and, he thought, was possibly showing off for Rosemary. There was definitely a flicker of something between the two, if even he was able to see it.

"But I imagine the waters were far too cold to be hospitable." The woman gave a delicate shudder, and Rosemary laughed, leaning forward and placing her fingertips on the desk, creating an immediate sense of intimacy between them that had the other woman's cheeks flushing.

"Indeed! Even Botheration, our hound, had no desire to touch paw into the waves. I shall have to return in warmer weather. But while we were there, we encountered a most curious old man."

Aaron smiled briefly, aware that neither of them were paying him the slightest attention. "Old" was a presumption, "male" was a guess. Determining the gender of most uncanny was notoriously difficult, and effectively pointless.

"Indeed?" As Rosemary had predicted on the way over, Miss Baker took the lure, leaning forward to match Rosemary's silent invitation. "A beachcomber, full of wild tales?"

"Certainly with a tale to tell. Of a serpent that lives in the waters with others of its kin, fully twenty feet long and able to swim like a whale, deep under the surface. It is full of magic powers, and if caught in your nets would tell your fortune, good or ill."

Someday when they'd retired, Rosemary would need to write down the stories she had spun over the years, and make them a tidy sum to live by.

"Oh dear." He came alert, without moving an inch. Miss Baker's voice was different now, a new note introduced into it, and Aaron flicked his gaze casually to her face, catching only the hint of something shifting in her expression. "I'm afraid he was having a bit of sport with you, Miss Harker."

Aaron knew he wasn't the best at reading people, but he hadn't imagined it. There was something in her voice that hadn't been there a sentence before. Not disbelief; he knew all the strains of that, intimately.

Fear.

His first impression had been right; something had frightened this woman. The uncanny they'd seen? Possible; if she knew the shoreline they'd walked, she might have seen it before; Rosemary's words might have brought it back. But that answer didn't feel right.

There was no way to alert Rosemary, if she hadn't caught it already. He could only hope that she had.

"Oh, we assumed it was nothing but a tale." His sister, not releasing Miss Baker from their shared gaze, waved one hand in airy dismissal of the nonexistent storyteller. "But he told it so very well, and you had spoken earlier of the creature said to live in Lake Erie, that I wondered if there was any such story of a beast living in Lake Ontario as well, or if the old man was simply transporting the beast for convenience in storytelling."

A heartbeat pause, and Aaron kept his gaze soft but focused, watching Miss Baker while appearing not to be paying any attention whatsoever. He saw her shoulders slide downward half a notch, and her head tilt to one side. Whatever she said, he thought, would not be what she was thinking.

"Lake Ontario may simply be too small for such things, although the local tribes had all sorts of stories, each one more fanciful than the last." The librarian ticked each one off on a manicured finger. "They claimed that the mist over the lakes was the spirit of a sacrificed princess, that a horned beast lived deep in the waters, and that the world was carried on the back of a turtle! Fascinating, to be certain, but not to be taken seriously. Magic and monsters are children's tales, as you said."

"A horned beast? Fascinating." Rosemary's voice was still

playful, but he knew that she was thinking the same as he: the uncanny serpent had ridges on its head, clearly meant to protect its eye sockets, which if seen only briefly could be taken for horns, low-curling like a ram's.

He closed his eyes, the better to focus on what they were saying. Willing himself to *hear* what was being said, not merely what was being spoken.

"But it did not tell fortunes, nor give luck," the librarian continued, clearly warming to her topic, whatever her earlier concerns might have been. "The beast was considered so dangerous, only the wisest of elders might speak with it, to distinguish truth from lies, and woe to the ones who chose wrong." She laughed then, a too-deliberately shimmery sound that rang flat and false in his ears. "Those are not stories I would tell to children, unless you wished to give them a fear of swimming!"

He couldn't see his sister, but from the soft scuffing and creaking noises, he imagined her moving her hands back to her lap and leaning back in her chair. "Of course, of course." A nod of her head, a half smile on her face. "But still, there are ways to turn stories, to make them more pleasant for the telling. And they are only stories, are they not?"

There was a pause before Miss Baker responded. If Aaron had been watching, rather than only listening, he might not have caught it, distracted by a sweep of the hand or a turn of the head, or a charming smile. But to the ear, it was as obvious as if someone had slammed shut a door.

Miss Baker did not believe that they were only stories.

The streets of Brunson were becoming nearly as familiar as those of their neighborhood in New Haven, although the town itself could not be more different, lacking the elaborately painted houses pushed up next to each other in favor of more somber stone and timber structures set flush against the street. Aaron lifted the umbrella over their heads and let himself enjoy the almost familiarity in quiet for a few minutes as they strolled down the street, before his sister spoke.

"You think she was lying."

"Lying is a strong word. I think she definitely knows something she isn't telling us. And whatever it is, it frightens her."

He expected Rosemary to argue with him, to defend the woman, but instead she said, "Not it. Us. She was frightened of us."

He considered that, looking at the memory of Miss Baker's face, and her voice. "Maybe," he allowed. "If she thinks we're the sort to buy into folderol like horned serpents and princesses in the woods, I could see where she'd think we were potentially dangerous lunatics."

"Don't be an ass. You saw the same thing I did: *she* believes it. I think she was worried that we might tell someone, and that she might lose her employment."

That wasn't an unfair presumption on Miss Baker's part. Unless you were born to a Huntsmen family, suggesting that there might be something other than humans walking upright in the world—or flying, or crawling in opposition to nature—

would certainly have your friends eyeing you askance, and likely worse.

"Employment and reputation," Rosemary went on. "A single woman, educated, possibly taking a job a man might have wanted? Here, no matter how modern they might think themselves? No doubt there are folk who would be happy to call her a lunatic and ship her off."

"Is that why you didn't push her?" He'd been surprised when Rosemary had ended the conversation soon after, making apologies for keeping her even the scant half hour they'd been there.

"A calculated risk. If she's that frightened, for whatever reason, she's not going to tell us anything. But I'd wager she'll need to spill to someone. Someone who knows as much as— or more than—she does."

He looked sharply at her, but their difference in height meant the brim of her hat kept him from reading her expression. "Something you want to share with your brother?"

Rosemary *hrmmmmed* under her breath. "It's human nature to share, especially a secret. What's the point of knowing, otherwise? You either hoard them or you share them, and no one becomes a librarian to hoard. She almost told me things when I first came by, but she pulled back. I think that she already has a confidante, someone who holds her secrets. And a woman who's afraid will go to someone she trusts to make it better."

"Her confidante. And you think that person might know more?"

"Unless I read her wrong, Miss Baker holds knowledge; she doesn't go out and find it herself. Yes, I think that her someone else knows more." She half turned and looked over her shoulder, intentionally tipping her hat to keep her gaze hidden. "And I think she's going to lead us to that person."

Aaron turned as well, holding the umbrella steady over them both, and saw Miss Baker, hat pulled down over her head to protect her from the rain, walking with demure haste away from the library.

"Well then. Shall we follow?"

The cold rain was now coming down just enough to keep the streets deserted, most people not at their jobs wisely hiding indoors. Thankfully, it was also enough to keep Miss Baker from pausing or looking around, since Aaron suspected they were hardly inconspicuous, lacking only the addition of Botheration to turn them into a parade.

"This is the better part of town," Rosemary observed, as the houses became slightly larger, with more ornate facades and the addition of low stone or metal gates. The streets were wider, too, with room for two vehicles to pass without scraping wheels, the macadam evenly laid.

"Not where one would expect a lady librarian to live, unless she had family money. Did you get the sense that she had family money?"

"Not in the slightest. Her clothing was in good repair, but not fashionable, and other than a single bracelet, her jewelry was paste." Rosemary's tone was rueful; she had sold most of her own jewelry after the Panic, when they were struggling to pay bills. Unlike Miss Baker, she had not replaced it with non-precious replicas.

"There." He tugged Rosemary to a halt, then turned slightly, as though admiring the thick-trunked maple growing in front of the nearest house, its leaves long-fallen and brushed away. "She's going into that house."

The house in question was set back from the street, a three-story structure of brick rather than timber or stone, with a graveled path leading to the front door, where Miss Baker was being let in by a woman in a maid's uniform.

"Very nifty," Aaron noted. "There's money in that house."

"She didn't have a key herself, so it's not her home. But there were no questions from the maid; they knew who she was, possibly were expecting her," Rosemary said.

A woman came out of the house they were standing by, accompanied by a young child bundled up so heavily against the weather they could not tell its gender. The woman gave them a curious glance; Aaron tipped his hat in return and pulled Rosemary forward so that they walked slowly past the house Miss Baker had entered.

"I know you liked her," he began, ignoring her indignant "Pshaw." "But we need to consider that Miss Baker may be actively involved with these deaths."

"You think *she* bound an uncanny?" Rosemary might be willing to accept that Miss Baker knew more than she was sharing, but that idea pushed her credulity too far.

"I—" and he had to stop, because the idea seemed impossible to him as well. The woman had appeared a twitchy but otherwise harmless thing. And yet. It happened. Particularly if the uncanny presented itself as beneficial. Like brownies; some households never knew they were infested, but others did, or suspected, and if a bowl of milk was left out overnight, or a few drops of blood spilled, it was a small price to pay for prosperity, and nothing could ever be proven, either way.

But, "People convince themselves of terrible things for a great many reasons," was all he said, and Rosemary sighed.

"And everyone has terrible needs, even librarians. But binding an uncanny? That takes nerves as well as knowledge." She shook her head. "I don't see it."

"Neither do I," he admitted. "But it would simplify things."

Her indelicate snort told him what she thought of that. "But if I'm right, and she does share her secrets with her confidante, together they might have both cause and nerve." She somehow managed to look back at the house they'd passed without visibly turning her head, a skill he'd never been able to learn. "We need to know who lives there."

"By shocking coincidence," Aaron said, poker-faced, "we happen to be expected for dinner at the home of a noted local gossip."

Rosemary smiled. "Indeed. Finding an excuse to ask will be the only difficult part. But once we have a name? If they're well-to-do, claiming to be relatives of Dr. Lovelace won't earn us entry."

"I have no idea," he admitted.

They paused at the corner while a brand-new Speedster jitney trundled by, kicking up bits of mud and ice with its wheels, its driver nearly invisible behind the large, long-haired dog sitting on his lap. "That can't be safe," Aaron said to himself, then went on. "Perhaps your story of searching out stories?"

"Claim that Miss Baker mentioned their name as a possible source?" Rosemary shook her head. "That's risky. If Miss Baker denies it, it will be her word against ours."

"And if this person is well-placed in the community, there goes any chance we have of finishing the hunt. The police would be all too glad to run us out of town on their say-so. Our only other option is confronting Miss Baker directly. It may be that she's heard rumors of an uncanny that lives in the lake, or it may be that she has seen it herself but doubts her own eyes. In either case, she's a dead end. But the off chance that she might in fact know more, that she knows of this thing that is"—and he made a gesture in the air with both hands—"'disturbing the air and water,' I think it's worth the risk."

They were almost to the boarding house now, and he could tell that his sister was having second thoughts about that plan of action. For all that she could be the fiercer of the two of them, she had a softness for people that he lacked.

"I will do it." He didn't like this plan either, but Miss Baker meant nothing to him. Once Rosemary liked someone, she tended to be more careful of them.

His sister didn't agree, but she didn't protest, either. "And what excuse will you have to go back there? 'Excuse me, Miss Baker, but we think you're withholding vital information, and it's a matter of national security that you tell us'?"

He huffed under his breath. "You mock, but it worked."

"Only because the man was a simpleton. No, you're right. A direct confrontation may be what is required. Needs must. Whatever is in this town needs to be stopped." Rosemary's hand tightened on his arm, and she rested her cheek, briefly, against his shoulder in solidarity. "No matter what it takes."

They had no sooner shed their outer garments than Mrs. Wesson appeared on the stairs, her hands planted firmly on her hips and tut-tutting so briskly Rosemary thought she might turn into a chicken.

"No more sense than children, to walk out in the rain," she scolded before they could so much as open their mouths. "Upstairs you go and change into something dry and warm. I won't have you risk dying of ague while you're under my roof. Dinner will wait, this once. Go, go, both of you, shoo."

Considering that they were in far better shape than they had been only an hour before, Rosemary thought the woman was overreacting, but she bowed her head meekly under the motherly scolding, handed over the mackintosh, and followed her brother up the stairs.

Rosemary would have changed her blouse, if only to appease the older woman, but a glance into the wardrobe reminded her that the blouse hanging there was the last clean one she had packed, and she'd still made no arrangements for laundry.

"Don't pack too much," she said, mimicking her brother's voice. "We'll be home in no time." She had no memory of why they'd been optimistic; they'd known coming in that they had no idea what they would be facing.

"To be fair," she said, turning away to unpin her hair and restyle it into a more casual knot, "it would have been difficult to predict even half of what has happened here, much less all of it. A pity that there isn't some Sight in the family after all; that would have been useful. We'll just have to wait and see."

"If you make them wait much longer, Mrs. Wesson may decide to make us go without dinner after all," Aaron said, causing her to jump; she had been so focused on tucking the wayward strands of hair under pins she hadn't heard him knock, much less open the door.

She let him pull her hand down the hallway, not particularly concerned that the woman would go back on her word. But when they got to the head of the stairs, raised voices made them both stop, just out of sight of the foyer below.

"You can't just come in here, Anthony Calune. Your mother taught you better manners than that!"

They exchanged glances, then descended the stairs together, stepping quietly. Sure enough, as they turned on the bend in the riser, they saw the patrolman who had accused them before standing in the open doorway. Mrs. Wesson was attempting to block him, with Jan a few steps behind, looking as though she'd half a mind to take a frying pan to someone's head.

"Mrs. Wesson, I'm sorry, ma'am. But this is police business." The policeman moved into the house, a second officer behind him. Their hostess huffed in indignation but gave no further protest. She glanced at Jan and gave a sharp jerk of her head; the girl nodded and disappeared back into the kitchen.

Calune raised his gaze to where they were standing on the stairs, now in clear sight, and nodded his head once in greeting. "Mr. Harker. Miss Harker. If you'd please come down, sir, ma'am?"

Behind the policemen, Mrs. Wesson now fluttered like a nervous bat, although Rosemary couldn't tell if it was due to the presence of officers in her parlor, or that said officers had come to see two of her guests.

"Are we under arrest, Officer?"

"No, sir. Not at the moment. Please. Come down."

There was a moment when, by the set of her brother's shoulders, she knew that he was considering the odds of refusing. But he came to the same conclusion she had: that they were better off bluffing their way through, if at all possible. They hadn't *done* anything that could get them into trouble . . . well, not that the police knew about. Hopefully.

By the time they reached the first floor, the second policeman was closing the door firmly behind him and placing a now-furled umbrella in the stand by the door. Their caps and shoulders showed evidence of rain despite that, she noted;

the weather must have worsened in the short time since they'd come home.

Rosemary cocked her head and recognized the sound of the wind over roof and chimneys, now that she was listening for it.

"I must protest this intrusion during the dinner hour," Mrs. Wesson said, making one last effort. "It's unseemly—"

"What's unseemly is allowing this pair to remain under your roof, ma'am, although I do not wish to tell you how to run your business."

Baxter's voice, coming from the hallway behind her; he had clearly been in the dining room, likely already seated for dinner. Dolph was nowhere to be seen; it was the first time Rosemary could remember not seeing the man standing in Baxter's shadow.

"Mr. Baxter, sir, we can handle this," the second patrolman said, and Mrs. Wesson spun on her other guest, skirt flaring, hands fisted on her hips like a fishwife. "Mr. Baxter. Have you something to do with this? Because if you do, guest or no . . ."

Rosemary's earlier imagining of the woman as a chicken returned, this time with feathers fluffed in anger rather than concern, and she felt an odd pang in her heart. But the patrolmen were fidgeting, and she couldn't see the woman's outrage going anywhere useful. "Mrs. Wesson." Rosemary reached out and placed a hand on the other woman's shoulder. "It's all right."

Mrs. Wesson kept looking at Mr. Baxter, who met her

gaze with the aplomb of a man who knew that he was perfectly in the right, until she gave a hard sniff and turned to Calune, ignoring the other officer. "In the parlor, then. And mind your voices. I'll not have you disrupt my house further."

"Ma'am. Of course."

"Jan was right about you," the woman muttered as she returned to the dining room, although it was unclear who the "you" referred to. "I should pay the girl better."

Baxter lingered, until Calune coughed gently. "We can handle this from here, sir. Why don't you go back to your meal?"

Assuming Mrs. Wesson let him sit down, Rosemary thought without any charity whatsoever, then looked at her brother, who had taken advantage of the distraction to fix a look of buttered innocence to his face. He opened the door to the parlor and gestured. "Gentlemen?"

Once within the parlor, Aaron took one of the overstuffed club chairs, sinking into it as though he had been the one who called this meeting, rather than being summoned. "Please, sit."

Rosemary took the matching chair, thankful that she'd taken the time to fix her hair before coming down; it would not have done to face the men looking like a drowned kitten. She smoothed down the fabric of her skirt, aware that the younger officer, a new face to her, was watching her hands carefully. He was young, barely Aaron's age, and a flush hit his broad, pale face when he saw her watching him. She widened her eyes, and he looked away, his blush increasing. It was inappropriate for her to smile at that, considering the circumstances, but Rosemary couldn't deny a touch of pride; she'd spent the past few days constantly washing dirt and sweat off her skin, and twigs out of her hair. Having someone admire her was definitely good for—well, perhaps not the soul, but certainly the body.

Officer Calune sat down in the upholstered chair opposite them, his cap balanced on his knees, his elbows held stiffly at his side. The Harkers waited, entirely at ease, for him to speak. When he did, the tone was half-apologetic but entirely accusatory.

"When last we spoke, you were given some excellent advice. And yet, you have not taken it."

"Of course we have," Rosemary said smoothly, placing a hand on Aaron's knee just in case he decided to take the offense being given. "You suggested that we not interfere in— what did you call them? The matters of labor in this town. As we had no interest in such matters, we have in fact kept ourselves away from them. Is that not what you wanted?" She didn't bother widening her eyes at Calune; she had already shown her hand there, and he would be rightfully suspicious of any attempt to flirt her way out of trouble. Particularly if, as it seemed, he was here not from any actions of their own, but rather Baxter's prodding.

And that would need looking into, once they were out of this.

"You expect the captain to believe that you are still here only to clean up your uncle's estate?"

Rosemary spread her hands out in a placating gesture. "As it is the truth, yes." It was in fact the absolute truth, for a vastly different definition of estate.

The younger officer's eyes followed her hands again, and she turned them over slowly, letting him look his fill. She didn't understand the fascination he seemed to have with perfectly ordinary fingers, but if it gave them an advantage, she would take it.

Calune wasn't distracted, nor convinced. "And yet, you remain. And your activities seem to have little to do with consoling Mrs. Lovelace, or taking care of Dr. Lovelace's effects, God rest his soul." He nodded to the other policeman, who jumped a little, then took a notebook from his pocket and flipped it open, reading out loud.

"Making a bother of yourself to upstanding families of this town. Harassing shopkeepers. Lurking in the streets when decent folk should be abed."

"You've been following us." Aaron didn't sound surprised, or offended, which was more than Rosemary could say for herself. How much pull—or push—did Baxter have with the local police?

Calune scoffed. "You've been acting oddly, stirring up trouble in a town where men, good men, have died. Of course we've been keeping an eye on you. This may not be a fancy city, but we're not fools, Mr. Harker. What did you think we would do, take you at your word?"

"Perhaps you will take mine?"

All four of them turned as though something had pulled

strings at their joints. Mrs. Wesson stood in the hallway, her expression still annoyed, but beside her stood Mrs. Lovelace, a cloak thrown over her shoulders and a man's hat pulled low over her forehead. She took it off, and hung it and the cloak on the rack by the door, water dripping onto the polished wooden floor. In that pause of quiet, Rosemary could hear the sound of rain and wind again, hammering against the roof and windows.

The storm they'd seen in the distance over the lake had settled in with a vengeance, it seemed.

"Ma'am." The patrolmen made as though to stand up when Mrs. Lovelace came into the parlor proper, as did Aaron, but she waved them all back, and instead made her way to the velvet-upholstered love seat, as regal as a queen.

Rosemary glanced over at Mrs. Wesson, whose lips were now curved in a faint, smugly satisfied smile, and Jan back at her side, looking flushed, her hair damp and tousled around her braid, as though she had just run to, say, a neighbor's house and then back again. The girl saw Rosemary looking, and lifted her chin and then dropped it in a subtle nod. Whatever unease Jan had felt around them seemed to have settled, although the shadows still lingered under her eyes, and Gert, half-hidden behind her, was chewing two fingernails, her eyes wide and worried.

"Thank you," Rosemary mouthed to both of them, then turned her attention back to the scene at hand.

The younger patrolman spoke up. "Mrs. Lovelace, ma'am, I—"

"And you hush, Jacob Weis. You may wear a uniform now, but I remember full well when you were in short pants, tugging at your mother's apron strings."

Jacob flinched and looked down at his own hands. Rosemary almost felt sorry for him.

"Mrs. Lovelace," Calune said, "we appreciate you coming all this way to put in a good word for your"—and there was the faintest of hesitations before he went on—"your niece and nephew. But they were given a warning and they ignored it, and now the chief told me to bring them in."

If Mrs. Wesson was a chicken, Mrs. Lovelace was an eagle. "The chief did, did he? Under what charges?"

"Mrs. Lovelace. Cousin Maggie." Aaron's voice, deeper than hers, stopped her mid-ire. "It's all right. These men have their job to do, same as we do." He held her gaze until she dropped hers, hands twisting in her lap. "And we will all do our jobs."

"Right," Calune said. "So that's—"

"But we will not be going anywhere," Aaron continued, cutting the man off mid-word. "Not until and unless you explain what exactly we are being arrested for."

"Arrested?" Calune looked at them, then looked at Weis as though he might have something to offer. The younger man looked back at him, slightly startled.

"No, Mr. Harker, not arrested. The chief just wants—"

"I have little care for what the chief wishes," Aaron said, interrupting the man again, deliberately, stripping off whatever verbal gloves he had been wearing and showing the bare knuckles of someone willing to fight. "My sister and I have become aware of the rumors being floated about our business in this town, and yes, we are also aware of where those rumors came from. And I will not deny that it crossed my mind to contact my solicitor, as such rumors could be harmful to our reputation. However, I did not think, even when you so helpfully offered your advice earlier, that it would go far enough that such an action might be required."

Aaron was getting wound up. Normally Rosemary would have interjected a calming word here, to give him time and space to calm down. But she rather felt that the patrolman had earned whatever was about to rain down on his head.

"I would presume, certainly, that before you took such rumors at face value, no matter how . . . valued the spreader of them may be to the town's interests, you would investigate them."

"And we have. We—"

"You followed us, yes. And what crimes did we commit, as you were lurking on our trail? Is speaking to fellow citizens now a crime? Is walking in the streets a crime?"

Rosemary hoped that the officers had not followed them all the way to the lake, although if they had, and reported truthfully, they might be having a very different conversation just then.

And had Baxter known to tip them the night they went to the graveyard . . . Well. Explaining ghouls would have been the very least of it.

Aaron was still hammering. "Have you investigated our

character? Have you checked with our friends and associates, determined if we have any connection, personal or professional, with the unions we are accused of promoting? Because if you have, and they have said we do, I would very much like to know who said such a thing, as it is patently untrue."

His voice remained calm, but his expression could have been carved from stone, and his gaze never left the senior patrolman. Calune's face became ruddier and ruddier as Aaron went on, his jaw working silently, and Rosemary decided it was time to intervene, before the poor man went into spasms.

"Aaron, I'm certain that this was all a terrible misunderstanding. Our earlier discussion at the dinner table may have put us on the workers' side, as indeed we are. A man who works for a living should be shown the same dignity and respect as a millionaire, don't you agree? But it is on the employer to take care of his men, as the good Lord said, not the government's position."

Actress. She could have been an actress, and had roses at her feet, instead of mud and muck and things with too many teeth.

"There is no need for any of this unpleasantness. We have no interest in the mills or the factories, or how they are run. Yes, we went to visit the families of the other victims, and we did so at our cousin's request, that they should know they were not alone in their grief, and that we trusted the police to find the creature that roams the streets and put it down." She paused, and twisted the knife. "You have found it, yes?"

She almost felt sorry for Calune at that point, as his gaze went to Mrs. Lovelace, who had pulled out Dr. Lovelace's kerchief again and was twisting it between her fingers, grief written in every angle of her body.

"Not yet. Ma'am . . ." His appeal to the older woman failed, as she lifted her chin to show a trembling lip.

"You haven't found it yet?"

"Ah. No. Ma'am, we—"

"Then you are spending your time abusing my family, rather than finding the beast that killed my husband." Margaret Lovelace might have looked delicate, but there was a rod of steel in her spine. "You have nothing to say to me that I wish to hear."

Rosemary took that unmistakable set-down as the opportunity to drop the coup de grâce. "If we are not under arrest, and you have nothing further to say to us, Officer Calune, might we be allowed to attend to our dinner in peace?"

When the door had shut on official backsides, a blast of wind trying to make its way into the house, the three of them looked at each other, the rain and wind outside even louder than before.

Aaron was the first one to speak. "That . . . could have gone badly."

"I am so sorry," Mrs. Lovelace began.

"No, this isn't on you, none of it," Rosemary said forcefully. "If anyone, it's those two interfering blowhards at the dinner table. Men like that, they take great offense at anyone who does not fall into abject awe over them." Rosemary looked at Mrs. Lovelace, and for the first time in days felt a stirring of mischief. "Jan!"

The girl appeared as though she had been waiting for Rosemary to call her, and Rosemary suspected she had been doing just that. "There is another chair at the table, is there not?"

"There is, ma'am." Yes indeed; the haunted look in Jan's eyes had been replaced by a vicious sort of glee. "And more than enough to feed another mouth. Mrs. Wesson would be most pleased to have a full table."

"Oh, I couldn't."

"You came at a moment's notice, no doubt abandoning your own dinner, in miserable weather. Of course you will dine with us." Rosemary took Mrs. Lovelace's arm and bent to whisper in her ear, "And think how uncomfortable we can make Baxter and Dolph."

Fifteen

THE TABLE HAD, in fact, been laid with an extra setting, as though it had been arranged hours beforehand, and Mrs. Wesson greeted Mrs. Lovelace by her first name, not at all surprised by her presence in the room. Aaron found himself wondering, not for the first time in his life, at the web of womenfolk at the heart of every town. Had Jan or Gert Seen a need for Mrs. Lovelace, or had it been Mrs. Wesson's decision to fetch her? If the former, how much of their Sight did she know about and depend upon to run her boarding house?

"And this is Mr. Baxter, Mr. Dolph, and of course, Mr. Wilder," Mrs. Wesson finished the introductions. "Gentlemen, may I introduce you to my dear friend Margaret Lovelace. She is only recently widowed, and I have been remiss in making sure she does not sorrow alone."

As a tactical move, it was brilliant. Neither Dolph nor Baxter dared say a word of protest, or be so rude as to ignore her as they did the Harkers, without also insulting their hostess.

And the widow, by reason of her recent bereavement, could say nearly anything she wished, without censure.

This promised to be as uncomfortable a meal for the two men as Rosemary could have wished.

Wilder, at least, took the addition in stride, having apparently met the late Dr. Lovelace during one of his earlier visits to the area. After appropriate condolences had been exchanged, he and the two older women fell into an animated conversation that allowed the others at the table to sit in their respective silences. Dolph gradually thawed enough to join in a discussion of the town's Christmas pageant, but Baxter responded tersely, and only when asked a direct question, clearly still nursing his displeasure. Or, Aaron thought, trying to be charitable, perhaps he'd had a bad day on the market.

They had just moved on to the main course when a terrible noise filled the air, a drawn-out roar, inhuman and unearthly.

"What the hell was that?" Dolph's already pale skin went white as a sheet, and Mrs. Wesson looked as though she might swoon, her hands clutched to her breast.

"Sounds like the hounds of hell come Judgment Day," Wilder said, frowning up at the ceiling, as though the answer might come crashing through there, and Mrs. Lovelace's eyes closed for a long moment, her hand fluttering down, only to reappear with her husband's handkerchief again. Aaron forced a chuckle, placing his fork down next to his plate with exaggerated care. "Hopefully nothing that dire. A deep-voiced fox or wolf passing through town on a cold winter night, perhaps?"

The kick to his shin was Rosemary, and he managed not to glare at her. What had she expected him to do, pretend he hadn't heard it?

"With luck, all the farmers have their livestock locked in for the night," Dolph said, looking oddly worried, for a city man.

"Indeed." Baxter patted his lips with his napkin and took a sip of his wine, the hand holding the cup steady as a judge. "And if it comes into town, the police will take care of it, no worry. I would suggest that no one take any midnight strolls, however."

Aaron, startled, wondered if that had been directed at them.

Mrs. Wesson made a noise of protest, and Baxter seemed to suddenly recollect himself, and who sat at the table with them. "My apologies, ma'am. That was thoughtless of me." His apology was stiff, as was the nod Mrs. Lovelace gave him. An uneasy silence fell on the table once more, the noise once again that of silver against china, the sound of chewing suddenly louder than the howl had been.

"I am surprised your own hound did not respond," Dolph said a few minutes later, clearly searching for the earlier ease of conversation. "It seems he is not so formidable a guard as you claim."

"Clearly, he does not consider the sound-maker any threat to us," Rosemary said, "or I assure you, he would have raised an unmistakable fuss. You cannot mistake Botheration's voice for anything else."

Rosemary had been entirely truthful: you could not mistake a Howl. The noise had not been a wolf, or a fox, or any other wild-roaming creature.

It was Botheration. Something uncanny had crossed his path.

––––––––––

The rest of the dinner seemed to take forever, Mrs. Lovelace and Mrs. Wesson still talking well after the meal was finished, and it was impossible for Rosemary or Aaron to leave while their supposed cousin was still visiting. Only after the girls had cleared the last plates away and the other guests had pushed back from the table and made their way to their rooms did Mrs. Lovelace finally begin her farewells, first to Mrs. Wesson, then to the Harkers.

"I am grateful to have been of help," she said, "and even more grateful that the evening ended so comfortably. But now it is time for this old woman to be home and in bed."

"Perhaps we should walk you home," Aaron said, as Gert brought the woman's cloak and hat. "It is quite late." And her husband had been killed on these streets barely a week before, although after the incident at the table, his shin still aching, he had the sense not to say it out loud.

Mrs. Lovelace looked uncertain, as though she appreciated the offer but did not feel quite right in accepting it.

"We can do that," Gert said, looking as though she was surprised the words had come out of her mouth. "We live just a bit past her house. It isn't a bother at all. And that way nobody need come out and go back again in the rain."

"That's kind of you," Rosemary said, "but—"

"It's no bother." Jan repeated her sister's words, and then nodded as though agreeing with something Rosemary had said. "We know these streets, and these streets know us." Her right hand smoothed down the apron tied around her waist, exactly where Rosemary's knife rested when she was on a hunt. "And nothing in this town gives us a fright."

"Well. If you're certain, my dears," Mrs. Lovelace said, casting a glance at the Harkers, as though to assure herself that they had no objections.

Aaron's eyes narrowed, studying the girls as though any lie would leap out and show itself. "You'll be all right yourselves, getting home?"

"We'll be fine," Jan said quietly, turning so that she spoke only to the Harkers, while Gert blithely distracted the two older women. "It's you three who need to watch yourselves." She finally looked Aaron in the eye for the first time since they'd arrived. "There's something wicked in the storm out there, and it knows your name now."

Rosemary sucked in a breath, reminded of what the brownie had said about the storm bringing something dangerous to town. "What do you See?"

Jan shook her head, ducking her gaze again, and Rosemary

half-expected her to deny anything. Then the girl's forehead creased, as though she had a headache, and she shook her head again. "Nothing clear. Nothing's been clear for weeks. Didn't See it coming, don't know what it is, only just know that it's here."

"A shadow?"

"Yes." She looked at Rosemary, as though curious how she'd known that. "A dark shadow, howling over rooftops, and a sense of . . . anger. Trouble.

"We didn't even know what to warn Mrs. W. about, way we usually do. Just trouble, hanging over everything. Bloody trouble." She swallowed hard. "And then people started dying, and then you came, and we could both See you were tangled in it already. But we didn't know then if you were part of it or were here to stop it. Until tonight."

Her sister came to her side, offering her a heavy cloak, and Jan slung it over her shoulders, then turned back to Rosemary. "Make it go away, Miss Harker."

Rosemary offered her hand, and, after a hesitation, Jan took it.

"We will. I promise."

Before anything else, though, they needed to check on Botheration. The Harkers did not bother to wait until the household was asleep this time, barely waiting for the girls and Mrs. Lovelace to pass the front gate before throwing on their own coats and slipping out the kitchen door. There were few secrets left to keep from the household now, and if the police were still keeping watch on them, they would do so no matter the hour.

Behind them, the electric lights through the windows were a beacon of warmth and dryness, but no safety. Not if an uncanny had been this close—an uncanny dangerous enough that Botheration would react thus.

The rain had slackened to a steady mist that obscured sight, the sky still deeply clouded over, the wind slapping wet branches against each other. The only light came from the lamps flickering through windows, the too-pale streetlamp not reaching this far behind the house. What little snow remained was pocked with ugly patches of mud, and the ground squelched unpleasantly under their shoes.

Something shot off on the ground to their right, a fleeing shadow in shadows, seeking escape from an owl's claws. Aaron would like to think the presence of prey animals meant the danger had passed, but that was a tyro's mistake.

He had readied his pistol for a hunt before they left the house, aware that Rosemary was likewise armed, cold iron and silver-laced lead. It would be easier to drop the pistol and pull steel if needed than it would be to do the reverse, and in a hunt, seconds mattered.

They hadn't spoken since they came downstairs, years of experience and training letting them read even the slightest movement or breath from the other, a pas de deux deadly to anything that might come at them, held in only by the awareness that they hunted too close to a house, a home. That they had no idea what waited for them, or if it waited at all.

But it had come looking for them. Aaron was certain of it. That had been no coincidence, that something would come to challenge Botheration just outside their door. Not just after they'd encountered the lake-bound uncanny.

It knows your name now.

It knew where they were. It knew *what* they were.

Aaron forced himself to breathe deeply. The uncanny might have been the Aksha, returning with more information. That was a possibility. But the hound had not reacted to it that way before; he would be even less likely to Howl now.

No, whatever it was, Bother had not known it, and had not liked it.

He exhaled, the sound too loud. Everything around them was silent, save for the crunch and squish of their shoes on wet ground, that single fleeting shadow the only sign of nonhuman life. Even in winter there should have been noises from the ground and bushes and the air above, the sound of things hunting, or hiding for their lives. But the closer they came to the kennel, the more the air itself seemed stilled, winter's wet bite freezing it in place. The delicate hairs in his nostrils felt as though they had frozen the moment they stepped onto the walk, and the back of his neck, left bare between collar and hairline, prickled. He cursed his foolishness in not taking a muffler. Not giving an uncanny something to strangle you with was all well and good, but his reactions would be dulled by the weather, not sharpened.

"Did you hear that?"

"What? No."

"Huh." Rosemary shook her head, trying to listen for whatever it was that had caught her attention. "It was . . . there. Don't you hear it?"

Aaron lifted his head and turned, his breathing quieting as he tried to catch what she had. "It . . . maybe."

Under the multiple layers of clothing, his skin prickled with something other than the cold. It was a whisper, a murmur, the crackle of something burning, the crack of ice, the snap of wood breaking, the scrape of claws across glass. And it was watching them. . . .

It was wrong, terribly, terribly wrong, enough to make him tremble. But they were Huntsmen. Their obligation was to go toward danger, not flee from it.

He kept walking, Rosemary at his side, and the sensation of being watched faded, but didn't disappear entirely.

The white roof of Botheration's kennel was a splotch in the darkness, and he could see the hound's shape moving beside the kennel itself, restlessly waiting for a command. The beast was silent as well, not even the usual whuffling noise of greeting; whatever had triggered its Howl might be gone, but clearly not forgotten.

But there was something else there too, just slightly off to the side. Dark, large, and too still. As though . . . He drew a breath in and gagged silently, reaching out with his left hand to tap Rosemary on the shoulder, then pointing toward the second shape, then toward his nose.

She nodded, lifting her head to sniff gently, then making a

face he could see even in the shadows, an expression of disgust followed by pained identification.

There was no way, once you'd smelled them, that you could forget the stink of fresh entrails.

"Dear God, don't let it be one of the cops," he said, and heard Rosemary murmur something under her breath that might have been a prayer, or a curse.

She tapped her leg twice, a flat slapping noise, and Botheration was at their side, a thick warm mass pressing between them, taking up a position half a pace ahead. Still silent, hackles down and tail alert rather than held low. That was confirmation enough that the threat, whatever it had been, had subsided: that was defense position, not attack.

With a sigh, Aaron secured his pistol but did not put it away. The smooth wooden stock was reassuringly warm against his palm, even as his fingers went numb from the cold. A glance sideways at Rosemary showed that she still held her weapon at the ready, elbow slightly crooked and her arm steady. With his free hand, he reached into his coat pocket for the flash he'd left there the night before, the fairy light mostly used up, and the rest left back in New Haven. His fingers were clumsy with damp and cold, and he fumbled briefly with the metal cylinder before pointing the lens end toward the ground and flicking it on.

The tungsten light, dimmer than an ordinary lamp, was still enough to make him squint until his eyes adjusted again. Botheration let out a huff of displeasure, his own vision momentarily ruined, and Aaron resisted the urge to apologize.

Slowly lifting the flash, he let the narrow band of light play back and forth over the snow, mud, and flagstones of the backyard, moving slowly toward the shadowed shape. Rosemary kept pace with him, Botheration falling back slightly the way they'd trained, so that if anything attacked, he would not be in the line of her shot.

The shape did not move, not that he had expected it to. Still, stranger and deader things had happened.

He took another sniff of the air as they came closer, and the smell, mixed with the damp, made his gorge rise. A low rumbling noise came from around his knees, and he almost laughed when he realized that it was Botheration's stomach.

"You had dinner," he told the beast, the whisper barely escaping his lips, and only then did he realize that the cold had numbed his face as well. Had it been this cold at sundown? No, or the rain would have been snow. It might be the normal nighttime chill, out here in the northernmost part of the country, but instinct and training both told him that this cold was not natural.

Something in the storm knew their name, the girl had said. No, she had said something knew their name *now*.

"What is it?" Now that he had spoken, Rosemary broke her own silence. He wondered if her face was as cold as his own, if her lips had trouble forming words. He resisted the impulse to lick his lips, aware that would only make things worse.

The beam of light reached the edge of the shape, and he lifted the flash slightly, catching what looked like a flayed-open limb, then farther up to show the entire body, draped over the gate of the kennel and torn open, the expected garish colors of blood and viscera washed pale by the light. Rosemary gagged slightly as they came too close and the smell wrapped itself around them, thick and bitter, with an almost-familiar tinge of brine.

"Did you do this, boy?" But even as he asked, Aaron knew he hadn't. Bother's kills were precise things; a neck torn out, or a spine broken. He worked with jaw and paw, and neither one could scrape open a body like this. And he would not kill without orders, not unless his own life had been threatened, and if it had been, they would have heard more than that single Howl.

"Aaron." Rosemary had gone a step ahead of him, then stopped. "Aaron, it's the Aksha."

The clouds, already thick, had dropped lower as the sun rose that morning, the skies over the Great Lakes swirling with rain and sleet. Brutal winds swept low over the waters of Lake Superior, driving in from the west and swirling across the shorelines, curling in on themselves like a child having a tantrum before exploding out, tangling with the currents over the remaining four lakes.

From the southeastern shores of Lake Ontario, another storm front appeared, a hard, compact swirl of wind and thunder.

Between them, dark clouds formed and flowed low on

the horizon, and skippers of boats from Canada to the United States took second and third looks at their charts, then back out at the waters before putting all steam forward in hopes of outracing the rising storm. Rain and snow fell in narrow sheets, moving across the water like advancing armies.

Ships relying on sight and radio lost all contact with the shores and each other, sailors cursing at their ropes and engines, passengers huddling together, pretending that everything would be well, that this was nothing more than the usual gales of November.

Meanwhile, the water's surface roiled, patches of ice tossed back and forth, while just a few feet below the surface, fish flicked and turned, and deeper down, great sturgeon swam restlessly, feeling something wrong deep under their skin.

And below them, an ancient uncanny moved.

This was its home. The things that swam within these waters, and even the things that floated upon it, they were its to hold; to protect or to eat, to frighten or to ignore. It knew the natural ebb and flow of the seasons, the tempers of the storms, and it knew that there was nothing natural about what was occurring above.

Something had changed. The killer had discovered the hunters on its trail.

Deeper still, deeper than ship's anchors could reach, deeper than listening sonar could detect, the uncanny sank, hiding itself from the storm, sheltering other beasts below it as rain turned to sleet, sleet turned to snow, but even fathoms deep, the storm's cry of rage could be heard.

It had warned the Huntsmen; what happened to them was of no concern to it.

The uncanny sank deeper, and deeper still, but could not escape the knowledge of what raged overhead, the dry, staticky cackle and spit of something no longer constrained by flesh.

Too strong. Too powerful. Too angry to be contained, too mad to be reasoned with. The malice in the eastern storm would not stop with humans. Gorged with power and rage, it did not know *how* to stop.

And with what might have been a sigh, the uncanny shook off the creatures sheltering in its bulk and slowly rose back to the surface.

Sixteen

ROSEMARY HAD ALWAYS prided herself on a strong stomach. A body, even one flayed open, should not bother her so. Particularly not an uncanny body, not when she herself had killed so many.

But Huntsmen did not kill without reason, and never for sport. Even on the worst, most terrible hunt, a Huntsmen should make the end as clean and quick as possible.

This creature had done nothing to warrant such violence. They had spoken with this creature, had seen nothing violent or hostile in it; to the best of their knowledge, it had nothing to do with the current situation save being used as a messenger. To come to such a grisly end, there was only one possible conclusion: the uncanny had been murdered and left here as a message to *them*.

That made it their responsibility.

She crouched by the remains, breathing shallowly to avoid both the stink and the cold.

"I'm sorry," she told the corpse, knowing it didn't matter

what she felt or regretted. She hadn't asked the uncanny to get involved, and she hadn't killed it. She hadn't been the one who turned it into a messenger. Vowing vengeance on its behalf would be pointless. They could only—

"We need to get rid of it," Aaron said.

That, too. "How?"

During a hunt there was usually time to burn or bury any bodies, or tip them into a convenient river. In the worst scenario, which still gave her cold curdles to think of, they'd run the carcass through a combine harvester. But here they were surrounded by homes, not open fields and handy barns. At any moment someone might come out, and they lacked even a sheet or tarp to throw over it. She considered for a moment stuffing it into the kennel, but that only put the problem off, it did not solve it. And trying to move it again in daylight . . .

Aaron was glancing around the shadows as though something would step forward and suggest itself.

"It's too cold to stand out here dithering," she told him sharply. "We need to . . . wait. The toolshed."

He glanced toward the house, where the shed butted against the side wall. "Someone will smell it."

"Not if it stays this cold, they won't." The wind had died down for a bit during the evening, but it was beginning to dance with the trees again, whipping the upper branches against each other.

Something in the storm knew their name. That wasn't ominous, not at all.

"We can find a tarp or something and cover it up, hide it

behind the tools. It's winter, nobody will be using them. By the time anyone smells it . . . I don't know, but we'll be gone by then."

He gave her a dubious look, but without any other ideas, finally nodded, handing her the flash. "Go open the shed. I'll"—and he winced—"drag the body."

Better him than her. She tapped her thigh again and Botheration moved with her, staying to her left in ready-guard position.

The shed door lock was a little more difficult to open this time; she needed to strip off her gloves to work the lockpick, and the cold made her fingers clumsy, but eventually it swung open. She put the pick back into her coat pocket and pushed the door open slowly. Once certain no surprises waited inside, she ventured within, while Botheration waited at the door, clearly mistrustful of anywhere with that many iron tools hanging in wait. She couldn't say that she blamed him.

Inside, there really wasn't enough room to hide a body, but when she cast the light of her flash across the floor, she found a pile of old, musty-smelling oilcloths in a corner, weighted down by a metal spring trap. She crouched to examine them, thinking they might be useful for wrapping the body.

"And what might you be doing in there?"

Rosemary managed, through sheer dint of training, not to shoot the patrolman who now stood in the doorway, half blocking the only exit. His pistol, a brutal-looking .32, was trained on her, but one eye was cocked at the hound a few paces to his left, who looked as though he were contemplating where best to bite, to drag the man down like a deer.

"You near gave me a fright," she said, making sure to keep her hand away from the pocket where her own pistol rested, turning slightly and placing a hand flat over her heart, while minutely shaking her head at Botheration.

"Them as creep around at night, in places they don't belong, might say they deserve a fright." Calune used his free hand to lift his own torch, its light stronger than her own, and cast the beam over her, flicking it aside at the last minute before reaching her face so as not to blind her. He was alone and she had Bother, but she did not make the mistake of thinking that gave her any advantage against a pistol ready to fire. One of them, her or the hound, would lose either way.

The wind thumped something against the side of the shed, and they both started, but his hand on the pistol remained steady, and his gaze never left her.

She could lie. She could make up some story about needing the tarp for Botheration, and pray that Aaron had shoved the body out of sight by the time they went back, patrolman likely, inevitably, in tow.

Or she could tell the man to follow her. Show him what it was they hunted, what it was that he should truly fear.

Every instinct, every bit of training, told her to lie, to hide. But this town had exhausted her, this hunt was confusing her, and this man was irritating her. Maybe it was time to show him, in all his arrogant assumptions, what lay below what he thought he knew.

If nothing else, she thought sourly, it would get him off their backs about the damned unions.

She pulled one tarp from the pile, moving carefully so she didn't startle Calune into shooting her, and folded it into a rough square. With a glance at the patrolman, to make sure he wasn't going to object, she gave Botheration the hand-sign to come closer, offering him the square. "Bring this to Aaron," she told him. Her breath formed a white cloud in front of her nose visible in the light of the patrolman's flash, and her fingers ached, reminding her that she hadn't replaced her gloves yet.

The beast took the cloth carefully in its mouth, muzzle wrinkling slightly at the taste, but backed out the door and disappeared into the damp, windy gloom. She looked around again, trying to determine if there was any way to move the tools stored there to better hide the body. There really wasn't.

The wind thumped against the wall again, and the tools rattled against each other.

"Miss?" The patrolman had let Bother go, likely unsure of how to stop him, shy of shooting the beast, but he kept a wary eye and steady gun hand on her.

"There's nothing for it now," she said, resigned, pulling her gloves back on. "You'll have to learn, and I'm sorry for that."

"Beg pardon?" He backed up slightly as she walked toward him.

For every person who learned about the uncanny, learned and accepted the truth, there were a dozen or more who looked it straight in the face and claimed later never to have seen a thing. As far as she could tell, they went on with their lives without a ripple of doubt or confusion, secure that the world was as they thought it was, and anything that might say otherwise was quickly forgotten.

That was what made a Huntsman's job possible. Made *Huntsmen* possible, really. Any oddity, any quirk in their behavior, people found excuses for. Anything not to have to think about what was *really* happening.

Her mother's death had proven that.

"You wanted to know what we were doing here," she said now. "Congratulations, Officer Calune; you're going to find out. Follow me."

What he'd do after that, she couldn't guess. If he was like most folk, he'd likely take one look and know that thing wasn't human, then bury what he'd seen deep and never speak of it again. If they were very lucky, he would do the same with their names, and any knowledge he had of them, and encourage his fellow officers to do likewise.

Harker luck had always been terrible.

He followed her, less from obedience than curiosity, back to the kennel where Aaron was waiting. The rain was shifting to snow, wet drifts of it catching in her lashes and chilling her face.

"What took you so long?" Aaron's voice dropped away when he realized there were two shapes, not one, and he tried to straighten up, the act made more difficult by the corner of the tarp he was holding, the cloth now weighted down by the remains of the Aksha's body.

"Damn," he said, then a few more words in what she thought was Russian.

"What the tarnation do you have in—" Calune started to say, and then the wind shifted and the stench reached his nose. Rosemary would give the man credit; he didn't shoot Aaron immediately, although the pistol did rise again. He did make the mistake of forgetting that Rosemary was as much a threat as her brother; she had reached into her own pocket, the slight noise of the Browning being cocked gaining both men's attention.

"Let's not do anything that would upset Bother," she said gently. "I promised you would learn what we were up to, didn't I? Well, here it is."

She looked toward the tarp, watching as the patrolman's gaze followed hers. Then he looked back to them, as though uncertain where the danger might be coming from.

"We're not the threat here, Calune," Aaron said. He put the corner of the tarp down and stepped away, using the back of his hand to wipe rain-slicked hair off his forehead, ignoring the fact that the moment he did so, another strand fell and clung to his forehead again. "Come see."

As the officer stepped forward, his weapon still at the ready and his other hand holding his flash, Aaron shot her a glance. Even in the dark she knew he was asking what the blazes she was up to. She could only shrug in response: she'd made a decision in the risk of the moment, and they would have to live with it.

The patrolman's flash played once over the corpse, then back again, before flicking back to them.

"What the hell is that?" Calune's pistol was now pointing more safely at the ground, and his voice was affronted, as though everything in his world had just been flipped upside down.

Which, she supposed, in a way, it had.

"That is an uncanny," she said, as gently as she could, before Aaron could say the wrong thing, the way he too often did. "A creature of the devil's own making."

She heard him swallow, a gulping noise, and then, "Did you—" And he jiggered the hand holding the flash at the corpse, water slowly pooling around the edges of the tarp.

"No. We found it like that, impaled on the kennel gate." He would either believe them or not. "Something left it there."

It was a message, but explaining what, when she wasn't quite sure herself, would require admitting everything else they didn't know. Better to be seen as the authority; Calune was trained to respond to that.

She debated telling him about the Howl, and decided against that, too. Accepting that Bother was anything more than an exceptionally large dog would also require more explanation than they could spare, to no point.

"Something . . . that could do that. Is still out there." His billed cap made it difficult to see his expression, but the reflected light caught the flick of his tongue as it wetted his lips. There was a pause, an infinite pause when all outcomes were possible: he could call them madmen and haul them in, he could decide they'd killed the Aksha and shoot them, he could pretend he hadn't seen anything and walk away—more possibilities than Rosemary could gather in the time it took for Calune to shake himself, a full-body shudder, and make his decision.

"You think what killed this . . . thing is what killed Hemry, and Dr. Lovelace, and the others. And you're after that thing." It wasn't a question.

"Yes."

"All right then." He didn't holster his weapon, but he wasn't pointing it at anyone. That was better than Rosemary had hoped for. "Not a soul would believe me, even after seeing this, but . . ." He shook his head, then did holster his weapon, lifting his cap and wiping his face with one hand before settling the cap securely on his head again.

"First things first: we need to get rid of that. Mr. Harker, if you'd be so kind as to pick up that side of the cloth." And he handed his flash to Rosemary before shifting around to pick up the other side of the oilcloth. The two men studied each other over the flayed corpse, then, seemingly coming to a decision about each other, picked up their ends. With a soft grunt from one of them, they lifted the tarp higher, and there was an unpleasant slushing noise as the body slid toward the center.

"We'd thought to put it in the shed until we could deal

with it," Aaron offered, but Calune shook his head. "No room in there that I saw; anyone opening the door would spot it right off, even assuming they didn't smell the thing from the street. There's a patch of marsh not far from here. We let it slide there and nothing but crows will find it, assuming crows will even touch this."

The fact that he knew where to dispose of bodies would worry Rosemary if she lived here.

"Well, if we're moving it more than a few feet, we can't do it like that," Aaron said with some asperity. "Drop your end—carefully, man!" When Calune did so, Aaron moved with the ease of practice, crouching to fold and tuck the edges into a lumpy but secure package.

"You always were better at wrapping presents," Rosemary said.

"You're a card," he retorted, not bothering to look up. "There." He'd created a makeshift shroud, longer and thinner than a human body would have been, but too recognizable nonetheless. They could only hope no one saw them. "Would be better with rope, but it should hold. Now help me with this."

The men each took one end of the bundle, careful not to let the folds come loose, trying not to notice how the contents shifted and gurgled wetly. The smell was even worse close up, and Rosemary was no longer certain even the night's deepening cold would keep someone from noticing the stink. Botheration, without orders, waited at Rosemary's heel, his one upright ear cocked for the slightest noise.

"There's a wheelbarrow out by the road," Calune said,

shifting his grip. "Saw it when I was coming in. We put it in that, I'll take it off."

Rosemary raised an eyebrow, although she knew he couldn't see it. "Alone?"

"Better for us all if you aren't seen with me, nor me with you." He could obviously sense their hesitation, even as they lugged the shroud to the street, Rosemary keeping her torch aimed at the ground ahead of their feet. "I'm the one takin' the risk here," he snapped when they didn't quickly agree, "lugging this thing off for you. But someone stops me, I can tell them it's an animal run afoul of the same thing that killed Dr. Lovelace and they'll believe me. You think they'll believe you?"

That was a fair point, well struck.

The wooden wheelbarrow was where he'd said it would be, left at the edge of a neighbor's yard. Botheration took up guard, while they pulled it free of a hedge, and slid the uncanny's remains into it, all three of them wincing at the wet, meaty thunk as it hit the bottom. There were worse, less graceful ways to end, Rosemary supposed, but she couldn't think of one just then.

"But you can find this thing," Calune went on. "Right? You can kill it. So stop your staring at me and go do that. We'll call it even steven and never speak to each other again. Get me?"

He didn't wait for them to reply but picked up the handles of the wheelbarrow and set off, lumbering down the road with his three-wheeled contraption and unsavory load.

"You trust him?"

"No," Aaron said, staring down the road after him. "But I don't trust anyone who isn't you. Do I think he'll do what he said?" He shrugged. "No reason for him to do otherwise."

"You mean you can't think of any reason for him to do otherwise, which isn't the same thing as him not being able to think of any reasons. Ugh." Rosemary wiped her hands on the sides of her skirt, the kid of her gloves feeling slick and greasy even though she'd not come into contact with the body itself. She took a cautious breath, then another when the cold, damp air carried only the smells of leaf mold and the bitter tang of snow. "What now?"

"You heard the officer. Now we go find the killer." He held up his left hand, a scrap of something hanging from it. Even in the cloud-stuffed darkness, she could see deep green and hints of gold in the long flutter. The Aksha. Either it had been torn loose during the attack, or Aaron had thought to cut it loose before wrapping the body, and pocketed it.

"You're going to burn those gloves, I hope."

"It's just skin," he said, rolling his eyes. "But whatever attacked it—"

"Would have left a scent on the body." She was going to blame exhaustion for not thinking of that the moment she saw the corpse. But—

"You don't think we should inquire about Miss Baker's friend first?"

He waggled the drape of skin and flesh at her, and she scrunched her face in disgust but refused to give him the satisfaction of flinching away. "Scent's not getting any stronger, not even for Bother. Anyway, as much fun as it might be to roust a wealthy citizen out of bed before dawn, we probably won't get useful answers that way.

"Besides," he said, a grin she hadn't seen in too long lighting his face. "Finally, this is the fun part."

She huffed at him, but he wasn't wrong.

"Bother," she said quietly, calling the hound from where it had been holding guard. "Botheration, come here."

The beast padded over to them, square head swinging to look from one to the other. By the time it reached them, even his flap-ear had come alert, body coiled in on itself and ready to be unleashed. Rosemary nodded at Aaron, who held the skin out and down for the hound to sniff.

Bother took a careful huff, then another, deeper one, dragging the scent into his mouth and nose. Rosemary held her own breath, hoping that the now-heavier snowfall wouldn't cover it up, that the hound would be able to find something in it, something he could follow.

It bothered her, sometimes, that they had come to rely on the beast rather than chasing down an uncanny on their own. But Huntsmen had bred his line to do exactly this, the things humans could not, and she wasn't stupid enough to turn away an advantage out of pride.

"Bother. Hunt."

He did howl this time, full-throated and raw, a sound that no doubt everyone in the house and all neighboring houses could hear. She imagined them digging deeper into their covers, some ape-based memory deep in their skulls telling them to hide, that the Wild Hunt rode the night.

Or some slightly tamer descendant of theirs.

The howl rose, challenging, and she let the sound race across her skin, her own heart beating faster, the dregs of fey blood rising in her veins at his call. She didn't grin, not the way Aaron did, baring his teeth at the world, but she *wanted* to.

Then she felt another presence swirl around them, the sense of being watched swiping back on a bitter-cold wind, the unease she'd felt in the town earlier now not a hint but a hammer, slamming at them. Her hand went to her throat, then slid to her chest, where her heart felt near to pounding out of her ribs, bile swirling hot in her mouth.

It knew their name. It was hunting for *them*.

Bother howled again, a deeper sound, a trumpet into the damp air, defiance and threat in one. The wind dropped, then renewed its assault, a scream rising in response, angry and despairing, and almost familiar.

And then it was gone, wind scouring across her skin, tossing the snowflakes into a whirl, and disappearing into the trees overhead.

Before Rosemary could gather her senses, the hound snapped around, faster than his bulk should allow, and raced toward the house, before pausing briefly and retracing his steps back to the kennel, stopping where the body had been.

"It went to the house first," Aaron spat in realization. "Damn the arrogance of the thing."

Rosemary shook her head, willing the echoes ringing in her ears to disperse, and glanced around. Through some miracle or common sense, no one appeared eager to come in search of what had caused all that noise. She had barely enough time to hope that the patrolman had gotten away unscathed, when the hound paused where the corpse had been left and dropped his nose to the ground.

"Hunt, Bother," she said again, although the beast needed no more command: once the hound caught the scent, he would follow it until he found the source, or the trail ended. If he followed the path to where they had dumped it in the wheelbarrow, and no farther, then they would have no choice but to roust Miss Baker's friend and hope for something useful.

And pray that whatever had been in that wind gave them time to find it.

The wind swirled around them again, but the sense of being watched, threatened, did not return. Bother lifted his head, lips pulling back to show monstrous white teeth and black gums, and then, without waiting to make sure they were ready, raced off into the road.

"Damn it," she heard Aaron say, even as she grabbed her skirt up in one hand and ran after, her brother hard on her heels.

Rosemary had long ago had all her skirts tailored so that she could run easily, if need be, and the heels of all her shoes were fitted well enough that she could walk, dance, or run in them without risk to her ankles or balance. But even with that, chasing after Botheration made her wish she could wear bloomers every day like a veritable suffragist, and be damned what people thought.

"Think he caught the scent?" Aaron had caught up with her, his slightly longer legs keeping pace, annoyingly able to speak without effort, while she could feel her breath coming short in her chest, the cold like a rasp against her lungs.

"Either that or he's leading us on the world's worst goose chase," she retorted, both hands reaching up to scrape her hair back, fingers moving to shove the wet strands out of her face, her hat left on the ground outside the boarding house. She spared a hope that nobody would find it before she could retrieve it.

They came to the end of the street and saw Bother half-way down the left turn, trotting with definite purpose. She beat down the urge to run to catch up with him; they were in public, even if it was late enough that sensible townsfolk were heading to bed. All it would take was one patrolman seeing them, and all of Calune's new goodwill in the world wouldn't save them from being hauled in, and likely forcibly put on the first train south in the morning.

"That thing, back at the house," Aaron said. "Do you think it lingered outside the house?"

"The Aksha? No, it was already dead, probably. Although I don't know if before or after it was impaled—"

"The killer," he said impatiently. "Do you think it was lurking? Waiting for us?"

She shot him a sideways look. "What, you think a human dumped the body? If someone has bound an uncanny, I can't see them not using it for all their dirty work."

"No argument. That's not what I meant. Do you think—"

"That it dumped the body and waited until we came out to see its work?" She shook her head, dodging a particularly deep-looking puddle after Bother splashed through it. "That's a human thing to do, not uncanny."

Sometimes she wondered if the others were right, that her brother honestly didn't understand the difference. That he couldn't see it, because it didn't exist for him. A little old blood was good, made Huntsmen what they were. Too much . . .

That was why they hunted together. So she could remind him, when he forgot.

But his instincts were sharper than hers, so she couldn't dismiss his worry entirely.

She'd been uneasy outside the house, true. They both had. But while human minds were excellent at picking up the hint of something uncanny around them, an instinctive reaction to danger, they could also create danger where there was none, and Huntsmen were not spared that. Beasts like Botheration did not have the imagination to build a threat out of nothing, which was why they excelled at hunting.

But Bother had sniffed the trail by the house, and they *had* felt the presence in the wind. That had been real, if fleeting. Something had lingered despite the proximity of a hound, despite the risk of discovery, and death.

That sound in the wind . . .

No. She was letting bad weather and vague hints spook her, and what kind of Huntsmen did that?

Bother slipped from view around a corner, and with a curse they walked faster, picking up the trail again between silent, unlit houses and through a yard, the mud and lingering snow slick underfoot, the low bark of a dog somewhere reacting to Botheration's passing.

The hound did not deign to respond, nor did he look behind him to see if the humans were keeping up; that was their responsibility, not his. Rosemary slowed as they came to a wooden fence, tightly built, with sharply slanted tips. A glance down revealed several broken slats still swinging gently, showing how Bother had gone through, but there was no way even Rosemary could slip through after him. She cast another glance at the slanted tips, trying to gauge the distance needed, as Aaron came up beside her, making a stirrup with his hands.

"Up and over," he said, even as she was stepping into the cup of his hands, one hand balanced on his shoulder and bracing herself before he jerked his arms up and forward. She caught at the fence with her free hand, swinging her legs up and over, careless of the flash of her ankles visible as she turned her torso and came down on the other side, the impact jouncing her knees and rattling her from hip to teeth.

She took half a second to catch her breath, and in that time Aaron had flung himself over the fence as well, landing with even less grace. When they were children, fences like these were barely an obstacle; at only twenty-six, Rosemary couldn't imagine how older Huntsmen managed.

"Onward," Aaron said, knocking his shoulder against hers as he scanned the ground with his flash and, picking up Botheration's trail in the wet, thinly fallen snow, set off again.

Thankfully, they were able to find the hound again easily; his tracks cut across the next yard and came out on a narrow street, where they saw him trotting down the center of it, his head low and his tail high.

"He's slowed. It's nearby?" Aaron had not drawn a weapon; running with a knife or pistol in hand was a good way to damage yourself or an innocent, and tended to gather unwanted attention, but his hand now slipped inside his jacket to where his holster rested against his ribs.

Rosemary just shook her head, speeding her pace from a fast walk to a slow trot, keeping Bother close but not drawing abreast with him; distracting a hound on a hunt was never a good idea. Thankfully, the weather and the hour kept everyone else off the street, the few lit windows they passed so warm and inviting she had to force herself not to look, for fear she would be drawn to them as surely as a will-o'-the-wisp would draw her into the marshes. "If it was, we'd feel it." She was certain of that now, that the unease they'd felt in town during their earliest walks was the same as the feeling she'd had outside the boarding house not an hour before. Whatever this uncanny was, it left a miasma behind, something her ape-mind recognized and feared. That was all. "What we felt before, you were right. It came close, deliberately."

The corpse had been warning, and taunt. Jan had been right. The hunters were being hunted.

She felt the weight of the iron knife in her sleeve and wished she'd brought her bow with her, too. They'd no idea what would be effective against this thing; better to be over-armed than under. Although running with the thing was always damned difficult, and she didn't think "hunting rabbits" would buy much belief here in town, were she spotted.

She breathed deeply in through her nose, exhaling through her mouth, listening to her nerves, trying to determine if there was any sense of the thing around them. If there was, it was too faint, or too old for her to find it.

"What we felt," he said, "do you think maybe it was an echo? Bloodlust and anger, lingering?"

"A remnant, maybe, yes. The science isn't proven, but—"

"I read the same journals you do," he said, a touch of snit in his huff. "That hounds aren't following a physical scent, the way they would a fox, but something intrinsic to their un-canny nature, something we can't smell or see. But then how *did* we feel it, back there? And not just feel, Rosemary. We both heard it."

She had no answer for that, none that wasn't flat-out denial, at least.

"Great." He glanced up at the sky, which remained thickly

overcast, no light from stars or moon slipping through. Shadows. Storms. "I wish I'd thought to bring a shotgun."

Just because his thoughts echoed her own didn't mean she'd let him get away with it. "Because that would have reassured people greatly, you brandishing that thing. The police would not have asked us to leave town in the morning, they would have escorted us both to the city limits tonight. Assuming they didn't lock you up for disturbing the peace." Long guns had their time and place, but a hunt in the middle of a populated area was not it. And unless Botheration took a left turn soon—

No, he took a right.

"He's leading us back to the house Miss Baker went to," she said quietly, her hand slipping down to wrap around the grip of her pistol.

"I guess we'll be waking them early after all."

The low sound of a hoarse chuckle drifted over her left shoulder, and she whirled to her right, pistol raised, even as Aaron did the same, a long hunting knife suddenly in his left hand.

"Did you—"

"What was that?"

They spoke over each other, the words cutting off abruptly as they scanned the street, moving at an angle to each other so they each had enough room to move but could protect the other's back, at need.

There was nothing. Just a dark, empty street, snow

swirling gently. Any sound would echo, making it almost impossible to pinpoint. Rosemary didn't relax, not just yet, but her breath came a little more smoothly until a familiar snarl cracked open the night, promising violence.

They looked up in time to see Botheration spin on his back paws without breaking stride, body elongated as he raced back, not to join them, but *past* them, muscles bunching as he leapt.

They hadn't been hunted, Rosemary realized. They'd been lured.

And it had circled around behind them.

"Damn it," Aaron cursed, clearly having come to the same realization. "Where is it? Where is the damned thing?"

He had shifted to the left, so she took the right, scanning the road where Botheration was snapping at the air, seemingly chasing the wind. She had just enough time to think that she might have been wrong about no uncanny being invisible, when something cold and sharp slapped at her face, knocking her sideways. She fell to her knees, empty hand coming up to her cheek, certain that she would feel the warm wetness of blood staining her fingertips. But the tips of her glove came away dry, only the cold burn of her skin assurance that something had indeed hit her. She slipped her finger within the trigger ring, raising the barrel despite not having a visible target to aim at. That had never stopped her from hitting something; their uncle used to blindfold them and put them one at a time in the gleaned cornfield with instructions to shoot only when they were certain. It had been a hard and often embarrassing lesson, but it had done its job. But there were too many other variables; her brother, and the hound, still snapping and leaping at something only he could see.

Aaron had the right of it; a knife would suit this fight better, for now.

She shoved the Browning back into her jacket pocket and twisted her lower arm so that the throwing knife slipped and fell into her hand, even as she was standing up, feet planted and knees loose.

Botheration was circling them now, gums flecked with spittle, teeth showing in a fierce white grin, while that low, angry snark echoed from his throat. Angry and . . . there was something else to it, but she couldn't identify it.

"He's afraid," Aaron said. Which was impossible. The hellhound line had been bred for centuries for courage, intelligence, and vigor; they did not have room for fear. And certainly not against the things they'd been bred to hunt.

Before she could respond, something slapped against her again, bringing with it the crackle of ice and aged oak, the howl of wind outside the door and down the chimney, all the sounds of danger and nature aimed against human flesh. Bother might not have been bred for fear, but Rosemary felt it prickling under her skin, sending cold fingers into her soul.

Aaron drew his own pistol, the knife still in his other hand, and the cackle grew stronger, as though his efforts amused it. The wind swirled around them, the temperature dropping until it stole all the moisture from her eyes and the tiny hairs inside her nose froze into a solid mass, making it difficult to breathe.

Invisible, cold, claws. Rosemary fought off the fear, chanted the elements of the uncanny to herself, racing in her own mind for any creature those things described. But there was nothing, not in all the sheaves of names and descriptions she'd been forced to memorize.

"A new uncanny," Aaron said, following her thoughts. "Can I say I told you so? Think they'll let us name it?"

"Only if we don't die!"

She felt something claw at her left shoulder and dropped into a twist to evade it, even as Aaron ducked to her right, a steady stream of curses falling from his lips. Botheration snapped and snarled, his heavy fur coat hackled up, making him look half again his already great size. She had only an instant to be thankful for the cold that left everyone indoors, and that whatever police force the town still had was occupied elsewhere, because there was no way to explain this, the three of them in the dead center of the street, in the center of town, surrounded by closed storefronts, fighting like a crazed pantomime against nothing at all.

A hot snarl sounded in her ear, and what felt like teeth grazed across her collarbone. On instinct, this time she didn't turn, but dropped into a crouch and stabbed up over her shoulder.

There was no reassuring thud or resistance to tell her she'd hit something, but the snarl cut off abruptly, and she dragged a deep, shuddering breath in through her nose, raw, but no longer blocked as the air around them warmed perceptibly.

"It can be hit," she said, and Aaron grabbed her forearm, swinging her up and around so that they had each other's backs, Botheration in perfect formation at their hip. "And if you can be hit, you can be hurt, you piss-dunked uncanny. D'y'hear that? I am going to *hurt* you."

"You made Rosie mad," Aaron said, forcing a chuckle. "Now you're for it."

Before the uncanny could respond, either in attack or voice, there was a sound at the end of the street, the heavy thud of a door slamming open and voices, male, raised in a shout. Drunk men, staggering into the street, two holding up a third by his shoulders in a vain attempt to keep him from falling on his face.

Rosemary swore under her breath, flipping the knife so that the blade rested against the underside of her forearm, knowing that she could turn it around again in less than a heartbeat, if needed. Civilians were bad enough; drunk civilians were every Huntsmen's dread.

But the noise had distracted their attacker as well. There was a rush of wings, as though a murder of crows had taken off over their heads, and another gust of wind slapped into them, cold and bitter, before swirling up like a funnel, tree limbs bending and loose shutters slamming against brick. The drunk men shouted in alarm, and Botheration let out a howl, equal parts challenge and triumph, as the uncanny, whatever it had been, fled up into the sky and was gone.

"Where did it go?" Aaron's voice was hoarse, as though he'd been screaming, although she'd been certain they'd fought in near silence.

"I don't know," and her voice was just as hoarse, her throat parched and prickling. "But we need to keep moving."

Before it came back, before the inebriated men too close on the street noticed them and staggered over to ask questions, before she fell over, as her limbs realized what they'd been put through and decided they were done for now. Whatever was waiting for them at that house was going to have to wait a little while longer.

A dose of Blast would get her up and going. She just needed to get back to her room, and she'd be all right.

She put a hand down and grabbed the coarse fur at Botheration's neck, her fingers digging into the musky warmth. She almost said *home*, but caught herself in time. "Back to the boarding house, Bother. But . . . slow."

She wasn't sure either one of them would be able to make it back without the beast's support.

Seventeen

THEY'D MADE IT down another street, moving slowly and trusting Botheration to lead them, when Aaron broke the silence. "That wasn't an uncanny."

Rosemary stumbled. Botheration moved closer against her leg in response, and she kneed him away gently. "What?"

"There's no such thing as an invisible uncanny, Rosemary. Not in all the research, all the books, all the notes."

"It would be difficult to research something if they couldn't see it," she retorted, feeling mulish.

"And the odds that we'd be the ones to discover it?" He shook his head. "You don't believe that."

They were being quarrelsome to stay focused, maybe not the wisest thing, but it was working; Rosemary felt more awake than a few minutes before. It wasn't as effective as Blast, but it would do. "Then what?"

"I don't know!" Aaron's frustration was a palpable thing, and Bother's upright ear flicked back in reaction, although the beast didn't pause in his forward trudge. "But it's impossible for anything living to be invisible."

"Once you eliminate the impossible, whatever remains—"

Her brother snarled at her. "Don't you dare finish that quote."

It hurt too much to laugh. The rain had given over completely to snow, falling in thick flakes, but the wind had finally quieted, the *shsssh*ing of snow filling her ears until the silence seemed more ominous than any noise. She didn't trust it.

Something knew their names.

Botheration remained alert as they walked, heads down and shoulders hunched, the damp cold sliding under their collars and up their legs. The flush of blood-warmth from the hunt and the fight had fled, leaving behind only the aching cold. Rosemary clutched the lead in her hand, trusting the hound to warn them, should anything move in the snowy shadows.

"The river," Aaron said suddenly.

"What?"

"Bother. He's taking us to the river, not the house."

Rosemary blinked and looked up, but the snow kept her from being able to identify any landmarks, even if she'd known them. The houses on either side were oddly distant shapes, the few lights in windows an impossible mirage. But now that she was paying attention, yes, he was right; there was the bench they'd seen, just up ahead on the hill where they'd first encountered the Aksha, and the river was on the other side.

She slid her hand forward until her fingertips found the hound's thick leather collar. Even inside her gloves, her fingers were almost too cold to curl around it and tug his head up.

"Bother. No. We need to get inside."

The hound whined and pulled them forward.

"Bother." She tried to make it a command, but his name came out as more of a question, her voice rising at the end. The thought of correcting him, of forcing him to go in another direction, was abhorrent. They either trusted him, or they didn't.

But if they died of frostbite, that would be embarrassing.

"Miss Harker! Mr. Harker!"

Rosemary thought at first she was hallucinating hearing their names, but when Aaron turned toward the sound as well, she tugged again on Bother's collar. "Wait," she said, both request and order, and was relieved when she felt his muscles ease, slowing to a halt. Forcing herself to remain alert despite her exhaustion, she turned to where Aaron was looking, only to see a dark figure come out of the snow toward them.

Beside her, Bother growled, but low; a grumble more than a warning. He recognized the shape before she did.

"I went to the boarding house but you were gone, and the maid told me you had gone out. I've been looking everywhere for you." Miss Baker was wrapped in a long coat and a fur-lined hat, only her eyes and nose visible, but Rosemary recognized her voice immediately. She was panting, as though she'd been running after them for a while. "You need to help me!"

That had not been what Rosemary had been expecting to hear.

"Help? With what?" Had she been the one to set the uncanny on this town after all? But no, it made no sense that she'd come to them for help then. Unless they were too late, and the creature had slipped her control already. . . .

"It's Jessika. She had a meeting with those men today, and it didn't go well. I've never seen her so angry, and it . . . she's not well. But you know all that already, don't you? You know about what she's become."

"Why should we—Wait. Jessika Matthews?" Aaron's voice was incredulous, and Rosemary was having trouble placing how she knew the name, until she remembered that Mrs. Wesson had mentioned the woman. Daughter of the mill owner, recent widow. Monied. Independent.

Suddenly it made sense. Jessika Matthews was the woman she had met that first afternoon, when she went into the library. The woman Miss Baker had been arguing with.

Jessika Matthews was Miss Baker's confidante—and the source of her fear.

"That was who you were going to see," Aaron said, his tone accusing. "That's who you were getting your information from. About the uncanny."

"The what?" It was hard to tell, bundled as she was, but Rosemary thought that Miss Baker sounded honestly puzzled.

"The beasts. The lake serpent," Aaron said, his tone clipped.

"The stories? Jessika always loved them, yes. She was

fascinated by the legends, used to tell them to baby Michael all the time. But they were just stories!"

Aaron swore, words Rosemary would have smacked him for under any other circumstances. "And now you know they're not. Did she bind one, Miss Baker? Did she bind an uncanny?"

"I don't know what she's done! None of this makes any sense. I just wanted to help, and she kept asking me for more stories. I thought—" She broke off, then, "This is all his fault! If he hadn't pushed her, hadn't been so rude, she would never have become so desperate."

"He who?" But Rosemary had a feeling that she already knew.

"That man, Baxter! Him and his partner! Everything was fine until they came to town!"

The pieces came together. Land-hungry speculators. A widow with land and a child to care for. A friend with access to myths and legends. And enough desperation to do unthinkably stupid things.

Aaron took Miss Baker by the arm, shaking her none too gently. "What did she do? What did you do?"

"I don't know!" the woman wailed again.

"Aaron." Rosemary shared his impatience, but they would get nowhere if he kept shaking her like that. "Miss Baker. Look at me. What happened when Baxter and Dolph came to town?"

Miss Baker gulped, either the cold air or her own emotions making her nose redden unattractively. "They wanted her land, the mill. Michael's inheritance. The men she'd hired, they were listening more to Baxter than they were to her. He was paying them off, she thought, but he was a man, and no matter how much she paid them, they didn't respect her the same way. They kept pushing her to let him buy shares of the mill, said it would be better that way. She was so worried, looking for anything that would give her leverage."

"And she found it?" If she'd had Huntsmen in her family, or simply acquired their estate . . .

"I did. I found a book, an old one, in the back of the library."

Or that.

"I didn't think. I brought it to her. It said there was a way to gain power. You made a sacrifice to the winds, it said, and gave yourself up to them, and . . . and it would bring you power. Make you powerful."

"Hocus-pocus witchcraft." Rosemary supposed she shouldn't be surprised; there was always someone willing to buy into that nonsense. And it might even work, if you had fey blood somewhere in your family tree. Like runes, you needed the right spells, in the right order. But it wouldn't help her bind an uncanny.

"It was nonsense! It was supposed to be a distraction, something to make her laugh! I hadn't heard her laugh in months." Miss Baker looked away, down to the ground, then back up at Rosemary. "But it worked. Whatever she did, it worked. I could tell; she was so much stronger, brighter, more vivacious. The men were listening to her! But then—"

Aaron shook her again, and this time Rosemary didn't stop him. "What. Happened."

"She started having trouble sleeping again. She never said so, not to me, but I could tell. One evening she went for a walk. We were supposed to meet, after. We'd have dinner, play with Michael for a little bit. But she came back late, and her hands . . . her hands were bloody. She said it was nothing, that she'd fallen by the river, cut her hands on some rocks. But she had a look in her eyes . . . and she said something about how he deserved it.

"I didn't want to ask. And for a few days, she seemed better. But then . . . we were at the milliner's. Jessika had ordered a new hat, and she wanted my opinion on it. And . . . she got angry, something about the hat wasn't right, and I saw . . ."

She choked a little, pulling her arm away from Aaron and pulling her coat more tightly around her. "Her fingers, they, they sparked, like an iron in the fire. And Mrs. Bücher, the milliner, she *flinched*, and there was a mark on her neck, like one of her hairpins had scratched her, deep enough to draw blood.

"I told myself I imagined it. Of course I imagined it. Everything was going so well, Jessika was herself again—

"But then they found Mr. Ottering. And when young Jimmy turned up dead . . . I knew that he'd been a thorn in her side, trying to rile the workers up, get them to form one of those unionizing things, and Jessika said that the mill wouldn't survive if they did that, and—"

"She was murdering people," Rosemary said quietly. "And you ignored it."

The woman didn't even try to deny it. "Who could I tell? Who would believe me? Oh hello, I'm sorry, my very best friend is killing people with *magic*? Until you came to town, asking questions, and I thought . . ."

"That kind of magic doesn't exist," Aaron said flatly. "She's bound an uncanny to her. One of the fire-based ones. A Salamander, maybe."

Rosemary scoffed. "Out here? In the winter?"

"You want to believe she's turned herself into a warlock?"

"Warlocks don't exist."

"Exactly!"

"Stop arguing about it!" Miss Baker practically screamed at them, causing Botheration to growl. "You need to save her! That's what the Wesson's girl said you were here to do."

Small-town gossip. The girls might have the Sight, but that didn't mean they had common sense. Had word of Dr. Lovelace's interest reached Jessika Matthews that way, marking him for death?

Rosemary could tell her brother was about to explain that it wasn't the *killer* they were here to save, when the wind picked up abruptly, sending snow and a few scattered leaves swirling in the darkness. Then it subsided, and another figure appeared, stepping into the faint, snow-coated light of the streetlamp. Miss Baker yelped, jumping behind Aaron, grabbing at his coat as though to use it as a shield.

"Matthews," Aaron said, as though Rosemary needed the identification.

Unlike Miss Baker or the Harkers, the woman was not swathed in a heavy coat or cloak, despite the bitter cold, but stood before them in a simple day dress, dark stripes over a cream underskirt, the buttons up the front shiny black, leading to an elaborate necklet of jet. Her cuffs were cream, but the gloves she wore were dark, making her hands look almost disembodied against the snow. And her face . . . her face was the most disturbing thing Rosemary had ever seen. She had been striking even a few days ago, but now her face had sunken to hollows, the rouge she'd used on lips and cheeks only highlighting her pallor.

Magic, the kind that humans could use, wasn't real, but if it were . . . if it were, Rosemary thought it might take this sort of toll on the user.

The snow swirled and rose again, leaving a clear, cold circle around them, and the sense of being watched, of being menaced, returned.

The uncanny was back.

"Jessika." Miss Baker's voice was a moan.

The woman's gaze flicked to her. "Madeleine. I thought I could trust you. I loved you, and I thought I could trust you."

"You could. You can! Jes, I was worried about you!"

That hollow gaze returned to the Harkers. "So you ran to Lovelace's kin, the ones trying to destroy me."

"No! They're here to help!"

Jessika's lips cracked upward in a grotesque parody of a smile, and she cocked her head in question. "Are you?"

"No," Aaron said. Rosemary repressed a sigh; her brother's occasional habit of brutal honesty was of course morally correct, but it was going to get them killed someday.

"You need to stop," she said. "This killing. Release the uncanny and stop. Walk away." Her hand in the deaths would be impossible to prove; even without her money she would never be arrested, much less convicted.

Matthews shook her head slowly, that grotesque smile never faltering. "No, I don't think so."

Hearing this, Miss Baker darted out from behind Aaron, stopping just shy of reaching for the other woman. "For the love of all that's holy, Jessika, please! Think of Michael, your baby!"

"Think of him? I'm doing this for him!" The smile was gone now, replaced by a snarl of anguish. "I thought you understood that! I thought you were with me. Instead, you turn on me." Her voice dropped low. "Just like everyone else."

"No! Jessika, I would never!"

"I met with them again. I told them I wouldn't sell. Do you know what they did? They *laughed*. Told me they'd have me committed."

Rosemary spared a moment to wonder if the unfortunate businessmen were still alive.

"And when I came to find you . . ." Matthews lifted her chin, glaring down her nose at the other woman. "Well, here you are."

Miss Baker reached out a hand, her gloved fingers trembling. "I wanted to help you."

The woman raised her hand in return, but rather than reaching for the offered touch, the sparks Miss Baker had mentioned crackled around her fingers, bent like claws. "I don't need your help."

"Jes?" Miss Baker's voice quavered.

"Kill them," Matthews commanded the air. "All of them."

"Holy mother of Jesus." Rosemary ducked just as she felt the wind pick up again, swiping at her face with something that felt dangerously solid. This was no uncanny, she'd agree to that now, but what in blazes *was* it?

Even as she was cursing, Aaron had grabbed Miss Baker by the arm and pulled her back, swinging her in Rosemary's direction. The librarian tangled in her skirts and fell, arms coming up to protect her head against whatever invisible forces were battering at her.

"Stay there!" Rosemary yelled. "Don't move!" Instinct would be to run, but if the thing went after her, they'd have no way to protect her from it.

Not that they were having much luck right now.

Something roared, and Aaron shouted his defiance right back, slashing at the air like he could see what he was aiming at before being slammed into the ground. There was a crack, painfully audible, and Rosemary winced: that had been a bone, likely the arm he'd landed on.

Her brother down, and Baker useless, Rosemary firmed

her hold on her knife and turned, not into the wind-creature, but the one controlling it.

Jessika Matthews stood with the storm at her back, her arms raised, miniature lightning swirling at her fingertips. She gestured, and the lightning cast itself toward Aaron, swirling and snapping over him as though it were about to tear into his heart.

One of his charges directly threatened, Botheration tilted back his head and howled, a promise of violence, before racing forward.

Uncanny eyes could see what human ones could not; he caught whatever it was in his massive jaw and snapped shut. There seemed to be something solid there, his teeth catching hold and turning bloody red. But the wind-creature fought back, slashing at the hound's side, shaking him in turn, until they tumbled off Aaron's body, a snarling and struggling knot.

Rosemary couldn't help Bother, couldn't run to her brother's side, couldn't look back to check on Miss Baker. Instead, she settled into her stance, sheathing her knife and raising her pistol, finger sliding under the trigger guard to rest against the curve of metal.

"Call it off," she said, her voice oddly firm. "Call it off or I will shoot you."

Whatever the creature was, without direction it should be nullified, and perhaps set free of its binding. Which would create another issue, but they would deal with that when it happened.

"You're threatening me? Another stranger telling me what I should do?"

Rosemary cursed to herself; that had been the wrong approach, after what Miss Baker had told them. Too late now to backtrack—not that Matthews was listening.

"You all think I'm just a pretty face, just a woman, that I can be ignored. But I won't. I won't be, not anymore. I have power, finally, and I'm not letting go of it." Her hands clenched, and Rosemary cried out as sharp talons raked across her face, and the heat of blood prickled along snow-cold skin. Her finger tightened against the trigger, when Miss Baker launched herself from the ground, scrabbling at Rosemary's free arm. The librarian's hair was torn from its pins, her eyes wide and wet. "No! You're supposed to save her!"

Aaron, panting heavily as he got back to his feet, right arm cradled against his body, called out, "We can't. There's nothing left to save."

"She's human," Rosemary said, but her voice sounded uncertain, even to her.

"Even the uncanny are terrified of her," he reminded her, and out of the corner of her eye, she saw that he'd drawn his own pistol, holding it awkwardly in his off hand. He was a terrible shot with his left; she couldn't count on him. Bother, where was Bother?

As though her thought had called him, the hound limped forward. His fur was damp and matted, splattered with what might have been blood, but he was upright and breathing, and that was all she had time to note.

"Please." Miss Baker held on to Rosemary's arm as though it were her rope to salvation. "Please. She doesn't know what she's doing. She's a good woman. She didn't mean to hurt anyone."

The figure in front of them didn't look like a good woman. Aaron was right: she barely looked human, no more than the Aksha had. There was something in her face, in the way she held herself. And in the wind that whipped through her hair, the lightning crackling under her feet, even as the snow stayed clear.

Whatever Matthews had done, whatever she had bound to herself, whatever impossible magic she'd swallowed, the lake-uncanny had been right: she had to be stopped, now.

If they even could.

Rosemary shoved that doubt down, biting her lip against it resurfacing.

"They wouldn't let me be, tried to stop me, wouldn't listen to me." Matthews was talking to herself now, half whispering, a bitten-off monologue that wouldn't have seemed out of place on a theater stage. "But now they will. The things that they whisper about me, the conspiracies they make, I'll make them scream my name when they apologize." She grinned, a horrifying rictus of white-patched skin and rouged cheeks and lips, like a corpse come walking, and Rosemary suddenly felt nothing but pity for her.

But pity wouldn't stop this. Bullets might.

"I'm sorry," Rosemary said.

Before she could raise the Browning again, Matthews

lunged forward. Rather than attacking Rosemary, she grabbed the front of Miss Baker's coat, dragging her away. The women threw their arms around each other in what might have looked like an embrace, save for the fact that Miss Baker was now placed between the woman and Rosemary's pistol.

"Damnation!" She tried to sight on Matthews, but the snow distorted the scene just enough that she couldn't be sure. There was too much risk that she'd hit—

The bark of Aaron's pistol sounded, once, twice, and then a third time in rapid succession. Matthews staggered but held on to Miss Baker, pulling them both backward. The snow swirled around them, almost a mockery of a bridal veil.

"This is my town!" she cried, her voice becoming less human throat and more wind and lightning crack. "It's Michael's birthright! None of you can take it from him! None of you can ignore me, not anymore!"

The uncanny's warning came back to Rosemary, now making perfect sense. Whatever Matthews had intended at first, whoever she'd meant to punish, or why, there would be no stopping her now. Not until she'd scoured this entire town—and possibly the entire state—of every living thing.

Whatever she had dabbled in, it hadn't been meant for her, and her sanity had snapped, the same as their father's had.

She saw his face again, distraught, crying, their mother's broken body at his feet.

As Huntsmen, they had an obligation: protect humans from uncanny who would harm them. But this was a *person*. Two people, one guilty only of being a fool.

"Damn it, Rosie!"

Aaron would have shot her already. *Had* shot her.

Before Rosemary could shake off her doubts, Botheration lunged with his full body weight, landing not on Matthews or Baker, but on something just to their left. His jaw snapped down, and dark blood splattered through the snow, a scream of pure rage sharpening itself on their ears. Whatever the creature was, this attack seemed to hurt it, because Matthews snarled, as feral as a hound herself, and threw herself at him, dropping Miss Baker to the snow as she did so.

Trusting Bother to hold the uncanny, Rosemary steeled herself, raising the pistol enough above Bother's height that she was reasonably certain not to hit him, and fired off two shots in rapid succession, the casings ejecting silently onto the snow-frosted ground.

Matthews's body jerked, her hand going to her shoulder even as she turned back to Rosemary. At least one bullet had landed, likely both, but the dark cloth of her dress made it impossible to see if she was bleeding.

Rosemary shot again, and she *knew* the bullet went true, hitting just over the heart.

But the woman didn't go down.

The Browning still had three rounds left. But before she could sight again, Aaron came from her off-side, charging Matthews from behind. His left hand swung down, the iron dagger he was holding landing square between Matthews's shoulder blades.

She staggered, hissing like a cat, and spun, her skirt swirling around her. "That wasn't polite."

"Unbelievable. Why won't this thing die?" Aaron muttered, abandoning the dagger and falling back, eyeing her with a mix of caution and disgust.

Matthews wiggled her shoulders and the blade fell to the ground with a soft thud, the bloody metal dark against the snow. She giggled, the sound of a child delighted by pain, and threw open her arms, the sleeves ruched up, her fingers splayed and bloody. Sparks flashed again, writhing up and down her arms like St. Elmo's fire, until the snow-cleared space glowed with them.

Miss Baker gasped, running toward—no, not running, being *pulled* forward, her shoulders and chest moving ahead of the rest of her body, until Matthews's arm caught her, pulling her back into a harsh embrace.

"No," Rosemary protested, the bloodless, horrified expression on Miss Baker's face an almost palpable, brutal blow.

"One more chance, Maddy," Matthews crooned, her arm around the other woman's waist. "One more chance." Together, they staggered backward into the swirling wall of snow and were gone, the impossible snow-clear circle collapsing, leaving the Harkers in blustery darkness again.

Rosemary swore, picking up the edge of her skirt and racing up the hill before the women disappeared from sight entirely, Botheration on her heels, and Aaron, she hoped, not far behind.

Before she reached the rise, something slashed at her, a burning pain across her shoulder, and she ducked and swung, even as Botheration leapt, his bulk knocking her free of her attacker.

She could almost see the creature now, with the hound's teeth deep in its insubstantial flesh. It was oddly clear, the snow seeming to float right through it, and she had a sudden memory of playing on the shore one summer and stepping on something near invisible, a sharp pain running up her leg. Not invisible, her mind supplied; clear, like a jellyfish. But what, and how? "Worry about that *later*," she scolded herself, even as Aaron passed her, reaching the top of the rise first.

A bloody slash opened on Botheration's flank, and he whined but didn't let go, dragging the uncanny with him. Rosemary abandoned him to it, chasing after Aaron.

The river was swollen, much higher on the banks than it had been a day before. But Rosemary didn't have time to wonder at it: Aaron had already reached Matthews.

The two of them were circling around each other, the snowflakes fluttering down around them. Aaron's arm was clearly broken, but Matthews was staggering as she moved; the bullets might not have killed her, but they'd done damage. Her hair fluttered as though each strand was alive, her once-perfect suit slashed and cut to ribbons, but an almost physical sense of menace, of *danger*, wrapped itself around her.

Uncanny or not, the thing was just a creature, however hard to see. This—the winds, the sparks, the way bullets didn't take this woman down—was impossible. *Magic* was impossible for humans. And yet none of this made sense, otherwise. What she'd said to Aaron came back to her: once you eliminated the impossible, whatever remained, however improbable, must be the truth.

Madeleine Baker had found a grimoire with magic that worked.

Rosemary paused a moment to wonder if Dr. Lovelace had known, had suspected, or if he too had thought it merely an uncanny gone violent. But the how didn't matter, why didn't matter, intent didn't matter. This sort of power was not for humans, and for good reason. It would kill them, eventually. But the damage done before then . . .

Huntsmen were called to protect against the uncanny, not humans. But they were the only ones here. The only ones who *could*.

Aaron was keeping Matthews busy, giving her time. *Think*, Rosemary ordered herself. *How do you stop a human, if bullets don't work?*

Matthews controlled the uncanny creature, somehow. She had suffered before, when it was attacked. They were connected. With luck they could use the connection.

Carefully sliding the poisoned dagger from its sheath, Rosemary moved forward, trying to judge from Botheration's movements where the creature was below him. She took a deep breath, sent up a brief prayer that her aim would be good, and, holding the knife with both hands, stabbed downward with all her remaining strength.

She hit something, blood spurting around the edge, and

felt the wet splatter hit her face at the same instant a woman's scream cut the air. Leaving the knife where it was, Rosemary turned in time to see Matthews stagger, screaming as if the dagger had been jabbed into her own flesh. Overhead, the sky lit up, the clouds crackling with lightning, the wind whipping down cold and sharp as a steel knife.

Behind her, Botheration whined, getting to his feet. The weight and warmth of him against her leg was a comfort; what was happening overhead was not.

Aaron was drawing sigils in the air with his left hand, but whatever he was trying, it wasn't having any effect on the storm overhead. Rosemary glanced back, bending at the knee to pull her knife out of the creature's body. It came free sluggishly, as though the now-dead flesh was doing its best to hold on to the thing that had killed it.

"Bother, to Aaron," she directed the beast, then, holding the knife carefully, moved so that she faced the other woman, pulling her attention away from Aaron, to give him time to finish whatever he was doing. Miss Baker was still nowhere to be seen, but Rosemary didn't have time to worry about her.

Whatever the creature had been, it hadn't been the source of Matthews's power.

"Call it off!" Rosemary yelled. "Whatever you're doing, call it off now!"

"Why? Why would I do that?" Matthews stepped closer to the riverbank and stretched her arm overhead toward the sky as though she were about to grab something, the winds swirling down around her like a miniature tornado. "Why would I give this up? Would you?"

Rosemary started to respond, then checked herself. No argument she could make would reach the woman, and neither killing the creature nor Aaron's sigils seemed to have any lasting effect. Firming her grip on the knife's handle, trying to ignore the wet stickiness running down from the blade, she took a step closer, then another. "Jessika. Those men. They're no friends of mine. We can help you—"

Lightning flashed down, hitting the ground in front of her. She jumped back, almost falling over Botheration, Miss Baker clutching the fur of his back as though he were a blanket, her hair completely loose and her face white as chalk. "Stay there," Rosemary hissed over her shoulder, looking back to where Matthews was standing. She was wreathed in miniature lightning, snapping and sizzling in the snow, and her eyes glowed like a wolf's in firelight.

Whatever Aaron had been trying to do, it hadn't worked.

"Damn it," she breathed, wondering how much poison was left on the blade, and if it would be enough, if she could throw it accurately enough.

Then something massive burst from the river, throwing itself up on the banks too damn close for any kind of comfort, and she flipped the knife in her hand, bracing herself for another attack. It was massive, serpentine, and there was an intelligence in the huge eye turned on them before the creature focused its terrible attention on Matthews.

"Rosie, down!" Aaron's yell made her drop and roll on her hip, coming up with skirts tangled around her knees in the snow-coated mud just in time to see a sinuous tendril slap up out of the water, uncurling and reaching, curling around Matthews's waist and yanking her back in an echo of what she had done to Miss Baker. By the time Rosemary realized what was happening, both tendril and head had disappeared under the water's dark surface, taking the woman as well.

The wind eased, then collapsed, leaving the air still. The snow began to fall again, clinging to their arms and shoulders. Rosemary staggered, the poisoned dagger still gripped in her hand, and Aaron went down to his knees, swearing the air blue.

"Oh God, Jes! Jessika!" Miss Baker ran past them, stopping just shy of the riverbank. "Jessika!"

"For the love of God," Rosemary said, exhausted and confused beyond civility. "Shut up."

Eighteen

THE NEXT MORNING, Aaron, his injured arm bound up for travel, watched from the hallway as a strongly built man who seemingly lacked the ability to speak—presumably Bernard—carried the weapons trunk down the stairs. Then he turned, entering into Rosemary's room without knocking. She was seated on the bed, her travel desk open on the coverlet next to her and a pen in hand, the words flowing smoothly onto the page.

Writing her report.

"We can't tell anyone."

She looked up, her pen poised over paper, her forehead furrowed in a frown at the interruption, and he bit the inside of his cheek to keep from commenting on how drawn she looked. She wouldn't appreciate it, and shy of telling her he knew about her use of that damned drug, there was nothing he could say.

"We can't tell anyone," he repeated, when she simply stared at him. "What happened."

He could see the moment realization struck her.

Huntsmen wisdom said that only the fey had anything that could be called magic, and part of the agreement between them and the fey was that it would not be shared with humans. That agreement was the uneasy truce Huntsmen had been born to enforce. If they reported that Jessika Matthews had killed people with magic . . .

"They'll assume the treaty was broken," Rosemary said, not putting down her pen. "No matter what we tell them."

Breaking the treaty meant that the fey would no longer be bound from interfering with humanity. Huntsmen would no longer be bound from hunting fey.

It would become war.

A war humanity would lose, eventually. But not before they wiped out every uncanny they could reach, malicious or not.

That was why the Aksha had interfered. Because they'd known it wasn't them—and that no Huntsmen would believe it. If he hadn't seen it for himself—Matthews, changed by the magic, no longer entirely human, the serpent coming upriver to join the battle, presumably sent by the Aksha—he wouldn't have believed any of it.

"Rosemary."

She put down her pen and sighed. "So what should I say? That we encountered an invisible uncanny who can control winds and lightning?"

"Maybe we don't mention the wind. Or the lightning." A

jellyfish-clear uncanny would be enough to keep the researchers busy for months, if not years.

"Lie."

He nodded. "Lie."

Aaron was surprised to see Miss Baker standing outside the boarding house, when he went down to check on their ride to the station. She wore a dark purple suit too closely resembling Mrs. Matthews's dress to be coincidence, and a hat with no ornamentation, and her face was strained with exhaustion and tears. "Miss Baker." He'd rather have ignored her, but he suspected she would make a fuss if he did.

Her gaze flitted over the sling holding his arm in place, then past him, then back again, seemingly unable to hold still on any one thing. "That . . . last night." Her voice was hoarse, scratchy, exactly as though she'd spent hours screaming. He supposed she had. "What happened?"

He bit back his temper. "You know what happened." Her former friend had tried to kill them all, and they'd been saved only by an uncanny heeding the sigils he'd hoped would summon aid.

"No." She shook her head, a twitching move. "That . . . What she did. That . . . Magic isn't real."

Aaron sighed. "Yeah, Rosemary keeps telling me that, too." Not that kind of magic, that a human could use. And yet.

His words seemed to break something in her. "It was all real."

"Yes."

"And Jessika." She stared at him, eyes red-rimmed but dry. "That . . . that happened, too."

The uncanny snatching her into the river. "Yes."

They'd told the story to Mrs. Lovelace, what they could piece together of it. A bereaved wife and mother, a friend thinking to be helpful. An uncanny, bound to serve. Grief turned to madness. It was something she could understand. Something that made sense, within the limited frame of what she knew. Something that wouldn't leave her with too many questions, once they were gone.

He supposed he should offer some comfort to Miss Baker, but he was exhausted, and his arm hurt like several devils, and even if Rosemary did all the paperwork for him, there were still going to be questions about the uncanny they'd seen—or not seen—and how Mrs. Matthews had managed to bind it to her so tightly that they'd apparently become one creature.

Not a lie, not entirely. Whatever she had called to her had changed her into something not-human. Something uncanny. Because magic—the kind of magic that called down storms from the sky, that wreaked havoc for miles, that might or might not have been responsible for the wreckage of a half dozen ships on the Great Lakes? Couldn't exist. For every-one's safety.

But four men were dead, maybe more they hadn't heard

of. And now this woman, who had fled the scene rather than help them stagger back to the boarding house, dripping blood and sweat every step of the way, dared show up and ask if any of it had *happened*?

If she had come here looking for absolution, he was no priest, and he had none to give. She had brought this all down on them, brought it down on the town, as much as her friend had. More, even.

He supposed having to live with that was more punishment than anything he might say or do.

"The book. The one that . . . I burned it."

"Good." That was one loose end that wouldn't come back to haunt them, at least.

"We won't ever find her body, will we?"

He suspected there wasn't much left to find. Even if the river serpent didn't eat it, something would have. He supposed they should be hunting down the uncanny for that; you never allowed them to kill a human and live. But he just didn't have the energy. Or, if he were brutally honest, the desire. For the record that Rosemary was upstairs writing, Mrs. Matthews died of wounds incurred during a hunt, when she got between them and the uncanny.

Not entirely untrue, either. As the uncanny had said: humans had caused this. Human fear, and sorrow, and greed, and maybe even love.

Maybe Baxter had been the one to push Mrs. Matthews to the edge. Maybe Miss Baker's well-intentioned gift was what sent her over that edge. You could blame the police, for keeping things secret. You could blame Dolph and Baxter for being greedy bastards. You could blame the world, for not taking a woman seriously. There was enough blame to go around.

"Her will named me Michael's guardian. I don't know what to do."

He shook his head, turning as the sound of the door behind him told him Rosemary had exited the house. She was moving stiffly, her own wounds bandaged and hidden under her dress and coat, and other than the red scarring on her cheek, she was still too pale for his liking. They were going to have to talk about that Blast, and soon.

When he turned back to the librarian, she had lifted her chin, firming it against a quaver, as though she would not allow herself to show any weakness in front of his sister.

His sister, who had almost died because of this woman. He found he had no pity for her.

"You'll do what's best for him," he said. "Listen to the men your friend hired to advise her." Baxter would buy them off, no doubt, and she'd probably foul it up even if they didn't, but if they were at all decent men, they'd make sure the baby— and his guardian—had enough to live well by, no matter what. "And stay away from old books."

It was a mean blow, but a necessary one.

"I'm sorry."

"Tell it to the dead," he told her, and smiled when she flinched.

Rosemary came down the steps, as a battered automobile rattled up in front of the house, Jan at the wheel, looking terrifyingly determined, as though expecting the vehicle to bolt out from under her at any moment.

"Aaron." She nodded a stiffly polite greeting. "Miss Baker."

"Miss Harker."

There was an awkward moment between the two women, one Aaron didn't even try to decode. Then, "We should go," his sister said quietly. "The train will be arriving soon."

Handing Rosemary carefully up into the car, he let Botheration jump up into the footwell, then settled next to his sister and nodded to Jan, who released the brake with the air of someone heading to her doom.

Behind them, Miss Baker turned and walked in the other direction, toward the center of town and the library. Neither Harker looked back.

They'd done what they'd come to do. The town would have to go forward on its own.

Nineteen

ROSEMARY SENT HER report off to Boston and heard nothing back in return. If there had been questions about her omissions, they were not being asked—not of her, anyway. Slowly, she stopped anticipating a knock on the door, or a telegram summoning them north.

Aaron, of course, had no such doubts of being believed. Or if he did, he did not share them with her.

Christmas Eve came with a surprise blizzard, reducing festivities in New Haven to those within walls and under roofs. Rosemary had been disappointed to miss the annual caroling on The Green, but a stubborn catarrh had sent Aaron to his bed a few days before, and it wouldn't have been the same without her brother. So it was simply the two of them, and Botheration, and an early to bed.

Heading into New Year's, the town was still quiet, the layers of snow now rutted with trails along sidewalks and streets, rooftops bare in patches where it had melted. Rosemary was seated at her desk, looking over the year-end accounts, when there was a solid knock on the door downstairs. Her chest constricted for a heartbeat, while at her feet, Botheration grumbled but didn't stir.

She waited, her hand suspended over the mechanical calculator, until she heard her brother heading down the stairs. There was the sound of muted voices, then the door closing again. She bent her head back to the list of numbers in the ledger book until a rough cough from the doorway drew her attention.

"We've been summoned," her brother said, holding a brown envelope in one hand and an odd, almost manic look on his face. Panic slid into her, before he continued, "To Baltimore. Uncle's found us a nest of harpies."

Under the desk, Botheration heaved to his feet, even as Rosemary closed the ledger and pushed back her chair, anticipation replacing the fear. "We can catch the eleven o'clock train if we hurry."

Acknowledgments

WRITING THIS BOOK during the depth of COVID, coming off my own illness and personal loss, was . . . an interesting experience, and by interesting I mean, "kinda hellish." I would be remiss if I didn't give a shout-out to the people who kept me going.

Burdock Broughton

Amanda and Andrew Cherry

Mindi Welton-Mitchell

Elsa Sjunneson

Megan Thyagarajan

Janna Silverstein

and a special thanks to Dr. Victor A. Friedman, of the University of Chicago, for checking my Macedonian.